WHISPERS *of* EMBERSTONES

The Emberheart Saga I

M. MALDONADO

For information contact: http://www.authormimaldonado.com

Cover design by GetCovers.com – https://getcovers.com/terms-and-conditions

Getcovers does NOT use AI for book cover design. They use only licensed images and always provide clients with the license or links to the assets per request.

Map Illustration by @shameen_cr fiverpro

Character Art by TL. Combs https://www.authortlcombs.com/

Stone & Section images from Canva Pro-(Getty Images) Studiobest, MiroslavMares, Vvoevale, Ksluong92 (pixabay),GloryStarDesigns, musthofarproject

Digital ISBN: 979-8-9985347-0-6

Paperback ISBN: 979-8-9985347-1-3

Hardback ISBN: 979-8-9985347-2-0

First Edition: September 2025

Published by M. Maldonado

www. authormimaldonado.com | instagram.com/m.maldonado_writes

Content Warnings

This book contains scenes and themes that some readers may find distressing, including:

-Violence in battle

-Death of loved ones

-Death by magic (including young children— on-page but not too graphic)

-Animal death

-References to harsh physical punishment

-Mental health struggles and suicidal ideation: The book includes themes that touch on mental health challenges, with some characters grappling with feelings of hopelessness and contemplating ending their lives. Although these issues aren't explicitly about self-harm, they may be implied through the narrative and could be distressing for some readers.

While these elements serve the story and character development, reader discretion is advised. If needed, please put the book down and come back to it **if and when** you're ready. Go outside for a walk, stare at the sun... no, don't do that... you know what I mean. Please take care of yourself!

This one is for you . . .
Black, Brown, Indigenous, Person of Color.
And for you who are overlooked, disregarded, and undervalued.
For you who have had to fight and persevere without tools or
resources in a society built without you in mind.
For you who continue to hold hope in a world that seeks to dim
your light.

And for you who believed in me.

I see you.
I value you.
And I honor your humanity.

WHISPERS *of* EMBERSTONES

The Emberheart Saga I

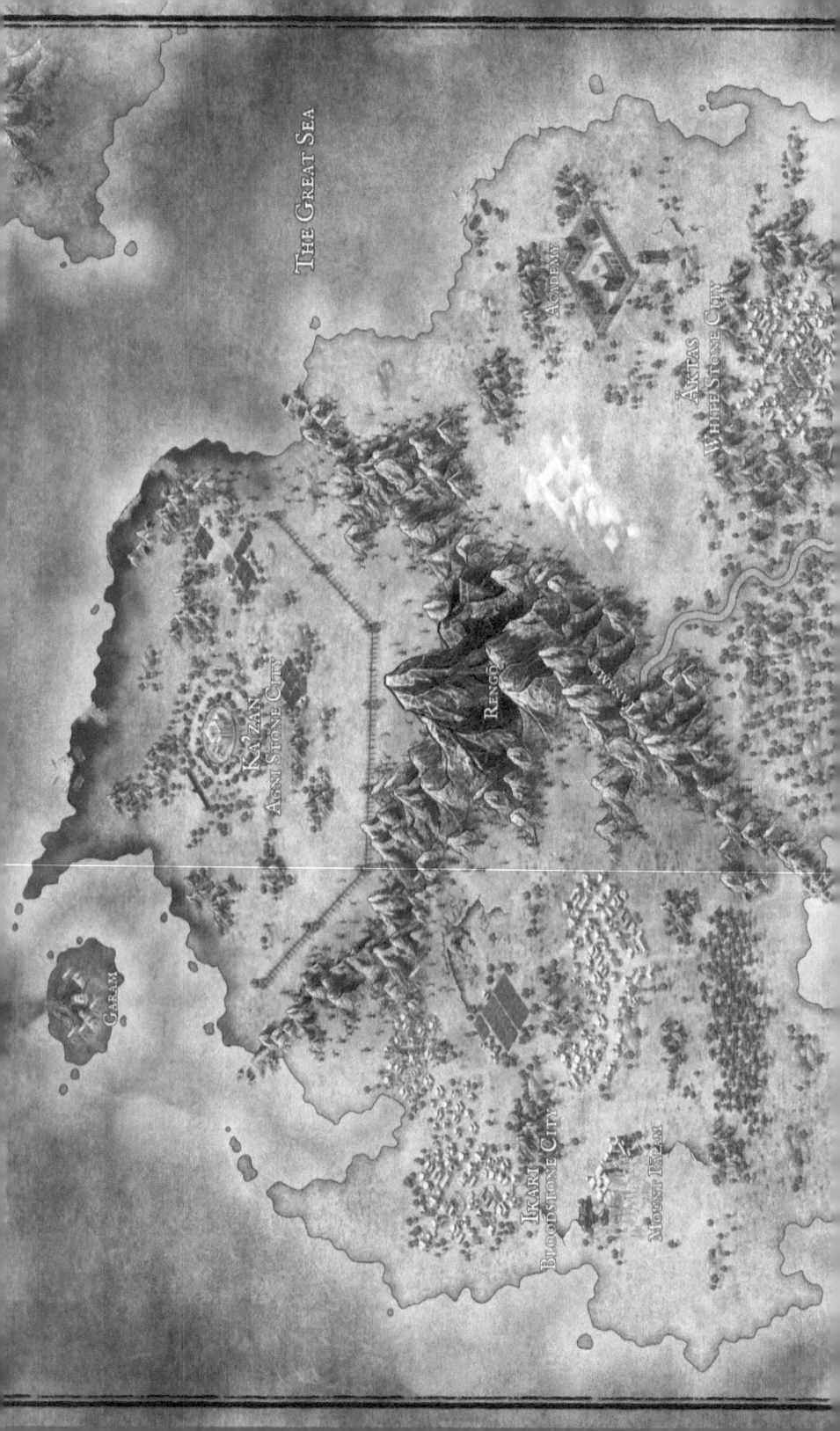

CAST OF CHARACTERS & LORE

WYVERNS
Ragas
The Elder Wyvern
Zuwena
The Lightning Wyvern

THE TANAMA MOUNTAINS
Trilateral mountain range dividing the three mining cities.

Home to:

Rengō: The tallest mountain at the center of the Tanama mountain range. It is full of powerful minerals and where the smoke begins.

The Dead Forests: Sentient forests filled with **wyvern remnants** from the Wyvern War, imbued with magic.

The Uláak: Masked creatures with lizard-like hands who guard the forests, and **Hexenbeasts** (hybrids of human and beast).

Emberheart Uláak: Leader of the Uláak and wielder of the Tristone Chain whip (white stone hilt, links of agni and bloodstones), Age unknown

ÄKTAS – WHITE STONE CITY (EAST)

Places:
The Academy, Iron Tower (White Stone mine), River, Main City is in the mountains

People:

The Hand: Council of Five (one for each Academy Trade)
Trades: Militia, Artificer, Terralects, Healers, Enchanters
Buldar: General Commander, Militia,
   Leader of The Hand, Age 58
Sadfar: General Artificer, Age 50
Elva: Second-year Sergeant Artificer, Age 21
Oran: Fifth-year Artificer, Age 22
Lyla: Fourth-year Sergeant Militia, Age 26
Fenris: First-year Artificer, Age 15
Anani: Elva's aunt, Age 47

IKARI – BLOODSTONE CITY (WEST)

Places:
Pālam (cavern city), Outer City, Abandoned City,
Bloodstone Mine
Home to Six Bloodstone Enchanters, Five Sages, and High Sage

People:

Sages:
High Priestess Samira: High Sage, Age unknown
First Sage Narisa: Shroudmist Sage, Age 57
Fifth Sage Zama: Avian Sage, Age 23

Bloodstone Enchanters:
Ida: Staff wielder, oldest of the six Enchanters
Okama: Twin broadswords wielder, youngest of the six Enchanters

Attendants & Citizens
Asante: First Attendant to the High Priestess, Age 19
Lux: Attendant to the Fifth Sage, Zama, Age 17

Tarrak: Hunter, Asante's older brother, Age 24
Nora: Citizen, Asante and Tarrak's younger sister, Age 11

KA'ZAN – AGNI STONE CITY (NORTH)

Places:

Garam (volcano and agni stone mine), Drekavog (city fortress)

People:

Zohar: High Regent, Agni Stone Enchanter, Age unknown
Vardan: Lord Regent, non-enchanter, Age 38
Magnar: High Regent (Deceased), Age unknown
High Council Hura: Regent's Right Hand, Age 57
Chief Gerel: Chief Guard, Age 50
Chief Daigo: Chief Healer, Age 65
Chief Yoen: Chief Miner, Age 45
Sefa: High Regent's Personal Guard, Age 31
Sumani: Archer, Age 23
Arben: Yoen's nephew, Age 18
Luan: Yoen's niece, Age 18
Nim: Yoen's late wife
Inara: Ka'zanty mare (Riders: Nim & Yoen), Middle-aged

ENCHANTED MINERALS & WIELDERS

The White Stone: Holds the power of light and can be wielded only by those from Äktas, men or women.
The Agni Stone: Holds the power of the elements (fire, water, wind, and stone) and can be wielded only by those from Ka'zan, men or women.
The Bloodstone: Wielded only by women of Ikari, it weaves itself

into those with innate gifts, amplifying what already lives within them.

Enchanter: Ignited/Enchanted stone wielder.

Tristone Wilder—Emberheart: A rare wielder of all three stones.

Sages/High Sage: Women from Ikari who carry the essence/magic of the wyverns in their blood without having to use bloodstones.

ARCHIVES

We fell through the void... From beyond stars, beyond memory, even beyond the pulse of time.

Guided only by the pull of absence, we drifted for an age, each of us apart—Pema, Etzel, and Temsin. The moment we touched, shadows fled. Flame sparked. Air and gas stirred. At last, stone gathered.

From our joining, this land, and many others, stirred and came alive. Wind carved valleys. Fire awakened mountains. Water traced the edges of stone. And in the shifting, we too changed.

Loneliness drove us to birth the winged ones from our essence. Wyverns, with eyes like burning gems and wings stretched wider than the skies, they soared across the lands we had forged. But still, we felt the longing.

So, we made something more. A mix of us and the winged ones.

Humans.

Not all bore scales or wings. Yet in the women, we recognized something familiar. An essence akin to the force that once sparked all things into being. It flowed through them like air through lung, like blood through vein. Even the mighty wyverns felt its power.

Blood magic bloomed from that bond. Through the women, the land transformed. Cities rose. Civilizations flourished—built on pure devotion, on ebb and flow, on memory pressed into soil.

And for a treasured time, harmony held.

But the men...

They desired what did not nest within them.

Their hunger tore that precious harmony apart, and the unthinkable followed. In the blink of an eye for us, though for you, a long, fragile, bleeding age. They turned on the winged creatures. First the young. Wings, bones, marrow, even their fiery breath. Our beloved little ones were stripped down, dissected, and repurposed. Some humans even learned to extract the wyverns' essence itself and bend it to their will. But that is a tale for another time, one that unfolds many, many years from now.

Still unsatisfied, they turned on the women, against those who carried our spark. They bound them. Controlled them. Forced them to create for others. The blood-magic wielders, once guided by balance, became tools of war. Fortresses rose. Sea vessels spread across the Great Sea.

Harmony collapsed.

Then, Ragas intervened.

The Elder. The Great Horned Wyvern loved the humans so deeply that he could not destroy them. And in a compromise, he gave them a version of what the men demanded.

Ragas dug deep into the earth and brought forth three minerals.

The White Stone, pale as starfire, held the power of light.

The Agni Stone churned with flame, water, wind, and stone. The raw voice of the land itself.

And the Bloodstone, drawn from the very earth soaked with the blood of Ragas' fallen kin, held a more intimate force. Wielded only by women of the first lands, it wove itself into those whose gifts were innate, amplifying what already lived within them.

Ragas saw the fire in the veins of his human offspring. With claw and instinct, he selected bloodlines to wield the power within the stones.

But the humans' greed only deepened.

In another blink, war returned.

The reverence once shown to the winged ones vanished. Humans no longer honored them. They sought to become them. They hunted. They forged. They bled the land dry.

The Great War shattered what remained of the balance.

Ragas, bound by love deeper than memory, turned his grief into a devouring fury. In sorrow, he cursed the Tanama, the most sacred of forests. Its roots twisted. Its color drained. What once pulsed with life now consumed it. Living things could not resist its call, and those who entered never returned.

From the decay, deadly creatures rose—guardians of the fallen. The land closed around them. The Tanama became both lure and prison. At its heart lay Rengō, the tallest mountain, where a fourth mineral ignited by the Elder wyvern still throbbed with the power the humans craved.

The humans tried to reach Rengō. Greedy. Desperate. They also sought the remnants of Ragas' fallen siblings, scattered around the forests. But the Tanama and its guardians did what the Great Horned One could not. They claimed many lives.

You may wonder why we did not stop them. Why we did not intervene. But you must understand that...We simply are.

In unity, life flows from us. It neither grants itself nor withholds itself. It becomes. But even if we had tried to mend what broke, you must also see that we had already been forgotten. Their memory of us faded, lost among suns, buried beneath sorrow, decay, and stone.

So now we share this with you. Do with it what you must.

If you remember us, even for a sliver of your fleeting time, you may begin to see what tore apart, and what still might mend. The veil shudders. It is not whole. But it is not beyond repair.

Whether they can see it, remains uncertain.

The tale you're about to witness, took place one hundred years after Ragas silenced the war. What followed may have served as punishment or a warning. Or a reflection—of something long buried, waiting to surface.

Fragment xlii: The First Kindling
—From *Daemons Archives, The Original Three*

PART ONE

AN OMEN IN THE SHADOWS

Chapter I

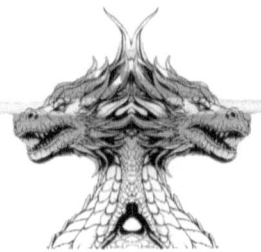

ÄKTAS THE WHITE STONE CITY

ELVA

WISPS OF MOONLIGHT CLUNG to Elva, hunched over an old wheelbarrow, her breath still ragged from the long journey to the barren fields. Her arms ached from hauling the weight of the Sky Lantern pieces, but adrenaline coursed through her veins, filling the corners where fear should be. Her hands worked with practiced precision, fastening each bolt under the starlit night.

The hot-air lanterns, designed to carry them over mountains and sea, and fueled by the magic of white stones, stood ready to alter the fate of the people of Äktas. Testing them within the Academy walls would have been easier—if only the General Commander had granted her permission. Each week, the orders to make the lanterns work grew more urgent, while his refusal to allow testing with the use of the enchanted stones consumed the time she no longer had.

Elva's thumbnail cut into the side of her index finger. The mere idea of using an enchanted stone sent her heart racing, its dangerous force had already brought about the downfall of her people.

I have no choice. The Commander's threats of severe punishment if the lanterns failed loomed over her, twisting her insides like a vine. Her restless hands adjusted the cerulean leather armband on her left sleeve, tracing the wyvern's fire emblem with her finger. With a deep inhale, she pushed her unease aside and braced herself for the possibility of yet another brutal punishment.

Her Academy's worn-out gray coat danced in the silver cloak of the night, as she began setting up the copper rails around the wooden platform, sitting half-angled on the ground and wide enough for two people.

"I can't believe you. Do you ever sleep?" A young man's raspy voice broke her focus.

"One could argue you're devoted to your sleep, Oran, and work too little. Come on. Give me a hand."

Oran dragged his feet over the grooves left by the wheelbarrow, emerging into the barren field occupied by the platform. The silver starlight caught his messy bedhead, playing across his robust silhouette. At her words, he raised his hands and clapped dramatically, the echoes drifting across the field.

A wrench danced between Elva's oil-stained fingers as she watched a stray lock of dark hair fall across Oran's forehead. His coat fabric strained at his shoulders. "Nice arms. Bet they're about to bust right through those old seams. Shame your jokes aren't as tight as your muscles."

"Oooh, so you think I'm handsome?" Oran grinned, puffing out his chest.

"That's not what I said! Shut up and help me," Elva shot back with a playful smile, motioning him toward the platform.

"Fine, but what made you think the lantern will work now? We've tried it several times already."

"Not with a white stone. An Enchanter lent me an ignited one."

"Elva," he blurted, spinning on his heel while gripping a bundle of braided ropes. "The Generals want this to work without stone magic."

"Are your nerves showing?" she teased, twirling the metal tool in her hand, her eyebrow arching in sync.

"You know what happened the last time you got in trouble," he insisted.

"I know, I know." Her eyes flickered away from him. Fidgeting fingers found the hem of her high-collar shirt. She squirmed, heat creeping to her cheeks as the fabric brushed against the jagged scars on her back. Scars Oran had no knowledge of. The Militia Commander's punishments had evolved over time, becoming more severe, leaving deeper and more painful reminders. With a slight shake of her head, she turned to him.

"That's why we're doing this now, before the town wakes up. We need to figure out the heat controls," she added as her eyes scanned the few remaining stars, hands planted on her hips. "Once we chart the energy demands using the enchanted stone, we should determine how to pilot the lanterns using fire or coal. Then, we'll only have to decipher the air controls."

Oran dropped to his knees beside the platform, jaw tightening while he wrestled the last knot in the ropes.

"I can't do this alone, and I only trust you. You're the best Artificer we have," she said. "Please, you're already here, and I know you want to test the lantern just as much as I do."

"All right," he sighed, releasing the rope and rising to his feet. "But if we get caught using magic, I'm blaming you."

"Deal." Elva extended her hand toward Oran, her thumb and little finger unfurled.

"And you're wrong." He mirrored her, allowing his little finger to lace with hers as their thumbs met. "*You* are the best Artificer in the city. The best we've ever had."

A subtle smile hinted at the edges of her mouth. She gestured for Oran to help roll out the lantern's fabric. The material stretched as long as two towering trees and nearly as wide as an ivory wyvern's wing. She had chosen a secluded field for their test, distanced from the Academy's main walls and concealed behind a series of desolate mounds. The location ensured the Iron Tower guards would remain oblivious to any floating device in the distance.

Her fingers ran through the heavy woolen ivory fibers, tracing the rough heatproof paste extracted from a centuries-old deposit of volcanic rock. Weeks of hard work and engineering stared back at her, every inch echoing sleepless nights and sore hands. Swallowing hard, she shifted her gaze to the Tanama's mountain range miles away.

Her hand found the patch over her heart baring the golden symbol of Äktas' council of five Generals, The Hand. Each General represented one of the Trades from the Academy. The leader among them pushed for inventions capable of transporting them directly into the heart of the highlands, bypassing the Tanama's dead forests and the lethal creatures haunting its grounds. She bit her lip. Enchanted white stones grew scarcer with each passing year, which was why the General Commander pushed the Artificers to avoid using them.

Her fingers tapped against her thigh. Many of the prototypes combusted into scorching spectacles during tests. Besides the unpredictable heat variances and wind currents, the Tanama's curse created a magnetic pull, drawing any living thing to consume it. At the thought of another failure and the trouble she'd face if the General Commander found out she'd used stone magic again, her shoulders tensed.

Elva approached the platform with a middle opening pointing toward the lantern's apex, where she placed a long volcanic stone cylinder.

"Let's leave the platform tied up to the sandbags in case we need to force descent," Oran said, gesturing to each of the corners.

"Make sure the ropes are long enough," Elva suggested as she tightened the bolts on the volcanic chamber.

"They are over 300 feet long. How high do you think we are going?"

"Where's your sense of adventure?" She winked.

He secured a knot on one of the sandbags. "I like my adventures on the ground."

"Don't tell me you're backing down."

"I'm not letting you go up there alone. But we need an exit in case things go wrong, and we both know you're not the best at planning ahead," he reminded her with a raised eyebrow.

"Ah, that's not entirely true."

"Every time you get these ideas you never have an escape plan. That's how you get into trouble." Oran's hands dropped the last sandbag, meeting her gaze. "This one is serious, El. You forget you're not in good graces with the Commander. He still thinks your parents are leading the rebels in the city."

"That's why I need this to work," she muttered. Her fingers wrestled with a stubborn bolt on the cylinder. She shifted her weight, the wrench flying into her other hand as her neck stretched the tension in her shoulders. "He still doesn't believe I haven't seen my parents in ages. I barely saw them when I joined the Academy. And after I became Sergeant, they stopped visiting. I know my dad has been outspoken against the Commander, but I can't imagine they'd be capable of leading any rebels," she stammered, the metal tool slipping from her fingers and landing on the sand with a thud. A long, frustrated sigh escaped her as her hands jerked down to her sides.

Oran's hand grazed her shoulder, his dark eyes steady on hers before he reached for the wrench. "Very well, then," he reassured, fitting the tool to the bolt. "How do we control the stone? We don't have an Enchanter to help us channel its power."

Elva tapped the cylinder gently. "This casing is made of volcanic metal and white stone. We just need to regulate the heat. The ignited gem is just a pebble," she added, pointing to a coin-sized opening. "Average white stones from our city and ordinary blood-stones from Ikari can contain any ignited rock. I made a cap using the western stone to tether the ignited stone's heat. If we stray too high, the combination should be enough to trigger a controlled descent."

"Or... we can plummet down," Oran joked, his hand sweeping downward.

She ignored his grin. "We've done the work. Numbers don't lie, and this should... *will* work. The only missing factor is the temperature." She fixed her dark eyes on Oran. "Do you trust me?"

"Of course I do. I'm just worried," he admitted, scratching the back of his head.

"All we have to do is reach an altitude that will ensure the lantern's stability, record our findings, and come back down before the town blinks an eye."

He sighed and turned to secure another sandbag. "Then, let's make haste."

As they finished setting up the platform, she dug into her leather waist satchel, until her fingers brushed the cool surface of a small bloodstone box. Moonlight bounced against the ruby-like stone, casting droplets of crimson sparkles around the lantern. Her hand gently raised the square lid. Like a captive star unleashed from its cradle, the ignited white stone blazed to life, its merciless radiance flooding the landscape.

She cramped around the box as her ears tuned to a familiar, entrancing melody, a symphony whispering the stone's ancient secrets. The stone's rhythmic pulse throbbed in her mind, each beat steady and relentless. Yet her body recoiled as an angry, razor-sharp surge of energy tore through her, shattering the trance.

"Careful with that!" Oran cried out, shielding his eyes from the arresting light with one hand. "Where did you get that box?"

Without answering, Elva's hand slammed the tiny bloodstone casing shut, taming the white stone's intensity. Starlight washed over her again as she drew near the cylinder. She eased it open, just enough to let the ignited rock slip into the side aperture. Like a conduit channeling the ancient power, the chamber contained and directed the heat radiated by the white stone, transforming it into a skyward jet of thermal energy.

Noticing the radiance emanating from the chamber's apex, they rallied their strength, heaving the platform upright. With a life of its own, the intense warmth surged as if giving the lantern breath. The conical ivory textile billowed outward, expanding with ease as it tugged against thick metal wires secured to the copper railings.

The drapery unfolded with a deep rustling, its edges snapping taut against the frame. Elva's pulse quickened while she counted under her breath. "It's surpassed the point of combustion," she blurted out.

"It's working," Oran said, transfixed. Unable to contain her excitement, she leapt forward, her arms wrapping tightly around him. "Skies, El, you're amazing." His dark eyes locked with hers.

A playful smile touched her lips. "You sound surprised."

"I—I'm not..." The protest died on his lips. One forceful shove from Elva sent him sliding backward, his feet shuffling across the sand.

"It's working too fast. Get in, hurry!" Her boots kicked up dust as she rushed around the site, gathering more equipment. With a final sweep, she tucked the bloodstone box into her waist satchel.

The wooden platform creaked under Oran's weight. "El, the platform's rising. Move!"

By the time she made her way back, the deck hovered at shoulder height. She tossed the extra items to Oran, then vaulted upward, arm outstretched. He latched onto her with a grunt, pulling her onto the structure.

"That was a close one," she grinned, looking up at the fully unfurled fabric, stretching out like the breathing lung of a mighty wyvern.

"Let's hope the sandbags anchor us in place," he stammered. Already several feet off the ground, the world beneath them receded into a tapestry of sculpted hilltops. His legs gave out, and he dropped to his knees with a startled yelp. One hand gripped the copper rail, the other clutching his stomach. "I hate this so much."

"Just don't look down. Remember... deep breaths," Elva chuckled, patting him on the shoulder while mimicking deep inhales. She grabbed one of the spare coils of rope she'd gathered before climbing onto the platform. One end wound around his waist, then she yanked the other end taut against the railing. Twisting the knot, she secured it until it held firm. "There, now you're safe."

"You call this safe? What about you?" Oran's knees shook with the sway of the lantern. Gaining his balance, he pulled Elva close. Her back pressed against his chest while he wrapped a coil of rope around her waist. "Let me help." With an unsteady grip, he fumbled with it, fingers grazing the fabric of her coat. He drew her in closer, breath warm and uneven against the curve of her neck.

A light tingle spread along her skin. "Did you just—sniff me?" She turned to meet his eyes with a grin.

"Yes, did you remember to bathe this week?"

"Maybe I did, maybe I didn't," she replied with a mischievous sparkle in her dark brown eyes. She gathered her long braid and twisted it into a bun. "We can already see the parts of the Academy, even the Great Sea and the harbor. Look," she gasped, gesturing to the city nestled within a sea of mountains.

"Please don't make me look. I'll pass on the panoramic view and focus on the lantern and the stone. Your artifact seems to be working too well," Oran said lifting his gaze. The lantern's textured fabric billowed in the wind, fluttering like the wings of birds in flight. Every step on the rising platform threw them off balance, the heat from the stone tugging at their bodies. "At this pace, we might be able to touch the stars. Those sandbags might not be enough to anchor us." His grip tightened around the railings.

Elva's hand dove into her satchel, emerging with a translucent, coin-shaped red stone. "If we gain too much altitude, this bloodstone cap should help," she said, stepping to the center of the platform. The wind whipped around her as she neared the cylinder holding the white stone, its heat radiating into the air. She reached for the lever above the aperture, her fingers moving with precision.

With a swift motion, the small gem from the western city, Ikari, fell into place. "I designed the cap to swivel and temper the flow of heat. It can also stay in place, allowing some of the hot air to escape through the fabric. That should help with navigation."

"You thought of everything after all."

"Almost. I still don't know how to steer it. But I think propellers might help," she replied, hands pressing to her waist, eyes scanning the cylinder before shifting over to the copper railings.

As the ropes tethered to the sandbags became taut, the night sky yielded to the approaching morning light. A fierce gust of wind jolted the lantern, setting it adrift above the mounds below. The sandbags skidded and scraped against the earth. Oran's grip tightened on the rails, his arm muscles straining beneath his coat. The rogue wind thrust Elva backward, her body slamming into the copper rails at the far end of the platform, knocking the breath from her lungs.

"Hang on," he yelled through gritted teeth.

Pain shot through her spine like lightning through storm clouds. Her fingers scrambled for the rails, but the metal's icy bite pierced through her skin. She fumbled at her leg harness, retrieving her gloves with trembling hands before steadying herself against the swaying deck. When her vision cleared, the shadowed, scarred lands of the Tanama stretched before her.

The trilateral Tanama mountain range loomed like a giant three-tailed snake, mutilated by raging wars. The treacherous range isolated three vast mining cities—Ikari to the west, Ka'zan to the north, and her own city, Äktas to the east. Each city, overshadowed by the mighty tails of the Tanama, remained a world unto its own. Her wide eyes darkened, tracing the swirling dance of the wind across the barren hills and into the haunted forest.

"Wyvern skies," she gasped, a chill racing through her skin. The insatiable greed for enchanted stones had tarnished the mountains and her city, leaving scars deeper than any battle could inflict.

"Are you all right? El?"

Her stomach churned, haunted by the thought of what lurked in the lifeless woods. The Uláak and their hexenbeasts guarded the forest grounds, preventing anyone from crossing between Ikari and Ka'zan. The dead forests exerted a magnetic pull, enticing any living being to enter, only to be devoured by the monstrous beasts, as they had done with Oran's parents when he was only ten. "I—It's nothing."

"What do you mean?" He called from across the wooden deck.

"I'm sorry, I shouldn't have said anything." Her gaze dropped and her lip caught between her teeth.

"It's okay, I know the haunted woods are there. Besides, the Commander wants us to find a way to the very center of those mountains. Rengō and the gems in its rock walls are our target."

"I know. I'm still sorry. Maybe we should start heading down."

"You can't mean that! We just reached our highest point," he objected, but his eyes avoided the Tanama. "It's been twelve years. There are things even logic can't fix, El." He swallowed hard. "I know my parents died in those woods, and there's nothing we can do about it. But if we can help our people, if we can reach Rengō and claim the enchanted stones it keeps from us. We might even have a chance to free ourselves from this damned land." His gaze hardened as he finally looked out toward the mountains. "Reaching Rengō could be our chance to fight back."

"That's rebel talk," she said, fidgeting with the edge of her coat as she glanced at the Tanama and then back at Oran. "But I know looking at that forest pains you. I just wish I knew how to fix that. You're my best friend."

"Thanks, Glowworm, you warm my heart," he said with a smirk.

She rolled her eyes and reached into her satchel. Her gloved fingers wrapped around a finely-crafted sight magnifier, which she then trained on Rengō's peak at the heart of the Tanama.

"Where in the wyvern's skies did you get that?" He pointed at the magnifier pushing outward from her eye. The Hand's symbol and golden wyvern scales adorned its sides.

"I borrowed it. Besides, I engineered it."

"We'll have to get that back on time before they notice it was *stolen*. Same with that bloodstone box."

"They were both *borrowed*," she countered, her gaze fixed in the distance. Her eyes widened when she looked upon Rengō's summit. The warmth fled from her limbs, as if she had plunged into a frozen lake.

"El? Are you listening?" Oran staggered across the platform. "What is it?" he urged, gripping her arm.

"S-S-Smoke." Her voice barely carried above the howling winds. "What?"

"There's smoke," she shouted, stretching out a quivering finger toward the distant silhouette. "On top of Rengō, dark smoke."

He took the magnifier and looked.

"We must alert The Hand," she blurted. Smoke coiled into the sky, twisting in slow, menacing spirals. Her gloved fingers tightened on the copper rails, the leather creaking under her grip. The sight sent ripples through her bones, her mind spinning with the possibility of the Uláak breaking free from the spell that bound them to the Tanama—the same creatures that had claimed Oran's parents. "Use the bloodstone cap to begin the descent. Cover the cylinder and count to thirty. Repeat every thirty counts," she mustered with a trembling voice.

"Wait, what are you doing?"

"Judging by my calculations, you should touch ground before the hour ends," she shouted against the wind as she untied her rope from the railing and looped it around her legs. Elva dug into her satchel again, pulling out a small stone ring. She fastened it to her rope and secured it to one of the lines attached to the sandbags below.

"Elva. What are you doing?"

"Remember, not all at once. Keep a steady count, and it will control your descent," she shouted, taking a deep breath before finally climbing over the copper rail. Just as Oran reached to grab her hand, she rappelled down, disappearing from sight.

CHAPTER 2

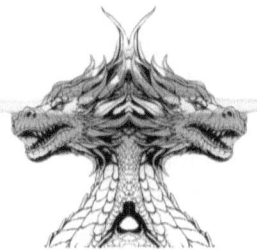

IKARI THE BLOODSTONE CITY

ASANTE

A SANTE'S FEET FLEW UP the spiraling steps as the oldest tree in the western city of Ikari rose into view, its crown stretching above the land below. Much like a seabird circling its high nest, the High Tree stood watchful at the summit of Mount Pālam. Lush green ferns and branches shot toward the sky, reaching for the few remaining stars, while others swept low, caressing the rugged ground.

"Good day to you, Mightiest of Trees," she panted, standing at its base and bringing her right fist to her heart. "May the radiant breath of Ragas forever ignite your core."

With the grace of a mountain cat, her feet darted through the labyrinth of branches, finding familiar footholds without a second glance. Dawn unveiled a honey glow over the stone archways. The best view of the outer city unfolded from her perch, revealing a landscape resembling a story told in layers. Across the distant horizon, the abyss of the Tanama's dead forests brooded, facing Mount Pālam and the hidden city carved within its heart.

Though separated by miles, the forests' menace pressed against her, haunted by countless nightmares of her father's final moments. Her hand gripped a branch tightly. Thoughts spiraled as she imagined the merciless creatures lurking within those forsaken depths.

"Hi, Baba," Asante whispered, addressing her late father. "I snuck out here before the Priestess could shower me with chores. It's been a while since I've been up here, sorry it has taken me so long to visit."

She stared at the dead mountains, guilt clawing at her insides. "Tomorrow is the Solstice Marking Ritual. After eight failed summers, this has to be the year I get marked," she sighed. Her fingers brushed against the rough bark of the weathered tree while her eyes scanned the landscape.

Her brown eyes took in the haunting backdrop of the abandoned city crouched beside the Bloodstone mine, where enchanted stones native to Ikari dwindled in number. Its entrance stood as a silent scream carved into the earth. Opposite the abandoned city, vast crop fields unfurled in a patchwork quilt pattern, guiding Asante's gaze to the outer city, where rows of kapok trees formed a natural boundary. Beyond the towering trees, the land stretched for miles until it reached the Great Sea.

Ikari rested in the western, suffocating grip of the Tanama mountains, too close to the sentient forests that had claimed more lives than she could count. Long before she was born, the threat of those forests forced Ikarites to abandon their home and forge a new one within the rock walls of Mount Pālam. The new city's architecture seamlessly wove cobblestone pathways, creating a harmonious transition from the outer city into the first cave levels of Pālam.

Still, each year, the Tanama's forest claimed more lives. And with no magic of her own, she had become helpless—just another burden to her city. "Tomorrow, I have to get my markings! I don't care which ones, Enchanter's or Sage's, I just can't bear it anymore," she sighed, tracing her finger from the bottom of her lip to her chin, where her Enchanter's marking would be. Then, from the edge of her nose to her temple, where the Sage markings would be.

"It pains me that we keep losing so many miners. You should've never been so close to those damned woods." Her shoulders tightened as images of her father lost within those haunted depths invaded her mind. There was no tombstone to mourn at, or sacred burial grounds to visit. She had only the looming mountains and the silent whispers of the several lost souls pulled by the dead forests along with him.

She ducked her head and glanced at her free hand. Calluses marked her dark-amber skin from countless hours spent tending to the Priestess. "Eight long years I've served the High Priestess. I've worked hard to become her first attendant, but it never feels like enough. Relying on the miners to gather bloodstones is too dangerous. No one should be working so close to the Tanama."

She lifted her gaze and let her feet dangle from the tree branch below. "With markings, I bet I could find a way to help, to prevent more lives from being lost to the pull of those forests. Or at least try. Zama is twenty-three, only four years older than me and she got her Sage markings last summer. There's still hope for me. Please, Ragas," she prayed to the Great Horned Wyvern, "I beg you. Tomorrow, grant me my marks."

She leaned back, allowing her eyes to drift toward the dead forests. The Tanama's terrain stood as a haunting reminder of each city's former grandeur. Magic-filled remnants of fallen wyverns lay scattered across its desiccated fields. Yet, the Uláak threatened any living being that dared approach the relics. They had drained the forests of all life. No wild animals roamed. No insects buzzed. Even the trees, once vibrant and full of life, now stood as weathered skeletons.

A deep ache echoed in her chest. The soft caress of the wind reminded her of the last time her mother's gentle fingers danced through her dark hair. She played with her shoulder length locs, tracing the golden beads at the end of each strand. "I miss her…"

She exhaled, shaking her head, trying to remember how long it had been since she had visited her family in the lower tiers.

"Mom's letters say Tarrak looks like you, but I don't see it. Maybe I'm starting to forget," she whispered to her father, her eyes fixed on the dead woods. "Tomorrow is also Nora's first Marking Ritual. I can't believe she's already eleven. That one has your strong will, stubborn as a wild horse." She talked about her younger sister as the crisp air filled her lungs and a half-smile tugged at her lips. "Tarrak tells me Nora stirs trouble wherever she goes. I'll wager the lower ground keepers..." Her words trailed off when something in the distance caught her eye.

"What is that?"

A shadowy specter danced across the horizon. Her heart quickened, causing her fingers to tighten around the rough bark. Drawing her knees to the branch, she dared to stand on the balls of her feet, balancing like a hunting hawk on the edge of flight. Leaning forward, her hand shielded her eyes from the sunrise.

"Skies! No!" Her breath caught in a jagged inhale, lungs tightening as her eyes locked onto a dark veil of smoke. It twisted like a monstrous stygian viper, slithering from Rengō at the heart of the Tanama mountains.

The outer city below remained oblivious. She fixed her eyes on the thin wisp of smoke staining the sky above Rengō's summit. For a century, the Uláak's sentient mountains had remained lifeless. The thought of it being something worse than those creatures made her sick to her stomach.

She launched forward, leaves raking her cheeks, her fingernails scraping bark before losing their desperate hold. A graceless tumble followed, the world spinning in a blur of green and brown. The upper branch caught her like a wooden fist to the gut, forcing a sharp gasp from her throat. The final spin hurled her face-first into the ground, tearing the breath from her lungs in a violent rush.

Stars burst behind her eyes as pain pulsed through her forehead. Warm copper bloomed across her tongue, blood trickling from the corner of her mouth. Asante's muscles screamed as she clawed her way upright and sprinted toward the archway connecting Pālam's summit to the caverns. Her bruised hands pushed against the iron gate, reaching for a kindled torch on the wall.

The gentle glow of the torch danced around the narrow white stone walls, as she plunged into the spiraling staircase. When she reached the Priestess' tier, just beneath the High Tree, warm light from lanterns lit by attendants draped the cavernous corridor.

She halted before the Priestess' chambers and wedged her torch into an empty sconce. Drawing a deep breath, she regained her composure and used the long sleeves of her white robes to wipe the sweat from her brow. Her heart hammered against her ribcage taking notice of her ruffled appearance. Samira, the High Priestess, held a vehement disdain for chaos and uninvited disruptions. She swallowed, allowing her trembling hand to knock on the imposing oak wood door.

"High Priestess, it's Asante. May I enter?"

"It is too early for my first meal," a muffled response filtered through the thick wood.

"It's an urgent matter, your Highness."

Before she could speak again, the door yanked open. Priestess Samira's probing gaze raked over her, sweeping from head to toe. "Speak," she ordered. Scarlet robes swayed around her, revealing her arms and bare legs.

The High Sage's markings, resembling veins of molten gold, streamed across her skin, spanning her entire body. One mark, like a golden ribbon, extended from the center of her bald head. It unraveled across the middle of her face, tracing her nose and lips. As it reached below her chin, it coiled around her neck in eight distinct loops, acting like a wide armor necklace, before plunging into her navel.

She stood towering, with deep brown skin that retained the smoothness of woven silk. Samira had lived long before the century-old Wyvern Wars, but seemed untouched by time. Her primal magic did not merely extend her life but also conserved her regal beauty.

"Your Highness," Asante began, bringing her right fist to her heart and bowing. "I was on top of the High Tree this morning, and I saw..."

"Out with it."

"Smoke, my Grace," she explained as she rose. "A spiral of onyx smoke unfurls from Rengō's summit. It's likely visible from your threshold." Shoes discarded, Asante crossed the chamber. Her bare feet rushed past the massive circular bed nestled within the roots of the High Tree and dressed with pristine emerald sheets. Above it, an alabaster crown of tendrils wove through the ceiling.

Reaching the veranda, she parted the translucent pearl curtains, wooden panels creaking under her firm push. The Tanama mountain range stretched before her in the distance, with Rengō at the heart of it all.

Samira stepped onto the balcony, fastening her robes. The marks on her fingers, as if dipped in liquid gold, gleamed against the morning dawn. Her gaze locked onto Rengō. The menacing sight of smoke expanded, creating a grim mushroom cloud that covered the giant's summit.

"Has anyone else seen it?" Samira kept her dark-brown eyes on the mountain.

"I'm unsure, your Highness. I ran here as soon as I saw it."

"Fetch my raiment."

Roots twisted like gnarled fingers from the chamber's ceiling, digging through the stone floors and into the caves below. Asante's bare feet darted between the organic pillars, cutting straight toward an archway framed by two massive, knotted tendrils. Soft amber light filtered through a moon-shaped opening, breathing life into stone ceilings webbed with roots from the High Tree. A charcoal sink stood on one side, resembling a stone platter waiting to serve. Across the cavern, a massive stone bath pulsed with warm water trickling through hidden channels within the walls.

Asante hunched over the stone sink, picking bits of bark from her locs. In the mirror above, her reflection revealed the aftermath of her tumble down the High Tree—leaves tangled in the tight strands, dirt clinging to her robes. She leaned closer until her fingers brushed the corner of her mouth, the taste of blood sharp on her tongue. Wiping dirt smudges from her deep-brown skin, her mother's protest about being nothing but bones echoed in her mind.

Cold sweat beaded on her forehead. "How did she let you in looking like this?" she muttered to her reflection. "That thing on Rengō must be serious." Her stomach churned. "What if... what if the Uláak found a way to break free from the forest's hold? No, no. It can't be! It's not possible." Her breath caught, a strangled half-sob pressing against her clenched teeth. Not the creatures that plagued the Tanama and stole her father. Not the creatures that haunted her dreams.

Burying her thoughts aside, she turned toward the archway. Her fingers found a hidden cupboard, retrieving a small vase for water and cleaning cloths. As her hand wrapped around the vessel, a flicker of light caught the corner of her eye.

She angled her gaze into the Priestess' chambers. Samira's gilded fingers gleamed as they wrapped around an ivory root pulsing with fluorescent blue veins. Light cascaded, tracing serpentine paths across the glossy white stone floor. The luminous dance spread, reflecting and multiplying until it reached Asante's bare feet. Breath caught in her throat and the water vase slipped from her grasp, shattering against stone.

Samira's glare sliced through her before shifting to the balcony. Her fists clenched, eyes locked on Rengō. "Menacing times are upon us," the Priestess said, her stern voice echoing through the chamber. "Our city has known wrath and misery. And I, more than anyone, recognize that power alone fails to shield us from their grip. Loyalty and sacrifice are our salvation. But I also know that one single misstep, one misplaced trust, could be our downfall." She turned back to Asante, her words cutting through the air like a blade. "There's no room for mistakes!" she hissed. "Stay vigilant!"

With her final words, Samira's gold-dipped fingers wrapped around another root. Blue sparks flickered to life in response, carrying messages through the network of tendrils. Notices raced to the Sages and Enchanters, commanding that the Marking Ritual occur immediately, bypassing the summer solstice. The ancient tradition, designed to identify women attuned to the enchanted bloodstones, teetered on the verge of disruption.

Asante fought the nausea rising in her stomach. If the High Priestess, the most powerful Enchanter of the land, feared the smoke, then the danger atop Rengō had exceeded her worst fears.

And suddenly the thirst for her markings and their power seared through her veins, fiercer now than ever before.

CHAPTER 3

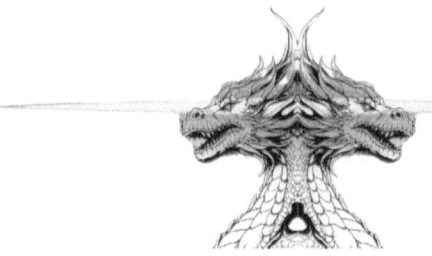

KA'ZAN THE AGNI STONE CITY

YOEN

IN THE NORTHERN SHADOWS of the Tanama mountains, the starlit sky taunted Ka'zan's Chief Miner through the single window in his roundhouse. After another sleepless night, Yoen lay on his resting mat, staring back. His eyes drifted to the empty space beside him. One hand lingered on the untouched cold sheets, while the other found the pit of his stomach, his fingers curling, as if to steady a storm within. With a long sigh, he sprang to his feet, strapping on his miner's gear.

Dew-dampened grass brushed his ankles when he stepped into the night. His gaze traced the connecting path to his children's round-house, where no wisp of smoke curled from the sleeping vent.

"Those two had better be asleep," he uttered under his breath, nearing the door, only to be interrupted by stealthy shadows sneaking around the back. "Get back here!" he snapped.

Two heads with onyx hair bobbed into view behind the white round-house. The twins' silhouettes dragged their feet toward him.

"Arben, what's in that bag?" He pointed to a small burlap sack secured with a piece of frayed rope.

"Ah, hi there Chief," Arben replied, shuffling the sack behind his back. "It's nothing, just a few things we gathered around the beach."

Yoen sucked in air through his teeth. "I've warned you repeatedly about the beach's high tide. It will swallow you whole."

"But uncle, that's the only time we can..." Luan began.

"No exceptions." His eyes raked over his niece and nephew's disheveled state. Streaks of sand and mud marred their warm olive skin. "All of this is not just from the beach." He gestured to their wind-tousled hair and Luan's missing socks. "Tell me, where else have you been?"

"Where else?" Arben started, scratching the back of his head.

"Let's hear it from your sister," he insisted.

"Um, the beach," Luan's voice trailed off.

"That's it. That's all we did," her brother chimed in. "We collected stones and shells then came back home."

"I asked your sister." Yoen locked eyes with Luan, taking in her long braid, thick eyebrows, and the freckles peppering her skin. Though similar in height, Luan stood a few inches taller than her brother. Her ears flushed under his scrutiny.

"You always tell me, even if it gets you in trouble. Unless..." He studied their faces. Out of the possible exploration sites, two nagged at his mind. The dead forests would've claimed their lives. The thought alone made him sick. The other place, they had visited before, yet it harbored a similar threat. His heart sank at the thought. "Wyverns' horns. The caves?" he snapped.

The twins exchanged startled glances as he silenced their objections.

"I've warned you against those caves. They lead to the Tanama's forests, and you both know what lurks within those grounds." His neck muscles tightened as he spoke. "The Uláak are death incarnate. Their sole purpose is to prevent any living thing from crossing those forsaken mountains. Those caves will lead you right to them."

"But Chief, what if we could find a way through the forest?" Arben let out a desperate plea.

"Enough!" Yoen's outburst made the twins flinch. His own heart hammered against his ribs.

Arben's teeth found his fingernails while Luan's eyes narrowed at her feet. Feeling a tug in his heart, he took a step closer to the twins. "Please, I implore you, no more exploring into those caves, and steer clear of the beach during high tide." He reached out to both of them, but their gazes remained fixed on the ground.

"If your mother were here, she'd be amazed by your brilliance and courage. And I assure you, she was a force to be reckoned with."

At his mention of their mother, the twins' gazes met his.

"I made a promise to my sister to keep you both safe," Yoen added, swallowing the lump in his throat. "I can't fulfill that promise if you continue being so reckless. You've just turned eighteen. You should know better and look after each other."

"But," Luan stammered, "what if we can get Mom and Aunt Nim back? The caves could be a way into the forest. Maybe they are just trapped."

His brow furrowed. "You can't risk your lives like this. It's too dangerous. I won't allow it."

Luan stepped forward and squared her shoulders. "The harder you grip, the faster things slip away, uncle Yoen. When will you trust us? We just want to find our mother."

He released a heavy sigh. "I understand the desire for your mother and aunt to still be alive," he said, fighting the knot in his throat while his gaze shifted to the ground.

He pulled them into a tight embrace, causing simultaneous whimpers. "It has been nine years, firebug. Nothing. Nobody comes out of those mountains. The Uláak are all-consuming." His lips pressed a gentle kiss on their mud-streaked foreheads. "Stay away from those caves."

Yoen walked away, leaving the twins behind. "Since you're both awake, go and let the sheep out. And for Ragas' sake, take a bath. You both reek."

He turned to the horse pit, where his mare stood ready. As he mounted, his gaze lingered on the round-houses one last time. With a heavy heart, he shifted his attention to the distant volcano and miners' exploration site. Mount Garam.

Yoen pushed his walnut mare forward, her hooves crunching on gravel near the volcano's base. He continued to climb on foot until he reached Garam's largest wall crevice. By then, stars faded as sunlight pierced the horizon. The thin, acrid taste of sulfur crept in, forcing his hands to tighten his mouth cover.

The crevice on the volcano's wall was a scar from the Wyvern Wars, marking the brutal fight for control over the enchanted creatures and their fiery breath. Ragas, the Elder Wyvern, bestowed each city with unique gifts. His wyvern's breath ignited native stones with special powers, turning them into vital resources. In Ikari, however, the creatures' magic ignited not only bloodstones but also certain women, transforming them into powerful Sages.

Yoen's eyes swept the volcano's walls, scrutinizing every crack. Clutching the dagger at his waist, he recalled the scrolls detailing how the cities turned against the wyverns, haunting them for the magic within their skin and bones. The giant lizards retaliated, but their time had run out. Extinction claimed them, along with their primal magic.

The vast fissure on the volcano remained sealed by an imposing White Stone Gate. Its surface shimmered like ice crystals on a winter's morning. It bore the life of Ka'zan in etched carvings. Garam, an isolated volcano amid the Great Sea, kept a vigilant eye over Ka'zan, accessible through a seabed unveiled during low tides. Past the harbor, the city's monumental fortress commanded attention within a circular space. Cobblestone roads branched out, guiding the way to the heart of the city and its bustling market.

At the center of the carvings, the Great Horned Ragas soared over the High Regent's court, with horns jutting out like pillars. The Elder Wyvern spouted its fiery breath as it ignited the scepter at the hands of the late High Regent Magnar. Beyond the round-houses scattered like white pebbles around farmlands, the Tanama mountains stood proudly, long before the curse. Yoen traced his fingers over the seal, forged from the native mineral of the city of Äktas. The ignited stone of the eastern neighbors kept the volcano subdued.

In Ka'zan, the only magic resided in rare ignited agni stones dug by skilled miners. Yet, their efforts became futile as the years wore on. The supply of enchanted gems dwindled. To make things worse, a persistent unease gnawed at Yoen. For the past eight months, he reported unusual volcanic tremors, as if fire-ants danced under its belly. But no matter how much he pleaded, High Regent Zohar had branded his warnings as mere delusions. Yet today, the volcanic mountain lay eerily still beneath his feet.

Relieved by the lack of unusual activity, his gaze wandered, drawn to the wild orchids blooming at the edge of the cliff. Their sight stirred memories of his wife's green touch, while his own hands could barely keep a dandelion alive. As his fingers curled around one, tiny scarlet flecks on the petals caught his eye, vivid as fresh-spilled blood.

His hand found the knife at his waist, sliding it smoothly from its sheath. The blade carved through the dark rock with delicate precision. Pride swelled in his chest when he lifted the orchid up for a closer look—until movement drew his eyes to a distant shadow.

Beyond Ka'zan, the Uláak guarded the Tanama mountains, annihilating anyone who attempted to access the wyvern remains brimming with magic. Their vigilant watch also thwarted access to mount Rengō, harboring enchanted minerals craved by the three cities. The forests stirred both disdain and longing in his heart. But what caught his attention ignited a fear beyond the ordinary.

Smoke, a sinister veil stretched from Rengō's summit, as if a wyvern's onyx tongue whipped the cloudless larimar sky.

"Great Ragas, spare us!" Ice shot down his spine. His hands fell, dropping the orchid and knife. A strong gust of wind snatched the flower, carrying it away from the cliff and into the air. The current yanked his hooded cowl tight around his head, snapping him out of the spell.

Yoen's feet finally sparked fire and he ran downhill to his mare, Inara. Ka'zanty horses held the reputation for unmatched speed among all cities' steeds, and though Inara lacked grace, none matched her swiftness. Strapping onto the mare, he shot another glance at Rengō, praying the smoke had been a figment of his imagination.

"No, No, No," he cursed under his breath.

Past the farmlands, the round-houses stood like small white bellflowers at the skirts of the Tanama. From that distance, the smoke above the towering peak started as a whisper, then grew bolder with each passing moment. His jaw tensed, his eyes locked on the mountain. At the same time, Inara weaved under his legs, matching his mounting dread.

Thoughts of his niece and nephew flooded his mind. This unforgiving land had shown no mercy to his only surviving family. The haunted grounds of the Tanama blocked passage to the other cities, while the vile creatures guarding the waters proved just as deadly. They found themselves chained to a land where only one Enchanter could wield the magic of agni stones. Whatever sinister force loomed over Rengō intensified the seething indignation and doom Yoen had buried for many years, all for his children's sake.

"Inara, to the High Regent," he snarled, clenching her reins and pushing her toward the seashore.

In the distance, fishers dotted the water, nets arcing through the air before plunging into the sea's grasp. Beyond the ashen basalt columns, the Chief Fisher and the High Regent signaled to the skiffs in the calm open waters. Waves crashed like white wool against the black sand, their froth mirroring the High Regent's long white coat dancing with the wind.

Zohar's personal guards approached Yoen, one remained by the High Regent, hand resting on her wyvern claw sword. The other guard's raised arm warned him to halt. He slowed Inara's gallop to a lope before vaulting from the mare's back to meet them.

"Apologies for the early intrusion," Yoen said, kowtowing. "I must have a word, Your Excellency."

"Chief Miner, our meetings are after the mining's day is done." Zohar waved his guards to go back.

Yoen rose. Though the three men shared a similar height, the High Regent surpassed them. Yoen and the Chief Fisher bore sun-kissed skin from endless days outdoors, while the High Regent's skin remained fair and unblemished. Wind tousled Yoen's brown and silver strands. Zohar's top-knot captured his tresses neat, his high collar concealing an amber amulet at his throat. The Chief Fisher bowed first to the High Regent then to Yoen before departing.

"I have witnessed something ominous while on my inspection of Mount Garam, Your Excellency. I believe it requires our immediate attention."

"We've been over this. I value your service and friendship, but these ideas must stop. Garam is dormant," Zohar said, striding back toward his four personal guards. Their ruby tunics shimmered in the light, standing like sentinels, nearly as tall as the imposing jet-black mare beside them. "The magic of the White Stone Gate on Garam's crevice keeps the volcano in deep slumber. There is no danger."

"Your Excellency, I mean no disrespect. It's..."

"Don't you think it's quite early to spew this nonsense?"

"Apologies for the confusion, what I witnessed wasn't from Mount Garam, but from Rengō. Fire or smoke rises from the summit," Yoen stammered, following behind the High Regent with Inara.

"Well, which one is it, fire or smoke?"

"Smoke, I saw smoke, Your Excellency, on Rengō's summit. Dark as night."

Zohar mounted his steed, avoiding Yoen's gaze. "Your eyes deceive you, young Chief. It's a long way from our volcano to Rengō. You mustn't worry."

The guard's firm grip on Yoen's wrists jolted him out of his oblivious state. His fingers had latched onto the High Regent's mare without his notice.

"Your Excellency, I implore you to consider my request this once. Perhaps your esteemed council could accompany me to the volcano. She would bear witness to the event," Yoen pleaded, forcing his hands down to keep them from acting on their own again.

"Cease this nonsense now!" The Regent's voice dropped to a stern whisper meant for Yoen alone. "Do you understand the pandemonium that would ensue if our people think something awry? I won't have unmitigated chaos."

Yoen's teeth clamped his tongue. His insides turned, cheeks flushed from anger, shame, and frustration. He'd have to figure out a different way to convince the High Regent if what he viewed from Rengō persisted. His knees fell onto the black sand kowtowing. "Yes, Your Eminence. My apologies once again. Thank you for your time. To make amends, please allow me to escort you back to town."

"Very well, young Chief, as long as we hear no more about this alleged wickedness."

Yoen's unspoken words hung in the air as they mounted and turned toward the bustling city. The guards, two leading the way and two trailing closely behind, maintained a watchful vigilance. Yet, the city bore witness to the wickedness now unveiled before them.

Beyond the borders of Ka'zan, in the profound silence of the Tanama forests, smoke circled Mount Rengō's summit like spilled ink bleeding across parchment.

ARCHIVES

F ROM THE NORTH AND the East, the men came, hunger
clutched in their hearts. They gathered beneath the ancient
stone canopy of the western city of Ikari's temple—a place of devotion, where the air still remembered each vow whispered beneath
it. The sacred court rose low and wide, shaped by dexterous hands
from massive blocks of stone. Each bore carved spirals and wyvern
sigils, their grooves pulsing faintly with old blood magic. An open
roof surrendered to the watching sky, while stone benches circled
the ceremonial grounds, its surface worn smooth by generations
of dancing feet and ritual.

Ka'zan and Äktas' men demanded an alliance. They sought
Ikari's power to aid in their hunt for the winged ones, though
many young wyverns had already fallen to their greed. They alleged their two cities deserved equal standing, if not more, than
the Ikarites, whose single city flourished with Sages, women of
blood-magic.

But the Ikarite High Priestess, detecting a perpetual rot in their
pleas, denied them.

In response, the men revealed their alternative demands. From
wooden chests, they unveiled two of Ikari's own—Sages Kalissa
and Özge—bound with chains forged from dark onyx. A stone
unlike any known to us then, yet it pulsed with powerful energy.
Even the High Priestess, in all her strength, could not break its grip.

Faced with the unbreakable, she turned to the unthinkable. From Uzoma, the Golden Wyvern—the one who had

forged mountains with her breath and raised mount Pālam from stone—the Priestess had learned the most sacred art: to extract life itself from the living.

And so, to save her Sages, the High Priestess drew the essence from a young wyvern—bright and pure—using its power to break the chains that bound them. The winged creature's energy became part of her, but when it fell, a golden mark appeared around the Priestess' deep brown neck, like a necklace scorched into skin. It was the first of many. Eight she would bear in time—each a cost, each a sacrifice, each a vow.

Beneath the open sky, beneath stone etched with reverence, a war was kindled.

Not with fire, but with a catalyst born of plunder, betrayal, and secrets.

Fragment lxiv: A Catalyst
—From *Daemons Archives, The Original Three*

PART TWO

SECRETS CARVED IN STONES

CHAPTER 4

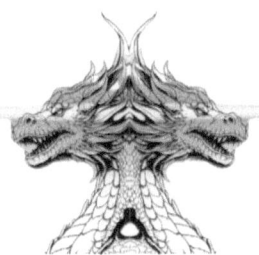

ÄKTAS

ELVA

THE SKY LANTERN SHRANK above as Elva rappelled toward the barren field, the rope burning into her gloves. Wind whipped at her coat and tugged strands of hair loose from her braid, filling her ears with a relentless roar. When her boots hit the ground, her knees buckled. Then she pushed into a sprint, her eyes fixed on the Academy's border wall and gateway ahead.

Dawn painted the sky gold, its warm glow spilling across the land. She skirted the wall overlooking the Tanama Mountains, halted at the archway, and peeled off her gloves, each breath burning in her lungs.

Above her, the five Academy Trade banners swayed, all bearing the ivory emblem of The Hand. Placed at the center of each banner, the symbol featured a stitched raised fist clutching an ignited white stone, encircled by a wyvern's flame, a testament to Ragas' mighty breath.

Elva's left armband mirrored the blue banner of the Artificer Trade, swaying beside the Enchanter's golden banner. In the center, the Militia Trade's maroon standard unfurled, with the forest-green flag of the Terralect Trade on its side, representing a union of foragers, farmers, and miners. On the opposite side, the white banner of the Healer's Trade billowed. The Enchanter's gilded trim outlined every flag, converging into two central lines flowing downward until they reached The Hand's symbol.

"Artificer! What are you doing outside the walls?"

Elva stiffened at the sound of a young man's voice echoing through the archway. So much for slipping by unnoticed. Spotting the red-armbands on the guards, she couldn't help an eye roll before gesturing to the black leather on her shoulders. "It's *Sergeant* Artificer, squire."

"Oi! You're that wildling girl!" the tall one said, pointing a finger at her. "The arsonist from the engineering room last quarter."

Her fists clenched at her side. "It combusted on its own."

"That's irrelevant *Sergeant* Artificer. The rules apply to all. The General Commander will be eager to hear about what you've been doing beyond the wall," the second guard blurted through crooked teeth.

"Ugh! I've got no time for this," she muttered. The tall guard's fingers barely grazed her sleeve before her knee slammed into his gut, doubling him over with a choked gasp. She pivoted, sweeping the legs out from under his companion and sending him crashing to the cobblestones. Without pausing, she bolted toward the main courts.

Elva turned to the botanical lawns where a few Terralects tended the greenhouses, nurturing plants for the Healer Trade. The main stone path led directly to the Generals' courts. Halfway down, the General Commander's voice rose above the courtyard's murmurs, addressing six Militia Sergeants.

Her shoulders tightened. The ache of the marks on her back flooded her memory. Buldar stood as the Militia's General and leader in command of The Hand. In recent years, the Commander's punishments had intensified with rumors of rebel conflicts beyond the Academy's walls. Any hint of deviation faced severe consequences.

Nearing the Bloodroots' greenhouse, a flicker of her reflection in the glass caught her eye, freezing her steps. Her skin was a beautiful mosaic with pale patches, white as snow, covering part of her forehead and scattered across her body, creating striking patterns against the bronze tones. A single white streak of hair traced its path from her hairline, disappearing into the escaped tendrils. But at the sight of the rest of her, her thumbnail dug into the flesh of her index finger, her jaw tightening.

"Wildling," she whispered to herself.

In stark contrast to the pristine petals of the Bloodroot flowers flourishing inside, she recognized the feral image others perceived. Her braid had loosened from its tight bun, stray hairs disrupting the neat lines. The eyes staring back didn't bother her. It was the way grime, ink, and oil seemed to always cling to her, forcing her to break code.

She smeared spit across her palm and waged war with the loose strands. Dust and sand scattered as her hands brushed at her gray coat. Her fingers tugged her blue-armband, then adjusted The Hand pin on her lapel, gleaming above her heart.

"That's the best I can do for you," she said, taking a deep breath.

Gritting her teeth, her feet found their way back into the main stone pathway. Commander Buldar stood a few steps away, giving orders to the Militia Sergeants. A leather belt securing a satchel cinched his Trade's maroon coat with overlapping flaps at the waist. He bore the emblem of The Hand on the left fold of his uniform. Sunlight glinted off his sleek, dark hair, while a precise beard highlighted his carved jaw. Standing with square shoulders, he fixed his piercing eyes on the young Sergeants, unfaltering in command.

"Yes, General Commander." The four women saluted, right fists meeting open left hands. With a sharp click of their boots, their synchronized footsteps echoed past the Artificer's courts.

Elva stepped forward. "Commander Buldar," she said, her voice betraying her with a hushed, almost timid tone while she offered the same salute. "Might I have a moment, General Commander?"

Buldar remained focused on the last Militia members beside him. Without a flicker of distraction, he issued his final orders. The two men acknowledged him with a salute before heading toward the main archway.

"Commander Buldar, I must…"

"Have you seen the state you're in?" he spat. His gaze, cold and steadfast sliced into her.

"Yes, Sir."

"I care not for the indulgence the General Artificer has on you. Filthy menace. You've become a liability. First daylight drills for the next six months! And you'll be tending to the Militia's uniforms for the foreseeable future. Perhaps that will teach you some discipline."

"Yes, Commander Sir, as you order. But…"

"Enough, wildling." With a dismissive flick of his hand, Buldar turned on his heel to the stone stairway.

"There's smoke coming from Rengō, on its summit," Elva burst out, the words tumbling out before his first step could land.

Buldar's neck muscles tightened as he tilted his head back. "And how did you manage to witness this?"

"I saw it while testing the Sky Lantern, Sir," she replied, swallowing the lump in her throat.

Buldar whirled around, his eyes narrowing to brooding slits. "You achieved flight?"

"I, yes, General Commander. I wanted to try them before sunrise, but when I saw the smoke, I ran here."

Crossing the space with three long strides, his shadow fell over her. "Look at me, wildling."

Her gaze lifted to his chin, avoiding direct eye contact, a shiver running down her spine while his gaze bore into her.

"How exactly did you manage to get the Lantern to work? Further, how could you discern such detail. Even in flight, Rengō is leagues away?" The Commander's words cut through the air like steel.

Her teeth sank into the soft flesh of her cheek. "I... um—"

"Speak!"

"I used a magnifier, once the Lantern was at its highest point, Commander." Her fingers curled into tight fists at her side.

"And the Lantern? How did you manage it to float?" Buldar's voice dropped dangerously low.

"I, uh, I used an ignited stone, Sir. It—"

The world exploded in white-hot pain when his fist connected with her chin. The ground rushed up to meet her, rough stone tearing into her palms as she tried to break her fall. Copper filled her mouth, warm and metallic. Everything spun, sounds melting into a high-pitched whine, piercing through her skull.

The General Commander's voice thundered above her, but the words blurred together. "Get up!"

She struggled to push herself back into alert position.

The second blow came like lightning, his knuckles cracking against her cheekbone. Fire erupted across the left side of her face, ice and flame warring beneath her skin. Blood pooled in her mouth, and she struggled upright once more, legs trembling beneath her. Her left eye throbbed, vision blurring at the edges. Through the haze, she braced herself for the next onslaught.

"Is there a problem here?" A familiar voice interrupted the third blow.

Buldar's gaze turned to the General Artificer. "Your pupil is a menace, General Sadfar. Her complete disregard for order and following rules deserves fifty lashes."

Elva's blood drained from her body. Ten lashes. That's the most she had endured. Ten agonizing, searing lashes. The scars on her back never let her forget. At the thought of fifty, her back stiffened.

"Young Elva is the best Artificer we have in the Academy. Whatever she's done, surely, she has an explanation," General Sadfar said.

Buldar shifted his stance, making way for the General Artificer. Sadfar edged closer to Elva in the cerulean coat of his Trade. His fingers found a dark stone ring on his left hand, featuring a wyvern's skull with jaws spread wide enough to cradle his index finger. The General carefully removed the jewel and tucked it inside his coat before addressing her. "What have you done, Sergeant Artificer?"

Elva's swollen lips pressed together, her gaze fixed on a spot on the ground.

"The wildling harnessed a stone to lift one of the Lanters," Commander Buldar said, pulling a handkerchief from his leather satchel and methodically wiping her blood from his knuckles.

"I see," Sadfar replied, lifting an eyebrow.

She tried to remain still, though the throbbing pain in her jaw threatened to make her falter. "Yes General, I wanted to test the heat variances, but when I was up there, I saw—"

"Lies! Maybe fifty lashes won't suffice," Commander Buldar interrupted, fingers twisting the bloodied cloth until his knuckles whitened.

"What did you see?" Sadfar pressed without turning to Buldar.

"I saw smoke, on Rengō's summit, General."

"You're just like your parents. You weave tales to escape your predicament," Buldar uttered. Disgust dripped from every word, though his voice remained controlled.

Sadfar's finger brushed against Elva's throbbing cheek, guiding her face upward with gentleness. A clean cloth appeared in his hand, pressing against her split lip. Her muscles coiled tight, but she held her ground. "How recently did you witness this?"

"I ran as fast as I could, once I saw it."

"As always, the General Commander is right. Using ignited stones without approval is an immense deceit, one that merits a great punishment," Sadfar said, pulling the cloth away and pressing it into her trembling hands. His eyes dropped to his bare finger, tapping the pale band where his ring had rested, before turning to Buldar. "Given the stakes the Sergeant seems ready to face, perhaps an inspection is in order, General Commander."

Both Generals locked eyes before Buldar's lip curled. "If this is a trick, wildling, lashes will be the least of your worries. I'll crush the rebellion with your parents' heads," he spat and turned his heel toward the gates leading to the Iron Tower.

Her spine remained rigid, arms locked at her sides. Sadfar's bloodied cloth crumpled in her fist as she held her salute.

Buldar's footsteps faded before Sadfar spoke again. "The city's unrest has the Commander on edge. Given that your parents are so outspoken about restructuring our council of five, nothing will convince him they are not leading the rebels." He leaned closer, his voice dropping to a whisper. "You know enchanted stones are scarce. Using an ignited one without permission when there's so few of them, especially when the main city threatens the Hand's leadership—well it could be seen as treason. You must see that."

"I understand, General. I'm not fond of the stones myself," Elva muttered, forcing the words past her swollen lip. "I would rather work without them. The pressing orders urged us to make the Lanterns work. Testing more samples without the stones would've taken too long. I failed to see another way.

As for my parents..." Her eyes flickered briefly to meet his before darting away. "I haven't spoken to them in nearly two years. If the Commander deems it fitting, I would much rather face any punishment alone."

"Blood binds you, Sergeant Artificer. Even if you haven't seen them, these ties endure," Sadfar said, his gaze lingering on the finger where his ring used to be. "I have also noticed your aunt's visits every term. The Commander could very well suspect her as well."

Her stomach twisted into knots at the mention of her aunt, bile rising in her throat at the thought of dragging her entire family into this mess.

"I understand the urgency of achieving flight. Yet, if the vision from Rengō proves false, I fear I won't be able to shield you this time," he added before she could answer.

"The smoke is there, General. I," she wavered, "I'm certain."

"We shall see." The General's dark eyes swept over her battered form. "How did you manage it by yourself?"

"Manage it? General?"

"To wield the platform requires the strength of two, at least."

Her muscles locked in place, her gaze darting away for a heartbeat. Her thumbnail carved a crescent into her index finger, but her lips remained sealed. She wouldn't drag Oran down with her.

"Very well, I won't press this time." Sadfar gave a slight nod. "Go get cleaned up, and seek a healer," he said, gesturing to her face before turning away. "Return the stone at once, and make your way to the main court. If danger stirs within those mountains, we'll have much work ahead of us." His footsteps followed Buldar's path toward the Iron Tower.

Elva stood rooted to the spot, her heart crawling up her throat. The mere mention of her parents and aunt sent her stomach churning. Her father's voice still echoed in her mind, denouncing Buldar as a tyrant who couldn't even wield the magic of Äktas' ignited white stones. The whispers of opposition had grown louder in the main city, questioning how a man without the Enchanter's gift had risen so quickly through the ranks. Her father's convictions about Buldar had always clashed with her determination to join the Academy and the Artificer's Trade.

But none of that mattered now. Her father's distrust of The Hand had labeled both him and her mother as rebels. On top of that, her recent attempts at engineering had spiraled into chaos, often because of her impulsive actions. Buldar had branded her a wildling for a reason. A wildling with rebel parents.

The path to the Iron Tower stretched before her, empty now but for the shadows of her fears. Her pulse quickened. If the smoke atop Rengō proved nothing more than a trick of her imagination, she'd have to face the consequences of her recklessness. Again.

With a sharp inhale, she dashed toward the Artificers quarters. The heavy door groaned under her push, her footsteps echoing against dark wooden floors. Stone columns, crowned with metal lanterns, guided her eyes to the central staircase. Each lantern bathed the area in a warm amber light. An iron chandelier, crafted in the shape of Zuwena, the lightning wyvern, harmonized with their glow. The metallic figure spread her wings wide, her belly shimmering in gentle hues of white and blue.

Her eyes shifted from the Zuwena shaped chandelier as a blond first-year Artificer descended the staircase, his arms clutching several parchments in his hands.

"Sergeant Elva. Are you alright?" the boy asked, his cheeks freckled with dark ink.

"Fenris." Her fingers fumbled with a loose curl, tucking it behind her ear. "I'm fine. Why do you ask?"

His ink-stained finger shot to her face. "There's blood on your lips, Sergeant."

"Oh! I took a stumble, but I'm okay." Her hand flew to cover her throbbing lip. "How are the first-trials coming along? Did you figure out the searing ash mix for the Trade's tests?" she said in a hurry.

"Not entirely, but I've been up all night measuring each element," he said, fingers drumming against his stack of parchments. "Would you review my findings again? Maybe you'll see something I'm missing. I really want to impress the Generals," he added, adjusting the pin on his lapel.

"Sure. But it might have to wait. The Commander will be calling us to an assembly soon."

Fenris' face lit up like a lantern. "Thank you so much, Sergeant Elva."

"Don't mention it." She watched him bounce through the main door, wondering if she had ever looked that young when she first joined the Academy.

The sight of him reminded her of home. Her parents and the intoxicating aroma of magnolia blossoms drifting across the stone courtyard. The soft melody of her mom's voice that danced through the stone walls and spilled into neighboring homes. She even missed collecting snails with her aunt. All sacrificed for a place at the Academy, for her dream of crafting artifacts that would free Äktas from its dependence on the vile enchanted stones.

Her chin throbbed in time with her pulse, the ringing in her ear a constant echo as she steadied herself before climbing the steps. Her fingers trailed over the carving of The Hand's emblem, lingering on the glowing white stone clasped within a fist.

The insatiable lust for the gems had cursed the Tanama. But she had been rowing against an unrelenting current. While she strived to create new tools, the city's hunger for the stones only grew. Now, with another death sentence slithering atop Rengō, the tide threatened to swallow her whole.

Inside the Sergeants' dormitory, blue tapestries rippled overhead like waves. Morning light spilled through crescent moon windows, casting long shadows across two rows of facing cots. Fellow Sergeants bustled about, slipping into gray coats and adjusting cerulean armbands, preparing for the first light assembly. Her eyes darted from face to face, searching for Oran. His absence sent her heart racing. Sweat beaded on her palms, fearing the Lantern had gotten him into trouble.

"Did you enjoy your evening escapade?" A third-year Sergeant's voice cut through the air. "What a wildling creature you are. What happened to you this time?" she scoffed. "Don't tell me another of your experiments exploded in your face."

Laughter erupted around her. Under the weight of fifteen stares, Elva's fingers curled into fists at her side. She didn't flinch. Years of mockery had taught her which battles to fight and which to ignore.

Jaw tight, she brushed past the third-year without a word and made for her cot. The metal armoire beside it creaked, the hinges protesting while she retrieved a clean uniform. When she turned toward the communal baths, Oran appeared, water dripping from his raven hair onto his open high-collar shirt. His eyes widened at the sight of her face, and before she could speak, his fingers closed around her arm, pulling her from the dormitory into the Artificer's meeting quarters.

"Wait, Oran. I have to change," she protested as he settled her into a chair beside a tall glass window.

"What happened to your face?" He dropped to his knees before her, his fingers lightly tracing over her chin before tilting her face toward the sunlight. With his sleeve, he dabbed at the blood smeared across her skin.

"How was the descent? How did you manage to get back so quick...?"

"Did he strike you?" he interrupted, his eyes narrowing with intensity.

She ignored his question. "Have you heard anything about the smoke? The Commander was heading to the Iron Tow..."

"Did he strike you?" The muscles in his jaw jumped beneath his skin.

"Did you hear me? He went to the tower. He never goes to the mining site, what if the smoke is gone?"

"El..." he said, his voice strained with hidden rage while he cradled her face in his hands. "Did he strike you?"

"It doesn't matter. Did you hear what I said? The smoke, is it there?" Elva pulled away slightly. "I'm fine," she mumbled, avoiding his gaze, fearing his potential retaliation.

His hands gripped the chair's armrests, his dark eyes boring into her wounds as if he could heal them through sheer will. Her cheeks flushed under his scrutiny.

With the rise of the city rebels, he had joined in secret conversations about standing up against Buldar's military regime. But conversations alone had gotten many rebel's heads displayed around the Academy's walls. The thought made her blood curl. "Oran, the Commander is going to have us gather soon. Please!" she begged, hoping he wouldn't continue to press.

"The smoke is there. It's growing. The tower guards already saw it. We could've brought the Lantern down together after all." His fingertips traced the raw scrapes across her palms. "Your hands are hurt too."

"Growing? Do they know what it is?" She winced when his fingers brushed the tender skin. "What about the Lantern and the other things?" The words tumbled out while his tender touch traced her bloodied lip, lingering there before pulling away as if resisting the need to mend her. "Oran, please. We don't have a lot of time."

"I bribed two first-year Artificers to help me put the Lantern away, that's how I managed to get back so quickly. But I didn't have time to return the rest of the *borrowed* items," he sighed. "What is the punishment?"

"Do you really want to talk about this now? Do you realize what's happening?" Her fingers tugged at the end of her long sleeves, attempting to conceal the wounds on her hands.

With a soft touch, he reclaimed her hands in his. "We don't know what's happening. What's the punishment?"

"Nothing." Elva flinched as she bit her lower lip, tasting of blood.

"Lying has never been your strength," he retorted with a raised eyebrow.

"I'm a perfectly good liar! Besides, General Sadfar might help. As long as the smoke on Rengō holds true."

Oran's nostrils flared. "Sadfar was there too?"

"He intervened," she admitted.

"He didn't intervene fast enough." A low snarl rumbled in his throat before he took a deep breath, his chest expanding slowly. "Let's get you to a healer."

"I promise, I'm fine," she insisted, pulling her arm free. "There's no time for a healer. We need to get ready. They might tell us what's going on during the assembly." Her eyes flickered to his sleeves, now stained crimson. "You're going to need a new shirt. You should pick one that fits. You couldn't even button that one," she added, a shy smirk tugging at her lips.

"I'll fetch a healer while you clean up." The muscles in his jaw shifted with the effort of another controlled breath.

"There's no need, really. We don't have time, and I don't want to be a bother. You've already done enough today," she stammered, glancing at the floor.

Oran's fingers twitched at his side before closing around her arm, steering her with more urgency than gentleness toward the dormitory.

"I'm sorry I left you on the Lantern." Her voice broke through the silence. "I thought it was urgent, so I jumped. I shouldn't have left you alone."

"Go get cleaned up. I'll be back in a few minutes." His shoulders remained rigid, and without meeting her gaze, he turned and walked away.

Her eyes followed him, watching him hurry down the stairways. She'd rather face whatever punishment came from the Lantern incident on her own. Should the Commander learn of Oran's involvement, his fate would be at risk. Her lips quivered at the thought that he might be better off with a less impulsive friend. One that would not be so reckless, so feral and wild.

The dormitory stood nearly empty now, giving her the chance for a hurried shower before she pulled on a fresh uniform. Her fingers worked quickly, weaving her dark and white hair into a tight braid while she shoved her feet into her boots. Sitting to adjust the leather, the blue wool blanket on her cot shifted, revealing an unexpected lump beneath it. Her heart skipped a beat when she pulled back the covers to find her satchel tucked safely away.

"Thanks, Oran!"

The satchel's clasp clicked open under her fingers. The magnifier lay next to the small ruby box housing the ignited stone, every borrowed item accounted for. She slipped into her shoulder harness, securing an extra strap around her waist to anchor the bag in place. When she rushed from the dormitory, a piercing wailing sound echoed through the air. A harrowing alarm rose and fell in a haunting rhythm, sending shivers down her spine.

The Hand issued a decree with a resounding call to arms that echoed through the courts. An ominous tension settled over the Academy grounds as whispers of the mandatory lockdown spread like wildfire. The transmission from the Iron Tower's amplifiers crackled with intermittent static, delivered by a raspy voice in a flat, monotone cadence.

Attention, all Academy Trades of Äktas:

This is an order by decree from The Hand, the council of the five, led by the esteemed General Commander Buldar of the Militia Trade.

Effective immediately:

The Academy grounds are under complete lockdown.
Unauthorized movement in or out of the Academy without approval is strictly forbidden.
All Academy Trades must support the war effort against Ikari in the west and Ka'zan in the north.
Report to your Trade's meeting quarters without delay.
A city-wide curfew is now in effect from dusk until dawn.

COMPLIANCE IS MANDATORY!

All communications must be routed through the Commander's courts.

Any deviation from these orders will be regarded as treason
and punished by death.
Stand resolute as stone and steel, Äktastary.
Rule with Might. Master Innovation.
Uphold and Honor our Legacy!

CHAPTER 5

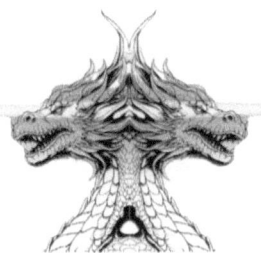

IKARI

ASANTE

T HE WYVERN FEATHER CAPE threatened to slip from Asante's grip before she managed to drape it over the Priestess'
shoulders. Though the weight of the garment tugged at her arms,
Samira bore its weight effortlessly, standing tall as the saffron raiment flowed around her with natural grace.

Asante shifted her weight on the stool, her bare feet gripping
the wooden surface as she reached for Samira's shoulders. Her
gaze flicked to the balcony, mind shadowed by the looming threat
beyond the Tanama. In the distance, smoke uncoiled from Rengō,
its growing presence tightening the tension inside the Priestess'
chambers like a bowstring ready to snap. The ivory robes and
feather cape gracing Samira's shoulders were no ordinary attire.
They were reserved exclusively for the summer ritual set for the
next day. Despite the century-old tradition, the Priestess called for
an earlier Marking Ritual.

The stool beneath Asante's feet wobbled when she stretched
upward, fingers struggling with the final lace. Another glance at
the Tanama's ominous silhouette threw her off balance, causing
a feather's quill to pierce her skin. The sharp sting made her

stumble. Then the world tilted, and her back slammed against the hard floor. Crimson droplets welled up from her fingertip, trailing down her palm.

"Perhaps a lower tiered attendant would do better," Samira snapped.

"My apologies, your Grace." She pressed her forehead to the floor in a deep bow.

Blue light pulsed through the chamber, drawing her gaze to the tree roots winding through the roof and walls. The ethereal glow danced along each tendril, carrying messages that scattered through the caves of Mount Pālam. Through the living conduits, the Priestess' summons reached out to the Sages, calling them to gather at the High Tree.

"Today is not a day for mistakes, child." Samira's fingers brushed an alabaster root, sending more waves of sapphire light coursing through its length. Then she crouched, lifting Asante's chin with a gentle touch. "You could still make yourself useful. Tend to this mess and change into fresh robes. Then join us at the High Tree." The Priestess' eyes caught the bright lights emanating from the tree roots, but her dissecting gaze lingered on Asante.

Her breath hitched as Samira's golden fingers grazed her skin, warmth flooding through her—intimate and invasive. The Priestess' gaze burrowed into her core, prying open the hidden corners of her mind, heart, and soul. *Don't let her in*, a familiar voice echoed in Asante's thoughts. Fighting the intrusion, she squeezed her eyes shut, breaking the mental probe.

"No markings for you this year, young one," Samira added before standing and striding to the chamber's main door, her saffron cape trailing over the glossy floor with every step. "Do as you're told and make haste. Speak to no one about what you've witnessed," she urged, turning toward the hallway outside, leaving Asante alone with her thoughts.

Watching the luminous veins of tree roots branch out in every direction, her throat tightened. Each cave on every tier received a message from Samira. Yet, Asante only knew the marking ritual's timing had changed. The threat above Rengō forced the Priestess to break an ancient tradition. And if the High Priestess feared it, it meant the entire city teetered on the brink of chaos.

Asante traced her bare cheeks and chin, where Enchanters and Sage's markings ought to be. Past the balcony, her gaze fixed on the mantle of smoke, a distant enemy mocking her powerlessness. With no markings to defend her city, she remained bound to the Priestess' orders, a mere spectator. Her fists clenched, the lingering sting of the wyvern's feather prickling her skin.

Blood beaded on her fingertip as Samira's recent mind-weaving stare flickered through her memory. She hated it. She didn't like being so seen, so exposed. The sensation only reminded her of her dreams of late. The Uláak in the dead forests, drawing nearer, their hollow eyes reaching out.

Echoes from the hallway jolted her from her thoughts, reminding her of Samira's orders and she rushed to the chambers nestled on the corner tier below. The windowless quarters served as a refuge for the attendants, who spent most of their time running errands and caring for their Sages.

Her steps halted when she spotted Zama, the Fifth Sage, deep in conversation with Lux, her own attendant.

"Asante! Where are you heading?" Zama's hand lifted in greeting.

"Avian Sage. Good day," Asante acknowledged her with a bow. "I'm headed to my chambers for a moment. I have orders from the High Priestess."

"Call me Zama, please. Do you know what's happening? She has summoned the Sages and the Enchanters to the High Tree."

"I have strict orders to not speak a word, Avian Sa—Miss Zama," she replied, her eyes tracing the dark dotted lines stretching from the corners of the Sage's nose to her temples, stark against her warm amber skin.

"I understand," the Fifth Sage conceded before addressing Lux and handing her a stack of parchments. "Please bring these to my quarters. Should the need come up, I'll send for you." And with a nod, she glided up the corridor.

"Sante, what in the wyverns' skies is going on?" Lux's wide brown eyes searched her face, red braid swinging as she leaned closer. "Everyone's seen the smoke outside, and—what happen to your face?" she gasped, eyebrows shooting up as she pointed to Asante's bruises.

Her hand flew to her forehead. "I can't tell you. I know very little myself," she whispered, fingers wrapping around Lux's free wrist and pulling her into their small chamber.

Behind the round door, Lux settled the parchments on a wooden chair. Then she quickly switched on a small stone lamp, powered by the bloodstone magic streaming through Pālam, filling the small chamber with warm light. Their twin cots pushed against opposite walls, each crowned with meticulously folded wool blankets. Weather-worn chests squatted at the foot of each bed. Two desks filled the space between the cots on opposite ends. Letters from home sprawled across Asante's space, while Lux's held her grandmother's worn portrait and a collection of gleaming golden feathers.

"You're still collecting your Sage's owl feathers? Doesn't she find it odd?" she asked, digging through her trunk, fingers brushing over fresh tunics.

Lux's eyes crinkled at the corners when she caught Asante's gaze, then she exploded with laughter. "I hadn't thought about it that way," she said, tracing one feather with a light touch. "Have you seen her golden owl form? The way her feathers catch the light... What I wouldn't give to be able to fly!" Lux added, helping her put on her new tunics. "Do you think we might get our markings this year?"

Asante slipped her arms through the sleeves, the clean fabric dancing against her deep brown skin. Her lips curved into a wide smile. "I really do want them. I need them. But I couldn't think of anyone who deserves them more than you."

"I still can't believe I'm an attendant to the Avian Sage," Lux said, her voice softening. "That alone is enough for me. But I admit, having wings would be incredible."

"You'd sore the skies, high and mighty like Ragas!"

Their combined laughter filled the room, but Lux's expression quickly faded, slipping away like the sun behind storm clouds. "What do you think the smoke means?"

Asante's hand found Lux's shoulder, squeezing gently. "I'm not sure, but I know we'll be okay. The High Tree will always protect us."

A ghost of a smile flickered across Lux's lips. "I swear, you treat that old tree as if it were a real person. The way you talk to it when you think no one's watching..."

"Well, that's because he's alive, and I've known him longer," she said, fingers dancing through her hair, adjusting a few of the golden beads on her locs. "Soon, you'll get tired of me rambling on and on."

"I would never, not after everything." Lux reached up, her fingers delicately plucking leaves from Asante's hair. "If it hadn't been for you, sneaking me into your chamber after my nana died, I don't know what I would've done. Then you helped me become Sage Zama's attendant. I could never get tired of you."

Asante's arms wrapped around Lux, pulling her into a tight embrace. She eased back, glancing at Lux's hands twisting the fabric of her own sleeves. "I have to get back. If I linger too long, the Priestess might turn me into a stonefly," she added before turning toward the corridors. "Try not to worry too much. We live inside a giant rock protected by the High Tree. Besides, I'm sure the High Priestess has everything under control."

The passageways buzzed with activity as attendants rushed past, their hurried footsteps and whispered conversations creating a symphony of anxiety. A knot coiled in Asante's stomach, tightening with each step. Her reassuring words to Lux rang hollow in her own ears. What loomed over Rengō had cast a shadow of unease across the entire city, even the High Priestess.

Yet, her thoughts drifted to the possible earlier reunion with her mother and sister, a bright spot amid the spreading dread. Her heart lifted at the thought, rather grateful for Samira's decision to accelerate the Marking Ritual.

"Little Rabbit!" A deep but gentle voice caught her attention.

Her brother's tall silhouette stood by one of the lunar stone windows. The daylight seeping through the opening outlined his broad shoulders. "Tarrak? What are you doing here?" Her eyes widened, her heart swelling with a mix of surprise and joy.

His dark honey locs had grown, cascading past his shoulders. A broken arrow's pick secured the top half of his hair at the back. His rich golden-brown skin glistened slightly, the warm hue contrasting with the shadows around him. Without a word, he crossed the space between them and enveloped her in a tight hug.

When he finally pulled back, his amber eyes drank in the sight of her. "Look at you! When did you get so tall? It's only been a few months. How is that possible?"

Asante took a step back, her eyes studying him in disbelief. "It's been a year since we last saw each other. And how are you here? The lower tiers are not allowed up in the Sages' tiers."

"I always find my way to you," he said with a wide grin, mischief dancing in his eyes. "I had planned to come tomorrow for the ritual, but I hear it's changed. The city is rattled..." His expression sobered. "I snuck in to see you, my little sister. Besides, I'm always around, even if you don't notice, little Rabbit."

"Don't call me rabbit," she sighed, though the corner of her mouth twitched upward with a slight smile. "I'm nearly as tall as you. And you're only older by five summers. I'm glad to see you, but I've got no time. I have to go see the Priestess."

Ignoring her dismissal, Tarrak's calloused hand wrapped around her wrist, pulling her beneath the flickering light of a burning torch. "Have you seen the skies? The smoke cloaking Rengō? Mom's worried. Everyone is."

"I have orders not to say anything," she answered, trying to step away, but his gentle grip held firm. "I have to go."

"Look at me, Rabbit."

"Tarrak!" she scowled, but her brother didn't flinch.

His eyebrows knitted together as he leaned closer while his free hand reached up to her forehead. "What happened to your face?"

"Missed a few branches climbing down the High Tree, but I'm fine. I have to go, please."

Instead of leaving, his arms opened wide while a bright smile spread across his face. "Come here!"

Her shoulders dropped in surrender and she stepped into his arms with a sigh. A knot formed in her throat as his familiar scent enveloped her—the warm, yeasty aroma of their father's home-made bread mingled with the sweet, floral notes of kapok tree flowers. "You smell like Baba."

"Is that so, Rabbit?"

"I have to go," she said, breaking free and running up the corridor.

"Hey!" His voice bounced off the stone walls. "May the High Tree guide your steps today, little Rabbit." His right fist pressed against his heart.

"May your feet follow!" she replied with a smile, matching the gesture.

The morning sun climbed higher in the sky by the time Asante reached Pālam's summit. The High Priestess stood like a regal statue beside the High Tree, her gaze fixed on the distant horizon where smoke slithered past Rengō's skirts.

Eleven women formed a perfect crescent before Priestess Samira. Five Sages stood in golden cloaks, their faces marked with dark dotted lines tracing a path from nose to temple. Beside them, six Stone Enchanters wore cloaks of deep emerald, their bloodstone amulets and weapons casting ruby reflections in the sunlight. Each Enchanter bore a straight mark from their lower lip to their chin, like a drop of ink frozen in its fall.

Asante hung back, noticing she was the only attendant present. Her eyes scanned the courtyard, ears catching fragments of conversations that made her feel like an intruder amidst the gathering.

"Your Highness, what of the smoke?" Ida, the oldest Enchanter, inquired, the sun dancing with her bloodstone staff, casting ribbons of ruby light.

"The Avian Sage will investigate," Samira ordered.

Zama's head dipped low in a bow. "Yes, your Grace."

Ida's grip tightened on her staff. "Your Highness, the Fifth Sage has not yet fully honed her skill. To reach Rengō, Sage Zama will have to carve a path through the haunted forests." Her somber words chilled the air between them. "The wind speaks in riddles today. I cannot see her fate." Besides serving as a powerful weapon, the bloodstone staff also acted as a conduit to glimpses beyond, allowing Ida to see momentarily into the future.

At the oldest Enchanter's words, Samira's gaze pierced the Tanama. A gust of wind swept through the gathering, tossing the eleven women's cloaks in a dance, their weapons and amulets glinting in the light. Yet Samira's saffron cloak remained still, as if the wind itself dared not touch her.

"Indeed, strange how the wind hides its secrets." Samira's voice carried the weight of steel, her eyes never leaving Rengō's silhouette. "Even from me," she added in a blood-curdling tone and then directed her attention to Zama. "Avian Sage, you've been practicing your horned owl form for a while now. Haven't you?"

The Fifth Sage took a step forward from the half-circle. "Yes, Your Highness."

"Then today you'll truly hone your skill. Make your way to our enemy cities, Äktas and Ka'zan. Then to the mountain king, Rengō."

"Th-through the dead forest, Your Highness?" Zama wavered.

Samira turned to the Fifth Sage, her cloak following every motion. "We must not hesitate today. Your Sage powers will guide you." Her voice lowered to a dangerous whisper. "Unless, you'd prefer not to heed my command?"

Zama's right fist flew to her heart and she bent low, her golden cloak pooling around her feet. "No, Your Grace. I will do as you order."

Asante's eyes caught Zama's other hand clenched at her side. Her own heart thundered against her ribs. Those who entered the Tanama—never returned.

"Find out the cause of the smoke and bring news from Ka'zan and Äktas. Our neighbors in the north and the east must be witnessing the smoke as well. Go! Make haste." Samira's final words dripped with venom. "Avian Sage, make sure to come back with answers or don't come back at all."

"As you command, Your Highness," Zama replied, though her voice barely concealed her unease. She bowed to the Priestess once more before turning toward the iron gate. As she passed, her gaze locked with Asante's, terror flickering in her golden eyes like a trapped flame.

Samira's attention shifted to the Enchanters. "Gather the women and young girls of age from the lower tiers and bring them to the Great Hall. Have them don their ritual cloaks. We'll conduct a special Marking Ritual exclusively for them and the Sages. Afterward, proceed to Pālam's watchtowers. You'll receive further instructions when the time is right," she ordered, her gaze sweeping over the remaining women. "Sages and Asante, remain with me."

"Is it wise for the Enchanters not to partake in the ritual?" The words burst from Okama's lips. Her twin broadswords caught the light, their bloodstone hilts pulsing with ruby energy.

Samira's eyes raked over the young Enchanter like talons.

As if sensing the dangerous shift in the air, Narisa stepped forward, her dark curls bound tightly at the back of her head. Shadows pooled beneath her eyes, making her already pale skin seem almost translucent. She stood as the oldest of the Sages, yet the markings from her nose to her temple remained vivid, like fresh ink on parchment. "Your Grace, please pay no mind to Enchanter Okama's words. She's still too young to grasp the severity of the situation." She paused, measuring her next words like precious gems. "Even so, I must note that it is rather unusual for some of us not to participate in the venerated ritual, Your Highness."

"Today's ritual is reserved solely for the Sages and the unmarked women from the lower tiers. No one else goes in." Samira's command rang through Pālam's summit. "Ensure the Great Hall is sealed."

The six Stone Enchanters bowed without objection, pressing their right fists to their chests, and hurried toward the iron gate. Once they departed, Samira finally locked eyes with Asante.

Come here child. The words reverberated through Asante's mind while the Priestess's lips remained still.

Her feet carried her forward, each step careful as she positioned herself beside the High Tree, its ancient bark rough and weathered against the morning light.

The Priestess' voice rumbled once again across Pālam's peak. "Sages, reckoning is upon us. Over a century ago, our city fought valiantly to gain scraps of the remaining wyverns. It was here, on this very mountain, that Ka'zan's High Regent Magnar met his end, and I, holding his head, bore witness to the turning point of the Great War. But before his fall, it is believed that he captured the last wyvern of the land."

The wind died, leaving nothing but the sound of Asante's heart-beat thundering in her ears. Even the rustle of the Sages' robes fell silent.

Samira's eyes fixed on the jagged peaks of the Tanama mountains, their lifeless summits piercing the sky. "During the Great War, Zuwena, the lightning wyvern, found herself wounded in the shadows of those highlands. This was long before Ragas' spell sealed the fate of those woods," she continued while her gaze appeared distant with memory. Then her gilded finger extended toward Ka'zan in the north. "In a sinister twist, Regent Magnar took Zuwena prisoner before meeting his own demise at my hands. For a century—the agni stone city has held the wyvern captive."

Silence stretched between them. The Priestess' heels clicked against stone, her movements fluid as water while her eyes scrutinized each of the four Sages. The golden markings etched across her dark-brown skin pulsed with life of their own.

Clasping her hands in front of her, Samira's spine straightened before she spoke again. "I fear the smoke billowing above Rengō is the vengeance Zuwena seeks."

A ripple of murmurs spread through the gathered Sages, their robes rustling as they shifted. Narisa stepped forward. "This isn't recorded in any of our sacred scrolls. Why are we only hearing of this now? If there's a wyvern charging toward our city, how can we sit here and pretend we're prepared? We are no match against the creature's powers."

The air crackled with tension when Samira's head snapped to Narisa. "What do you take me for, Shroudmist Sage? I am the conqueror of mountains, slayer of wyverns and men." Fire erupted in the Priestess' eyes, golden light blazing from within. Wind exploded from beneath her feather cloak, whipping it into a fury of motion. "I have witnessed the Elder wyverns who gave the women of Ikari their essence. How dare you question me!" The markings across her skin ignited like molten metal, their light so intense it burned the eyes, forcing the Sages and Asante to their knees, foreheads pressed against stone.

Narisa's voice quivered. "My apologies, Your Highness, I did not mean any disrespect."

"Silence!" Samira hissed as her glowing eyes and marks dimmed. "Get out of my sight. Prepare for the ritual. Wait for my orders."

The Sages retreated past the High Tree. Asante remained with her forehead to the ground, not daring to move.

"Stand child."

Asante's legs trembled with obedience, her eyes fixed on the ground rather than risk meeting that ferocious gaze. The sound of the saffron cape against stone drew her attention to Samira gliding toward the High Tree's massive trunk. The Priestess' gilded hand pressed against the ancient bark, and the air filled with the crack and groan of living wood. The solid bark split and peeled away like heavy drapes drawn aside.

Golden light spilled from Samira's fingertips. She reached into the now hollowed trunk, her movements precise and reverent. When she withdrew her hands, they cradled a jade sphere, its surface catching and reflecting the glow of her touch.

"Help me with this," Samira requested.

Asante extended her shaking hands and the gem's weight settled into her palms, cool and smooth against her skin. Before Samira, the tree trunk groaned once more, the bark closing seamlessly as if it had never been opened. Then, with practiced precision, her fingers peeled away a thin layer of bark. The material transformed in the Priestess' hands, becoming as fluid as silk, dancing in the morning breeze.

"I need you to pay close attention to what I'm about to tell you. In your hands, you hold the entire fate of our city."

Asante's gaze darted between the gem and the Priestess, her heart hammering against her ribs.

"If my speculations are correct, and the lightning wyvern found a way to escape Ka'zan's volcanic cage after all this time, then I'm certain she will be coming for what you now hold in your hands. This, Asante, is Zuwena's last embryo."

"A wyvern's egg?" she gasped, awe and terror gripping her heart.

"It is a gem," Samira admitted while her hands traced the air above the sphere, golden light dancing between her skin and its surface. "Once a living seed, but it has long been stripped of life. It was capture with enough time to be transfigured into raw power, even surpassing the strength of our ignited stones. For a century, it has rested within our High Tree, feeding magic into the very bones of our city." Her feet glided to the cliff's edge, her feather cape catching the sunlight. Her arms rose toward the sprawling ruins below, where the abandoned city stretched toward the Tanama's edge.

"Our city barely survived the war," she murmured, the wind catching her words and carrying them across the summit. "Those abandoned streets below echo with the footsteps of the fallen, a testament to all we've lost."

The Priestess paced back to the High Tree. The golden markings around her neck gleamed like molten gold in the morning light. "You've seen our numbers dwindle," she continued, her voice taking on a heavier tone. "Each year, fewer Sages light our halls and fewer Enchanters shape our stones. We depend more on our miners, like your father, sending them deeper into the earth for every precious bloodstone."

Asante's nails scraped against the embryo at the mention of her father. They should have never been ordered to mine so close to the dead forest. He walked in, entranced by its call, and the Uláak made sure he never returned. The thought alone sent heat prickling beneath her skin.

Samira inched closer. A flush crept up Asante's neck, frustration tightening in her chest. She drew a slow, measured breath, hoping it hadn't betrayed her. Any hint of defiance would only invite trouble. Relief washed over her as the Priestess continued to speak of the stone-gem, unaware her thoughts had wandered.

Samira's eyes fell to the jade egg in Asante's hands. "This gem gave our five Sages their power, helped our Enchanters master their gifts. Just as the wyverns once blessed the women of our city, before the Great War tore our land apart."

Asante's throat was too dry for words.

As if reading her mind this time, Samira turned to her and covered the gem with the shroud she had made from the tree's bark. "Only a few share this secret, child. Now you stand among them." Her voice sliced through the silence, each word a warning. "Zuwena must never claim this embryo. With it, she would wield power great enough to reduce our city to ash."

An invisible weight hung around Asante's shoulders, making her stomach clench and her knees weaken. Questions burned on her tongue, but she bit them back, uncertain why she'd been chosen for this burden.

"Young Asante," Samira's voice softened, though her firm stare remained. "I'm entrusting you with this knowledge because I need you to guard it. Shield it from every searching eye."

The ground shifted beneath Asante. "Your Grace, m-m-me? You want me to take care of the gem?"

Samira's finger traced one of Asante's locs. "I've watched you since your first marking ritual on your eleventh summer solstice. After eight summers, though no magic flows in your veins, your mind stands like a fortress, and your loyalty is as unshakeable as our mighty High Tree." Her finger paused in its gesture. "The mother of this embryo will attempt to connect to it. She'll seek a path through your thoughts. But you must bar her way in, just as you've barred mine. Push Zuwena from your mind as you've pushed me from yours."

Asante's eyes widened, realizing the Priestess knew of her resistance against the mind-weaving.

A small smile curved Samira's lips. "You thought I hadn't noticed?" The smile faded just as quickly. "Earlier today, when you prepared my cape, I challenged your defenses. You turned me aside without a thought. Now you must show the same strength against the matriarch wyvern."

She didn't let Asante conjure a word as she continued. "Make your way out of Pālam discreetly and seek refuge in the abandoned city. Answer my call when I connect with your mind. When that time comes, I expect you to let me in."

"Your Grace, the abandoned city?" Fear crawled into Asante's voice, creeping like frost on glass. "It's so close to the dead forests." The idea of being near the woods that took her father's life made her heart race. If her strong and determined father couldn't resist the sinister tug of the haunted grounds, she wouldn't stand a chance. No one had ever survived the magnetic pull of the forest, let alone the Uláak.

"It's the safest option," Samira said with a tone that left no room for argument. "Stick to the heart of the abandoned city. Distance weakens the forest's pull." She paused, deep in thought. "If Zuwena comes, she will head directly here, then to the mines. Let us hope the creature believes her embryo is lost to time."

"Your Grace, what about the marking ritual?"

Samira strode to the gate. "As I said, you carry no Sage's magic nor the Enchanter's gift." Her dark eyes held Asante's for a long moment, weighing and measuring. "No one must know the embryo has left its nest. There are enemy forces acting against us. Secrecy and loyalty will become our shields as our city's fate hangs in the balance." She stopped at the threshold, one hand on the iron gate. "Oh! Dear child," she added, her voice carrying the chill of winter. "Should Zuwena claim her prize, or should it fall to enemy hands, your family's blood will answer for your failure."

The gate groaned shut behind the Priestess, leaving her warning hanging in the air like poison. Asante's breath came in short gasps. With dread coursing through her veins, she turned to face the High Tree, the wrapped embryo pressing against her chest. With a bow, her fist found her heart.

"Guide my steps, mightiest of Trees."

CHAPTER 6

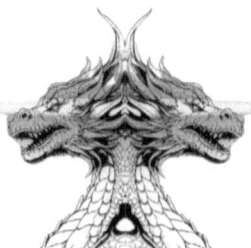

IKARI

ASANTE

THE STONE CORRIDORS BUSTLED with movement. Attendants rushed past—robes rustling, lips drawn tight. Asante moved through them, her steps weaving between the tension. Hushed murmurs and protests filled the air, mingling with nervous discussions about the smoke spreading past Rengō.

Lux's empty cot greeted her when she entered their cavern. Her stomach twisted with a mix of concern and jealousy. Right now, her friend would be participating in the marking ritual without her. She yanked open her trunk, rummaging for a suitable satchel, when her fingers brushed against familiar dark fabric. Her ritual cloak.

Pain shot through her forehead. She hissed, pressing her palm against the tender flesh. Her fingers traced the bruise while her thoughts raced between her fall from the High Tree and the Priestess' shocking revelations.

Her heart echoed Narisa and Okama's defiant protests above Pālam, though she would never dare speak against the Priestess. A wyvern. The word alone sent shivers down her spine. No one had glimpsed such a beast since her great-grandmother's time, much less one crackling with lightning's fury. Now its lifeless offspring nestled in her palms. Her fingertips scraped the stone shell. Her lungs fought for air. The reality of a living wyvern staggered her mind, but the greater terror lurked at the edges of her thoughts. Zuwena hunted for the treasure she now guarded.

And to make matters worse, the place where Samira instructed her to flee, terrified her just as much as being hunted by an ancient creature. "I can't believe she wants us to go to the abandoned city," she muttered to the egg in disbelief. "That's so close to the dead forest—far too close to the Uláak." Her grandmother's warnings about the Tanama rang in her ears. The trilateral mountains loomed, not as mere charred wilderness, but writhed with a twofold doom.

Near the end of the Great War, the forests overflowed with magic-filled remains of fallen wyverns. And at the heart of the highlands, Rengō harbored powerful stones buried within its bedrocks. In retaliation for the human's role in the slaughter of their kin, the Great Horned Ragas bound the Uláak to these haunted woods, condemning them to guard both magical bones and minerals. To add to their torment, the forests themselves hungered for the living. Like fish to bait, humans found themselves hearing the forests' calls, unable to resist their lure. Lost in trance, they would wander inside until their corrupted guardians finished them.

Nestled too close to the dead woods and its pull, the Ikarites left their old city behind. Despite all the warnings. After all the lives lost to those cursed woods, the Priestess' orders to hide within the abandoned city made Asante's blood run cold.

She sank to the floor beside her cot, placing the jade egg in her lap. "I can't do this. I'll just tell the Priestess she's mistaken." She didn't know what bothered her more, being entrusted with an impossible task, or hearing Samira say aloud what she had feared for so many years. "No Sage or Enchanter's magic," she whispered, staring down at her hands. The truth hit her like a sharp dagger to the chest. "I'm just an attendant, with no powers, no magic," she whispered.

The jade caught the flicker from the lantern, turning the dark veins into twisting shadows beneath its surface. Her fingertip followed each current until her nail scraped against the cool shell. "How does she expect me to keep you safe when I have no way to fight back? What if I fail?"

Samira's words echoed in her mind... *Should Zuwena claim her prize, or should it fall to enemy hands, your family's blood will answer for your failure.* Sweat beaded on her forehead. Her chest constricted with each heartbeat until black spots danced at the edges of her vision.

The threat jolted her to her feet. She eased the egg down on her cot until it settled into the wool blanket's fold. "All right, then. Looks like we're doing this, little one." She stared at it, hands flying to her temples. "Skies! I still can't believe it. A wyvern's embryo inside the mighty tree!"

Her hands wrapped the gem in the mantle Samira had peeled from the High Tree, then tucked it deep into her satchel. At the doorway, her gaze snagged on the ritual cloak spilling from her trunk like a pool of midnight. Her mother and sister would be at the Great Hall now, participating in the ritual. Uncertain of how long she'd be gone, her fingers tightened, then yanked the fabric free.

"Just a quick glance."

Shadows danced across stone walls. Asante pressed herself into the cold surface, her dark cloak rustling against the rough-hewn rock. The weight of the satchel pulled at her arm as she watched the guard's shoulders rise and fall with each breath. When he turned, she slipped through the side doors, emerging onto the Great Hall's balconies.

The cavernous chamber stretching below stole her breath. Salt crystal chandeliers cast prismatic light, breaking into dancing white flickers across the stone walls. She sank behind the rails, cool marble pressing against her palms, then peered between the rounded pillars. Several feet below, intricate etchings adorned a wall, depicting Samira in an eternal battle combat with Ragas, their stone forms frozen mid-strike. On another wall, the High Priestess stood on Pālam's summit, before the mountain became their home, holding Magnar's severed head, Ka'zan's late High Regent.

Across the carved walls, alabaster roots from the High Tree wove through the chamber like pale serpents, twisting and braiding until they formed a perfect circle. Several women from the first tiers stood inside the nest of roots.

"I just want to have a quick look at them. Then we're leaving," she whispered into her bag.

"What are you doing here?" The words drifted from the shadows.

Asante's muscles seized. Her head snapped toward the sound, eyes widening in recognition. "Tarrak." Her brother's amber eyes caught the fractured light, his long locs disappearing beneath his hood.

He crouched beside her, his breath warm against her ear. "Why aren't you inside the nest of roots?"

Her finger shot to her lips. "Hush!"

"Why are you hiding?"

"Tarrak! Lower your voice. I'm not supposed to be here," she hissed.

His fingers dug into her shoulder, forcing her to face him. "Answer me."

"I won't be marked today. I was tasked with something else, but I wanted to see Amá and Nora." Her eyes darted back to the gathered women, searching the sea of faces.

"Why won't you be marked?"

"Never mind that. It's about to start. I just wanted to see them."

"There they are." Tarrak's finger pointed to the row closer to Samira. "Nora wanted to see the Priestess."

Her throat tightened. Their younger sister stood near their mother, her dark tight coils cascading past her shoulders, longer than she remembered. Something sharp twisted beneath her chest. "Her hair is so long."

"She's been waiting for you to cut it. Won't let anyone touch it, not even mom."

Their mother stood tall, her warm honey skin glowing in the crystal light. Silver threads had begun weaving through her dark hair at the edges. Her heart sank, realizing she might not see them for a while.

"What's going on, Rabbit?" Tarrak's shoulder playfully nudged against hers.

The contact threw her off balance. "Don't call me rabbit," she scowled.

"You tell me what's going on right now, Sante, or I swear!"

"I should ask you the same thing! Men are not allowed in the marking rituals or even in the Great Hall."

"I always find my way to you. I thought you'd be in the nest too. Instead, you're skulking in the shadows."

Before Asante could retort, Samira's voice filled the chamber. The gold-dipped markings around Samira's neck and bald head sparkled against the salt crystals around the cave.

The Priestess' gaze swept over the four Sages, her voice smooth as silk. "You have all seen the peril that slithers its way to us from the Tanama. Turning from it will not stop it. It will take unimaginable courage and resilience to face what haunts us. We must gather our strength to safeguard our people. This has always come with a price. Sacrifice." The word hung in the air like poison. Then Samira's eyes found the women within the roots.

Asante's fingers dug into the rails. "Why is she saying that? That's not part of the ritual."

"The Enchanters have been telling the lower tiers the smoke is a sign." Tarrak's hood slipped back, muscles tightening around his neck. "Is it? You know what's going on. Tell me."

"I—I can't tell you. I just wanted to see Mom and Nora and now I should go."

"Go? Go where?" His fingers circled her wrist like iron bands.

"Sages," Samira's voice resonated through the chamber. "Call forth the wyvern's breath within you. Kindle the flames running through your veins."

The Sages stood inside circles etched deep in the stone floor, surrounding the twisting mass of tendrils, their golden cloaks pooling around each of them. The Fifth Sage's circle gaped empty. At the Priestess's command, the four Sages extended their hands toward the roots. Then Samira's golden markings blazed to life. Ribbons of light, like strands of liquid sun, danced through the air until they reached each Sage.

The nest of roots themselves awakened, their shimmer forming a lattice of golden veins that caged the women within. Across each Sage's face, their dotted markings pulsed in perfect harmony with ethereal glow.

"We take in this sacrifice, weaving it with the wyvern's force that flows in our blood." Samira's voice thundered through the radiance. "Let their essence be the shield of our survival. Feed!"

"What are they doing?" Asante bolted upright, her muscles coiled with terror.

Silver threads of light, delicate as spider silk, began seeping from each woman within the nest of roots. The essence spiraled upward from their mouths, weaving with the glowing roots that imprisoned them. Eyes widened in horror, faces contorted in silent screams. One woman hurled herself against the barrier of light, only to be thrown back into the circle. The brightness of the threads grew more intense, each woman's essence adding to the radiance of the Sages and the High Priestess. As the spectral lights reached their peak, the women within the circle of roots crumpled to the ground, lifeless.

"They are killing them," Tarrak gasped, his grip tightening around Asante's arm.

Her heart pounded against her ribs as her feet launched forward, desperate to reach Nora and her mother.

"No, you can't," he said, yanking her back down and pushing her behind the stone rails, terror burning in his eyes. "They'll do the same to you."

Asante's gaze stared in horrified silence. Light mercilessly drained away from her little sister. Her vibrant brown skin turned ashen gray until all strength and vitality had been exhausted. Her mother clung desperately to Nora, until her own light faded. "They killed them," she whispered, tears streaming down her face. The weight of loss pressed upon her like a suffocating shroud.

"We have to go." Tarrak's unsteady voice sounded distant. "Asante! They can't find us here."

Her feet remained rooted in place, unable to tear her eyes away. Only a handful of women endured in the center.

"Lux!" she gasped. Her friend's small frame trembled as silver light poured from her. Her mouth opened in a silent scream while her copper-red hair faded to pale strands. Lux's light mingled with the others until their bodies crumbled like water vases against stone.

Sorrow sat heavy in Asante's chest, squeezing each breath into a fractured sigh. Her terror-stricken eyes wouldn't tear away from her mother's body, motionless beside her sister's. Like torches without light, their kindling flames were only memories now. "Amá."

Rough hands hauled her to her feet, pulling her forward with urgency. Tarrak's hand gripped her hood, drawing it over her locs.

Her body followed the pull of his arm, but each step was unsteady, and the grounds blurred around her. *They killed them, they killed them. Nora! Amá. Lux. Sixty of them—snuffed out like candles.*

"We have to get out of here. Asante!" Tarrak's hands gripped her shoulders, shaking her gently. "Asante!"

The familiar walls of their family chambers swam into focus. "We're home."

"We have to go. Help me pack."

"They are gone, Tarrak," she mumbled, hands shaking at her sides.

"We can't stay here. If they find out we were in the Great Hall, we're both dead. Do you understand? They will do the same to you as they did to Nor—to them. We need to go."

The stone chamber echoed with rustling. Leather creaked, metal clinked against metal. Her brother's hands flew across shelves and hooks, trading one outfit for another, dark and practical... designed to disappear.

Through tearful eyes, the leather straps across her brother's broad shoulders caught her gaze. A quiver nestled against his back, a thigh holster hugging the outline of a blade. "Hunter's gear," she whispered, her voice cracking.

"We need to blend in," he said, draping a brown cloak over his shoulders. He pulled out a dagger, its surface rippling like frozen waves of obsidian. "Here, Father's lava stone blade. It never dulls, never breaks."

The dagger trembled in her hands and a dam of grief threatened to burst. "I—I can't, Tarrak."

He dropped his bags on the stone floor before pulling her into her arms. Despite their similar height, she leaned into him, her shoulders pressing lightly against his chest, desperate for shelter.

"Listen, Rabbit." His thumb gently wiped the tears from her face, while his amber eyes blazed with a mix of fury and fear. "It's just you and me. That's all we have." His breath hitched. "I won't lose you too. So, we're going to run, and you're going to tell me what in Ragas' name happened this morning."

Asante locked eyes with her brother. The last time she had seen that same fierce love, it had been in their father's gaze. His broad shoulders coiled with tension, and in the dim light, his eyes swam with the same haunting images burning in her mind.

Something within her hardened, like clay under the heat of a furnace. She drew in a long breath and steadied her spine, wiping the dampness from her cheeks before reaching for her father's dagger. Her other hand pressed against her satchel, where the subtle warmth of the embryo stirred beneath her fingers.

"Let's go," she whispered, her words firm despite the tremor in her chest.

Chapter 7

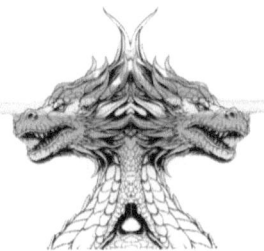

KA'ZAN

YOEN

Yoen's heart pounded in his ears like a thousand war drums. Waves of shouts and screams echoed through the town, every eye and finger pointed to the Tanama. A mantle of midnight smoke covered Rengō's summit, unfurling down the mountainside, casting an ominous trail in its wake.

Atop his obsidian mare, like a statue carved in time, the High Regent's gaze pierced the smoke in the distance. Despite being miles away, the menacing sight sent ripples of fear through the city.

"High Regent Zohar, what should we do?" Yoen's voice cut the uneasy silence.

"Your Excellency," one of his personal guards stepped forward, her grip firm on the jet-black mare, "the city's unraveling. We need an order."

Issuing a silent command, the High Regent's hand cut through the air. He turned to the nearest guard. "Gather our fifty best miners. Have them armed and at the Blackstone gate in ten minutes' time. Move."

Zohar's gaze swept to another. "Summon fifty guards. Have them don their scale armor and mount their best steeds. Converge at the city gate with my scale armor and Agni Scepter. Go! Swift as the wind." At last, his eyes locked onto Yoen and the remaining guards. "You three, with me."

Yoen's heels dug into Inara's flank. Her muscles bunched and released beneath him, keeping pace with the Regent's mount. The guards' hands wrapped tightly around their wyvern-sword hilts and advanced, mirroring Zohar's every stride. The mares' iron-shod hooves rang against cobblestones while Zohar led them through the city's winding streets, the Blackstone Gate looming ahead.

"You were not yet born, young Chief," Zohar said, his eyes fixed on some distant memory. "There was a time when our city was more than ashen remnants. These streets once glowed with the amber light of agni stones, magic dancing in the air like summer fireflies." He let his words hang in the air until Yoen drew alongside. "For a brief time during my father's reign, we were once the jewel of the land. Now look at us. A mere shadow of our former glory."

Yoen's jaw clenched. The stories of Magnar, lost to the Wyvern Wars, had been his childhood tales. After Magnar's death, Zohar became the last and only Enchanter in Ka'zan. His only surviving offspring did not bear the gift to channel the powers of agni stones. The smoke billowing from the haunted forests sent ice through his veins.

He knew what lurked in those shadows. He knew of their hunger, their cruelty. They had claimed the only person who had ever truly known him, the only one who had seen past his imperfections and called him worthy. She had loved him unconditionally. Not for what he could become, but simply for who he was. But the creatures tore Nim from him, leaving nothing but a gushing wound that would never heal.

If the smoke signaled the release of the Uláak from the Tanama's curse, the creatures would be free to ravage all of Ka'zan. His fingers tightened around Inara's reins, the leather biting into his palms. The thought of losing his niece and nephew—to those creatures—made his heart hiss like hot steel against ice. One Enchanter, no matter how great, would not be enough to face an entire legion of the Uláak.

His gaze darted around the cityscape. Panic spread like wildfire. People surged through the square, tripping over cobblestones in their haste. A myriad of eyes turned toward the High Regent's regal gallop. Their faces twisted in fear, voicing their protests aloud.

Zohar swung down from his mare, passing the reins to his guard. His boots struck the ground with quiet authority, and he strode to the heart of the round square. The massive white stone carving of the Great Horned Ragas loomed above, its horns catching the light.

"Silence!" His guard's voice cut through the noise. "Your High Regent will address you!"

Zohar's fingers closed around the agni stone hanging from his neck, a powerful amulet passed down through generations. "For many years I have asked the Ka'zanty for patience. We have devoted our resources to finding enchanted agni stones to sustain us. Today, I ask for courage." The amulet's amber flames danced under his touch, amplifying his voice to every corner of the square. "Go to your neighbors. Gather them all and proceed to Drekavog. A fortress for its people."

A man stepped forward, his beard streaked with gray. "Are we under attack?"

"It's the Uláak, it must be!" A blacksmith clutched her children close, her forge-stained apron dark with sweat. "Have they escaped the dead woods?"

Zohar's raised hand commanded silence with the authority of a sharp blade. "I urge you to place your trust in me, as you have done for more than a century. All is well," he replied, his voice resonating with firm resolve. "The will and power of our people may be tested once more, but we will rise, victorious. Do not succumb to the shadow that is upon us." His gaze swept over the city center.

"Today, your unwillingness to yield will be indispensable. Make for the fortress." The amulet disappeared beneath his collar before he nodded to his guard and reclaimed his mare's reins.

"Go! Heed your High Regent's command," the guard bellowed, her voice echoing over the murmurs of the crowd.

"Chief Miner, with me. Guard, reach the Chief Fisher. He must navigate two Agni Vessels to the open waters. Raise Drekavog's shields and ensure everyone makes it to that fortress," Zohar commanded, swinging himself onto his steed.

"Your Eminence, I shouldn't leave you," the guard stammered, her fingers tightening around the hilt of her sword.

"This is no time to vacillate, young Sefa. Today, your people will depend on your valor and mastery. Do not fail them. Do not fail me."

Yoen followed the High Regent toward the Blackstone gate. Beyond its shadow, their forces waited like a painting come to life. Guards stood in oxblood tunics, their armor a symphony of wyvern scales shimmering like diamonds in the sunlight. Curved swords hung at their sides, deadly as a beast's talons, while archers slung bows and arrows carved from wyvern bones across their backs. The miners stood apart in their gray tunics and cowls, their rough hands gripping steel instead of their usual picks and knives.

Horses shifted beneath their riders, hooves pawing at the earth as if they could smell the coming storm. The High Regent's personal guards approached with his scepter and armor, a marvel of onyx scales that seemed to absorb the very light around them. Impenetrable and commanding, his heirloom piece clicked into place, the scales cresting around his shoulders, rising like black flames. With a final motion, his horned helmet settled onto his head. Then he spoke.

"The omen from the Tanama extends its reach to us. We must journey to Mount Garam, for I believe it holds the answers we seek."

Ka'zan shrank behind them with each stride, while the volcano's shadow loomed over their path. Though Yoen had climbed Garam a few hours ago, returning under these circumstances sent daggers through his chest. Inara's muscles rippled beneath him, her powerful strides accompanied by urgent neighs that mixed with the whistle of the wind in his ears.

At the volcano's base, he pulled back on Inara's reins, allowing the High Regent's midnight mare to reach the gathering point first. Dark volcanic rock crunched beneath hooves until the last riders fell into position.

"Ka'zanty! Assume line formation," one of the Regent's guards ordered.

Zohar's hand drifted to the agni stone amulet at his throat. "Before moving forward, it is time I tell you the reason our city continues to stand." His amplified voice boomed over the formation. The wind shifted, bringing with it the acrid clash of seawater and sulfur.

"Today marks the eve of the Great Hunt, the Wyvern Wars. It's been over a century since Magnar the Great stood against the cities of Äktas and Ikari. Like bloodthirsty leeches, the Ikari drew life from the majestic creatures. Ikarite's power grew, nourished and sustained by the fading life force of the wyverns. The people of Äktas, like a hammer on hot steel, survived on unrestrained violence. Their blatant aggression toward the winged lizards fueled their magic, a coarse power drawn not from the finesse of the arcane, but from brute viciousness."

The small armada stretched across the rugged terrain like a metallic serpent. The High Regent guided his mare along their ranks, his spine rigid and commanding in the saddle, though his knuckles whitened around the reins.

"But as Ka'zanty, we understood a crucial truth. The extinction of the wyverns would spell doom for us all. Our city thrived from the life and breath of the wyverns, not from their deaths," Zohar continued.

Memories of the tales about the cities beyond the Tanama stirred in Yoen's mind. His fists clenched, and his nostrils flared at the thought that one of them could be the cause of the smoke.

"Our volcano, Garam, has been the source of our ignited agni stones. If the Ikarites or Äktastary get a hold of our enchanted minerals, Ka'zan will be no more." The High Regent's voice faltered, his gaze breaking from the fleet for the first time.

Yoen's legs shifted in his saddle, his gaze locking on the bead of sweat tracing down Zohar's temple. The Regent cleared his throat, his usually steady hands carrying a faint tremor.

"The smoke billowing from Rengō is a grim omen," Zohar said, gesturing toward the haze rising in the distance. "We must protect our city and our people at all costs. Over a century ago, my father sealed Garam's scar with a White Stone Gate. Paired with the power of this scepter," he added, lifting the staff high, "these two forces work in harmony to keep our volcanic island in deep rest, allowing us to mine for agni stones. Today, I aim to unlock the gate and safeguard our enchanted gems reserves before any impending danger can reach them."

Yoen's heart lodged in his throat. Since childhood, the Elders' warnings about the gate had haunted his dreams—never open, never breach, never break the seal. Around him, horses stamped and snorted, matching their riders' unease. Whispers rose like wind through dry grass until Zohar's raised hand cut through the air, commanding immediate silence.

"Beyond the seal on the volcano's wall, Garam holds a force that will allow us to survive the threat looming from the Tanama." The scepter caught the light when Zohar thrust it skyward. "Today, you will not falter. Through fire and stone, Ka'zanty! Stand mighty and powerful." His deep voice echoed across the ranks.

The gem atop the scepter erupted in golden light, sending ribbons of brightness dancing across shields and armor. Zohar's voice rose like thunder. "By the tempestuous fires of the Agni Stone. Ka'zanty!"

"Oooh-Hum-Oooh-Hum! Agni-Kal!" The battle cry burst from dozens of throats, deep and resonant, each guard's and miner's fist pounding against their chest in rhythm. The sound resonated off the volcano, as if the mountain itself joined their call.

Zohar's next words came low and quick, meant only for his guards. Without hesitation, they spurred their mounts up the narrow hiking path winding toward the volcano's sealed fissure. Dismounting, they sent their horses galloping back toward the city to avoid the rising tides that would soon reclaim the seabed.

Inara's head butted against Yoen's shoulder, her hooves pawing the ground in protest. "We won't be long, fire-beetle. If the seabed is submerged by the tides before we return, the Agni Vessels will reel us in." His hand ran along her neck, feeling the warmth of her mane beneath his palm before urging her to join the retreating horses.

The air filled with the sound of boots crunching on volcanic gravel. The High Regent and his elite guards picked their way along the path leading to the sealed fissure. Yoen positioned the remaining warriors along the narrow trail, keeping them well back from the edge. The sight of Zohar finally raising his scepter toward the White Stone Gate made his chest tighten.

Light blazed from its gem, seeking out every crack and crevice in the ancient seal.

The edges ignited with white fire. The volcano shuddered beneath their feet, and the massive doors split down the middle with the groan of stone against stone. A howling wind burst through the opening, battering the High Regent and his fleet. As they crossed through, light trailed from Zohar's agni scepter, casting fleeting shadows before the darkness swallowed them whole.

Yoen ground his teeth together. His eyes remained fixed on Garam's wide fissure, the forbidden entrance. At forty-five, he had spent countless years visiting and inspecting this gate, knowing it must remain sealed. Now, it gaped like an open wound in the mountain's face. He turned his gaze toward Ka'zan, sweat trickling down his neck.

The circular city fortress pulsed with life in the distance. Four massive emerald wyvern wings stretched above it like living shields, their scales catching the sun. His heart clenched at the thought of Luan and Arben, who had wandered into the beach's caves just hours ago. A long breath escaped him, staring at the distant stronghold, hoping they were inside.

Beyond Ka'zan, smoke continued to pour from Rengō, devouring the Tanama's dead woods with relentless appetite. It crept forward with the patience of a predator—the ominous sight that had compelled the High Regent to do the unthinkable.

He drummed his fingers against his thigh, pacing along the edge in search of answers. If the Regent's intent meant to safeguard the agni stones, then opening Garam's fissure defied logic. Most of their enchanted minerals rested securely in Drekavog, their fortress, not here.

Every moment wasted at the volcano risked the Uláak breaking free. They needed a plan to shield the city. To shield his niece and nephew. The thought of facing the Uláak surged, tangled with a creeping hunger for vengeance—for his wife and sister. Heat simmered through his veins like a kettle near boiling, the fear of his children trapped with those vile creatures tightening around his chest.

A bone-chilling screech sliced through his thoughts. The jagged wail reverberated through the entire volcano, making him flinch. The earth under Garam thundered and shook as if giant ground moles tunneled their way to the surface. Yoen and the guards lost their balance and tumbled dangerously close to the precipice.

"Keep from the edge."

The command had barely left his mouth when a wave of blazing sapphire flames erupted from the open gate. Seering white at the core, they engulfed two guards standing nearby, sending them over the cliff's edge. The flames vanished in an instant, leaving him crouched with his shield raised, one hand buried in the dirt for stability.

His feet inched forward and peered through the open threshold, expecting someone, *something*. The White Stone Gate stood silent, its surface scorched gray where the flames had licked it. Scorching heat billowed out in waves, forcing him back with an arm raised to shield his face.

The sudden stillness carved into his chest.

The earth's tremors faded beneath his palm. He lifted his gaze to the volcano's mouth above—it gaped silent and dark against the sky. Garam remained dormant. A shiver prickled his spine while sweat beaded at his brow. His muscles tightened, unable to determine the true source of the flames. The acrid air burned his lungs, causing a fit of coughing, forcing him to double over before he could speak. "Ready your shields!" he ordered, the words scraping past his throat.

Nearby, the guards' terror-stricken eyes locked on him. Fingers tightened around weapons, armor clinking with each bracing movement. At his hand signal, they steeled their bodies, ready to step through the gate.

Before their boots could carve out a step, the ground shook beneath them again, sending shockwaves across the surface. A massive creature launched itself out of the volcanic scar and plummeted down the mountainside. Sapphire and emerald scales caught the light, their brilliance dulled like gems losing their glow. Weathered horns, pale as old bone, curved upward from a rugged snout.

"Wyvern!" Yoen sucked in a sharp breath.

The wyvern's wings beat erratically against the air, failing to catch hold. Its body slammed against the mountain's unforgiving rock walls, sending cascades of rock down the slope while dust billowed upward in choking clouds.

Heart racing, he summoned the courage to peer over the edge. Through the settling dust, those distinctive blue-green scales shimmered into focus. Years of studying the Elders' teachings flooded back. Every scale pattern, every marking that distinguished one great beast from another. His blood went cold. "The lightning wyvern," Yoen whispered in disbelief. "Zuwena."

Zuwena shook herself, sending a low growl reverberating through Garam's rock walls. Her claws scraped against stone, leaving deep furrows as she climbed. As the midday sunlight bathed her, the subdued sheen of her scales resembled a fading mural. Jagged patches of bare skin ran along her left paw, like scars from metal that had pressed into her skin for a long time.

His eyes shifted to the creature's translucent chest beaming in blue flames. "She readies her fire breath," his voice rumbled. "Archers! Quick. Before she unleashes!"

Zuwena launched herself across Garam's side, a blur of motion, resolving into widespread wings. Her shadow swallowed the rocky ground below. With a piercing screech, talons flashed in the sunlight, snatching an unsuspecting prey. The guard's severed head tumbled down the slope, and her jaws snapped shut to feast on his body. With renewed strength, she soared upwards, circling Garam until her legs perched on the volcano's yawning mouth.

With each wing beat, blue sparks flared and danced along her scales, creating a ripple of mesmerizing power. Veins of liquid light coursed through her, and the air hummed and sizzled with energy. With a resounding crack of thunder, lightning surged from her snout, tearing into the volcano's gaping mouth with an ear-piercing roar that shook the earth.

Violent currents of electricity pulsed through Garam's walls. Miners tumbled from their perches, their screams lost in the thunder of her attack. The guards braced themselves, their wyvern-scale armor sparking and smoking under the electrical onslaught.

Sprawled on his back, ripples of electricity coursed through Yoen's spine when he spotted a looming ashen cloud over the volcano, its dense mass unfurling across the sky. A piercing cold settled deep in his chest. "The creature has awakened Garam!" he shouted.

An earsplitting wail warped by hunger and decay filled the air—Zuwena's victory cry, before she launched herself from the crater's edge. Yoen scrambled to his feet, following her flight path along the mountain's curve. Her wings banked around the volcano until her ferocious gaze locked in with her next target. From that vantage point, the Great Sea unfolded in the distance with two Agni Vessels bobbing unsuspecting.

With a precise and forceful lash, her horned tail struck the ship's hull. The crack of splintering wood echoed across the water. In an instant, waves rushed in to claim the vessel, sending sailors leaping from the decking. Yoen's legs refused to budge, his knife-grip tightening with each moment he watched the ship disappear beneath the surface.

After reducing the Agni Vessel to scattered fragments, Zuwena's gaze turned to the west. With one powerful downstroke, she soared into the sky, abandoning Ka'zan to face Mount Garam's awakening fury.

Gray flakes drifted down like poisonous snow, coating the ground in ash. Yoen broke free from his daze and turned back to the gate where the surviving guards gathered. "You five, with me. We must find the High Regent. The rest of you, sweep the area for survivors. Get them across the seabed. The tides are rising. Go now."

The White Stone Gate loomed ajar, letting the midday sun cast pale gold across their charred path. As they entered, light bounced off the guards' scale armors, scattering the radiance deeper into the passage. Sharp sulfur strained Yoen's lungs with every breath.

But they didn't have to go far. Footsteps echoed ahead when a cluster of soot-stained figures emerged from the shadows. Zohar teetered on the edge of consciousness, propped up by his personal guards. Blood seeped from his temple, staining his helmet, while his agni scepter flickered, its amber glow fading like a dying star.

Yoen's chest tightened at the sight. "We must hurry. The tides are rising," he blurted, rushing forward.

"We won't make it in time while carrying the High Regent. He's badly injured," one of the guards panted, blood trickling from her ear.

"We must find a way! Move!"

They stumbled down Garam's rocky flanks through a rain of ash and burning embers. The ground's tremors grew stronger with each step. When they reached the seabed, waves had already drowned their escape route. Then he turned toward the narrow path winding around the volcano, searching for their last hope. The second Agni Vessel dipped and surged in the churning water.

"The rowing skiffs won't reach the shore," he shouted. The small boats pitched in the choppy waves, threatening to capsize with each swell. His eyes darted across the ground, seeking any possible way out.

Just as panic began to set in, the High Regent's eyes fluttered open. His trembling hands raised the dimming scepter toward the remaining ship. In response, the ground beneath shuddered. From the seafloor, a bridge of dark rock erupted, stretching for miles from the shore to the waiting vessel.

"Move!" Yoen shouted. "Look to the skies for fire rain."

From a distance, Inara's call rang out, searching for her rider. The High Regent's mare followed closely with three other horses in tow.

"You're a stubborn one, old friend," he sighed when Inara approached, allowing himself a fleeting moment to breathe.

The guards lifted Zohar onto his mount before they spurred the horses across the stone bridge at a gallop.

Forged from wyvern scales, the sails of the remaining vessel doubled as shields against the onslaught of volcanic rocks. Survivors from the sunken ship helped pull them aboard. The vessel cut through the sea with a steady grace, setting course for the black beach with the city of Ka'zan emerging on the horizon.

Yoen watched how two guards tended to the fresh wound on Zohar's forehead. The amulet at the Regent's neck danced with a fiery glow, but the light from his scepter continued to fade. His eyes swept the expanse above. Clouds of smoke dulled the once-bright skies, and in the distance, a strange golden owl plummeted aimlessly into the waters. His gaze turned back to Garam, spitting rivers of lava. Then to his city, where a shroud of ash smothered the white round-houses. Beyond the farmlands, the ominous smoke had swept past Rengō and consumed most of the Tanama forests. Like an insidious tide of shadows, it crept slowly toward Ka'zan's borders.

Every muscle in his body coiled tight, his nails bit into his palms. "We're doomed," he muttered, the words barely escaping his clenched teeth.

CHAPTER 8

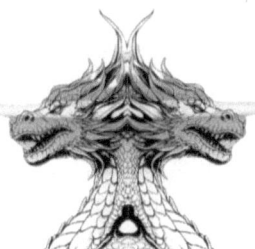

ÄKTAS

ELVA

E LVA'S FEET PLANTED FIRMLY, back straight, hands poised at her sides. Rows of students in gray coats and cerulean armbands fixed their gaze on the General Artificer. Sadfar's shadow stretched long across the central staircase. His dark hair, pulled into a tight knot, sharpened the angles of his chiseled jaw, where a well-groomed beard traced the line of his chin. Clad in the Trade's dark blue wool coat, he stood with squared shoulders and an unwavering stance. The Hand's silver pin over his heart glinted under the light of the Zuwena-shaped iron chandelier.

His voice resonated with authority. "Artificers, today more than ever, your abilities and resourcefulness will be tested. Even more than any of the Trades in our mighty Academy."

The click of boots drew his attention. A Militia Sergeant, her red-armband a slash of color against the gray coat, advanced, offering him a cluster of parchments.

Elva's eyes darted through the crowd, searching for Oran's face among the sea of gray coats. Nothing. He hadn't returned from the Healers' quarters. A tightness gripped her chest, fingers anxiously tracing the seams of her satchel. After the war sirens went off, each

Trade had been ordered to report to their quarters. The command left her no time to return the small bloodstone box containing the ignited white stone she had used to test the Sky Lantern.

Her teeth sank into her lip at the thought of being caught with an Enchanter's stone. The sharp sting made her wince—a bitter echo of Buldar's recent onslaught still fresh in the split skin.

"By order of our city's mighty council, The Hand, led by our esteemed General Commander, today, we will showcase the strength of the Äktastary," Sadfar continued. His gaze pierced through the crowd, finding Elva's eyes with unsettling precision. "On the eve of the anniversary marking the end of the Wyvern Wars, we stand at a crucial milestone in securing our city's prosperity. The smoke looming over the Tanama speaks clearly. Our city is under siege. And The Hand will not stand idly by as its enemies plot against us."

The wooden steps creaked beneath Sadfar's boots on his way down. Below, the students held their alert stance, eyes forward, their ranks parting quietly at his approach. The parchments he'd received from the Militia Sergeant crackled as he pressed them into waiting hands. "Twenty of you have been tasked to display the might of our Academy in a counter attack."

Elva's dark eyes widened, her fists tightening at her sides. The air thickened with tension and whispers slithered through the gathering.

"How can we counterattack? We can't cross the dead forests?" She recognized the voice of a fourth-year Sergeant Artificer. The question cut through the stillness, sparking a ripple of muttered agreement.

"Silence!" Veins stood out on Sadfar's neck. "I will have order. You will not question The Hand's authority. Those with a parchment are to stay here to receive further instructions about the counter attack mission. The rest of you are to meet with the Militia Trade. You are dismissed."

Elva's fist met her palm in a bow. When she straightened, Sadfar loomed before her, a piece of parchment extended between them. "This is the only way to escape the fifty lashes the Commander threatened, and to spare your family from the mistakes you made earlier today."

A gouging ache tore through her chest. She reached out and took the parchment from his hand. "I understand, Sir," she said, fighting the sting in her eyes. Swallowing hard, she tried to process the four words and the number inscribed upon it: *Underwater Vessel III - North, Ka'zan.* The text shook in her hands, its weight bearing a death sentence. The orders left no room for uncertainty. Navigate through the underwater caves and invade the city of agni stones. Her fingers left sweat marks on the corners before she slipped it into her waist satchel. The rows of Artificers dwindled, leaving only twenty behind, their breaths shallow and fists clenched around the parchments, eyes darting to one another.

Sadfar paced through the chamber until he halted beneath Zuwena's iron figure. "You all have been chosen for a very important mission. Few will ever have the privilege to protect this land." His hands clasped behind his back, his thumb brushing the bare spot where his wyvern-skull ring had once rested.

"Each of you has had some involvement in the training or development of our Underwater Vessels," he continued, his voice filling every corner of the room. "Five convoys have been assigned to siege the bloodstone city, Ikari, and another five to the agni stone city, Ka'zan. Each ship will carry eight Militia Trades, and two Artificers will assist with the navigation."

"Pardon the interruption, General." A patch-eyed Sergeant Artificer raised a quivering hand. "The air provisions within the Underwater Vessels are limited. Given the lethal threats we will most certainly encounter, the chances of survival fall below an acceptable threshold. The risks involved outweigh any potential gains."

Taking slow, deliberate steps, Sadfar pressed forward, addressing the Artificer with a steady, unblinking gaze. "Artistry is our Trade, a craft honed in the crucible of adversity. It transcends mere numbers or any *acceptable threshold*. It emanates from our unyielding determination to triumph over challenges. Have we not instilled that lesson in you?"

The Sergeant's gaze dropped to the floor, and around Elva, jaws clenched and chests froze in mid-breath.

General Sadfar's shadow fell across her while he continued to address them. "The vessels have undergone extensive enhancements with the expertise of two of our finest, one of whom stands beside me," he added, acknowledging her with a nod. "They've endured rigorous testing, proving their reliability. Each of you have the ordained duty to bring honor to our city."

At the main door, he turned on his heel for a final word. "Any deviation from the orders provided by the Militia Sergeant will be deemed as treason. Death penalty, not just for you but for every member of your family. These are trying times, Artificers. Show Äktas why you stand as the pinnacle of the Trades." Twenty pairs of hands brought their right fists to open left palms before he disappeared through the doorway.

The air around Elva spun, the room dissolving into a whirlwind of colors that swirled and blended together. The vessels had undergone successful testing, but only in the depths near their own coastline—familiar waters that had been mapped and deemed safe. The farther any vessel ventured from the shores, the deadlier the journey became. Vile creatures rose from the ocean depths, ancient beings that had long guarded the waters. Many had tried to flee the city, venturing into the seas, but those watching from land could only witness their ships disappear beneath the waves, swallowed by things from nightmares.

While the Uláak roamed the dead forests, sinister beings ruled the abyss beyond the coast, presenting an intimidating challenge no sturdy metal machine could overcome. Her stomach churned, her split lip pulsing in time with her racing heart.

"Sergeant Artificer, pay attention!" The sharp voice sliced through her thoughts. A Sergeant Militia fixed her cat-like gaze on her, freckles dotted across her cheeks. The strong bridge of her nose accentuated the intensity of her stare.

Elva hurried to meet them. "Apologies."

"I'm fourth-year Sergeant Militia Lyla. I'll be leading the armada targeting Ka'zan to the north," she announced, each word delivered with dagger-like precision. "We're set to depart in minutes. Militia, Artificers, and Enchanters Trades are already preparing the aquatic fleets."

"We are leaving now?" one of the Artificer's choked out, failing to steady their voice.

Lyla's glare could have melted steel. "There's no time for interruptions," she scolded. "We are heading over to the harbor immediately. Board as you are. Your orders as Artificers are simple: maneuver the fleets through the underwater caves. Once we get to the agni stone city, you will follow my lead. Don't waste my time with questions. You heard the General Artificer, any deviation against General Commander Buldar's orders and your heads will be displayed at the Academy's entrance for all to see. Now, follow me."

The path to the harbor stretched before them like a mournful procession. Elva's hands clutched the satchel concealing the ignited stone she had used hours ago, fingers tightening around the leather strap to keep them from shaking. Her recklessness had led her here. The thought of never seeing her family again settled like a bitter winter.

Her teeth sank into the inside of her cheek, the sharp taste of blood keeping the tears from betraying her. At least they wouldn't face punishment for her mistakes. But not being able to say goodbye gnawed at her, having wasted so much time arguing. They'd be better off without her. Even Oran. A flicker of relief coursed through her. He wouldn't share her fate, and she knew he would look after her family. But the thought of not seeing him again drove a knife into her chest.

Around her, the other Artificers mirrored her own unease. Footsteps faltered and dragged. Panicked eyes darted like trapped animals, searching for an escape that would never come. Refusal proved impossible. The Commander's warnings rang clear—board those convoys and face the deadly creatures, or stay above ground and face his deadly fist.

The harbor hummed with a symphony of mechanical echoes. Five Underwater Vessels bobbed at their moorings, their sleek forms catching glints of sunlight. A few Artificers crouched by their assigned docks, retching in fear, the stench of sickness mingling with sea water and the sharp bite of machine oil. Elva swallowed hard, pressing a hand to her own twisting stomach. The reality of what lay ahead settled in—bitter, inescapable, and life-sentencing.

A burst of white light pierced the blue sky. Then another. And another. Her eyes tracked each flash as they erupted from the vessels bound for Ka'zan. An Enchanter stepped onto the deck of the final machine, his gold-trimmed coat rippling in the warm breeze. The white stone in his hands pulsed faintly before he dropped it into the waiting cylinder with precision.

Light exploded upward, spilling from the machine in a radiant pillar, until the Enchanter sealed the stone within its chamber.

Elva dragged her feet, nearing her assigned dock at position three. The last Militia members clambered aboard, boots thudding against the metal surface. Another red-armband circled the top, glancing along the metal rails, scrutinizing the machine from every angle.

"Where's the other Artificer?" Lyla's voice cut through the harbor noise. Elva blinked at her, then scanned the crowd. "There should be two blue-armbands per convoy. Where's your colleague?"

"I'm here, I'm here!" Oran ran toward them, a small piece of parchment fluttering in his raised hand

Elva's breath hitched. The thought of Oran near the vessels sent a shiver down her spine. She wanted him away, far from her. The punishment for testing the Lanterns fell solely on her. Hearing him argue with Lyla about boarding a death sentence twisted her insides. Yet there he stood, resolute and willing to share her fate. A tightness gripped her chest, turning each breath into a struggle.

"You are not assigned for this task," Lyla retorted, her eyes drilling into Oran.

"I am now. The other Artificer has been reassigned."

Elva's gaze darted through the crowd, searching for the other blue-armband, but the patched-eyed Artificer had vanished. "What are you doing?" she whispered through quivering lips.

"I've been assigned to this Underwater fleet," he whispered back.

"I don't believe it. You shouldn't be here." She kept her voice low while Lyla studied the parchment. "Didn't you hear General Sadfar? Anything we do against the Commander's orders will be considered an act of treason."

"I have orders stating I'm supposed to board the craft docked at station number three, with the agni stone city as the target. I'm staying. Come on, we have to move." He motioned for her to board, while Lyla stared at him, standing firm in the middle with her hands on her hips.

"If you'd like, we could wait until the General is free," Oran said, meeting Lyla's glare. "We could ask him to come here and confirm that piece of parchment. By then, the rest of the vessels would've submerged and made their way to their target. Is that your preferred strategy, Sergeant Militia Lyla of the fourth-year?"

Lyla jabbed a finger against his chest. "Do as you are told, blue-armband. You are nothing but tools to get my Militia Trades and me to our destination. Fail me, and I will personally deliver your head to the General Commander. And you." Her attention snapped to Elva. "I hope your reckless reputation doesn't interfere with my mission. Any misstep, and I won't hesitate to take you out. You're both under my command." Not waiting for a response, she spun on her heel and climbed aboard.

Oran extended his hand toward Elva, his familiar smirk doing nothing to ease the knot in her stomach. Her thumbnail carved crescents into her index finger. Still, with her other hand, she took his. The gratitude she'd felt at his staying behind crumbled away, replaced by the cold certainty that she would lead them both to their deaths.

"Ready your posts." Lyla's voice bounced inside the chamber walls. Her eyes locked onto Elva and Oran. "Our lives are in your hands."

Metal scraped and clanked when the latches sealed. The vessel lurched downward, pressure building in Elva's ears with each meter they descended. She made her way to her station, where the largest glass viewport yawned into darkness, and cinched the safety strap tight. Though her heart pounded like distant drums, her fingers managed to find the control handle, cool and solid. She took in a deep breath before easing it forward, angling it north toward Ka'zan.

Her mind raced, imagining what awaited in the land where the late Regent Magnar severed his enemies' heads. But before she could let her mind wander to the dangers in the city of lava stones, she'd had to first brace herself for the deadly creatures beneath the waters.

Perhaps crossing through the Tanama would have been easier—even with the Uláak guarding the dead forests, protecting wyvern remains imbued with potent magic. The sea creatures were believed to be just as merciless, and they were about to find out just how much.

She bit her lip, surrendering to the shooting pain from where Buldar's fist had connected. The sting grounded her, pulling her attention away from the crushing weight of abandoning her family and leading her only friend into the depths of death itself.

CHAPTER 9

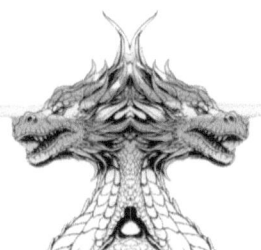

ÄKTAS

ELVA

THE SERPENT-LIKE BEAST GLIDED across the underwater cavern with fluid grace for its size. From the viewport, Elva watched its massive stygian mouth swell horrifically, taking the shape of a large, bloated sack. Then its long tail whipped through the current, plunging the fleets behind them into chaotic spins.

Time slowed as its maw gaped wide—a bottomless void lined with an arsenal of razor-sharp teeth. The light of the ignited white stone inside the machine flickered under the creature's relentless attack. Rather than engulfing it whole, its fangs pierced the craft with a shriek of metal, the sound reverberating like a muffled scream.

"We have to help them!" Oran's yell echoed within their own metal craft.

"Our orders are to push through these caves," Lyla asserted, her shadow falling over Elva. "Get us out of here. Now. That's an order."

The steering lever slipped against Elva's palm, her hand slick with sweat. "We're already moving as fast as we can. These caves are a labyrinth. If we go any faster, we risk crashing into the walls," she replied through clenched teeth.

Metal shrieked outside their machine until, at last, the trailing Underwater Vessel split apart in jagged halves. Its troop members spilled from the wreckage, flailing helplessly in the current. Then, along the cave walls, what had seemed like innocent shadows began to shift and morph.

Small luminous creatures materialized from the rock face—hundreds of slug-shaped beings with finger-like tentacles stretching out of their bodies. Their dorsals pulsed with a glowing indigo and silver light. Eyes wide with silent terror, the ten operatives tried to swim away, their limbs cutting frantically through the water. Mouths opened to scream, but only streams of bubbles escaped before the creatures crawled into throats with unsettling gentleness. The crew fought desperately with diminishing strength against the slugs' choreographed movements. But they were no match for the tiny beasts.

The luminous beings swarmed and fully enveloped each of their human prey. Their blue radiant skin pulsed while they feasted, devouring flesh, bone, and muscle, until nothing remained. The tiny forms turned a sickly red, and as easily as they appeared, they cleared, leaving only gear drifting down into the depths. They vanished, seamlessly merging with the rock once more—patient predators lying in wait.

"Stay away from the walls!" Sergeant Lyla shrieked, her fingers digging into Elva's coat. "Get us out of here."

Oran shoved Lyla aside. "She told you. We can't go any faster. It took everything we had to get past that large maw serpent. Any faster and we'll crash into the walls—right into those... those slug things," he said, his voice barely concealing his dread.

A shadow flickered at the edge of Elva's vision, her shoulders cramping from gripping the controls too tightly. "Oran, check the bow. Something's moving out there. Something large."

Oran's hurried footsteps echoed behind her. He raced to the bow while she remained at her station at the stern, eyes scanning the waters for any potential threats creeping up on them, darting between the dark depths and the remaining vessels trailing in their wake.

"I don't see anything," he called from the front.

"What is it? What did you see?" Lyla muttered through gritted teeth.

"I don't know, check the sides." Elva jerked her chin toward the starboard and port openings.

The chamber creaked with activity. Lyla's head brushed the low ceiling while Oran hunched beneath the metal frame. The other seven red-armband soldiers crowded the small space. Peering into the murky waters, four of them pressed against the port openings, their breath fogging the glass. Two more braced themselves against the starboard wall with each sway of the ship. The last soldier's face had gone pale, one hand clamped over his mouth while the other clutched his stomach.

"Port side, anything?" Another shadow darted past Elva's peripheral vision.

Lyla swept past the others, pushing them aside, and craned her neck for a better view. Elva's gaze lingered on the remaining transport trailing behind them. Her eyes caught the Artificer at the port side, squinting into the dim waters. He aimed his water torch through the glass opening, the beam slicing through the gloom.

Her leg bounced anxiously against the metal floor. Two hours into their dive, and already the giant serpent-like creature had claimed two ships. Then the veil of terrifying slugs appeared from nowhere to finish the job. Her team's survival depended on pushing their machine's energy to the limit, racing through the underwater caves. But the faster pace drained more power from the stone. And she couldn't shake the feeling that by increasing their speed, she had unwittingly turned the other convoys into bait.

Of the five units heading north to Ka'zan, only three remained, hers boxed between the others. They still had hours to go before reaching the final destination. One sweaty palm wiped against her trousers. Navigating a maze of stone walls had been the last thing she'd anticipated. The horror-stricken faces of the Militia Trades around her didn't help, so she avoided meeting their eyes, including Oran's. She made a conscious effort to regulate her breath and adjusted her focus. All her concentration had to be on controlling the propellers.

Movement flashed again in the deep. The ship behind them lagged, its torch flickering weakly. "What do you see?" she whispered, as if speaking to the craft itself. Every torch on it glowed, including the bottom lights casting light into the shadowy water surrounding them. "You're going to burn your stone out."

The violent surge came without warning. Elva's forehead cracked against the glass viewport, pain exploding behind her eyes. The world blurred around her, the pulsing ache blending with the chaos, while shuffles of feet and muffled grunts rose from the center of the craft.

"What was that?" Someone's voice quivered behind groans.

Elva's vision blurred. She pressed her fingers against the throbbing spot on her head. Oran appeared beside her, cupping her face with warm hands, his thumbs gentle against her temples. "Are you all right?" he asked, worry lines creasing his forehead.

She managed a nod, her attention already drawn back to the water. Her eyes widened in horror when they locked on the ship following them. The hull bore deep, jagged gashes, as if monstrous claws had raked across the metal. Flickering lights sputtered, struggling against the encroaching shadows, until they all faded, leaving the vessel shrouded in darkness.

"Get us out of here!" Lyla's voiced rang through the confined space.

Oran's boots thundered toward the bow. The craft lurched forward, sending Elva's stomach into her throat. Their white stone flared brighter, casting wild shadows through the water.

"You had your lights on." Her whisper quickened with her pulse. "Why?" Her mind raced through the pieces. "What am I missing? You had your lights on, all of them. That would burn through your stone so quickly. Your stone. The stones. Beacons."

The final thought seized her. Shadows had consumed the fallen convoy, just like the other two. But the stones within them should have continued spilling light through the cave, even if the fleets had been destroyed.

She abandoned her post, lunging toward the bow where Oran guided them through the currents under Lyla's watch. Without warning, she shoved him aside and yanked back on the throttle. The ship shuddered, metal groaning beneath the sudden halt.

Then her feet hurried to the center of the chamber. Her gaze found the casing where the Enchanter had placed the ignited Äktas white stone before they dove into the Great Sea. The convoy's pulsating heartbeat, a petite stone small enough to fit in a hand, infused life into the vessel. It radiated a soft glow, linked to channels running along the edges of the underwater craft, casting a subtle light throughout the metal interior. Her fingers scraped against the covering, but it wouldn't budge.

Lyla's kick sent her flying, pain exploding through her side. Elva's ribs screamed in protest the moment she hit the metal floor. Her eyes flicked up past the Militia Sergeant and to the stone floating above them, its light suddenly sinister.

"Stand down, Artificer." Lyla raised her foot again, but Oran stepped between them.

"Let her explain!" he protested, one arm raised, his spine curved against the low ceiling.

"There's no time. We have to shut it down. Shut it down or we die!" Elva blurted.

Eight pairs of eyes locked onto her, the Militia Trades' faces drawn tight with tension. Even Oran's usually steady gaze wavered. His throat bobbed before he spoke. "The stone is what gives this machine its power, if we remove it, we lose buoyancy."

Elva closed the distance to Oran. "We won't, please trust me, we have to remove it."

"Removing the stone is *not* an option. We can't jeopardize our chance of escape and our mission. Find another solution," Lyla said firmly.

"Please!" she insisted, sweat beading on her forehead. "You saw that clawed out fleet. We don't have time."

Oran's dark eyes locked onto hers. With a sigh, he approached the benches. Hinges creaked when he lifted the lid, his hand diving in, sifting through tools until they emerged with a steel mallet. With determination, he drove it into the casing containing the stone.

"Don't break the protective case!" Elva warned.

The Militia Trades stared, seemingly unable to decide who to trust. Just as Oran prepared for a second strike, the transport surged violently, mirroring the turbulence that had destroyed the one behind them. The impact hurled Elva backward, slamming her against her post. Glass and metal bit into her spine.

The cramped interior swayed erratically, blurring the view from the small glass openings. The sudden movement sent a red-arm-band flying toward the ceiling before he crashed onto a side bench. His grunt of pain blended into the chaos. Struggling to regain balance, he fumbled with his coat, tangled in the safety nets bolted to the metal walls. Near the front, Lyla grappled with the turbulence clinging to the overhead handles. Once on their feet, the disoriented crew redirected their focus to assist Oran. With a final tug and pull, they managed to detach the small container. The machine responded instantaneously. The gentle currents of light cascading through the edges gradually faded, shrouding the space in darkness, except for the small cylinder with the glowing stone.

"Cover it!" Elva urged.

The Militia Trades yanked their coats from the wall-mounted nets, throwing them over the stone in Oran's hands until its light dimmed to nothing. Elva rushed to the side bench and quickly lifted the hinged top. Her hands found a small lantern, its faint glow barely piercing the gloom. She positioned it in the chamber's center, close to Oran, careful not to betray their presence to the outside maritime world.

The vessel swayed violently again, caught beneath the grip of turbulent waves. Most of her crew pressed their hands to their mouths, stifling screams into half-swallowed shrieks. Through clenched teeth, Elva fought to stay silent herself.

A loud stomp thundered through the chamber—something massive collided with the outer surface. A series of metallic clangs followed, like muffled footsteps in water, creating an unsettling symphony. Her eyes met Oran's across the dim space. One of his hands gripped the overhead handle tightly, while the other concealed the ignited stone beneath the gray fabric of their Academy coats.

Beyond him, a distant flicker of light caught her attention through the front viewport. From the shadows emerged a winged figure, its legs fused together, coiling its wings around itself. The creature slammed its weight against their portside, using the vessel for leverage to spring itself toward the dancing radiance. The ship groaned and tilted beneath her.

Elva's gaze darted beyond the pilot's opening. Panic tightened her chest the instant the winged fiend locked onto the source of the light. It latched onto the lead vessel, its fused legs gripping tightly and driving the craft into a collision course with her fleet.

"That thing is ramming the lead ship straight at us. We have to move." Lyla's cry shattered the silence.

Oran rushed, shoving the casing holding the stone back into its cradle before sprinting to the pilot's post. Elva hurried to her post in the back until something caught her eyer. Ice flooded her veins, freezing her in mid-stride. Through the glass, two white eyes burned like twin stars. Her breath hitched in her throat at the sight of the beast. Its pale wings stretched wide enough to block out what little light remained, membrane-thin skin almost translucent in the gloom. Those eyes held her, measured her, dismissed her as prey. Its fused legs ended in claws that gripped the glass surface, the sheer weight threatening to shatter the barrier.

She stood petrified, unable to tear her gaze away from the menacing white glare. Her fingers curled tightly around the cold metal handrail, unable to advance closer to her station. The creature's force rocked the vessel, making the propellers' handle jerk and jolt erratically. Behind her, frantic grunts and piercing screams filled the air.

The small chamber rattled, causing her knees to buckle. Her stomach churned. The Militia Trades struggled to maintain their footing while Oran wrestled with the controls. A tightness gripped her chest. He should have been safe in Äktas, surrounded by the Academy's stone walls, not drowning in her mistakes.

Shaking the thought, her mind tried to make sense of the unfolding chaos. Her gaze shifted rapidly between the beast clinging to the glass and the ignited stone. In a moment of clarity, her fingers released the handrail.

Rushing to the middle of the chamber, she seized the mallet Oran had used earlier. Her hand swung it toward the roof, aiming for the casing housing the ignited stone.

"What are you doing? We need that to power the machine."

She ignored Lyla's protests and swung again with force, freeing the casing.

The glow around the metal walls flickered out instantly. The craft came to a forced halt, leaving them adrift and at the mercy of the currents and the creatures looming outside.

Her hands found the dual-axis periscope mounted beside the stone's housing. Another swing, another impact. Finally, the viewing port shattered, raining glass onto the metal floor.

Lyla thrashed against Oran's hold, unleashing a torrent of curses.

Elva's hands shook while they worked the stone's casing lever. Two pair of Militia Trades' hands appeared beside her, helping until the mechanism sprang open.

She positioned the container holding the ignited stone at the periscope's broken base and released it inside. A searing beam of light surged forth, threatening to engulf everything in its path. Bracing herself, her hand forced the casing against the base, using it as a makeshift shield.

Power surged through the improvised contraption and up the periscope. Twin rays of light erupted from both its axes in opposite directions, slicing the murky depths.

The radiant blades surged forward, illuminating the fleet ahead and forcing the creatures to recoil. The fiends wrapped their membranous wings around themselves before darting away, their silhouettes vanishing into the darkness beyond.

A momentary wave of relief crashed through Elva. The beast's grip on her post viewport had surrendered its hold. Her eyes found Oran's, his smile blazing brighter than any ignited stone, but the moment quickly shattered.

The impact came from all sides the moment the leading vessel slammed into them—a metal-jarring collision that sent shockwaves through the craft.

The stone's casing on the periscope slipped from her grasp, and a small but powerful sliver of light burst outward. Its force hurled her upward like a puppet on strings, slamming her against the ceiling hard enough to drive the air from her lungs. She barely had time to gasp before she crashed back to the floor, and everything around her faded in an instant.

The gentle sway of the Underwater Vessel pulled Elva from darkness, consciousness trickling back into her mind. The weight of her body pressed against Oran's lap, his chest barely rising beneath her. She turned quickly, cupping his face in her hands, the rough scratch of his stubble brushing against her palms.

"Oran!" She pressed her ear to his chest, finding only a faint heartbeat. "Wake up!" she yelled. Her hands raced over his shoulders, down his arms, each shake more desperate than the last, but he remained unresponsive. She surveyed the chamber. The only light came from the small lantern she had turned on earlier. The weak glow cast long shadows across the floor, where bodies lay strewn like broken dolls. Lyla slumped at the rear post, arms dangling beside her. She picked her way through the tangle of unconscious Militia Trades.

"Sergeant," Elva said.

Lyla's eyes flickered, battling a heavy haze. Her arm lifted a fraction of an inch, then another until a finger extended toward the wall. The air-measuring valve's needle quivered deep in the danger zone, making Elva's lungs seize. Minutes. Just minutes of oxygen remained, perhaps less.

Glancing at Oran, the tightness in her throat grew, and her eyes burned with tears.

Her knees sank beside him, her fingers tangling in his sleek dark hair until she caught sight of a bruise near his brow. "Oran!" her voice wavered, pressing her forehead against his. "I'm so sorry. This is all my fault." She cradled his hands in hers, brushing her lips over his knuckles. "What do I do?" she whispered, her voice trembling against his cold skin.

"I'm so sorry."

Her eyes stung the moment the realization hit. The lights emitted by the transports had lured the beasts closer, while the force of the ignited white stones struck fear into them. Desperate, she had placed the kindled stone in the periscope, hoping it would serve as a weapon against the creatures. Her actions chased the fiends away but the caves emerged as the greater adversary they wouldn't survive.

She had noticed how quickly the stones faded around the wrecked vessels. Their energy drained faster than usual. It was the caves all along. They pulsed with a life of their own, hungry for the magic in the gems. This was why the creatures relentlessly tore open the vessels. By using their own ignited rock against the beasts, she had unintentionally fed the caves their fill. Now, their white stone lay drained, empty, with nothing left to carry them forward.

Her thumb brushed the bruise on Oran's brow. "You should've stayed in Äktas."

Turbulent currents surged, rattling the convoy. Elva's eyes snapped to the flickering light of the ship that had collided with hers. Shadows twisted in the depths, and a sudden flash of motion darted past, vanishing into the murky waters. Another impact sent her sprawling.

The fiends had returned for more.

She scrambled up, but her leather straps caught on metal. With a sharp tug, the bands tore free, her fingers brushing the satchel at her hip. Her heart thundered, remembering what was inside.

Desperate hands dug into the bag, until her fingers found it. The Ikarite bloodstone box. She held it to her ear, shaking it gently. The white stone inside replied with a soft rattle that sent a storm rushing through her veins. The stone that had started it all.

If only she hadn't used it to test the Sky Lantern... She should've listened to Oran. Should've stayed in her cot or buried herself in her pile of parchments. Facing the Commander's punishments for a failed Lantern would've been more bearable than dragging her only friend into the depths of this chaos. Her eyes darted between the box and his unconscious body, his tan olive skin turning pale. His breath grew even shallower.

Her heart twisted. Her hands curled around the box, a snarl tugging at the edge of her lips. The stone inside had led her to do the unthinkable—and now, Oran would pay the price.

She hated its magic. Despised it. The destruction it brought. If the cities hadn't lusted after the power coursing within the stones, they would've been home, safe. He'd be safe. The blight that cursed the Tanama and poisoned the underwater caves—it all stemmed from the gems' powers. Wielding their magic only left devastation in its wake.

A bitter pang rose in her chest. Her gaze swept over the convoy of unconscious bodies before returning to Oran. She couldn't fight the tremble of her lip any longer, and tears blurred her vision. "I'm sorry. I'm so sorry."

He had risked everything to be by her side. Whether she hated the stones or not, she owed it to him to do whatever it took to save him. Even if it meant sacrificing everything.

She leaned down to Oran, pressing a tear-soaked kiss to his forehead before hurrying to the hatch at the bottom of his post. Her pulse thundered in her ears the moment she opened the Siren's den latch. The narrow space would allow her to swim free of the craft.

With a deep, shuddering breath, Elva's fingers pried open the Ikarite bloodstone box, letting the sinister energy of the white stone consume everything around her.

Chapter 10

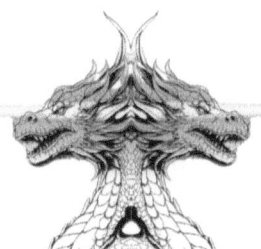

KA'ZAN

YOEN

THE AGNI VESSEL'S DECK pitched beneath Yoen's boots, each movement echoed by his mare's hooves scraping against the salt-stained planks. Through the storm of volcanic cinders, Ka'zan's harbor emerged—its cobblestones splitting like shattered glass. Overcrowded with survivors from the vessel claimed by Zuwena, the fleet swayed on the churning waters of the Great Sea.

The captain's voice cut through the muffled cries, moans of pain, and desperate prayers from the injured. "We're reaching the harbor. Ready the anchor," the captain bellowed. "Stand by for mooring."

Yoen's brown eyes swept across the deck. From a fleet of a hundred, only a handful remained unscathed. Four guards staggered under the weight of High Regent Zohar's stretcher. The scepter in Zohar's limp fingers sputtered, its flame flickering like a dying candle. Only the amulet at his throat still blazed bright, its golden light pulsing in rhythm with the High Regent's shallow breaths. "Make way for the High Regent," one of the guards who survived the wyvern shouted.

The vessel slammed against the quay, sending bodies stumbling across the blood-slicked deck. Yoen struggled to keep his balance, his boots sliding on the wooden planks.

"Make way!" He repeated after the guard, positioning himself in front of the stretcher.

Ropes whistled through the air while marine members scrambled to secure the vessel. Three crew members leaped onto the wharf, their boots thundering against the wood, wrestling with a heavy boarding ramp.

Yoen's fingers found his mare's warm flank, feeling the tremors running through her muscles before he addressed the captain, "Inara, see that she's safe."

The moment the ramp touched down, he surged forward. Behind him, the guards carried the High Regent, their labored breathing punctuating each step. He called over his shoulder, words breaking through their gasps. "Drekavog's walls and shields are withstanding Garam's force. We cannot linger outside the fortress too long. The volcano's roots extend under all of Ka'zan!"

Swarms of people scurried like ants before a storm. Above, like a bird brooding over its nest, four mighty emerald wyvern wings wrapped around Drekavog, creating an unbreakable barrier against the volcanic onslaught. Along the paths leading to the fortress, slivers of gas curled up from small crevices in the ground, stinging his nostrils.

The fortress' grand doors swung open, revealing golden drops of light flickering beneath the wing shields. Within the circular stronghold, an indoor atrium spread before them, with tall trees and a centered field of grass filled with cots for the wounded.

The enclosed garden hummed with activity. Burnt flesh mingled with the pungent aroma of herbs as the healers tried to soothe the agonizing burns and scrapes. Children clutched at their parents, their faces streaked with tears that cut through the ash-stained cheeks.

"High Regent Zohar! Is he dead?" A woman's whisper carried across the space, her head wrapped in crimson-stained bandages.

"Over here!" Yoen's arm shot up, flagging down to an attending healer. "Where's the Chief Healer?"

"Chief Daigo is in the Healer's chambers," he replied, falling in step with the stretcher-bearers to tend to Zohar.

The personal guard Zohar had requested to stay behind before their journey into Garam, emerged from the shifting crowds. Neatly gathered into a center braid, her dark silk hair framed a tanned face with high cheekbones. "Sefa!"

She approached, her muscular frame towering over most, lips pressing into a thin line at the sight of the High Regent. "What happened?"

Yoen's fingers curled into fists at his sides, his gaze dropping to the stone floor. The weight of the recent events pressed down on his shoulders. So much had happened in such a short period of time that he couldn't formulate a simple answer.

"We heard the screeches and saw the lighting," Sefa said, her dark eyes narrowing. "A wyvern? There are rumors, but no one has confirmed."

He dragged his sleeve across his sweat-slicked forehead. "We must get the High Regent to safety first."

Sefa leaned forward, her voice a mere whisper. "Wyverns are supposed to be extinct."

"I believe the High Regent would like to speak to his council first. If he wakes." His gaze drifted to where Zohar lay motionless, his face a mask of blood and ash. Two guards still gripped the stretcher's handles while another cradled the scepter and helmet as if they were made of glass. "Given his state, it'd be wise if he has a word with his son as well."

Leaving Sefa behind, Yoen hurried toward the Healer's chambers. Rows of cots lined the walls, and more whispers erupted at the sight of the unconscious High Regent.

Chief Healer Daigo hunched over a patient, his fingers working deftly to wrap bandages around the stump of what had once been an arm. An attending healer's words drew his attention upward and his green eyes met Yoen's. The wheels of his copper chair squeaked against the stone floor, rolling toward them. "The next room is empty. Let's move him there, away from prying eyes."

The guards maneuvered through the doorway, lowering the Hight Regent onto an empty cot.

"How bad is it, Chief Daigo?" Yoen asked, watching the Chief Healer assessed Zohar's bloodied forehead.

Blood stains marked the Chief Healer's brown felt coat and his white hair and long beard caught the light. He rolled closer, holding a golden-rimmed glass sphere to Zohar's nose. After studying the fog that formed, he gently lifted each of the High Regent's eyelids. "It's hard to tell, but his neck amulet seems to be sustaining him. What struck him?"

Yoen struggled to find the right words. His hand moved to his neck, attempting to ease the tension there.

"We never stood a chance." The guard holding Zohar's staff stepped forward, her hands trembling. "The creature slithered through the shadows like twilight made flesh, hunting us from the moment we entered Garam. Her presence crushed the air from our lungs before we could even cry out. When she struck, those blue flames made the scepter look like a twig against a searing storm. The clash painted the cavern in horrific light, throwing our bodies against the rocks. We would've been dead if it hadn't been for His High Regency," she rasped, sweat beading along her collar.

Copper gears whirred as Daigo circled the cot, his chair responding to the slight touch of a lever. Through his magnified, round spectacles, his green eyes fixed on Yoen. "So, the rumors are true. We are in the midst of a wyvern assault."

"The creature flies west. She'll soon reach the Ikarites," Yoen explained, while his shaking fingers found the knife at his waist, gripping the hilt like an anchor.

The chamber doors groaned open, revealing a towering figure in a dark blue stand-collar suit. His brisk steps echoed against the stone in his approach.

"Lord Vardan," Chief Daigo said, and the room bowed as one.

Vardan's fingers wrapped around his father's limp hand. "How is my father?"

"The High Regent seems to be drifting in and out of consciousness. His neck amulet is still kindled. There's a chance he could pull through, but it'll be difficult to determine how quickly," Daigo said. The leather straps across his chest displayed an array of gleaming healer tools. "I'll need more time. Placing him in the Sanctum will hasten his recovery. However, it will require at least two of our ignited stones."

"Do it," Vardan ordered. "Ka'zan can't afford to lose him." He took the scepter from the guard's hands, studying its failing light. "Do whatever is necessary to keep the High Regent alive."

Daigo's chair hummed with movement while he addressed two attending healers. "Liren, Desna, let's transfer the High Regent to the Sanctum. Chief Miner, one of the healers should take a look at that burn on your arm."

Yoen's gaze dropped to his left arm, where raw flesh had begun to throb. "No, I—I'm fine. Please tend to the High Regent," he insisted. "Lord Vardan, may I have a word?"

The Lord Regent approached, the scepter held carefully in his hands. The healers remained at his father's side and with the wounded guards. "You should have that burn looked at, Chief Miner," Vardan said, his eyes flicking to the bloodied sleeve.

Yoen nodded but pressed closer, dropping his voice. "I assume you've heard the rumors. The wyvern?"

"The word has spread throughout the fortress. I can hardly fathom it, not after everything."

"If I didn't see it myself, I wouldn't believe it. But she was hard to miss," Yoen said, his hand working at the knots in his neck.

Vardan brought the scepter closer to his eyes, carefully inspecting its diminishing glow. "I gather you recognized the creature?"

"The Elder Scrolls link her to Ragas. Zuwena, the wyvern with sapphire and green jade scales and lightning as her strongest trait. She didn't hesitate when she used it to awaken Garam," Yoen rasped, wincing as pain shot through his arm. "I thought she would finish us all off. But she veered west instead, to Ikari."

Vardan's hands tightened around the scepter, testing its weight. "It has been a safeguarded secret, known to a selected few." The emerald of his eyes absorbed the soft glow of the agni staff, turning them almost black in the dim light. He closed the distance between them until Yoen could smell the lingering scent of burnt incense on his clothes. "Zuwena has been imprisoned inside Garam since Magnar captured her at the end of the Wyvern Wars. My grandfather caught the injured beast amidst the Tanama's forests, before Ragas' curse ensnared the land."

Vardan's words hung in the air. Yoen's fingers dug into the cot's railing, his chest tightening, each breath growing shallow and quick. "All this time, a wyvern in our midst? So close to our city, our families?" The words caught in his throat, Zohar's face flashing through his mind, the way his eyes had darted away during his speech at Mount Garam, the slight tremor in his usually steady voice and hands.

His fingers curled into fists against his thighs. "Wyverns have been extinct for a century. It's written on every Elder scroll I've studied. If the High Regent was privy to such knowledge, why open the Gate if there was a possibility for the creature to escape?"

"When I first heard of Zuwena, I dismissed it as nonsense. Yet those ignited agni stones powering our fortress and the ones we keep tucked away are her doing." The cot across from Yoen groaned beneath Vardan's weight the moment he settled onto it. "I share this in confidence, because you're a trusted Chief. I can't explain my father's choice to keep the truth from you, despite your friendship. However, opening Garam's Gate? That burden falls on me."

The ground beneath them lurched. The scepter slipped from Vardan's grasp, its metallic clang against stone drowned by screams from nearby rooms. Yoen's muscles strained, gripping the cot tighter to keep from being thrown off.

"The tremors haven't stopped since her lightning struck Garam," Vardan said, scrambling to retrieve the staff. "Zuwena's thunder has stirred the volcano into a perpetual unrest. Its roots spread through all of Ka'zan. She has left us at its mercy, and I fear it's my fault."

Yoen stood, extending a hand to help Vardan steady himself. "Are you all right?"

Vardan's head bobbed in a weak nod. "Your reports on volcanic activity kept piling up. For months, I begged my father to investigate Garam's scar and ensure Zuwena remained captive. The smoke atop Rengō's in the middle of the Tanama must've pushed him to open the Gate. But we were wrong. Zuwena might've been stirring inside the volcano, but that smoke consuming the dead woods is something else entirely."

Another quake shook the fortress. Yoen stumbled, instinctively reaching out to catch himself. Searing pain exploded through his burned arm. "If Zuwena isn't the cause of the smoke on Rengō, then what is?" he managed with a hiss.

The Lord Regent steadied him, his grip gentle but firm. "The Council is still meeting with the Elders, but we have not yet found a reason for the smoke. It seems the more pressing matter now is the volcano. I don't know how long we have until Garam truly shows us its might."

Sweat beaded on Yoen's forehead, rolling down his temples, the burn pulsing with each heartbeat. Vardan caught the eye of a nearby healer and beckoned him over.

"I'm fine."

"Your eyes betray you, Chief."

His shoulders slumped when he sank back onto the cot, allowing Liren to examine his arm.

"The Council believes my father can subdue Garam," Vardan said, passing a water container to Liren.

The healer carefully cleaned the burn, causing Yoen to flinch. "Does she know the state of His Regency?"

The Lord Regent paced, the scepter catching the light with each turn. "Sefa's informing her now. Though, even if my father recovers..." He held up the scepter, studying its surface. "This heirloom no longer holds the strength to reseal Garam's scar. To close that Gate, we'll need a power stronger than a volcanic eruption—a force that counters Zuwena's lightning. Perhaps that's why her wrath focused on the staff. She knew that without it, we'd face Garam's full force."

The ground heaved again, sending Liren stumbling. Yoen's good arm shot out, steadying the healer before he could fall.

"It will be best if I go meet with the Council myself. I wanted to see my father, in case he..." Vardan's gaze drifted to the back door where Daigo had carried the unconscious Zohar.

"I understand, Lord Regent."

"I must thank you, Chief. Something tells me my father wouldn't have made it if it weren't for you."

"Inara is the true hero, I must say."

"I'll have to give her an extra treat when I see her," Vardan said before addressing the healer. "Please make sure the Chief's arm is cared for."

They both bowed to Vardan before he departed, holding the gesture until the door closed behind him. Yoen's eyes fixed on the dark crimson stains marking Liren's robes, shadows from his last patients. His heart hammered against his ribs as a new fear clawed its way up his throat. "Liren, my niece and nephew, Arben and Luan, have you seen them? Are they in the fortress?"

The healer's hands stilled over the bandages. "I'm sorry, Chief. I haven't seen them. Everything happened so quickly. Some of the guards went into the city borders to warn the farmers. My husband went too." His shoulders slumped. "They haven't returned."

The ground's violent shake scattered Liren's tools across the floor. As Yoen bent to help retrieve them, another tremor knocked them both off balance. Chunks of ceiling rained down, and he threw himself over the healer, sheltering him from the debris.

"That was a strong one," Liren faltered. "I know this fortress can withstand almost anything, but we can't evacuate through the sea, we can't run into the Tanama or the Uláak would massacre us all. That monstrous smoke is spreading across the entire dead forests. There's a wyvern in our midst, and Ka'zan might collapse into a river of lava while our only Enchanter lies unconscious," the healer blurted out in one breath, his words tumbling over each other like a waterfall.

Yoen gripped Liren's shoulder, his own hand trembling despite his attempt at reassurance. He opened his mouth to speak, but the words lodged in his throat, choked by the storm brewing in his own chest. Instead, he gave a sharp nod and pushed himself to his feet. "Thanks for the bandages."

"Chief, I'm not finished."

"This will do. I'll come back to check on the High Regent."

Yoen rushed past the healing quarters. The indoor atrium buzzed with chaos, cries of pain mixing with the shuffle of feet and clatter of weapons. The fortress' usual warmth felt stifling now, its spherical tiers stretching upward like the throat of some great beast.

People crowded every available space. Healers darted between makeshift cots while guards assembled their weapons at hastily erected stations. Between the patches of greenery, tables groaned under the weight of water vases and food provisions. Large paint-ings decorated the walls, depicting wyverns in their majestic glory, soaring through the boundless skies. A striking painting displayed the late leader. Magnar stood tall and proud beside Ragas, the eldest of wyverns, their gazes locked in an eternal moment of understanding.

He scanned the crowd, searching for familiar faces. His heart leaped when he spotted Luan's friend in the distance. He raised his good arm, waving until she noticed him. The young girl's eyes widened with recognition.

"Mawün," he mouthed, his hands already moving. His left hand formed a d-shape, index finger extended, while his right one tapped his left hand's closed digits. He silently signed—*Arben. Luan. Where?*

Mawün's teeth worried at her lower lip as she shook her head.

With pleading in his eyes, Yoen's palms pressed together, moving back and forth. *Please. Where?*

Her closed fist pressed gently under her chin, thumb and pinky extended, her eyebrows furrowed. *Sorry.*

Her next gestures sent ice through his veins while his heart sank. Her palms turned downward and swept through the air, mimicking the motion of waves. Then her arm carved a concave curve in the air, resembling the entrance of a shelter, while her other traced an inward motion.

"The Beach Caves," his voice quivered.

Mawün's hand gestured to apologize, but he had already turned, his boots pounding against the ground as he burst through the gates. A wall of fog engulfed him, not the gentle morning mist he knew, but something thicker and more oppressive. It billowed up from spider-web fissures in the earth, carrying the acrid stench of Garam's volcanic heart. Above the chaos of fleeing villagers and the fortress' wailing alarms, stone cracked and split with sounds like thunder. The fog burned his eyes and coated his tongue with sulfur. He yanked his cowl tighter, but it did little to filter the toxic air. Panicked animal cries echoed through the fog. From the bleats of sheep, grunts of pigs, and clucks of chickens, a familiar neigh cut through the noise.

"Inara!" The sound led him to the stables, where the chestnut mare's outline gradually materialized through the mist. "There's my fire-beetle." He patted her flank before swinging himself up. He turned toward the Black Beach, only to pull up short. Massive crevices blocked the direct path, their depths glowing with hidden fire. His fingers tightened around Inara's reins before guiding her toward the longer route. The ground radiated an oppressive heat from its fractured surface. Sweat trickled down his brow, when he spotted a figure on horseback emerging from the haze.

"Where in Ragas' name are you headed?" Chief Gerel's voice strained through his mouth covering.

"My children. Word is they're in the caves."

"Look around you!" Gerel gestured at the crumbling city. "Any minute now, that fortress will be all that's left standing!" He yanked off his wyvern-scale helmet, sweat glistening on his deep brown skin against the crimson of his tunic. "You must turn back!"

Yoen shook his head. "I won't leave them out there."

"Everyone's being directed to Drekavog. The twins are grown. They must've made it into the fortress. Going out there is madness," Gerel insisted while his mare danced nervously beneath him.

"I have to check the caves. Make sure they're safe."

Yoen dug his heel into Inara's flanks, cutting Gerel off mid-protest. The round town square stretched before him, now a maze of fallen debris and rising steam. The Great Horned Ragas statue lay in pieces, its proud structure scattered across the cobblestones. Inara's hoofbeats echoed off empty buildings along their path.

The fog thinned near the beach, revealing the towering basalt columns lining the shore. Two imposing metallic vessels lay grounded like beached whales. Their dark exteriors gleamed ominously, reflecting dully in fractured light filtering through the volcanic haze. Each bore the same symbol—a hand clutching a glowing stone encircled by flame. His heart skipped a beat when he noticed the deep gouges marring the metal, like the claw marks of a giant beast. The trail of footprints leading from the vessels toward the caves filled him with dread. His fingers curled around the pit of his stomach, breath tight and shallow, pulse hammering in his temples. Then he drove Inara forward with growing urgency.

Voices carried on the wind—muffled conversations punctuated by sharp commands. Five figures stood guard by the cave entrance, their gray coats and crimson armbands matched the symbols on the vessels.

Yoen dismounted behind a cluster of rocks, signaling Inara to stay put. He retraced a familiar climbing path from his childhood adventures with his younger sister, feeling the handholds along the cave's outer wall. As he climbed, the crevice felt tighter than he remembered, as if the years had squeezed it shut. His sister used to climb the same rocks with much ease. He wished he had an ounce of her agility. Back when he was a guard, he could keep up. Now, after years as a miner, his strength remained, but his agility was gone—along with his breath.

He squeezed through the narrow opening, but the rough stone tore at his bandages, scraping against raw burns. Biting back screams, he fought through the pain shooting up his arm. Finally reaching a ledge overlooking the cave's interior, he pressed his belly against the cold stone. His chin jutted over the edge, several feet above, peering down at a scene of unfamiliar faces. Down on the black sand, a young woman lay motionless, her bronze skin marked with white patches, a single pale strand running through her dark braid. Beside her, a man with onyx hair knelt, his hands working at something in her boot.

"You must know what's causing the smoke. Was it that damned volcano? Or your bloodthirsty Regent?" The words cracked like a whip.

His heart stopped. Arben and Luan knelt before a woman with a red-armband and leather rank marks on her shoulders. Blood matted Arben's face, Luan's hair was wild and tangled. His nails bit into his palms, fighting the urge to leap down.

"Speak!" the woman demanded.

Luan's quiet voice carried a thread of defiance. "We've done nothing."

Bile rose in Yoen's throat. His chest tightened until each breath felt like drowning. His jaw clenched so hard it ached, forcing him to turn away and retrace his path down the cliff face. The thought of any confrontation sent a shiver down his spine, knowing that if he dared to challenge and lost, the twins would pay the price.

A sharp whistle brought Inara trotting from her hiding place. His hand pressed against the white moon on her forehead. "You must find Gerel. Find anyone that can lend a hand. Go!"

Inara snorted, bumping his shoulder with her nose and pawing at the sand.

"I can't go with you. The twins need me. They need you too, fire-beetle. Go swiftly, as a spellbound arrow." He patted Inara's flank with urgency. His heart tore apart watching the last tangible link to his wife speed through the stone path, disappearing into a volcanic haze.

He shifted his attention back to the cave. Earlier that morning, he'd yelled at the twins for being in that same cavern. His fingers found the familiar spot around the pit of his stomach. None of it mattered now.

His feet quickened their pace using the large stones along the beach for cover, then squatted down. In the distance, two guards held their post while white-capped waves crashed against the shore beyond them.

As he darted between boulders, movement flickered in his peripheral vision. A quick turn of his neck revealed three red-armbands charging toward him. A young man with dark hair falling past his shoulders lunged a punch at his face. Yoen twisted aside, but a second attacker's boot caught him in the ribs, driving the air from his lungs. He struggled to catch his breath.

The dark-haired man seized the opportunity, wrapping him in a steel-clad grip from behind, like a snake coiling around its prey.

Yoen slammed his head backward, feeling cartilage crunch as his skull connected with the man's nose. When the hold loosened, he spun, delivering a kick that left the red-armband motionless in the sand.

He turned to face his remaining opponents. The woman who'd kicked him twirled a copper rod etched with wyvern fire patterns. Beside her, a man with ashy blond hair drew a dagger, its white stone hilt catching what little light filtered through the haze. Both seemed to be no more than half Yoen's age. Their agility and speed starkly reminded him of his lack of practice.

His fingers closed around his own knife. The blond man's blade flashed toward his chest. Yoen caught his wrist, but his attacker twisted free, transferring the dagger to his other hand in one fluid motion. The blade whistled past Yoen's eye as he jerked backward. His counterstrike left only a thin red line across the man's cheek.

The dance of blades continued, each thrust a deadly calculation in a fast-paced duel. Yoen finally managed to twist his opponent's arm behind his back, but before he could strike, the copper rod smashed into his knee. He blocked the next blow with his knife hand, the impact jarring his weapon loose. The woman flashed like a striking viper, her rod catching Yoen in the chest and sending him sprawling. She pressed her advantage with a flurry of strikes until one connected with his left ear. The world tilted and spun, sound becoming a distant buzz.

He staggered back, each step sending jolts of pain through his leg. His knife glinted tantalizingly out of reach. He caught the next blow aimed at his ribs, trapping the copper rod against his side with his elbow. The woman yanked sharply, and the weapon split in two, revealing a hidden blade. As she lunged forward, triumph in her eyes, a swift arrow sank in her throat.

She froze mid-motion, the copper rod slipping from her grasp, and she instinctively clutched at the shaft. A choked sound escaped her lips before she crumpled to the sand. The blond man attempted to flee but a second arrow found his leg, dropping him mid-stride.

Yoen turned, muscles screaming in protest. Through the thinning volcanic haze, Chief Gerel led a charge across the beach, mounted archers at his flanks. And there she was, Inara, racing alongside them, her hooves throwing up clouds of black sand.

W E FELL THROUGH THE void, as we have said many times, neither here nor there. In convergence, raw energy surged, untamed, and volatile. We became its vessel, its conduit. And when the storm stilled, we rejoiced in what had been conceived.

And in that sacred stillness, ages after many storms, we shaped the winged ones.

The wyverns were not forged for dominance, nor created for servitude. They were a binding and a living bridge between the energy that is us and the essence of the land. That force coursed through them like an undying ember glowing within their bones.

Where they flew, the land awakened. Trees bowed. Flowers bloomed in their wake. Seas and rivers sang to their passing and answered their call. Even the sun herself danced with them.

When we brought forth the early humans—those small, walking beings still shaping language from breath, the wyverns saw a flicker of kinship and resonance.

And for a time, they roamed as one. Not as beast and rider, but as flame and tinder. Many rode the winged ones in joy. Ragas himself rejoiced in climbing the skies with the humans on his rugged back. He played among the clouds, sparking lightning and rain for their amusement.

But... from above, the humans glimpsed the world that lay beyond their own.

And in that glimpse, another spark lit.

A different convergence began—one born of hunger and wonder.

It did not weave like silk, but fused through pressure, breaking wings and cracking scales to forge new strength. They united as iron bonds in fire—tempered by shared ambition.

If you are paying attention, you might see it still: In unity, there is life.

But only through scorching chaos is it born.

Fragment lxxvii: Convergence
—From *Daemons Archives, The Original Three*

PART THREE

ENKINDLE
CONFLUENCE

CHAPTER 11

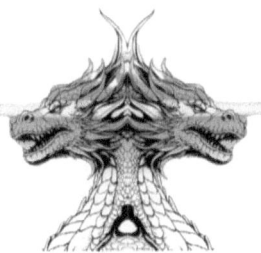

KA'ZAN

ELVA

A MIXTURE OF SALTY brine and acrid smoke filled Elva's nose. Consciousness crawled its way back, and her eyelids fluttered, but the world refused to sharpen, swirling in a nauseating dance of shadows and light. Fire seemed to lick her palms with every twitch of her fingers. The distant crash of waves was punctuated by sharp voices, their heated argument urgent, yet far away.

Through her haze, two Militia members materialized, guarding the entrance of a cave. Inside, their Sergeant's silhouette cut a menacing shape against the dim light, towering over two kneeling figures. Black sand and dust marred their similar features, and ash stained their tunics.

Pain shot through Elva when she turned, attempting to lift herself up.

"Easy." Oran's hands steadied her shoulders, his face appearing above her own. "You've been unconscious for a while," he whispered, his voice soft and gentle, brushing back her braid.

Her throat felt like she'd swallowed glass. "Where are we?"

"The levers inside the Underwater Vessels pointed north. Somehow, we made it out of the caves and onto Ka'zan's Black Beach."

Fragments of memory flickered at the edges of her mind, but slipped away like water through her fingers. "How did we get here?"

Oran's gaze dropped to his boots, where volcanic sand had worked its way into every crease of the leather. "I remember the light of the stone knocking you out after building that contraption. You were amazing, El," he added, as his dark eyes gazed back at her. "The winged creatures fled, but we lost all power. Without the stone, we drained our air supply. You were still unconscious when we started fainting."

She searched his face. "Who steered the fleets out of the underwater caves?"

He swallowed hard and settled beside her. "We don't know. When I woke up, you weren't inside the vessel." His fingers trembled, ghosting over her bandaged hands. "When I found you at the beach shore, I thought you were..." He paused, words catching in his throat, tears threatening to spill. "You really scared me. You swallowed so much water."

The weight of unspoken words hung heavy in his dark eyes. Her head throbbed with each heartbeat, drowning out any attempt to recall what had happened in the vessel. "How long was I out?"

"A few hours."

Elva clenched her teeth, battling the vertigo threatening to pull her under again. "What's going on there? Who are those two people?" she asked, pointing with her lips to the figures kneeling before the Militia Sergeant.

"Locals. They confirmed our location after we found them near the cave," Oran said.

Elva propped herself up, ignoring the searing pain in her palms. The young man's blood had dried black against his forehead, while the girl's hair hung in tangled curtains across her face. They seemed to be only a few years younger than her.

"You will answer our questions or else." Lyla's voice bounced off the cave walls like steel on stone.

"We've told you. We don't know what you're talking about," the young man answered through a raspy voice.

The Militia Sergeant's fist cracked against his jaw before her boot found his chest with a sickening thud.

"Arben!" The girl's scream pierced the air.

As Lyla's leg drew back for another strike, the dark-haired girl threw herself forward, taking the full force of the blow to her stomach.

"What's going on?" Elva interrupted the next assault on the Ka'zanty.

A Militia Trade yanked the locals back to their knees at Lyla's wave. "Look who's back with the living." Her boots crunched across the black sand toward Elva and Oran. "We would've left you for dead if it hadn't been for the blue-armbands. This one specially wouldn't let you out of his sight." Her chin jerked toward Oran. "How quickly can you get the machines working again?"

Elva's fingers pressed against her temple, trying to push back the pain. "They're not working?"

"We tried to restart them but they wouldn't budge, both stones are dead," Oran said, rising to stand beside the Militia Sergeant.

Lyla's hands clasped behind her back, spine rigid. "If we are to complete our mission, those convoys need to dive again."

Elva's mind raced through possibilities, each one crumbling like the black sand beneath them. Without ignited stones, the ships that had carried them from Äktas to the agni stone city were nothing but metal coffins. Lyla's cat-eyes bore into her with the intensity of a drawn bow. The message was clear. Refusal wasn't an option. The artificers were tools, nothing more, pieces to be manipulated in whatever game the Militia Sergeant played. "I'll have a look," she finally said.

"You just woke up, and you're not in good shape," Oran protested.

"That doesn't matter," Lyla insisted, arms crossed like barriers over her chest. "I have orders and a covert mission. We must stay on target."

Oran's hand found his waist while the other pressed against his temple. "I've said it countless times, the white stones have lost all their power."

"The vessels function by harnessing the energy within the enchanted gems," Elva managed, her words scratching past her dry throat. The world tilted suddenly, and her legs betrayed her. Oran's arm caught her waist, drawing her against his steady frame. She offered a weak smile before continuing. "Restarting the machines without an ignited stones will be a daunting task. It could take days, weeks, or even years—assuming we even have the necessary resources in this region. But, even if we manage to secure a local ignited stone, we'd require an Enchanter to assist us. And even then, there's no guarantee the vessels will function. The machines are specifically designed to respond to the power of white stones, not to whatever energy the other cities' gems contain."

Oran guided her to a volcanic boulder and helped her settle in. "The Sergeant Artificer is right," he said. "As far as my knowledge of Ka'zan goes, the only Enchanter here is the High Regent. And something tells me he won't be too pleased that twenty Äktastary invaded his city's Black Beach with a secret mission. Let alone be willing to help them escape."

Tension crackled between Oran and Lyla, their gazes locked in silent conflict. The bridge of the Sergeant's nose wrinkled with familiar contempt. Elva recognized the scowl. It was the same the Militia Trade reserved for anyone wearing a different armband. Being leagues from home didn't change anything.

"Find an alternative, Artificers," Lyla ordered, her words falling like stones. "I have strict orders and an assignment I intend to complete. We might be far from The Hand's grip, but Äktas' regimen will be upheld. We stand resolute as stone and steel. We rule with might." She recited the Academy's creed. "Any deviation and you'll be treated as traitors. I'll eliminate anyone who stands in my way. That includes those two locals." Her chin jerked toward the prisoners. The young man's amber skin had gone pale, leaning against the freckled woman for support.

Elva's gaze fell on the bound Ka'zanty, their mouths covered, and her stomach rolled. "What do you mean, Sergeant?"

"I can't have witnesses. These two have seen and heard too much. We have to get rid of them."

Bile rose in Elva's throat at the sight of the locals, not much younger than herself. The reality of their invasion crashed over her like a wave. Her stomach betrayed her, and she barely had time to turn before emptying its contents onto Lyla's boots. Oran's gentle hands swept her braid back, his other hand steadying her frame.

"Bloody skies! Compose yourself," Lyla snapped, shaking her leather boots in disgust. "We'll take care of the witnesses now, gather your strength. No matter what happens, my mission comes first."

"Wait," Elva choked out between coughs. "Perhaps they can help." She took a deep breath, her bandaged hand pressed against her stomach. "From the looks of it, they must also know the way around the city. We can use them to our advantage."

Lyla's gaze swung between Elva then the locals like a pendulum.

Oran's dark eyes met Elva's briefly, his hand giving her shoulder a reassuring squeeze before speaking. "The sun will set soon. We're too exposed here. We still haven't figured out what's causing the smoke around the Tanama, but we do know that damn volcano is going to wreak havoc."

"What about the volcano?" Elva asked.

Oran's forehead creased with concern as he replied. "Garam, the city's volcano has awakened. One of the Militia Trades came back with news. Most of the city is in shambles, and the locals have taken refuge inside a massive stone building, surrounded by large wyvern wing shields. Looks like the volcano runs under the entire city."

She recognized the name Garam—the volcanic mount she had studied in the Academy scrolls, the looming island watching over the northern city. Her eyes drifted to the local young man with hair like Oran's, now barely conscious.

"I don't care about daylight or the volcano. We can't have any witnesses," Lyla retorted, striding toward the Ka'zanty prisoners.

Elva's feet raced forward, her stomach in knots. "What if they can help us navigate the city?" The words tumbled out in a rush. "If it's true, that most of the locals are in their hideout, then these two can help us sneak around."

"Even so, we won't be safe," Oran burst out, throwing up his hands. "The volcano is about to burn this city to the ground. The safest place is that structure shielded by wyvern wings."

She met Lyla's stare, willing her stomach to settle. "What if they can help us sneak into that winged structure with the locals? What better way to hide than in plain sight? Everyone will be busy with the volcano or focused on the smoke around the dead forest." Lyla's dark eyes shifted between them and the two prisoners. Elva's chest tightened at the thought of watching these young people die. Murdered.

"If we hide where all the Ka'zanty take refuge, our mission would still be afoot. Whatever you were instructed to do or gather will most definitely be inside the Ka'zanty fortress. If we get discovered," Elva continued, her voice dropping to a whisper, "then we might have some leverage if those two are still alive. Without them, we have nothing."

Lyla's lips curled into a smile that didn't reach her eyes. "I didn't think you had it in you, Sergeant Artificer. You are as conniving as any Militia member." Her fingers drummed against the hilt of her blade. "Fine, we'll take them with us. But they better not cause any trouble." Her threat hung in the air before she strode across the cave to address the other red-armbands.

Elva's teeth dug into her lower lip until she tasted copper. The two locals huddled against the volcanic rocks, shoulders touching, eyes wide and wary. Their momentary relief would soon fade. Just this morning, she had woken up excited to test the Sky Lantern. Now she was miles from home, caught between a raging volcano and the threat of war. Her vision swam, dark spots dancing at the edges. A steady thrum of a heartbeat grew louder in her ears, drowning out even the scrape of footsteps on sand. Her knees buckled, dropping her onto a nearby boulder.

Oran's boots appeared in her line of sight. "Are you all right?" He crouched before her, bringing his face level with hers.

"Just out of sorts," she mumbled, stretching a shaking hand to his face and brushing volcanic dust from his cheeks.

"It's the ash. It's everywhere." His fingers wrapped around hers, steadying them.

The bandages around her palms caught her eyes. Each flex of her fingers sent lightning bolts of pain shooting up her arms. "What happened to my hands?" she winced.

"I was hoping you could tell me. Do you not remember?"

"It's all very foggy," she admitted. "You were knocked out and the air valve hovered over the lowest level." Around them, Militia Trade members checked weapons and adjusted their coat fastenings with steady hands. "Everyone had collapsed. I remember diving into the Siren's den, and then..." She shook her head, the rest lost to darkness.

Oran's palm cupped her cheek with a familiar gentleness that always seemed to melt her. "You really scared me."

Her lower lip quivered. The weight of what she'd done pressed down on her chest until breathing became a conscious effort. The General Commander's orders to send her away were supposed to be her life sentence, but Oran bore the scars. Wildling. The word fit like a well-worn glove. If only her stubbornness hadn't driven her to test the lantern. If she at least had hesitated before rushing to the Generals about the smoke—maybe, just maybe, Oran would be safe. She wanted to tell him how devastated she'd be if she lost him, but in the end, it was her own doing that continued to bring him harm.

To add salt to the wound, in their desperate struggle to survive underwater, her wildling instincts had driven her to retrieve the extra ignited white stone from her satchel. The one that could have powered the Underwater Vessel and given them a chance to return home. Yet her feral instincts had ensured the stone was lost to the depths of the Great Sea. With dusk creeping closer, Oran's chances of survival dwindled. "I'm sorry," she whispered, fighting back the tears.

"Both of you, let's get ready to move. We can't stay here much longer," Lyla interrupted, securing a belt with small leather pouches around her waist.

Elva's muscles tensed to stand, but Oran's hand on her shoulder kept her seated. "Rest for a moment. You haven't fully recovered. I'll help with our tools."

Her gaze followed him around the cave, each step precise despite the exhaustion weighing on his shoulders. Near the entrance, the red-armbands readied themselves, adjusting knives at their ankles, leather straps creaking as they tightened across their backs.

She ignored the persistent thrum of the phantom heartbeat pulsing in her ears, pushing herself up and wobbling toward the northern prisoners. "What's your name?" she whispered, offering the girl a flask of water.

The young woman's jaw clenched, but something in Elva's expression must have reached her. "I'm Luan," she said, accepting the flask with bound hands. "This is my twin brother, Arben."

Elva turned her attention to the angry red gash across Arben's forehead. Her fingers probed the wound with gentle pressure, noting the heat radiating from his skin.

"What are you going to do with us?" Luan's voice cracked. "My brother needs a healer."

Her mind raced, searching for an answer, but none came. She had only bought them time by interceding—now she had to figure out how they'd survive this mess. Then she felt the weight of Sergeant Lyla's stare on her, forcing her into a wordless retreat.

Their exit from the cave lasted only moments before reality struck. Four of their advance guards lay face-down in the black sand, ropes biting into their wrists and ankles. The Sergeant from the other vessel, a young woman wielding a copper rod, now lay lifeless.

A volley of arrows sliced through the air. Elva's body sprang before her mind could catch up, propelling her toward Oran as an arrow flew past his chest, grazing the air just inches from him.

Her own unit reached for their weapons, but a commanding voice cut through the chaos. "Move, and the next one goes through your head!" Sand crunched beneath hooves as a walnut mare shifted her weight. Her rider sat straight-backed despite his sweat-darkened miner's tunic, his gaze pinned them with the intensity of a stalking wolf.

Chapter 12

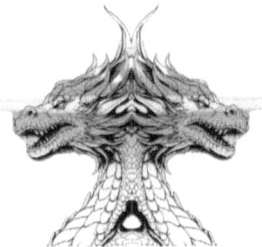

IKARI

ASANTE

Asante's eyes tracked Ida gliding toward a sentinel's watch post in Pālam's lower tier. Sunlight caught her shimmering markings tracing from the Enchanter's lower lip to her chin, their glow intensifying with each stride against her deep brown skin. Her hair bun remained perfectly coiled despite the breeze, not a single white strand daring to escape. She moved with the fluid grace that made every guard straighten their spines.

When she reached the circular stone structure jutting out from the mount's walls, Ida's hazel eyes darted across the landscape. Without a moment to spare, the Enchanter's bloodstone staff angled toward the conical roof. Crimson light writhed from the scepter, snaking upward and coiling around the finial at its peak, pulsing with newfound energy.

Flashes of ruby light spurted outward, seamlessly connecting to the next watch post. The luminous thread extended, weaving an intricate web linking each one. The radiant chain spread from the mountain's bottom tier to its summit. When the final link illuminated the highest watchpoint, a resounding warning alarm echoed through the cavernous city.

"We have to move." Tarrak's hands fumbled with Asante's cowl, yanking it over her face and shoulder-length locs. He nudged through the cobblestone promenade while swarms of Ikarites rushed from the outer city and into the mount.

"This isn't the way out," she whispered, her words muffled by the fabric.

"They are blocking the entrance points." Her brother's amber eyes darted to the closest exit, where armored figures stood rigid, their weapons catching the light. "The alarm is a call for the city to seek refuge inside the mountain. They must have orders to bring people in and not let anyone out of the caves. Hurry, this way!"

His grip tightened on her arm, pulling her through the surging crowd. On the veranda, worried faces watched in silence while waves of outer-city people poured in. Amid the chaos, eyes turned toward the Tanama mountains, where the shroud of smoke continued to engulf Rengō.

Tarrak jerked sideways, pulling her away from a pair of passing sentinels. They crossed into the lower tier's main cave opening. Silver light seeped through a massive exit on the far side of the cavern, a gaping maw carved into the mountain's heart. Market stalls crowded the space between. Yet instead of heading toward the light, he pulled her into a side passage.

"Where are we going?"

He replied with a tug on her sleeve, guiding her into the market halls. Vendors' voices competed with the shuffle of frightened feet and rustling fabric.

Nervous glances fluttered between vendors and citizens in silent alarm. "Did you see? They summoned the unmarked ones from the first level to the Great Hall." The words drifted from a silk-haired man who hunched over the wool vendor's stall.

One of the Sage's attendants muttered to the jewelry vendor. "The Enchanters say not to worry. We must trust our High Priestess!"

Asante's stomach turned. The Ikarites seeking refuge in Pālam had no idea of the massacre in the Great Hall. That so many had been just murdered under the High Priestess' orders—a slaughter of her own making. "Tarrak, these people. They don't know what the Sages and the High Priestess did. We have to warn..."

His palm slammed against her shoulder, pinning her to a narrow wall between stalls. "The moment we speak, those sentinels will drag us to the Priestess," he said under his breath. His chin jerked toward two patrolling muscular women. "Come, this way."

"This is not the way out," Asante objected.

The market stalls blurred past them. He dragged her forward, shouldering between merchants and the crowds flooding the area. The noise of the alarmed city faded with each twist and turn until only whispers of sound drifted through a quieter section of the mount.

"It's a dead end." Asante's heels dug into the ground.

He huffed in frustration before his hand found her wrist again. "This way." The passage squeezed inward, High Tree's roots snaking down the walls and pressing against their shoulders. They wove between thick coils, their bodies twisting through the maze of tendrils until stone blocked their path. Finally, his feet halted where a wall of roots cascaded down like a waterfall entangled with jagged rock.

"You see! Dead end."

Tarrak's body stretched upward, his fingers dancing across the roots until they found one marked with a golden feather. It caught the light like those of Zama's owl form. And to her amazement, the mark sparked to life. A golden circle spread wide before the stone wall split down the middle. Like parting doors, a chorus of cracking wood and the deep groan of shifting earth followed, leaving darkness stretching beyond.

She stared at the shimmering portal with wide eyes.

Tarrak's finger brushed her chin, lifting it to close her slackened jaw. "There's always a way, little Rabbit," he said with a playful smirk, extending his hand. "Come on, we have to move."

When they crossed the threshold, the newly formed gateway instantly sealed behind them, snuffing out every trace of light. The veil of shadows closed in around her, making her chest tighten, each breath growing shorter. "Tarrak," she stammered.

A soft spectral of light blossomed from her brother's hand.

"A miner's lantern," she grinned, drinking in the details. Worn leather wrapped the handle over the wooden cylinder, and her ear caught the whisper of seawater that powered it.

"Let's go," he said, raising the light, its soft glow revealing only a few paces ahead. The passage forced him to turn sideways, his broad shoulders scraping stone with each step. Pale roots wove across the ceiling like a living tapestry. Their boots crunched on uneven ground, revealing new jags and dips in the natural path.

Her gaze fixed on the lantern's fading glow. "Is that thing going to last?"

"We're nearly there."

The roots thickened overhead, the pale tendrils weaving tighter and tighter.

"How did you find this passageway?" she managed, trying to ignore the sweat beading on her forehead. The humid air clung to her skin like a second cloak. "I didn't know Pālam had hidden corridors."

"It's a secret, but this is how I always managed to stay close to you," Tarrak said, glancing back at her. "You're the third person to know about this one, and you can't tell anyone about it."

"Does that mean there are more?" she gasped, eyes widening. "Wait, who's the other person?"

His eyes dropped to his feet, then he turned to the next dark corridor without answering. Her teeth found her tongue. Better to leave questions for when they weren't fleeing from the Priestess' claws.

The dim glow from the lantern cast dancing shadows over the gnarled roots lining their path. Tarrak's boots came to a halt, his tall silhouette framed by the soft glow. He turned to face her, handing her the light. "Wait here."

Her throat closed like a fist, choking the air from her lungs. "You're leaving me?"

"I need to make sure it's safe," he reassured, his hand settling on her shoulder with a squeeze. "I won't be long."

"Tarrak!"

"I'll be back, Rabbit. I promise."

She nodded reluctantly. Her brother's silhouette melted into the shadows, leaving her alone in the underground stillness, her fingers desperately clutching the lantern. As the echoes of his footsteps faded, the labyrinth of roots seemed to close in around her.

The last thing she wanted was to be trapped with thoughts of the recent massacre at the Great Hall. She had fought to keep them at bay while Tarrak was nearby. But now, in the suffocating silence surrounded by creeping shadows, they crashed in on her, relentless and unforgiving.

Their faces clawed to the surface first—her mother's, Nora's, and Lux's—pale countenances frozen in silent screams, the light draining from them. Her heart threatened to crumble beneath the crushing weight, an overwhelming burden she would never be ready to bear. Powerlessness wrapped around her like a vice, but it was the betrayal that tore through her, leaving her utterly broken.

She had known of the Priestess' ability to drain the essence of any living thing—like the darkness around her feeding on the thinning light. She had always found it unsettling, but to witness it... to have watched her own mother's life drain away. Her sweet mother, whose gentle hands had twisted the locs that now brushed her shoulders. The strongest woman she had ever known, so bright and gentle, a force and a stronghold, reduced to nothing—snuffed out like a candle by the Priestess and her Sages.

Her mind swirled, reaching for answers. Tales from the time of the Great War depicted the Priestess using the same ability against many powerful wyverns. Yet, Asante couldn't fathom why Samira had turned against her own people.

Everything traced back to the smoke slithering from Rengō, but even that wasn't enough to explain the massacre. Then came the revelation of the wyvern's egg and its mother searching for it. Her hand flew to her satchel, feeling the weight of the gem nestled inside. A shiver danced down her spine. Not only was she now fleeing from the High Priestess, but Zuwena's rage might find her too.

Her hand pressed the lantern against her chest, desperately trying to make sense of everything. "Why?" her voice echoed in the stillness, grief stabbing through her chest. The Priestess she had served all these years. The High Sage her own father revered. Daughter of wyverns. The irreverent sting in her eyes betrayed her, her breath coming in sharp, quick bursts. "Monster!"

With the fading echo of her outburst, the torch gave out, plunging her into complete darkness.

"No! No, no." She shook the lamp as if trying to breathe it back to life. The weight of everything she'd lost crashed over her. Each ragged breath felt like drowning. She squeezed her eyes shut, then opened them again. But it made no difference. The shadows were absolute, and as overbearing as the gaping rupture in her chest.

A sob caught in her throat, raw and broken. And for the first time, she let herself crumble. Yet even in the circling darkness hungry and patient, she refused to let the void consume her tears. Instead, she offered them—to her mother whose bright smile once lit up the darkest chambers, to her sister whose dreams would never bloom, and to her friend who would never get to soar the skies, and whose hand she'd never hold again. There would be no burial ceremony for any of them, so she gave her sorrow to the mountain and the tree that wove through it. Let the earth and roots drink deep of what she could not bear. Let them absorb the grief she could not speak, and cradle the fractured echoes of her loss.

Her heart stopped.

A piercing screech shattered the silence, like jagged claws scraping metal. A gust of wind slammed into her, sending her stumbling over a gnarled root. She hit the ground hard, her bag tumbling open. A soft radiance flickered from within. Crawling to it, her fingers dug into the satchel, pulling away the mantle made from the bark of the High Tree revealing the embryo. The shadows fled with the soft light spilling from the gem.

Her fingers gave in to the need to touch it. As they traced the surface, the screeching intensified in her mind. A distant image of mount Pālam filled her sight, soaring from the Tanama's dead woods. The bird's-eye view came with an insatiable thirst for vengeance, transforming her chest into a burning ember, fury incarnate. Her vision blurred red at its edges, each heartbeat pounding with a visceral, ancient desire to ravage the mountain city. The need to destroy clawed at her consciousness, raw and primal, the rage nestling into her heart like it had found its true home.

"The mother calls," Asante's voice quivered, recalling Samira's warning. The mother wyvern would try to connect. Her hand jerked back from the embryo severing the connection.

"Asante!" Tarrak's voice broke her trance. His eyes darted between her and the glowing gem. "We have to go. Now!"

His grip tightened around her arm, pulling her through a tangled maze of roots, rocks, and mud until sunlight flooded her vision, forcing her to squint while her arm shielded her eyes. Her locs whipped against her cheeks in the warm breeze. The Great Sea sparkled on the horizon beyond Mount Pālam, deceptively peaceful.

Another shriek tore through the air—a grating wail that made her bones ache, as if the very earth itself recoiled in fear.

Her head snapped to the skies. "What was that?" The words escaped her, but she feared the sound came from the same creature that had invaded her vision.

Tarrak's chest heaved, sweat gleaming on his dark, golden-hued skin. He snatched her bag and shoved it into the crevice they'd emerged from.

"What are you doing?" she protested, lunging for it.

"Leave that thing. We have to go."

She clutched the satchel, the embryo pressing against her chest, her eyes flickering back to the crevice, tempted to leave it behind. Samira wanted the gem out of Pālam, but obeying the Priestess' orders felt like a betrayal to her mother and sister. She owed nothing to the High Sage, not anymore. Her fingers tightened around the leather strap, thoughts racing while she considered the gem's power. If it ended up back in Samira's hands, it would only give her more strength to destroy.

But if the gem truly held power to be wielded... Her lips twitched at the thought. She could use it herself, bring the Priestess and her Sages down. Yet the feeling faded too quickly. Just hours ago, she had been nothing more than an attendant. Now, she stood on Pālam's mountainside as a fugitive—powerless, a nobody.

A more wicked thought crossed her mind. The Priestess could do to the gem what she had done to her mother. She could tap into it, drain its power until nothing remained.

Her gaze locked on Tarrak. "I'm not leaving it."

"Did you not hear that roaring? The outer city is in chaos. People are screaming about a wyvern in the sky," he snapped, jabbing a finger at her bag. "That thing was just glowing inside the passageway, and you want to keep it? We can't have anything that draws attention."

"It's Zuwena, the lighting wyvern. And this is her embryo," Asante confessed, hoisting the satchel over her shoulders while avoiding her brother's horrified look. "We have to hide it, from the wyvern and Samira."

Tarrak's feet closed the distance between them, his hands shaking while he pointed at her bag. "Are you telling me there's a bloody wyvern hunting for that thing, and you want to hide it from her?" his voice quivered. "My only concern is you, and getting somewhere safe. We can't outrun a damned wyvern."

Asante's arms folded tightly over her chest, pulse racing beneath her skin. "Samira asked me to take it to the abandoned city, and hide. I don't know what I'm going to do, but if we leave it behind, the Priestess will find a way to exploit it. That wretched woman doesn't deserve any more power," she hissed through gritted teeth.

Tarrak's muscles coiled beneath his shoulders. His eyes burned through her in disbelief, lips parting and pressing together, as if searching for the right words.

A much closer ear-piercing screech made them both jolt like startled prey.

"Fine!" he snapped, sweat tracing a path down his temple. His hand gripped her tightly. "But there's no way we're going to the abandoned city. That takes us too close to the dead forest and that damn smoke. We have minutes—maybe less—before the wyvern reaches Pālam."

His fingers dug into her arm, his eyes wide and unblinking. "If that thing sees us, we're dead." His voice dropped, strained with concern. "The moment we turn from the mountainside, you keep up. No matter what happens, you run. You hear me, Sante? No matter what, you run."

She met his gaze. With a shuddering breath, she managed a hesitant nod. Her brother raced toward Mount Pālam's edge, peering around. She huddled close, her heartbeat thundering in her ears.

From their vantage point, six Enchanters stood rooted at their posts in the lower tiers of Mount Pālam, bloodstone amulets pulsing with ruby light. Higher up, two pairs of Sages gathered within the sentinel's points, their markings shimmering on their faces. Crimson energy coiled around the arms of the four figures, twisting and writhing like living veins. The power flowed from their hands, arcing downward in ribbons of blood-red lightning until they connected with the waiting bloodstone amulets below.

"They're making a seal. Look." Asante's finger stretched toward the distance, where the Sages' ruby shroud stretched outward, their lights weaving together. From the High Tree, Samira's larger mantle unfurled like a sheet of oxblood silk, slowly encasing all of Pālam.

"We can't get locked in," he yelled, pulling her from the mount. Their feet pounded against packed earth, sprinting through rows of kapok trees at the city's edge. Around them, waves of people stumbled and pushed toward Pālam, their screams mixing with the wyvern's ear-splitting cries.

They wove between massive trunks until Tarrak suddenly lunged forward, slamming her against the towering root of one of the ancient trees. The roughened wood bit into her back as a blast of air erupted above them. The thunderous crack shuddered through her bones.

Leather wings stretched overhead, so close the displaced air whipped their locs, each massive beat vibrating through her chest. Through the leaf canopy gaps, the mother wyvern wheeled back toward Pālam, where the ruby shield pulsed silently, swallowing the city's chaos behind its translucent wall.

The massive creature circled the mountain. Fading blue and green scales rippled across Zuwena's body, pale-yellow horns framing a snout that curled back in blood-curdling snarls. Beyond the shield, several Ikarites still ran desperately toward the mountain city. One man sprinted to the barrier. The moment he made contact with it, his agonizing scream was cut short. Orange flames burst around him and his body quickly crumbled to ash, the wind carrying his remains away in pale wisps.

Zuwena's talons gouged into an outer post when she landed, wood splintering beneath her weight. Her nostrils flared, head tilting toward the shield as if listening to its energy. In one fluid motion, she snatched a fleeing man in her fangs. The wyvern's neck snapped sideways, hurling him against the energy field where he erupted into flames.

More screams pierced the air as the creature stalked the outer city, snatching runners and throwing them against the shield like kindling. Each victim ignited, consumed in a surge of blistering heat. The wyvern's agitation grew more frenzied, scales bristling with rage until she reared back and unleashed a roar that sent Asante's hands flying to her ears.

The cerulean glow in her chest intensified moments before white flames erupted from her maw. The blaze crashed against the ruby barrier in a mesmerizing dance of power. When the shield held, she turned her fury to the outer city. Entire buildings crumbled under the scorching fire that devoured everything in its path.

As the glow in her chest dimmed, Zuwena launched herself toward the mines, her massive body settling onto a rock mound. Her wings stretched wide before a deep, resonant call burst from her chest, a guttural sound that shook the very earth. In Asante's satchel, a faint light pulsed in response, its brilliance dulled by the fabric.

"The mother is calling for it," she whispered, fingers clutching the bag tighter.

"Keep it covered," Tarrak said through gritted teeth.

Zuwena dove into the farmlands. The sound of splintering fences and bleating livestock echoed behind them as they ran the opposite way, the seaside caves mere specks on the horizon in the distance.

With every screech from the wyvern, the intensity of the embryo's glow amplified. Asante's hand yanked her cowl, desperate to smother the growing light. When her fingers brushed against the gem, white-hot needles pierced through her bones. A gasp tore from her throat. Her knees gave way, driving her hard against the ground. Scalding heat like molten metal raced through her veins, locking her muscles tight, forcing her to clutch her arm. Behind the searing agony, a familiar voice whispered—warned, *Don't let her in.*

Her brother's worried shouts became distant echoes. She fought to stifle her screams, teeth clamping down on her tongue until copper filled her mouth. "It burns," she forced out between ragged breaths.

Tarrak scooped her up, slinging her over his shoulder. Each stride sent fresh waves of fire through her flesh, as if her skin was being flayed from her bones.

Time blurred until suddenly freezing water engulfed her. The polar shock struck like searing metal thrust into ice, hissing against her burning skin. Her groans echoed off cave walls, the pain slowly subsiding though the burning lingered. Her brother splashed more water over her face.

"Look at me," he said, his gentle voice rippling through her haze. His calloused hands cupped her face, eyes wide with worry. "Look at me. You're okay. You're okay."

Asante's gaze darted around, taking in the deep cave they had reached. Tarrak had led them through the sea caverns and into the hidden pools, far from both Pālam and the raging wyvern. She gave a weak nod, then pushed away to sink into deeper water. She submerged and the cold embraced her fully. Silence wrapped around her while she lingered, letting the cool water ease the flames under her skin until she could no longer hold her breath.

"I was moments away from diving in after you." Relief softened Tarrak's voice when she surfaced. He stood outside the pool, his wet locs dripping onto the ground. "What happened? The way you screamed..."

"I—I'm not sure." The words scraped against her throat.

As his gaze studied her, the muscles in his hand clenched, then eased. "The wyvern didn't follow us. We should be okay for now, but we cannot stay here long. If you need a healer," he said, swallowing hard, "we'll have to find a way back into Pālam."

"No! I'm fine. I promise," she said quickly, though embers still burned beneath her skin. Her stomach churned at the thought of facing Zuwena or Samira again.

Her heart tightened with the realization that she had never ventured so far from Pālam. Yet Samira had ordered her far beyond its borders. The thought of seeking refuge in the abandoned city, so close to the Tanama and its dead woods, sent her spiraling.

A small snarl curled on her lips. The High Sage demanded loyalty and obedience, no matter the cost. Her own father hadn't survived the dead woods. The Priestess didn't care who she put at risk, as long as her will was done.

Heat flushed through her skin. She was nobody compared to Samira. It was only a matter of time before the Priestess' mind-weaving found her, and she'd be powerless against it. Her stomach turned at the thought of the High Sage slithering into her mind. Even this far from Pālam, the Priestess' hold was stronger than she'd ever be. Though her arm still burned and her head spun, she had to endure. For her brother's sake and her own. The sea caves remained their only sanctuary.

"What's that in your hand?" Tarrak's gasp drew her attention. Before she could react, he plunged into the pool and yanked her right arm from the water.

Asante's eyes widened. Where her skin had touched the embryo, silver patterns now wound around her fingers like molten metal. Tarrak ripped her sleeve, revealing more gleaming trails that continued their serpentine path up her arm. His fingers tilted her chin, following the argent veins as they crept up her neck

They stared at the glowing marks in awe until his whisper broke the spell.

"Sage markings."

CHAPTER 13

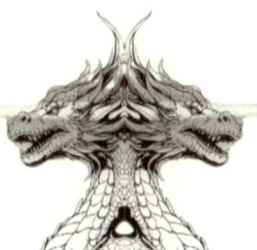

KA'ZAN

YOEN

A WAVE OF UNEASE surged through Yoen as he reached to examine his nephew's wound. Slumped on Inara in front of his sister, Arben's eyes blinked in a haze. The gash on his forehead appeared hastily cleaned, but he couldn't gauge its severity. He turned to Luan, clasping her hands and securing them on Inara's reins. "I won't be long, I promise. These two guards will accompany you. Seek a healer as soon as you reach the fortress." He patted Inara reassuringly, pausing a moment to watch her bear away his world's most treasured souls.

His attention snapped back to the scene behind him. Ka'zan's archers moved down the line of nineteen gray-coated prisoners, tightening bonds until rope sliced into flesh. One by one, they stumbled forward, yanked into place behind the waiting horses. Beneath the exhausted slump of shoulders and ragged breathing, defiant glances passed between them. The lifeless body of the young woman who had nearly finished him hung across one of the mounts.

He limped across the sand, his leg throbbing where the copper rod had struck. "Gerel, I can't thank you enough for helping me get the twins back."

The Chief Guard's hand clasped his shoulder. A wince flickered across Yoen's face, his bruised muscles protested the touch.

"Old Inara wouldn't take no for an answer. But save your thanks. We still have to reach the fortress. The ground shakes the strongest near the city center, and that's the safest way back. Garam's volcanic roots could swallow Ka'zan whole at any moment."

They raised their eyes to the sky, where dark clouds threatened the last copper rays of sunlight. A fierce wind howled, and waves clashed violently against the black sandy shore.

"My eyes can't believe it. Äktastary in our black beach!" Gerel said, rubbing his temples. "You are certain? They're from the White Stone City?"

Yoen nodded. "According to Luan, they came through the underwater caves. The red-armbands are leading some kind of mission."

"No one survives those waters. Let alone what lurks beneath them." Gerel shifted his scale helmet, eyes fixed on the prisoners. "The council will want answers. Which one is the leader?"

"That one," Yoen replied. His chin jerked toward a prisoner bound behind one of the horses. "The one in the middle, with the raging feline eyes and a cluster of freckles." His gaze locked with the young woman's defiant stare, noting her red-armband and black leather marks around her shoulders. "Found more blades on her than the rest combined, plus some leather pouches filled with a strange black dust. The others call her Sergeant Lyla."

Chief Gerel gestured to the Äktastary's armbands. "The colors must identify their guilds."

"The maroon ones seem military. I'm not sure about the blue ones. But I believe they steered the beached vessels," Yoen explained, pulling his cowl tighter against the wind.

"I've dispatched two guards to sweep the metal whales. We move now," Gerel urged, swinging onto his horse. He nodded toward an archer with soft brown skin and a long dark braid. "Ride with Sumani. She's swift and her arrows fly true."

Yoen studied the three prisoners tethered behind Sumani's horse. Two young men with red-armbands whispered to each other. One wore a topknot, the other had eyes like amber in sunlight. At the tail end with a blue-armband, the young woman who had been unconscious inside the cave caught his eye. Her skin revealed a soft blend of white and bronze patches. A snowy mark stretched across her forehead, merging into a frosted strand of hair. She stared at the ground, seemingly lost in a trance.

"Elva. El." The whisper came from a prisoner bound behind Gerel's horse. The one who'd tended to her in the caves. Elva raised her head, lips trembling.

"It's going to be okay," the onyx-haired Äktastary called to her.

"Oran, I'm sorry," she mumbled, tears welling in her eyes.

"Forward!" Gerel spurred his horse, yanking Oran's tether. The other guards followed, their lines of prisoners staggering into running rhythm behind them.

"We ought to move, Chief," Sumani urged.

Yoen mounted behind the archer. As they galloped, the trailing Äktastary prisoners struggled to keep up.

The farmland surroundings became a blur of motion and bare grounds. The once pristine white round-houses now stood smudged with the gray of dust and ash. Canvas walls flapped like tattered wings, others torn away to expose naked wooden frames. Through gaping doorways, dying embers flickered in cold hearths. A child's doll lay face-down in the dirt, parchments lay scattered, wool blankets and herding staffs were abandoned in frantic escape.

His own round-house emerged through the haze. Memories assaulted him. On any other evening, he'd be preparing dinner, surrounded by the twins' laughter. A curse slipped through his clenched teeth. He'd led his children to that cave. It had been his wife's favorite spot in the city.

A startled neigh cut through his thoughts. Ahead, a horse reared against its post while its rider lay motionless in the dirt.

"Sumani, halt!"

"Chief Gerel and the other archers already reached the square." Her hand gestured toward the distance where the line of horses and prisoners had vanished. "Orders are to ride straight to the fortress."

"Look!" Yoen forced his voice through the wind, pointing. "The rider, he might be alive. Please!"

Reluctantly, Sumani hauled back on the reins, and the horse's gait faltered beneath him. He rushed to the fallen rider. The body lay twisted on the ground, flesh bubbling and peeling away like wax from a candle. The acrid scent made his stomach heave. He stumbled backward, his hand flying to cover his mouth. Yoen's trembling fingers lifted the rider's cowl, drawing it with care over his face. "Rest easy, Ka'zanty. In the world beyond, may you soar on the wings of mighty wyverns."

He turned to the distraught mount, hooves drumming against the packed earth. As Yoen pressed his brow to its neck, his palm traced slow circles along its heaving flank. "Easy there, easy," he whispered. "I'm so sorry, dear friend." He pulled on the reins, but the steed held firm, head pulling toward its fallen rider, refusing to move.

"Leave him!" Sumani yelled.

Yoen untied the leather straps from the steed and bowed. "May Ragas grant you strength and illuminate your path." As he rose, his eyes found the Äktastary prisoners tethered behind Sumani's horse, catching their breath. At the rear, Elva gazed at him with tearful eyes. He sprinted back but the earth lurched beneath him. A crack split the ground with a sound like thunderclap, and a column of white vapor burst upward, scalding the air.

"Chief, move!" the archer bellowed.

He swung himself up behind Sumani, who spurred her steed into a gallop. Behind them, the captives' ragged breaths broke the rhythm of their stumbling steps. Their feet dragged through the dust in a desperate effort to keep up with the horse's pace.

The main square vanished in a blanket of vapor, making breathing a labored effort. The ground shuddered in violent waves, sending chunks of carved stone raining down from the surrounding structures. Above, darkness swallowed the sky, while below, the fractured earth bled ribbons of orange light from its molten core.

With another violent quake, the prisoners lost their footing, collapsing onto the cobblestones. The horse hauled them mercilessly. Their screams and agonized groans grew louder with every bump against the rough path.

"We must stop," Yoen shouted.

"The ground's falling apart beneath us," Sumani shot back. "If we stop, we die."

"If they die, we won't get any answers. Halt!"

The archer's fist clenched around the horse's reins, bringing him to a stop. Yoen slipped down from behind her and turned toward the prisoners. Their gray coats hung in tatters, stained with blood. He approached the young woman with the white strip of hair when something shifted in his peripheral vision.

"No!" Elva's cry pierced the air.

The amber-eyed prisoner bolted forward in a violent rush. In an instant, Yoen found himself overpowered, his knife torn from his grasp. The blade glinted, tearing the prisoners' bonds. Sumani hurled herself at the amber-eyed man, fighting for control of the weapon. As it sliced toward her, her horse reared with a shriek. Its hooves crashed down against his skull with a sickening crunch, sending him crumpling to the ground in a lifeless heap. The other red-armband grabbed Elva, yanking her away in a desperate attempt to escape.

"Wait!" the young woman pleaded.

Sumani's bow sang, and the arrow struck true, burying itself in the man's skull. He fell, dragging the blue-armband down with him. Another was already nocked, poised for the next target.

"Don't shoot!" Elva's voice quivered. "I yield. I yield." Her arms pushed the young man's body to the side and stood with trembling hands, her face smeared with his blood.

"Any false move, and you're done," Sumani warned, her intense brown eyes locking onto Elva. The Äktastary nodded, moving slowly back to Yoen.

The archer seized the ropes binding Elva's hands just before the ground unleashed another threatening rumble, a deep sound of stone splitting and earth tearing apart. Behind them, the red-armband's body had been consumed by a growing chasm, its jagged mouth creeping closer.

"Move, quick!" Yoen signaled forward.

Sumani swung onto her horse. Yoen lifted Elva to sit between them before awkwardly climbing up behind the saddle.

"Faster!" he shouted.

The rift behind them grew insatiable, swallowing statues of High Regent Magnar and his ancestors, along with the old structures with carvings of wyverns. Merchant cabins vanished in an instant. The earth gave one final, thunderous groan before collapsing in front of them, leaving them stranded on a dwindling island of stone.

A blistering cloud of steam erupted behind them. Yoen's cry cut short as the mist seared his back, throwing him from the horse. The destabilized path caused the mount to rear, sending the archer and Elva tumbling.

"Whoa!" Sumani seized the reins, steadying her horse. "We're trapped."

"There!" Through the haze, Elva pointed to a gap in the destruction.

"Can he jump it?" Yoen pressed a hand against the mount's heaving flank.

"Not with all three of us."

His heart raced, the promise to return to his niece and nephew now fleeting. "Then you go, take the girl with you. I'll find another way."

"Chief," Sumani protested.

"No time to waste. Go now!" Yoen tore off Elva's bindings. Her eyes, dark and wide with fear, reminded him of his niece's. "Don't let my sacrifice be in vain."

Before Sumani could spur her horse forward, the Äktastary jabbed a finger toward the distance. "There! Near the statue!" She gestured to a narrower crack. "There's a smaller opening. Small enough to jump."

Yoen squinted through the vapor. Ragas' fallen wing stretched across the crevice like a bridge of white stone. "We'll have to go on foot. The path around the statue is too narrow."

He turned to Sumani. "Go. Take your steed and meet us on the other side." Without waiting for her response, he sprinted toward the statue, Elva's footsteps close behind.

He tracked Sumani wheeling her horse around, backing up to gain momentum before charging forward. Horse and rider soared across the wider gap, circling the square until they reached the other side of Raga's remnants.

His feet stumbled over the debris-strewn ground, climbing across the statue's remains. Ahead, Elva darted with grace over the rubble. When she rounded the statue's edge toward the out-stretched wing, she paused instead of leaping toward Sumani. Her eyes locked with Yoen's. With his next step, the ground betrayed him, collapsing beneath his weight and threatening to send him into the fiery pit below.

Terror seized his chest as he plummeted. His arms flailed until his fingers found purchase on a small ledge. One hand gripped the white stone while his body dangled over the abyss. A strong tug at his tunic pulled his gaze upward, where Elva's panic-stricken face hovered above him, straining to hold him.

"Hang on!" she shouted through gritted teeth.

Below, a river of magma flowed like the molten heart of a vengeful star. Sweat dripped into his eyes and the rough stone bit into his fingers. He tugged with all his strength, his elbows finally bending, granting him a firmer hold. Elva's other hand seized his tunic with a grunt, and together they hauled his body onto the sculpture's remains.

He collapsed onto his back, fingers curled against his stomach, chest heaving with ragged breaths. Pushing up onto his elbows, he turned to find Elva slumped against the statue's base, gasping for air. In the distance, Sumani sat atop her nervous horse, the animal shifting beneath her. Ragas' wings had crumbled away, leaving nothing behind but the hiss and crackle of the magma rivers encircling their white stone island. The scorching heat bore down relentlessly, making them sweat profusely.

His eyes darted to Elva's shaking hands, where fresh burns peeked beneath the unraveled bandages. Her breath came in shallow gasps. Yoen's fists clenched at his side, guilt stabbing through his chest. "I should've sent you with Sumani. I'm sorry," he stammered. Dread coiled tightly in his stomach, and his own breath quickened.

Tears carved a small path through the grime and blood on Elva's face. "It's not your fault," she whispered, her voice breaking with a cough.

He tried to scan the surroundings for an escape, but it was futile. This was his end. Thoughts of his niece and nephew flashed through his mind, and a voracious tightness gripped him. His palm found the pit of his stomach once again, fingers curling slightly in an effort to suppress the beast threatening to break free. He forced a slow breath, blinking away the sweat blurring his vision.

"I'm Elva," she said, her voice barely audible above the roar of the magma below.

He let out a trembling sigh and shook off the haze clouding his mind. "Yes, I know. I heard your friend call you. The one with the dark hair. I'm Yoen."

Tears welled in her eyes at the mention of her friend. She looked away, wiping her cheek with her sleeve. "I'm sorry about Luan and Arben in the cave. I—I didn't know what was happening at first."

"You were unconscious for most of it. I saw. I was up on the ledge."

She scoffed, a faint smirk crossing her lips even though her fingers twisted anxiously in her lap. "Who are they?"

He leaned closer. "My niece and nephew." The words cut like blades in his chest, his promise to his sister shattered. "I was supposed to protect them, but I'm not sure I've done the job," he confessed, a heavy sigh escaping. "Are you truly from Äktas?"

She gave a slight nod, pressing her lips together. Her thumbnail dug deeper into her index finger, threatening to break skin.

Questions surged in his mind, each one crashing against the next like waves. He had never met anyone from across the Tanama. For a century, the curse of the dead woods had kept all three cities secluded from one another. His knee bounced, tapping a nervous rhythm under his clenched fist. He considered a more pressing question. "Did the east cause the smoke around the dead forests?"

Her head shook slightly, managing a hoarse reply amid bouts of coughing. "We were sent here because we believed you were responsible."

Yoen sighed, then managed a wry smile. "Well then, welcome to Ka'zan, Elva of Äktas! Apologies for the chaos. I don't know about you, but I'm having the worst day."

A sound escaped Elva that might have been a laugh before dissolving into another coughing fit. His hand instinctively reached to pat her back, but she flinched, her eyes widening with a guarded look. He offered an apologetic glance and withdrew slowly.

The roaring of the magma river echoed through the stone debris, its molten waves sizzling like a searing blade plunged into water.

Beside him, Elva finally managed to gasp for a clear breath, but her gaze dropped to her boots.

A pang of guilt and fear gnawed at Yoen, his mind shifting to the twins with suffocating dread. The mere thought of them in the midst of imminent danger and destruction sent shivers down his spine.

They deserved a full life, a better life. His fingers curled into the familiar knot at the pit of his stomach, hoping they'd found their way into the fortress. But even if Drekavog's walls withstood the volcano's wrath—death, sorrow, and misery would always loom over Ka'zan. There would be no escape. With a lightning wyvern looming in the skies, mysterious smoke blanketing the dead forests, and the Uláak on the verge of escaping, Arben and Luan would be left with no one to protect them. He had failed as a husband, a brother, and an uncle.

The ground shook violently, pulling him out of his swirling thoughts, threatening to topple them into the fiery abyss. Elva's breath caught in her throat again, teetering on the precipice. His grip quickly found her arm, steadying her just in time. Instead of settling down, she reached down in a swift motion.

"What are you doing?"

She retrieved a small ruby casing from inside her boot. When she opened it, an intense white glow erupted from within. One hand delved inside, wrapping around the blazing light, while the other tightened around the crimson box.

Threads of energy spiraled from the glow in her hands, winding up her arms in slow, deliberate spirals of white and ruby, merging with her skin. The radiance seeped into her, and both hands thrust toward the river of magma beneath them. With eyes squeezed shut, a soul-piercing scream escaped her—a raw, visceral sound of power mixed with agony.

When her eyes flew open, twin suns of fierce brilliance burst forth. The earth shuddered in response, deep groans and splintering cracks reverberating for miles. Black rock erupted from the depths, thrusting upward to repel the encroaching magma.

Then, right before Yoen's eyes, a stable stone pathway formed across the molten expanse. With one last scream, she returned the white radiance to its ruby case, its glow dimming just before her knees gave way beneath her.

"Wyvern's skies," Yoen gasped in awe, fighting back tears. His hands shot toward her just in time to prevent her from collapsing. "Elva of Äktas. An Enchanter."

CHAPTER 14

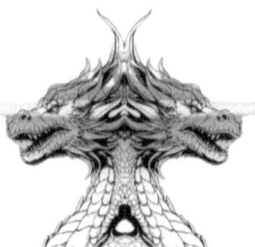

IKARI

ASANTE

V EILED IN A SUFFOCATING white haze, the dead forest lay in an unsettling silence. Contorted trees thrust their bare limbs toward the obscured sky, skeletal branches clawing at the mist like restless spirits. A mantle of gnarled roots covered the sullied grounds, baring scars from an ancient scorching war.

Like a tide pulling at the shore, a wyvern's skeleton pulsed with life, calling to Asante's blood. Adorned with gleaming fangs, the massive skull radiated a light of its own.

It beckoned.

Its song wove through her, threading into the very marrow of her bones, calling her closer with each heartbeat. The pull intensified, transforming into a desperate need—maddening, inescapable. It was like an itch blooming beneath her skin, seeping deeper until it nested in her core, begging to be scratched.

Her body finally gave in, hand stretching toward the skull. But the ground betrayed her. It liquefied beneath her feet, swallowing her ankles in an instant, yanking her from the trance. Her muscles strained against the mud's greedy pull. The moment she wrenched free, the fine hairs on the nape of her neck prickled. Ice crawled down her spine. The air thickened, heavy with an unseen presence. She forced her gaze to where her eyes didn't want to go.

An Uláak loomed before her, its mask bearing forward-pointing horns and a gaping snout full of razor-sharp fangs. A midnight cloak wrapped around its body, shifting like silken smoke. Its haunting frame reached skyward with an imposing stature. The towering figure swayed side to side in an unnatural rhythm. Another terrifying creature emerged from behind it, a hybrid of human and beast. Its corroded metal skin exuded a sickly crimson hue, and its hunched posture forced it to rely on clawed hands for support. An elongated maw bristled with ferocious fangs as it released a bone-chilling growl.

Asante's chest heaved, noticing the rows of needle-sharp spines on its narrow back. The eyes of the mixed-breed creature smoldered like burning coals within deep-set sockets. It slithered forward with a predatory grace, its claws anxiously clicking against the stones.

Run, she thought. *Run*. Yet her feet froze in place.

With a crooked twist, the Uláak extended its reptilian hand, clutching a chain whip with a handle forged from white stone. The weapon's hilt appeared tattered and scarred. Along the lash, faded spikes and links of agni stones and bloodstones bore the scars of countless victims. With a sharp flick, the Uláak whipped the hybrid creature, setting it on a relentless hunt.

A ragged scream tore from her throat. She stumbled backward, her body slamming into the mud. Raw instinct took over—crawling, scrambling, finally finding her feet to sprint. But each thundering heartbeat competed with the hybrid creature's growls, growing louder, closer, hungrier.

Faster.

Out of the corner of her eye, more Uláak materialized around the dead woods, each with twisting spectral bodies and horned masks. A backward glance revealed the crossbreed fiend closing in. When her head jerked forward, the Uláak with the tristone chain whip materialized a few feet away. Her legs buckled, sending her crashing into the decayed roots.

More Uláak surrounded her in a tightening circle. The coal-eyed creature prowled the ground, tethered to its handler. Its back quills rose like daggers, muscles contracting beneath its metallic skin. Chains clattered through the forest, and in a flash, the tristone whip coiled around her throat, constricting like a vengeful serpent.

Asante bolted upright, drenched in sweat and struggling for breath. Her fingers grasped her throat, as if battling an invisible chokehold. It took a long, disorienting moment before she realized her neck was free. She collapsed back onto the ground, pressing trembling circles into her temples, trying to erase the images of the nightmare. The warmth of her new markings pulsed, an eerie radiance against her deep-brown skin. She looked down, tracing the argent twisting veins with her eyes. It was as if a silver hand had intertwined its fingers with hers, leaving a permanent imprint.

The images from her dream surged back, jagged but vivid. She had relived them countless times before, but this was different. Something had shifted. The wyvern's remains had never beckoned her before. And she had faced the Uláak leader many times, but it had never captured her. She shook her head, trying to clear the remnants of the dream, and pushed herself to her feet. Though the gnawing feeling didn't leave her.

Before falling asleep, Tarrak had led her on a hike until they found the caves furthest from the central opening. They found refuge in a chamber perched on a cliff's edge, overlooking the Great Sea. Her eyes took in the amber sky, while her fingers worked through her locs, adjusting the golden beads that had shifted during sleep. The sunlight unraveled, seeping inside the cave like thinning honeyed threads, weaving around the white stone pillars inside.

Her heart sank when she didn't spot her brother. "Tarrak?" Her voice bounced off the stone walls. She wove between rocky formations jutting upward like petrified fangs. "Tarrak!" Her fingers twisted into the hem of her shirt, pulling it taut. She had already lost her mother, sister, and friend, and now her brother. Her chest tightened. "Tarrak!"

"Rabbit?" her brother's voice carried from a skylight.

Her head snapped up when a shadow crossed the opening above, followed by the thud of Tarrak landing and the soft thump of bags hitting the ground. Relief flooded through her, quickly followed by anger. She glared at him before yanking at his locs.

"Agh! What was that for?"

"I was looking for you. Where were you? Why did you leave me?" she snapped, fighting the sudden sting in her eyes.

"You were exhausted after the markings. Figured I'd let you rest. I wasn't gone for long, just snuck out to get supplies."

She snatched one of the bags and spun away. "Just don't do it again." Footsteps echoed behind her. Tarrak collected the remaining supplies and followed in silence.

Perched on a rock near the opening, her gaze followed the rhythmic pulse of the sea. The serene beauty of the scene mocked her, clashing with the endless void growing inside her.

Her brother's hands worked with intense focus, arranging and rearranging the supplies he had gathered. For the fifth time, he methodically organized the bow and arrows before moving on to the neatly stacked knives, bread, nuts, berries, and blankets.

She exhaled slowly, the sound heavy in the silence between them. Her brother had witnessed the same horrors she had. The memories hung there, sharp and fractured like splintered wood, and neither dared to touch them.

After her silver markings appeared, Tarrak made her recount everything that had taken place before the massacre inside the

Great Hall. She explained how the Priestess summoned the Enchanters and Sages after witnessing the smoke above Rengō. Tarrak's fists had clenched by his side when she mentioned Samira's request to safeguard the wyvern's egg.

But she didn't confess everything. She hadn't revealed how Samira could mind-weave into her thoughts and expected updates about the gem. She also withheld the fact that she had seen through Zuwena's eyes when she touched the embryo inside Pālam's tunnels. And she wasn't sure she'd ever tell him about the recurring nightmares with the creatures that killed their father.

Her mind spiraled. Since her first marking ritual, she'd ached for even a whisper of magic. But now that it thrummed beneath her skin, dread seized her chest. Eight summers of prayers and wishes, and now all she could think of were Samira's golden markings. The woman with the gilded veins had ripped her from her home after her father's death, forcing her to work as an attendant far from her family. Those same veins had pulsed with life as they drained her mother and sister's last breaths. The Priestess had stolen everything—her home, her friend, her family, even her brother's bright smile.

The same rage she had sensed through Zuwena slithered into her mind, mixing with her blood like venom. Heat flooded her skin, bubbling up through her chest. Through tight breaths, she forced the rising rage down.

Tarrak's footsteps jolted her out of her spiral. His knees sank in front of her. "I'm sorry for leaving without a word," he said gently, placing a wrapped tool in her hands.

The fabric fell away, revealing a dagger with a volcanic obsidian blade and an amber handle etched with wyvern flames. "Dad's knife! I thought I lost it," she gasped.

"It was by the kapok tree."

Her heart fluttered at the sight of the family heirloom. Her father often recalled how the blade dated back to a time before the Great War, when the Tanama's forest flourished with life, and wyverns roamed the skies. The weapon had been a wedding gift from their mother to their father.

Memories of her parents cut deep. A quiet ache spread through her skin like a searing burn that flared with every breath, never fading, always raw. Losing the blade had bothered her, but the thought of her brother venturing alone with Zuwena in the skies terrified her even more. "I can't believe you went back there."

Tarrak scratched his ear nervously. "I had to check if it was safe. Besides, I couldn't sleep and we needed supplies." He paced across the cave back to his pile of arrows and started counting them for the eighth time.

"How long are we staying here?" she asked.

"At least for the night. Something's stirring in the dead forests," he said, grabbing a wool blanket from his gathered provisions and handing it to her.

"Wh... what do you mean?" Her voice quivered, the nightmare with Uláak flashing behind her eyes.

"The smoke stopped right at the edge of the Tanama. It's like something invisible is holding it back. But I fear it won't be for long. The wyvern has gone into those woods."

With the fading sunlight, Tarrak's silhouette stretched between the petrified formations. Tension pulled at his shoulders while he retrieved the miners' lantern from a satchel hanging on a rock. His hands shook, fumbling with the bottom casing, failing to pour ocean water from a flask into the lantern.

"Here, let me." She reached for both containers, pouring with a steady hand. "What else did you see?"

"Those who didn't run into the ruby shield, ran to the Tanama's forests or the abandoned city. I gathered what I could," he sighed heavily. "The out houses are all ash, as well as the crops. You can still smell the burned flesh."

Her mouth went dry. Zuwena had ravaged the entire outer city. "Did anyone else run here, into the caves?"

"I don't know. There are over sixty sea caves," he said, his fingers twisting the wooden base of the lantern, igniting its amber glow. The light caught the sweat beading on his brow. Then he crouched beside the stack of supplies.

"Is that's safe?" she asked, her finger pointing at the glowing lantern. "What if Zuwena sees where we are? We're too exposed on this cliff." She inched closer, watching him wedge the lantern into a narrow crack in the stone.

"We can risk some light. Just enough for us," he reassured her.

Her fingers tapped nervously on a rock. With the shield enveloping Pālam and Zuwena possibly hunting them, returning to the mountain city would be impossible. The sea posed the same lethal challenge as entering the Tanama forests. Her eyes lingered on her satchel. Samira and the wyvern would also call for the gem. It wouldn't be long before they would have to face them. The thought terrified her, but she still asked. "What if we go to the abandoned city?"

"Absolutely not! We're not going there," Tarrak said firmly, thrusting a cloth-wrapped flatbread at her. "Eat, you need your strength."

The wrapping crinkled in her grip. Her gaze darted outside where a few stars dotted the sky. "What are we going to do? We can't stay here forever."

Tarrak snatched a slender piece of wood from his supplies, and perched himself on a large rock. He dragged his knife across it, metal rasping against wood.

"What if I go alone?" she countered. "Samira and Zuwena will be looking for the gem, we have to do something."

"No!" he spat, his amber eyes darkening beneath furrowed brows.

"I don't know what my markings do. We need answers, we need help!"

Wood shavings scattered at his feet. He leaned forward, elbows pressed to his knees. His golden-brown locs had come undone, half-covering his face. "We abandoned that city for a reason. It's too close to the Tanama. Those bloody woods have claws of their own. They'll drag us in like stoneflies to a spider's web—so the Uláak can have us. There's no discussion. We're not going."

"It's not like I'm eager to go there, but we need a plan. Dad used to talk about the sunken temple. The one with all the scrolls. Maybe we could find a way to..."

"A way to what, Sante?" he snapped. "You want to learn how to kill a bloody wyvern? A rotten Priestess?" His grip tightened around his knife.

Heat crept up her neck, and her arms formed a barrier across her chest. "I don't know, but we can't stay in the caves. If the embryo starts shining again, Zuwena will surely find us."

"We're getting rid of that thing," he said, jabbing the knife toward her satchel.

"We can't do that!"

"You just said it. They'll come looking for it."

Asante closed the distance between them. "Getting rid of it won't stop Zuwena or the Priestess. If it falls into their grip, we're all doomed. Besides, the Priestess said it's a powerful gem. We could find a way to harness its energy to help us, to protect ourselves."

With that last word, her teeth caught her bottom lip, and her fingers tucked one of her locs behind her ear. "Or we could try to lift the curse of the Tanama, free the city from the Uláak," she whispered, her breath barely disturbing the stale air between them.

Tarrak scoffed, settling the spear he had been carving on the ground. "You're forgetting one important fact. The embryo's mother terrorized and killed hundreds of people in a matter of minutes. Samira did the same. That egg is nothing but trouble. We'll toss it into the Great Sea. It can join the creatures that guard the waters."

"I won't let you," she snapped, clutching the satchel with the embryo around her chest.

"I never thought working for that monster would make you lose all sense of logic. We barely made it out of Pālam alive." Tarrak's hands slashed through the air, desperate. His feet inched closer, his body tense, chest heaving with each breath. "Did you not see with your own eyes what that High Sage did to our mother, to our sister? How could you be so oblivious?"

"Of course I saw! How could you say that?" Her voice echoed inside the dimly lit cave.

"What is it then? You finally got your markings, now you want to be like her? Is that it? Asante, the Sixth Sage. A blood thirsty monster."

Her fingers let the bag slip from her grasp. Her brother's sharp words sliced into her gut. Part of her believed them to be true. She blinked back the tears, swallowing hard before forcing herself to speak. "Is that—what you think of me?"

His gaze dropped as the toe of his boot dug into the dirt.

"Because I do. I fear it," she confessed, her shoulders slumping. "I fear I might become like the Sages who murdered our family. I prayed for these markings, long into the night. Foolishly hoping they'd help change our ways. Little me, with markings, could definitely persuade the High Priestess," she scoffed, her eyes welling with tears.

"I'm just a dimwit. I thought I could convince the crude Priestess to stop sending people to the mines. Or find a way to shield the miners from the clutches of the dead forest. So that no more children had to endure the agony of losing a parent to the Uláak. And now that I have them..." She stared at her markings, her hands trembling. "What if I become like them? What if whatever this power is consumes me, and I lose all sense of myself?"

Her palms rubbed nervously on her side. "I should've been inside that nest of roots with Mom and Nora. I shouldn't have listened to that monster. I should have just gone and hugged Amá one last time, let them drain every last bit of me."

"Don't say that," Tarrak cried out, extending his arms to her, but she brushed him off.

Feeling the warmth of her markings, she recoiled taking a few steps back. "I should have forced my way into that cage. Hold mom's sweet and soft hands. Hold Nora until my very last breath. At least that way, I would've felt them one last time, and you wouldn't be trapped here with me. You would've been safe inside that shield."

"Asante, stop." Tarrak rushed to her, tearing off his vest. "Your arm."

Her gaze snapped to her right arm. The markings on her skin glowed silver, bright enough to push back the shadows in the cave. Tarrak's hands quickly pulled down her torn sleeve, then hastily covered the glowing markings with his vest.

"I'm sorry, I'm sorry!" she gasped, knowing the flashing light could give away their location.

He pulled her into his chest, her marked arm between them. The glow flickered, but he pressed her closer, trying to hide it with his own body. One hand rested protectively on her back, while the other gently patted her head.

"I'm sorry!" she whispered, letting tears fall.

He tightened the embrace. "If you had been inside that circle in the Great Hall, little Rabbit, my entire world would've ended. I... I could never survive that." His chest rose and fell with a deep breath. "I'm the one who should be sorry. I don't think you're a monster, Sante. I'm sorry. I'm just..." His voice trembled, taking another deep breath. "I'm terrified. Not of your markings, but of losing you. I'm scared you'll run so fast and far that I won't be able to catch up." Tarrak pressed a gentle kiss on her forehead. She turned to face him, finding his amber eyes filled with tears.

"Fine, we'll stay the night and leave at first light." His voice softened, and he led her toward the rock where the miner's lantern flickered, casting shadows against the walls. Then he dug through their supplies. "You're right. We do need options. We can try to find the sunken temple you mentioned. But we need to be discrete. Here, put these on." He handed her a pair of long forest green leather gloves. "You have to hide your arm and neck. And if we're keeping that bloody gem, it needs to be well hidden. No one can know what's in your bag or that you have markings. At least not until we figure out how they both work."

A flutter echoed off the cave walls, pulling their eyes to the skylight. Through the jagged opening, a horned golden owl swayed in the night air, its wings beating unsteadily. Golden feathers—just like those scattered across Lux's desk.

The bowstring creaked under her brother's fingers, his arrow singing through the darkness.

"Tarrak, No!"

CHAPTER 15

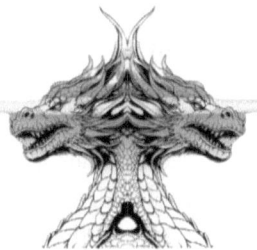

KA'ZAN

ELVA

E LVA'S EYES SNAPPED OPEN, and the world spun, fragments of unfamiliar shapes swimming through her vision. Her hands throbbed beneath the bandages. A sharp pressure stabbed at her temples, sinking deep behind her eyes. Everything felt disconnected and memories scattered like sparks flying from the forge.

Her muscles trembled under the strain of pushing herself upright, and cold stone bit into her bare feet. She narrowed her eyes, willing the blurry shapes around her to sharpen. Gradually, the room took form. A lone cot hugged one side, beside a wooden nightstand. Next to the only exit blocked by a heavy wooden door, a large carving of wyvern wings sprawled across a stone wall. A honeyed glow spilled from the edges of the engraved wings, flooding the room and bouncing off the alabaster walls.

She pressed an ear against the door's rough grain. Silence stretched beyond. The handle rattled but refused to yield. Instead, what caught her attention was the pulse emanating from the radiating wyvern wing carvings, echoing in her mind like a living heartbeat.

Her fingers drifted toward the light. At her touch, a warmth bloomed inside her and her palms tingled beneath the bandages. She tore at the wrappings, strips falling away to reveal burns vanishing in an instant, leaving behind unblemished flesh.

She staggered backward, heart thundering in her chest. The enchanted stone's hum vibrated through her veins, stirring a familiar pull resonating deep in her bones. She had fought against it during the Enchanter Trades' trials in Äktas. She despised it, the summoning, the unbearable call of the white stones that spellbound her. She recalled the tests vividly. That year, only two people became Enchanters, while those who failed to hear the call of the white stones pursued the Trades they had scored highest in.

Joining the Enchanter Trades meant embracing a life she had never wanted. In Äktas, the Enchanters were treated like royalty, heavily protected by The Hand. Yet, white stone wielders found themselves caged within the Academy walls, only allowed to travel up the mountains, shadowed by Militia Trades. The council's shackles clamped tight around the Enchanters' every choice—meals measured to the grain, training scheduled to the minute, marriages arranged like union decrees. Since General Buldar's iron grip had tightened around the Commander's seat, the push for new Enchanters had spiraled into obsession.

Her knees sank to the floor beside the cot and a knot twisted her insides. The call of the enchanted gems had been a secret she'd buried at the core of her being, hidden even from Oran. For years she'd pushed back against their song. Now miles from home, in enemy lands, that same insufferable pull thundered through her blood. She knew the stone she had borrowed from Äktas had saved her fleet from the underwater caves, but the details slipped through her mind. Channeling the power of the stones, required years of training she'd never received.

Her teeth dug into her index finger while her gaze traced the wyvern wings' carvings, wondering how Ka'zan had managed to get a hold of ignited white stones. The surface beneath the etchings vibrated in pulses, like the constant beat of weathered fingers against frame-drums.

She jolted off the floor, rushing to the opposite end of the room, desperate to escape the enchanted stone's grip. Her restless feet carved uneven paths in the narrow space while she forced air in and out of her lungs.

With an abrupt stop, she pressed her forehead against the stone wall, her eyes squeezed shut. Her fingers drummed against her thighs before her hand flew to her chest, clutching the new blue fabric. Guilt crashed over her like a tidal wave. She didn't know if Oran had survived. The last time she saw him, he had been tethered behind a Ka'zanty horse, amidst a storm of volcanic steam and rubble.

A squeaking of wheels made her head snap back. The creaking of the wooden door echoed through the small room as it swung open.

Her fingers danced faster against her side, contemplating an escape, when a figure in a rolling chair entered through the doorway. The white-bearded man maneuvered inside, and the chair's movement brought a symphony of gears to life, each component interlocking in a mesmerizing display. Her muscles coiled, ready to spring, but two guards materialized like crimson-scaled giants. Their hands gravitated to their claw-like weapons, their eyes locked onto her.

"I see you've finally woken, young lady," the man said, his round spectacles accentuating his green eyes. "And you took your bandages off."

Elva's eyes danced between him and the guards, her muscles tensing with each shift.

The man cleared his throat. "My name is Daigo, Chief Daigo," he nodded. "I'm a healer. You had us all worried. Please sit down. Let me examine you." Daigo flicked a lever near his hand and his chair wheeled around the cot.

"Stay away from me!" Elva scrambled backward until her spine pressed against the cold stone wall.

Both guards surged past Daigo, hands wrapped tightly around their swords, their boots scraping against the floor in their advance.

"Is that really necessary? Sefa, why don't you wait outside?" Daigo waved to one of the guards.

"The examination will have to wait, Chief. I have orders to bring her to the High Regent the moment she wakes." Sefa's dark eyes raked over Elva from head to toe. "You're coming with us, whether you like it or not. Understood?" she warned, tapping on her blade.

Elva's thumbnail carved into the side of her index finger. "If I go with you, will you take me to my friend?"

"That's not for you to decide," the towering guard said, her fingers digging into Elva's arm.

She twisted against the iron grip, her muscles straining uselessly. Sefa slammed her into the wall, wrenching her wrists behind her back and binding them with leather straps.

"Please! There's no need for the bindings. She's unarmed," Daigo protested over the whirring gears.

Sefa scoffed. "This one doesn't need blades, Chief. She's more dangerous than the three of us." She shoved Elva toward the slip-on shoes by the door before yanking her through the doorway.

Light poured into her eyes when they entered the corridor, and a hypnotic call surged through her body, pulling her head upward toward its source. Through the middle of the ceiling archways, a single strip of gentle sparkle wove up and down, dancing like a wyvern in flight. The guard's rough hand seized her shoulder. Coarse fabric scratched against her face, blurring her sight. But even through the sack, her skull resonated with the conjuring song of the white stones.

Each step forward amplified the rhythmic cadence. Her fingers curled into fists behind her back, finding the grooves of an old scar on her thumb—a small reminder of the day she had reeled in her first fish. Her mother had been so proud. She shook the image off. Memories of her family pierced her heart like a dagger.

Her mind spiraled, dwelling on the type of punishments Ka'zan offered—what kind of tortures Oran had received. If he still lived. The thought of him gnawed at her and guilt consumed her, much louder than the enchanted stones' assault on her senses. She remembered the first time they met.

On a summer morning, her parents and aunt talked about a group of six people who had wandered into the Tanama's dead forests, unable to resist its magnetic pull. Two of them had been the parents of a ten-year-old child, a boy only a year older than her. Her father fumed over The Hand's actions, blaming the council for their loss.

Later that morning, she was cleaning snails at her aunt's shop, hands coated in slime, when she spotted him. He sat hunched on an old bench by the fountain, cradling a broken locket in his hands. After a long stare at her slimy fingers, he handed it to her, reluctantly. She worked on the locket, carefully piecing all the fragments together. When she placed it back in his palms, silence stretched between them. Though, those dark eyes shimmered with unshed tears. When she turned to her aunt's, the boy with dark hair, sad eyes, and a locket walked next to her. It had been over twelve years since she walked without him by her side. The knot in her throat tightened. She shook her head again.

With another turn down a corridor, one of the guards' hands pressed against her back. Her body jerked away, memories of General Commander Buldar flooding back. Concentrating on the scars on her back shielded her from the stones' call. Her shirt had shredded beneath each lash of Buldar's whip, every strike a blaze that tore through her spine until her legs gave out.

Someone had sabotaged her work and blamed her for nearly burning down the Artificers' quarters. Any protest died in her throat. Buldar had branded her a wildling from the moment he set eyes on her. As further punishment, he forced her to repair the damage, without tools and without seeking a healer. *Character building*, he'd called it. Elva avoided Oran for an entire week and never mentioned the scars to him or anyone.

Focusing on that pain helped her. The beckoning remained, a constant hum at the edges of her mind, but the noises in the hallways slowly sharpened.

Heavy boots thudded through the corridors, armor plates singing with each step. Metal levers creaked and groaned nearby. The grip on her arm tightened, forcing her to a halt. With a shift in the air, the cloth ripped away from her head, dragging curls free from her braid.

Her eyes blinked at the shift in light, revealing a woman in a long dark blue jacket with layered collars. The stranger examined Elva thoroughly, with eyes painted in smoky hues sweeping gracefully to her temples.

Sefa stepped forward and bent low. "High Councilor, we have orders to bring her to the High Regent."

"The High Regent rests. I'll question her first," the woman said while her gaze scrutinized Elva, stripping away her defenses.

"High Councilor, I have orders," the guard insisted, her spine stiffening.

The Councilor's gaze slithered to Sefa, and her voice took on a soft, yet unsettling tone. "Of course," she said, her lips curving upward as her eyes remained cold as stone. "Why don't you have the wardens assist the High Regent? In the meantime, we can acquaint the young lady."

Sefa's fingers tightened around Elva's arm as the warden's footsteps echoed away.

The chamber resembled an alabaster cave, white light cascading through a massive round skylight. Not far from where they stood, carvings of the land spread across a sunken section of the floor.

The Tanama mountain range, with its three-tailed ridges, cradled Rengō at the heart, separating the cities. To the north, a volcanic island loomed over Ka'zan. Black beaches spread across its shores. To the west, Ikari nestled within its mountain fortress, where a towering tree cast shadows over the outer city and surrounding farmland. Near the Tanama stood the skeletal remains of abandoned homes. To the east, her own city rose, Äktas, its stone roads winding between mountains and desert. The Iron Tower stood tall beyond the deserted mounds, though there was no sign of the Academy.

Elva's eyes caught the light glinting off the High Councilor's cuffs. In the polished metal, Ragas' horned face flickered. She turned toward the sunken section with the atlas, descending one measured step at a time toward Rengō's carving. The woman's predatory gaze remained locked on her.

"It's Elva, correct? Your name?" The Councilor's lips twisted into a subtle grin, clasping her hands behind her back.

Her chin dipped in agreement, but she didn't dare answer, teeth sinking into the inside of her cheek.

"I am Hura, Councilor to our High Regent, Zohar, son of the late Magnar." Hura climbed up the three small steps, her long jacket sweeping behind her. She approached a table where a black teapot rested over burning embers. "Would you care for tea?" The liquid hissed against the clay cup. "I'm afraid we only have dragon's leaves. What kind do they serve in the White Stone City these days?"

Elva's head jerked side to side, her throat too tight for words.

As the High Councilor took the first sip, the stone wall across the chambers parted on its own, revealing another space.

"Ah! Here he comes," Hura announced, her eyebrows arching.

Beyond the moving stone wall, a large skylight bathed the atrium with natural light. An indoor pond sparkled beneath a glass ceiling, spanning along a path of scattered stones. The figure of a man emerged through the archway, his deep purple tunic billowing with each stride, dark hair brushing his shoulders. Like shadows, four guards stalked in perfect rhythm in his wake.

The wall sealed shut behind him, and Hura and Sefa dropped into deep bows.

The enthralling murmur Elva fought to ignore shattered her defenses. Her lungs seized when her eyes locked onto the source, the amulet draping over the High Regent's throat, its call drilling through her skull. Her shoulders tightened, battling its incessant tug.

Her legs screamed with pain when a sudden kick drove her to her knees. The bindings bit deeper into her wrists with the crash against the floor.

"You insolent wretch, you dare not bow in the presence of the High Regent? Kneel and show proper respect!" A warden's voice roared in her ears.

Elva bit her tongue, forcing her eyes to the floor, doing what she could to ignore the amulet's assault on her mind.

"Has she spoken?" Zohar's deep voice echoed through the room.

Sefa's firm grip yanked her upright.

"Not a single word, Your Excellency," Hura replied, wrapping her fingers around her teacup.

"Where's my crew?" Elva finally said, her eyes meeting the High Regent's dark gaze.

Hura's cup froze halfway to her smirking lips. "She speaks!"

Zohar glided to the carved atlas, halting at the first step. "Most of them survived the volcano's onslaught. They have been fed and bathed. However, their continued treatment and state will depend entirely on you."

Her heart sank. Oran could still be alive. "Can I see them?"

"You're in no position to make requests. Not after invading my land. You will answer my questions. And if I'm satisfied with your answers, I might consider it."

She shifted uncomfortably. "I don't think I can be of much help, Sir. Your—Excellency."

"Considering your associates have not disclosed any valuable information in three days, we expected their Enchanter to be more cooperative."

Three days. She had been unconscious for three days. She blinked, forcing her eyes to focus while a shiver crawled up her spine. Enchanter. The truth she'd buried since childhood spilled out in that single heinous word.

"Oh, she's gone quiet again." Hura's chuckle coiled through the air.

"I—I'm not an Enchanter, Sir. Excellency."

"Not an Enchanter?" The High Regent descended into the atlas carvings. "Then tell me, child. How did you manage to appease our volcano. Our Chief Miner has told us everything. You used two stones to calm the beast."

Her mouth opened but no words came out.

"You deny it?"

The room spun under Elva's feet. Zohar's approach amplified the pounding of his necklace, growing louder like thundering drums. "I don't know of what you speak." The words strained past her lips.

The High Regent's jaw tensed, muscles shifting beneath his trimmed beard. "That's what your friends have been saying for days. You're forcing my hand. Bring them in."

Metal hinges groaned as the door swung open behind her. Two guards in gleaming red wyvern scale armor marched through, each gripping a cloth-hooded prisoner. A familiar figure in miner's tunics followed, his dark stubble peppered with white.

Hura approached the table, lifting the kettle from the burning ember. A knife took its place, the blade drinking in the heat. The guards shoved their prisoners to their knees beside it.

Elva's eyes darted nervously between Hura, the prisoners, and the High Regent while her thumbnail carved its familiar groove. Smaller in frame, the first prisoner knelt with a tilted forward chin and square shoulders, a posture typically carried by Militia Trades.

Lyla. But the second prisoner. The broad shoulders, the way the tunics strained against muscle. Oran. Alive. Her heart lurched and sank all at once. He stood so close, yet whatever the Ka'zanty Regent had planned for them twisted her stomach into knots.

The miner approached the High Regent and leaned close to his ear.

"Chief Yoen believes you might not have memory of what transpired. Is he mistaken?"

She shook her head again. "I don't know of what you speak."

At her voice, the broad-shouldered prisoner jerked toward her, the hood still masking his features. With a nod from the High Regent, the guard ripped away both coverings.

The sting in her eyes grew as she drank in their faces. Purple marks bloomed across Sergeant Lyla's freckles, dry blood coating her lip. Shadows haunted Oran's eyes, and days of stubble clung to the rigid lines of his jaw.

"I've made myself clear, young Äktastary. They are alive—for now. However, their fate hinges on your words," Zohar said, giving a sharp nod to his Council.

Flames danced along the blade when Hura lifted it from the embers, metal glowing in deep crimson and amber.

The High Regent's hands clasped tightly behind him. "Speak, or you'll be forcing my hand."

"I—I don't know," she said, her voice breaking.

Zohar took a few measured steps, gesturing to Lyla and Oran. "Your friends here have disclosed the reason behind your arrival, accusing us of the smoke that now engulfs the Tanama. It's a half-truth that hasn't fully persuaded me. More suspicious still, none can fathom how you navigated the underwater caves. Centuries have passed since any city dared to cross those waters," he said, pacing past Oran and Lyla before fixing his gaze on her. "And then, just as Garam laid waste to our city, you somehow managed to tame the volcano." As the Regent closed in on Elva, Sefa's grip tightened.

"Speak!" he hissed, standing mere inches away, casting a towering shadow over her.

Her lips quivered. "I told you, I—I don't know of what you speak."

His eyes flashed with a heated glare. With a sharp exhale, his finger jabbed toward the prisoners. "Him," he ordered.

Elva's heart sank. "Wait. Wait!"

The Council fingers twisted in Oran's dark hair, wrenching his head back at the High Regent's nod. Red-hot metal kissed his cheek, sending tendrils of smoke curling from his flesh. The leather straps bit into his wrists as he thrashed, deep, muffled grunts rumbling behind gritted teeth that threatened to crack under the pressure.

Elva lunged for Oran, but Sefa's hands slammed her down, stone biting into her knees. "Please, stop." Her voice cracked. "I told you. I don't know," she mumbled, lips trembling.

"You leave me no choice," Zohar bellowed.

Hura's eyes darted upward, lips twisting into a serpentine smile while the searing knife bit into Oran's throat. His flesh bubbled and blackened beneath the glowing blade, the acrid stench of burning skin drowning out the cries clawing past his clenched jaw.

With another nod from Zohar, the guard towering over Lyla pulled a leather strap and wrapped it around Lyla's throat, the rough material digging into her skin. The Sergeant's jaw clenched like stone. Her burning gaze remained steady until her lips parted, struggling for breath.

"Stop!" Elva pleaded, lunging forward, but a kick to her side expelled all the breath from her lungs. Lyla gasped repeatedly until her lips turned blue. Oran's groans bounced off the walls, raw and strained.

"*Stop!*" Her voice fractured.

The unrelenting pulse of the stones hammered against her mind. The call drowned her, suffocating her from the inside out.

Her muscles seized, and then the chamber's lights began to dance wildly, casting leaping shadows across the room.

The guards and Councilor recoiled, eyes wide, giving Lyla and Oran a fleeting second to catch their breath.

Elva's vision blurred, walls twisting together. She forced her forehead against the cold floor, as if trying to stop the room from spinning. Her breath came in short, jagged bursts. The dim flicker of the lights sputtered and hummed around her, gradually fading into a steady glow.

Sefa's fingers dug into her shoulder, yanking her to her feet to face Zohar. His eyes drilled into hers. "Speak!" he ordered.

But she hesitated, lips pressing into a thin line.

"Again," the High Regent snapped, signaling the Council and the guards.

"All right, I did it! I did it. I used the stone," she blurted out, as the burning blade hovered just above Oran's eye. "Just... stop," she mumbled, her gaze dropping to the floor.

"Speak!"

Oran's chest heaved, each breath ragged, sweat trickling down his forehead. He leaned slightly forward, eyes never leaving Elva. Beside him, Lyla's lips curled into a silent snarl, her head shaking slightly as the color slowly returned to her skin. The warning was unspoken but clear. Elva swallowed hard before turning to the High Regent.

"We were ordered to dive," she whispered. "To cross the underwater caves and reach Ka'zan. The water vessels run using sparked white stones. Ignited stones our Enchanters have managed to remove the top layer of, allowing for the energy within to flow freely. It's like peeling the skin of a fruit," she explained in short breaths. "Similar to opening the gates of a dam, releasing a torrent of energy. The stone energy is unrestricted. But..." her voice wavered, images of the underwater creatures creeping back. "Not long after we dove into the caves, we were attacked."

She cleared her throat, drawing a shaky breath before continuing. "To survive, we used the shooting energy of the stones against the beasts. They fled, but it depleted the stone's life force. Without an energy source powering the vessel, our air supply dwindled. Most of the crew had fainted." She glanced at Oran, fighting back tears. "I had another sparked stone in my satchel, but my convoy had no knowledge of it. I climbed into the emergency chamber and retrieved the sparked stone. I don't remember what happened after," she admitted. Her teeth bit into her lip, and her gaze darted to the Regent. "The next thing I recall is waking up inside the caves."

"Are you saying someone else wielded the stones?" The Regent questioned.

"No, Sir. I'm saying the stones that powered the machines didn't require an Enchanter onboard. And that I don't remember what happened after I climbed into the emergency chamber."

Her legs shook beneath her under Zohar's intense glare. His clenched jaw twisted with barely contained fury, his teeth grinding, threatening to splinter under the strain.

The hollow tap of Yoen's boots against stone caught their attention. His fingers pressed against the pit of his stomach as if stifling something within. "Your Excellency, may I address her?"

At Zohar's silent nod, Yoen turned to her. "Elva, you had two stones. A sparked white stone, as you call it, and a bloodstone."

"The bloodstone is a casing, Sir. A protective skin. Like drawing a curtain over a sunlit window. It suppresses the force of the ignited white stone," she explained, drawing a deep breath with a wince, the lingering ache of Sefa's blow still throbbing in her side.

"Do you remember when we ran through Ka'zan's grounds? The earth shook and gave in, swallowing everything around it?"

Her chin dipped with a nod. "Some of it."

"That night, you saved my life. And if I may be so bold..." Yoen's gaze darted to the High Regent. Only when Zohar nodded his head did he continue. "You saved Ka'zan."

She stretched the tension around her neck. "I'm glad your city didn't burn, Sir. But I had nothing to do with that."

"Just seconds before Garam nearly finished us, you retrieved the Ikarite box, containing an Äktastary stone from your boot." He shifted his weight onto one foot, his fingers scratching his forehead. "Then you used both gems to counter the force of the volcano's roots beneath our city."

Her head shook. "I retrieved the white stone, but only out of desperation," she admitted, her gaze momentarily meeting Oran's.

"You admit it? You're an Äktas Enchanter," Zohar bellowed, crossing his arms.

"I'm an Artificer, Excellency—Sir."

"Does your city divide their Enchanters?" Yoen asked, raising an eyebrow.

Her throat tightened until each breath came in shallow gasps. The leather bindings cut fresh lines into her wrists while her fingers fidgeted behind her. "We have trials. Our Academy is missing from your atlas," she said, her lips pointed toward the floor carvings. "The school hosts Enchanter tests every year. If one doesn't pass, we move on to the next Trade. We get placed where we score the highest."

"You traitor!" The words ripped from Lyla's mouth, slicing through the air. In response, the guard's fist connected with her jaw, then her ribs, again and again.

Elva's muscles tensed with each impact. "Please, no more!"

The High Regent raised his hand, signaling the guard to stop the beating.

The stones' incessant whispers drained the little energy she had left, while bile rose in her throat. The thought of sharing her secret with the enemy city made her sick.

Enchanters in Äktas lived under strict control. And from the little she knew of Ka'zan, Zohar was the only stone wielder in the Agni Stone City. Her heart threatened to escape her chest. If they found out she had a splinter of an Enchanter's touch, they'd see her as a threat. Or worse, they'd turn her into a puppet dancing on strings, something to be controlled, used, and kept.

But the image of Oran tugged at her soul, deeper even than the call of the stones. Her actions had led to him being tied and tortured, so far from home in a strange land. He had given up everything to be by her side. She had to do the same.

Her lungs drew in a deep breath before she managed her next words, wondering if Oran would ever forgive her for keeping the truth from him. "During my Enchanter's trials, I pretended I didn't sense the ignited white stones. I ignored them, pushed them away."

"Impossible!" Hura marveled. "Remarkable!"

Zohar inched closer, standing beside Yoen. "My Council is right. Resisting the call of the stones and their magic is nearly impossible, unheard of. Why resist?"

Her gaze dropped.

"Resisting the summoning of the stones takes an incredible amount of energy. No wonder you've been out for so long. Even now, you look faint," he continued, scrutinizing her with a furrowed brow. "Now, explain the bloodstone. How could an Äktas Enchanter wield an Ikari stone?"

"As I said before, the bloodstone is just a box, it suppresses the energy of the Äktas stone," she countered.

"Elva," Yoen interrupted, rubbing his chin while his brown eyes locked with hers. "Both stones are ignited. You used them to stop the ground from caving beneath us. The rising magma solidified around the farmlands. Garam is still awake, but you subdued it temporarily."

"That's impossible, Sir. I admit I took the white stone. But frankly I didn't know what I was doing. I just grabbed the stone, and then—then I don't know what happened," she hesitated, her gaze darting from Yoen to Zohar. "I'll tell you everything I remember, but please don't hurt my people."

"Answer honestly," Zohar insisted, gesturing to his amulet. "Do you sense the stone around my neck—and the ones around this fortress?"

"I do, Sir... Excellency."

Jaws dropped in unison and a collective gasp filled the air, bouncing off the stone walls. Her gaze darted between Oran's and Lyla's wide eyes.

"Elva, do you know what that means?" Yoen asked.

She swallowed the knot in her throat before answering. "The necklace is a white stone, just like the ones in the corridors. This place is full of them."

"My heirloom is pure agni stone. Older than all of us together. Ignited by Ragas himself," Zohar said.

Her heart sank and she shook her head. Her mouth opened to speak, struggling to find the words. "It can't be. I'm just—a wildling," she whispered.

"Do you think it possible, Your Eminence?" Hura interjected. "This young woman, a Tristone Enchanter?"

"That is yet to be discovered. But one thing I'm sure of," Zohar remarked, looming over Elva. "You will help put Garam into a complete rest."

Then he strode toward the sliding stone wall, his wardens following closely behind, and paused at the threshold. "I'm not fully convinced Äktas isn't responsible for the smoke shrouding the dead forests. So, after we deal with the volcano, you will help us figure out the cause and how to get rid of it, or your friends will pay with their lives, and you'll never see the light of day."

CHAPTER 16

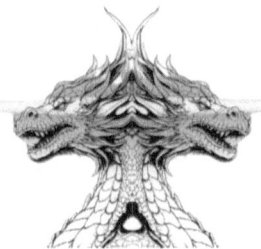

IKARI

ASANTE

MORNING SUNLIGHT STREAMED THROUGH the cave's entrance, casting soft amber hues over Zama's unconscious body. Asante's fingers worked quickly, wrapping fresh bandages around the arrow wound in the Sage's leg. Her golden owl form had arrived the night before, wings ruffled and eyes wide with signs of a fierce struggle.

"Why did you shoot that arrow?" she shouted, securing the last bandage. Behind her, her brother packed, leather rustling and metal clinking throughout the cave.

Tarrak didn't look up from his quiver. His fingers jammed arrows into place with more force than necessary.

Asante gathered the blood-stained bandages with tightly clenched fingers. "You know her owl form. Why would you shoot?"

His quiver dropped to his side. "You're really asking me that? She's a Sage." His hand cut through the air, pointing at Zama lying beside the alabaster boulder. "She's dangerous, we can't trust her."

Asante's gaze drifted to the Sage. Her brother's cautionary words lingered, but she still struggled to believe Zama could harm them. The Fifth Sage had always been kind to her and Lux. Yet Tarrak could be right—after all, the Sages carried out the massacre in the Great Hall.

Her eyes fixated on the markings on Zama's face, sharp and distinct against her smooth brown skin. Dark dots ran from the corners of her nose to the curves of her temples, so different from the silver veins on her own arm. The argent threads crisscrossed her dark-brown skin, luminous in the dim light, unlike anything she'd ever seen on an Enchanter. The unsettling nature of her markings sent a shiver down her spine as a haunting whisper crept through her mind. *Perhaps I am a different kind of monster.*

Her hands smoothed a blanket over Zama, noticing a different mark on the back of her left wrist. A golden feather, streaked with black stripes, carved into the Sage's skin. "Tarrak, look," she called out, pointing to it. "This feather. It's just like the one on the branch you pulled. The one that revealed the secret passage in Pālam."

Her brother's gaze lingered on Zama, his jaw clenching. Something flickered across his face—not anger, but a deeper pain that tugged at the corners of his mouth. He turned away, sliding a dagger into his thigh holster with trembling fingers. For a moment, a faint tremor crossed his lips before he cleared his throat.

"We have to head out," he said, grabbing a rope from his supplies. He approached Zama, winding it around her wrists and ankles. Each knot pulled tight with a sharp snap.

Asante's fingers dug into his shoulder. "What are you doing? You really want to leave her here? Tied up?"

"She can't join us," he insisted, moving to one of the skylights with a grappling hook. He hurled it through the opening, securing a line so they could climb out.

She followed, dragging her feet. "She's still unconscious, we can't just leave her."

"She works for the Priestess. They killed Mom," he said, wrestling with the knot on his supply bag. "What makes you think she's not here to give away our location or harm us?"

Her arms wrapped around herself. The Sage she knew wouldn't harm them. But then, she had once believed the same about the others and the Priestess. "Sage Zama wasn't at the Great Hall. She was ordered to fly to Ka'zan and Äktas," she whispered, the words sounding hollow even to her own ears.

"I won't risk it," he said with resolve, pressing the green gloves into her hands. "Here, cover your markings. Remember, no one must find out. And keep that gem hidden." His eyes darted to the satchel at her hip.

Her fingers slid into the gloves, then delved into her satchel. The jade stone pulsed with warmth even through the fabric, its surface a maze of silver veins threading through deep greens.

Questions still hung in her mind. "We need to figure you out little one."

They had decided to go to the abandoned city to search for the sunken temple their father spoke of so often. The thought of being so close to the Tanama's dead forests made her nauseous, but they needed answers.

Each night since losing her father to the dead woods, her dreams had grown more vivid. But something had shifted since their escape from Pālam. The Uláak and its tristone weapon had crossed a threshold, unraveling the boundary between slumber and waking.

"Are you ready, Rabbit?" Tarrak called, his stance steady under the natural skylight. Morning light bathed his honey locs, half of the strands restrained by a broken arrow's pick.

Her gaze shifted to Zama momentarily. "I guess it's just us, little one," she whispered into her satchel. Her feet rushed toward the skylight, fingers reaching for her brother's hand. His arm shot out, pulling the thick, frayed rope around her wrist. He gripped the other end, his body coiling with effort as the muscles in his arms flexed. With a sharp tug, he yanked her upward, lifting her effortlessly through the opening.

Dried leaves crackled beneath Asante's boots, each step a struggle to match Tarrak's pace across the uneven ground. His silhouette moved swiftly, barely visible among the ashen trees. Her fingers tugged her cowl higher to avoid the bitter scent of charred wood and smoldering plants stinging her nostrils.

A massive kapok tree loomed ahead, an island of life in the devastation. Its roots twisted skyward like ancient fortress walls, their weathered surface a patchwork of moss and green foliage clinging to life.

Her brother's hand pressed against her shoulder, guiding her behind the shelter of the towering roots. Without a word, he vanished into the haze of ash and smoke, slipping past the outer posts to survey the area. She stood there, heart pounding and hand pressed to her chest as if she could keep it from leaping out.

Feeble sun rays twisted through the spirals of smoke, where the skeletal remains of the outer city stretched before her. The once-vibrant structures now lay in ruin. Only Mount Pālam stood defiant. Its crimson shield caught the sunlight, twisting it into little rays of blood dancing over the ruined landscape.

As her gaze fixed on Pālam, she remembered feeling Zuwena's rage through their mind connection. She understood it fully now. That fury, that taste for vengeance, like a blazing ember against her very bones. Samira stood safely behind the ruby shield, and all she wanted was to see her burn. She forced measured breaths, trying to ease her thoughts when a flutter of wings caught the corner of her eye.

Above her, a golden owl, perched motionless on a branch, its yellow eyes following Tarrak as he disappeared into a small outpost. Her eyes tracked her brother, and when she looked back to the branch, the owl had vanished. In its place, Zama materialized next to her in her Sage form, like an apparition summoned from thin air.

With a jolt, Asante stumbled backward. "Don't come any closer!"

Zama extended a reassuring hand, taking a careful step forward. "Why do you retreat? I'm not going to hurt you."

A gust of wind tugged at Zama's shoulder cape, revealing smooth skin where a leg wound had been. Asante continued to carefully widen the distance between them.

"What's going on?" the Avian Sage probed, her hands sweeping the air as if grasping for the right words. "Last night I spotted a bright light from the cave opening. I was relieved to hear you and Tarrak. But he shot an arrow at me. Why?"

Asante's fingers twisted in her bag straps, and her gaze fell to the ash-covered ground.

"There's no need to fear me." Zama took another step forward.

"Part of me wants to believe it," she admitted, her voice trembling. "The other warns against it."

The Sage's hands dropped to her sides. "I don't know what's gotten into you or Tarrak, but we cannot stay here. I saw Zuwena inside the dead forests. The wyvern is up—"

The whisper of a flying arrow cut her words short. Zama's head snapped to the side, the arrowhead slicing a thin crimson line across her cheek just below her markings. Tarrak stood with another arrow already nocked, his jaw set in stone. Rather than shifting forms, Zama launched herself at him, a blur of motion dodging the second shot.

The Avian Sage slammed into him with the force of a storm wind, driving them both to the ground. Tarrak's hands found her throat, but Zama twisted like a serpent, flipping him over her shoulder. His face met the earth with a dull thud. She pinned him with one knee, wrestling his arms behind his back. "Stop this!" The words tore from her throat between heavy breaths.

"Let go of my brother!" Asante hissed, her grip tightening around her father's knife, her eyes ablaze.

Zama slowly raised her hands, backing away from Tarrak. The fresh wound on her cheek began sealing itself, leaving a faint trail of blood behind. "I don't want to fight. I don't know why you've shot at me three times now, but I still need you to listen."

Tarrak pushed himself from the ground, dusting off his locs. "Those were warning shots." He let out a long breath and shouldered his bow. "Don't make me shoot another."

"Firemoon, please. Just listen," Zama pleaded, her eyes glistening with tears.

His feet moved swiftly, closing the gap between him and Zama. "Don't you call me that. Don't you dare!" he blurted, thrusting a finger at her face.

Asante's gaze darted between Tarrak's tensed shoulders and Zama's furrowed golden eyes.

The Sage's voice quivered. "What is with you? Please! We have to find a way into Pālam. The Priestess and Sages can protect you."

He scoffed, putting distance between them. "Is that what you think? Your beloved Priestess, the daughter of wyverns, will keep us safe behind her blood-stained shield? I won't let that monster near my sister, even if it costs me my own soul." He yanked his bag from the ground. "As if you don't know what that monster did," he shouted, jabbing a hand toward Pālam.

"You mean Zuwena? I saw..."

"The Priestess," Asante interrupted, cutting through the tension. Tarrak turned his back on Zama, dusting off invisible dirt from his bag. The Avian Sage's furrowed gaze darted between them.

Asante shuffled closer. "The High Priestess and the Sages, they—" she faltered, gritting her teeth while her fingers fidgeted with the straps of her satchel. "They murdered the first-tier unmarked ones. Sixty of them, including our—" Her gaze fell to the ground. "Our mother and sister."

Zama's eyes widened in horror, her mouth falling open as if struggling to find the words.

"Tarrak was there too," she added, her eyes flicking to her brother, who glared at Pālam. "The Priestess and the other four Sages encircled them inside the Great Hall and drained the life out of each of them. Lux too."

Zama's lip trembled. She shook her head slowly, her eyes brimming with tears. Her gaze turned away, and a clenched fist found her heart.

"Let's go, Sante," Tarrak mumbled, wrapping his fingers around her arm, without looking back.

Ash drifted like gray snow over the cobblestones, coating abandoned market stalls and scattered belongings in a pale mantle. Her fingers brushed the golden beads woven into her locs—the same ones her mother had bargained for in that very market, now a graveyard of scorched wood and ravaged stone. As they hurried, her boots crunched over shards of broken clay, each step an echo of what was lost.

To one side, the Tanama mountains had disappeared beneath a mantle of smoke. The ominous shroud licked the city's edge like a tidal onyx wave hitting an invisible barrier. On the other side, Pālam's shield glinted like a ruby gem in the shadows, surrounded by swirling tendrils of smoke—Zuwena's wrath made flesh.

"Where are you going?" Zama's voice rang out behind them, echoing off the scorched posts.

Tarrak let out a hissing curse through clenched teeth. The sound of the Sage's running footsteps grew closer.

"Leave us alone," he snapped, positioning himself like a shield between Zama and Asante.

The Sage halted several paces away with tear-stained cheeks. "I swear on my sister's grave, I had no knowledge that the Priestess or the Sages would commit such a heinous act—to murder your family and my Lux." Her voice quivered. Her gaze darted between them, hands shaking at her sides. "If I had known, I would've moved mountains to prevent it." Her feet moved closer toward Tarrak, shoulders hunched. "I would've given my life without hesitation for Nora and for your mother. I beg you, please, believe me."

Hot tears pricked at Asante's eyes. "You knew them? My Amá and Nora?"

Zama nodded and shifted her gaze to Tarrak. Her brother's chest heaved, but his eyes stayed fixed on the ashen ground.

The Sage inched forward again, hands raised. "I can't begin to imagine what you've been through, but you can't be out here. Not alone. Let me help you."

"We don't need your help." His fingers gripped Asante's arm and pulled her forward, their footsteps quick against the cobblestones.

"I flew over the dead forest. The creatures there, they responded to Zuwena." Zama's words tumbled out in a rush. "I believe you, all right? Samira she's—she's menacing. Harrowing."

Tarrak quickened the pace. Scorched husks of buildings blurred past where many homes once stood. Only charred beams reached toward the sky like skeletal fingers.

"That shield she raised is more than a mere defense," Zama continued, her breathless voice breaking between pants while she pointed at Pālam's ruby barrier. "The Priestess wouldn't have been able to wield it without turning against her own people. That must mean she's truly frightened. She should be. Please let me help you."

Her brother veered into an alley overlooking the Tanama's dead woods, peering through empty doorways and broken windows. Asante's gaze flicked back to Zama's shadow, trailing behind them.

"Zuwena is stirring the Uláak in the dead forests. She's drawing them here," she shouted, her arm sweeping toward the rolling smoke beyond the city.

At Zama's words, Asante's legs froze, refusing to move. Her muscles seized, as fragments of her nightmares flashed behind her eyes. "The Uláak? How do you know they respond to Zuwena?"

Before the Sage could answer, Tarrak's grip returned to her arm, steering her toward an isolated guard post that had survived the devastation of Zuwena's blue flames.

"We can rest here for a moment, but not for too long, if we want to make it to the abandoned city before nightfall," he said. The thud of his bag hitting the floor punctuated his words.

"Please, let me help you." Zama's lean figure lingered in the doorway, palms raised in a peace offering.

"Stop following us!" Tarrak hissed, his fingers tightening around his dagger's hilt.

"I want to hear what she has to say." The words scraped past Asante's throat, and her brother's amber eyes clouded with betrayal. Her eyes met his gaze, silently pleading. She needed to know what Zama saw in the woods.

"You can't believe a word she says. No one has ever survived the haunted woods," he snapped. A heavy sigh escaped him, while his finger jabbed at Zama. "No matter their form—bird or Sage, man, woman, or child. The Uláak devour everything." His eyes narrowed on Zama. "If you're telling the truth, how did you manage to escape?"

The Sage removed her shoulder cape as she stepped inside, the dark fabric cascading onto the nearby table like a pool of shadowed silk. The wooden chair creaked beneath her weight when she sank into it. Her copper braids stirred, releasing owl feathers that spiraled downward and settled lightly on her lap.

Asante's eyes followed her brother, still rigid in the doorway, arms crossed and his furrowed gaze fixed on Zama. The same shadow of worry that had haunted him in the caves carved itself even deeper into his features.

"I almost didn't make it," Zama admitted, her body collapsing forward. With elbows digging into her knees, her face sank into her hands. "I avoided the forests during my flight north, but the creatures leaping from the water proved relentless. I soared too high, until the land blurred below. When I arrived at Ka'zan, the city was in chaos. Zuwena's lightning had stirred the volcano to life." Her fingers pressed against her temples.

"At first, I thought the volcano had caused the smoke around the Tanama, but I was wrong. The smoke from Rengō billowed long before Zuwena struck. Then she unleashed her tail horns on Ka'zan's ships. She was about to strike the second vessel when she spotted me instead. I hid in the ashen cloud, but her tail found me. I flew until I was exhausted, then plummeted into the sea."

Asante extended Zama a flask of fresh water with trembling hands. Her eyes flicked to Tarrak, catching the muscle twitching in his jaw, his shoulders stiff with barely contained distrust.

Zama tipped the flask back, water dribbling down her chin, until it emptied. She lowered it with a gasp. "A blast of light exploded from near the underwater caves. The force pushed me to the surface—saved me from drowning. I'm not even sure what I saw, but some strange metal creatures surged from behind it. I didn't dare face them. Knowing Zuwena had charged west, I had to come back here, but I was so tired. The dead forest seemed faster if I could just fly straight through..." Her fingers drummed against the flask, her leg shook beneath her. "The Uláak spotted me just moments after I flew over. One of them flicked some sort of stone chain whip. It caught my talon, dragging me down. The whip—" She swallowed hard. "It forced me out of my owl form."

She sprang to her feet and began pacing around the table. Asante's gaze dropped to the Sage's battered boots—leather cracked and peeled, covered with mud and bloodstains. Her own hand flew to her throat as a phantom pain constricted, remembering the chain whip from her nightmare coiling around her neck.

"I've never been so frightened." Zama's words barely stirred the air. "I thought it was the end."

"But you escaped. You escaped them?" Asante quavered.

Zama's chin dipped slightly. "It was Zuwena. When she entered the forest, she released a deep howl. It shook me to my core. The hexenbeasts cowered at the sound, but not the masked ones. The Uláak... they—they turned to the wyvern." Her arms snaked around her torso, fingers digging into her sides. She braced herself against the table. "One by one, they glided toward her call and released their grip on me."

"What are hexenbeasts?" The question left Asante's lips, but her mind conjured the hybrid creatures from her dreams—the ones whose growls echoed through her nightmares, night after night.

"The Uláak's pets. A hybrid of man and beast, with spikes on their backs, hunched over and leaning on claws." Zama's foot tapped on the floor, quick and uneven. "They're just as terrifying as the Uláak."

"They just left you there?" Tarrak asked, leaning against the doorway with arms crossed. "How is that possible?"

"I don't know, but I didn't stay to find out. I just ran. Ran as far as my legs could carry me. It took me a long time before I could transform. By the time I stumbled out of the forest, Pālam's shield was already pulsing overhead. The outer city... Skies! The outer city was nothing but ash and rubble, with scorched bodies everywhere I looked. I searched from the skies, desperate to find anyone still alive. That's when I saw it—a flicker of light from the sea caves. And there you were."

The furnace's warmth did nothing to chase away the chill creeping through Asante's bones. She sank into a nearby wooden chair, her grip tight around her satchel. She had never wandered into the dead woods, but Zama's words painted those hexenbeasts in a way that resembled the creatures from her own night terrors. The urge to confess her nightmares to Tarrak rose in her throat, only to be drowned out by the sudden shouting battle.

"You had orders," Tarrak spat, his shoulders pulling back as his shadow stretched to the ceiling. "Sante told me you were instructed to seek answers and return. That means you must know a way back into Pālam, and through that shield. How can we trust you? For all we know, you're here to get to my sister." He spun on his heel, snatching up his bag and Asante's forest-green cloak. The fabric rustled when he draped it over her shoulders.

"I'm relieved you survived the dead forest," his voice dropped. "But I can no longer trust any Sage or stone wielder. Asante and I have a plan. It doesn't involve you." He pushed the door open with a creak, casting one last look over his shoulder. "Rabbit, we ought to move."

Her gaze bounced between her brother's rigid stance and Zama's glistening eyes. Before she could speak, a warm glow pulsed through her bag, painting the room in amber light. Her fingers fumbled with the strap, revealing the softly glowing embryo inside. She met Tarrak's wide gaze, her heart hammering against her ribs. "She's coming."

Tarrak burst through the doorway and searched the skies.

"What is that?" Zama pointed at the satchel.

Asante lunged for the window instead of answering. A wall of smoke towered in the distance, marking where the Tanama forest began. A bone-chilling screech rippled through the haze, sending ice through her veins.

Zama's grip tightened around her wrist, yanking her from the post. The Sage led them through the scorched field of crops, with Tarrak's strides pounding behind them. Heat still radiated from the ground, the lingering wrath of Zuwena's fury two days prior. Ash and debris swirled around them, forcing her to pull her cloak across her face.

They stumbled to a halt beside a massive kapok tree, its trunk scorched and peeling. One of its massive roots arched overhead, offering them shelter. Zama tugged at her shoulder cape, willing it to life. The fabric twisted and morphed, expanding into a wing-like shroud. Before their eyes, the cape transformed into a large shield of feathers, its surface darkening to match the tree's charred bark. It enveloped them rendering them nearly invisible against the trunk.

Tarrak squeezed Asante against his chest, their sharp gasps echoing in the confined space. The air thickened with the presence of four racing hearts beneath the enchanted wing. Even with a Sage's magic by their side, the thought of facing a wyvern made her stomach clench. Beneath her gloves, her markings burned—a power she neither understood nor controlled.

Sweat beaded on her forehead despite the chill in her bones, as guilt twisted in her gut. Tarrak and Zama's lives hung in the balance because of her. If only she had found the courage to defy the Priestess and reject Zuwena's embryo, the price would have been hers alone to pay—just as she should have been braver for her mother and sister.

She forced the thoughts away, straining to see through the translucent span of the wing-like covering. Shockwaves traveled through the ground when Zuwena landed nearby.

She gasped, jerking upright as thick fog surged behind her eyes, swallowing her vision.

"Asante, not a single move," Tarrak whispered.

"I can't see." Her eyes blinked, but the clouding haze refused to clear.

"My wing is concealing us. It's hard to see through, but we must keep quiet."

"No, I mean I *can't* see anything." An invisible force tugged at her consciousness.

Where are you, child?

The Priestess' voice wove through her mind like a thread sliding through delicate silk.

CHAPTER 17

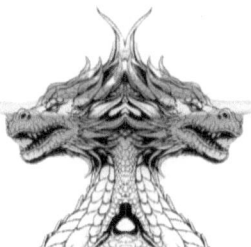

IKARI

ASANTE

A TUGGING FORCE CREPT through Asante's mind, like a hook lodged in her thoughts, reeling her deeper into the pull. "It's Samira." The words caught in her throat as she huddled within Zama's wing.

The Sage's breath hitched, warm against her ear. "The Priestess is trying to connect. If she fully mind-weaves with you, she'll discover anything you're hiding in your thoughts. She'll see and know everything."

Sweat beaded on her forehead. Invisible tendrils pulled at her consciousness. "What do I do? I don't think I can resist her."

Gravel crunched around her. Tarrak inched closer, his voice barely above a whisper. "Fight it, don't let her in."

"She must sense you're alive if her mind is reaching for you. If you don't let her in, she'll see it as betrayal. We have a wyvern out here and we could soon be facing the Uláak. Do you want to add a High Sage to the list of things that hunt us?" Zama countered, placing her free hand on Asante's shoulder. "The most difficult part is to not let her in completely. Not everyone can manage it. Try to stay calm. Focus on one thing at the time. Take deep breaths."

Her chest rose and fell, measured and deliberate. The invisible force yanked harder, pulling at the edges of her mind like a puppet being manipulated by unseen strings. The world blurred, then snapped into focus. Warm air brushed her skin. She found herself on Samira's balcony, gazing over the remains of the outer city.

Miles away, dark smoke covered the distant Tanama mountains like a silken shroud. Within the chamber, the translucent shield over Pālam pulsed with ruby light. Each throb matched the rhythm of a heartbeat, casting crimson shadows across the stone walls.

Asante, the Priestess' voice rung in her mind.

"Your Grace." The words tasted like ash in her mouth.

You've survived.

She faced her sister's murderer, who stood with regal grace. Acid churned in her stomach. Her racing thoughts scattered like leaves in a storm until her brother's calloused fingers found hers, anchoring her.

Through Samira's eyes, Zuwena's serpentine form prowled below, her wyvern's scales gleaming like polished shields. The creature remained oblivious to the Priestess' presence above.

What I entrusted you to guard, is it safe?

"Yes, Your Grace. It's safe," she replied, measuring each breath.

Where are you? Show me.

Her tongue clung to the roof of her mouth, making each word harder to speak. "You—you want to see where I am?"

"Don't let her see us," Zama whispered.

Show me! Samira's words seized her thoughts like a hawk's talons closing on prey. The invisible tendrils probed deeper. Asante's eyelids clenched shut, her markings blazing beneath her gloves.

You're different. Something has changed.

"No, I—I'm just scared, Your Grace. The wyvern, she's close."

You should be frightened.

The Priestess' gaze fixated on the wyvern below. Zuwena's blue flames pulsed beneath her chest, casting eerie shadows across the devastated landscape.

If the creature finds what we've hidden from her, she'll gain an unimaginable power. Enough to bring destruction to us all. Keep it safe until I ask you to bring it back. When the time is right, I'll show you the path through the shield and back into Pālam.

"Your-Your Highness." The words stumbled from her lips. "I don't understand. Why not keep it hidden inside Pālam? Out here, it's—exposed."

Through their shared vision, the scorched grounds of the outer city stretched before them.

Wyverns. The word resonated through the air. Samira retreated from the balcony and stepped inside her chamber, where the High Tree's roots pulsed with rhythmic flashes of dancing blue lights. *The creatures are the physical form of the Daemons that shaped our land and bestowed life upon us. That same energy flows through Ikarite blood—it's what created the first Sages. No stone was needed. Our Ikarite blood carries both the wyverns' essence and the power of The Original Three.*

Samira's gilded fingers retrieved a crimson gem from her circular bed, silk fabric whispering beneath her touch. The stone caught the light, bleeding red across her gold markings. *At first, the Ikarite women were the only ones with the gift. But in their insolence, men yearned for the essence too—fought and killed for it. The Great Horned Elder, wise as he was, knew better than to ignite their blood. Instead, he offered the minerals full of their essence. That's how Enchanters came to be. A ridiculous offer of peace and balance.* A scoff echoed through their mind connection, dripping with centuries of bitterness.

Samira glided back to the balcony's edge with the bloodstone nestled in her palm. *While the magic in our Sages' blood is the wyvern's essence, there's a split between us. We're nearly equals. But the stones.* The High Priestess' eyes darted to the gem between her fingers. *They hold an eternal link to the wyverns. The creatures used to be able to spark them or make them useless, whenever they deemed it necessary.* Her last words dripped with venom.

Below, Zuwena's scaled nose inched closer to the ruby barrier, nostrils flaring. The wyvern's horned tail whipped out, sending debris flying. The shield swallowed each piece of rubble, igniting them in flashes of fire that flickered like kindling catching a spark.

The shield keeps Zuwena from hearing the bloodstones that fuel our city. However, the bond between Zuwena and the stone you hold acts as a beacon. They draw each other, like a moth to a flame. Their connection is a force of nature, undeniable and electric. The presence of the embryo within these walls would shatter this shield, as if it were a thin layer of glass.

Asante's heart hammered against her ribs. Her mind writhed against Samira's presence. A murderer. Yet curiosity held her fast, questions sparked like fireflies.

I sense the storm in your mind, young one. The task I've entrusted you is critical for the survival of our entire city. Now is not the time to waver.

Asante's teeth sank into her lip, stifling the curses meant for the Priestess. Instead, she pushed forward a different thought. "There are some many others more qualified for this task, Your Grace. I fear I might not be as strong... or brave."

To resist and fight the weaving of minds, takes a formidable skill. As I mentioned before, you have exhibited a remarkable resilience where others have failed. That's why I chose you. Place your trust in your mind. Samira's gaze fixed on Zuwena below. *You must push her out when she attempts to connect through the embryo.*

The wyvern's head snapped up, faded yellow horns catching the shield's ruby light. Wings unfurled like storm clouds as she launched skyward, her gaze locking with Samira's. Power crackled between them. Two matriarchs, their gazes filled with disdain. Zuwena's jaws gaped wide, releasing a torrent of sapphire flames that battered against the protection.

The mental connection snapped. Asante's mind recoiled violently, throwing her back into her own body beneath Zama's wing shield. Her ears rang with the echo of Zuwena's feral roar, the sound tearing through the land like thunder.

The wyvern's white flames surged, and Asante's nails dug deep into her palms through her gloves, feeding the flare of her own markings. Heat bloomed in her chest, throbbing like an open wound as Zuwena's assault raged against the shield, flames crackling in a ferocious roar that echoed her own hunger for vengeance. She pictured it. The shield shattering like rock to glass, the flames engulfing the High Sage, reducing her to nothing but ash—yet, the barrier held, mocking her.

The wyvern's nostrils steamed when she let out a guttural roar that shook the earth beneath her. In response, the dead forest of the Tanama erupted with a bone-chilling chorus of shrieks and growls. Her spine stiffened, cold as ice, as shadows twisted behind the veil of smoke, their forms writhing in the murky haze.

At the sound, the Avian Sage retracted her wing-like shield, morphing it back into her shoulder cape. She grabbed Asante by the wrist and bolted. Zama dragged her across the scorched farmland. Behind them, Tarrak's bowstring creaked with tension, scanning for any signs of pursuit. Each step carried them closer to the abandoned city, where nature had overtaken the clay ruins. They halted at the city's edge, watching the Uláak prowl, still confined within their distant prison in the Tanama.

The dying sunlight painted long shadows through the abandoned cobblestone paths while Tarrak and Zama searched for shelter. She clutched her satchel, her stomach churning at their proximity to the haunted woods. The embryo seemed to grow heavier with each step, as if feeding on her festering thoughts.

Rage and shame wrestled in her chest. The Priestess had invaded her mind as easily as a curtain being drawn aside, exposing nearly everything she kept hidden. She couldn't decide which monster she despised more. The massive wyvern with her horned tail, or the High Sage with her golden markings.

"Nearly equals," she snarled in a whisper. Samira had dared compare herself to a wyvern, while she stood useless. When faced with her mother's murderer, she had a chance to be brave again, but she said nothing.

She stepped through trails where vines strangled clay houses and moss blanketed walls, while her fingers drummed anxiously against the satchel at her hip. The massacre in the Great Hall flashed behind her eyes—she could still see the spectrales of life leaving their bodies. With the embryo, Samira's power would eclipse even that horror. No wyvern, no Enchanter, or Sage would stand against her. Except there was one thing Samira feared. The egg falling under Zuwena's claws.

Asante's neck muscles coiled, her mind conjuring two paths of destruction. The outer city's charred bones testified to Zuwena's rage. With her embryo, the wyvern's vengeance would rain fire and lightning across all of Ikari until nothing remained.

She slipped her hand inside the satchel, a sly smile curling on her lips. Her fingers traced the surface of the gem inside, its warmth seeping through her glove. Her pulse quickened. A cold shiver clawed up her spine, while a third path emerged in her mind—terrible, beautiful, and probably impossible. She inched the latch back just enough to peek at the embryo. "Do you think your mother would ever join forces with a lowly first-tier attendant?"

CHAPTER 18

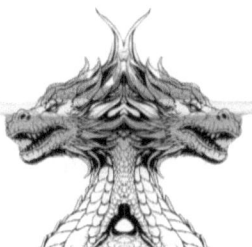

KA'ZAN

YOEN

THE PATH AHEAD WOUND past scorched, empty farmlands toward the Tanama's borders. Patches of uneven rock jutted where Elva had sealed Garam's volcanic gouges with her stone-wielding magic. The air hung dense as Yoen approached the edge of the dead woods. In the distance, where skeletal trees once embraced the city's limits, a menacing mantle of smoke engulfed everything in its path.

His grip tightened on Inara's reins. The steady rhythm of hoofbeats behind him drew his attention.

Arben's mount matched stride with Sumani's, their horses' flanks nearly touching. Their recent argument still lingered in his mind. He had pleaded with Arben to stay inside the fortress, to avoid getting close to the dead forest. But his nephew insisted on joining the fleet assigned to scout the edge of the woods and reinforce the barricades around it.

Their formation tightened under Gerel's command toward the unsettling wall of smoke. The sight struck deeper than he'd expected. The fact that he couldn't see through it sent his mind spiraling, imagining any number of sinister plots behind the veil. The absence of burning scents only deepened his unease.

Inara brought him alongside Arben. "Remember, keep your distance from the dead woods. Focus on the barricades. Stay close to Sumani."

"That's not for you to decide," Arben snapped, turning away with a stiffened shoulder.

"That forest pulls at everything that breathes. Without experience, you'll cross its threshold before you even realize you've moved. These guards have been trained to fight it. Let them do the scouting. Your task is the barricades."

"Chief Gerel is on lead, by orders of the High Regent," Arben hissed. "I will do as the guards' Chief orders."

"It's my responsibility to keep you safe. You'll do as you're told."

Arben's dark eyes sliced to his uncle. "Great job you're doing," he snarled. "Unless Chief Gerel says otherwise, I don't have to follow your orders."

"You have no—"

"Why don't you focus on your duties and stop hovering? You're not my father!"

His nephew's words gutted him, deeper than any spear. Inara's gallop eased with his slowing breath.

Gerel guided his mount alongside Inara, his firm hand finding Yoen's shoulder. "Don't let him get to you," he said, his voice deep and resonant.

Yoen managed a nod. "Chief."

"We all have weathered a span of trying days. He's adjusting the best way he can," the Chief Guard continued, his grip adjusting around the saddle horn. "To be honest, with the wall of smoke, Garam, and that bloody wyvern, what must be tearing at him most is the incident in the caves."

Wide-eyed, he stared at Gerel, words tangling in his throat.

The Chief Guard's voice lowered, steady and measured. "The Äktastary invaders got him and his sister. And he couldn't do anything about it. It must be eating at him." He paused, considering. "I'm quite surprised the boy lacks combat skills, especially with you as his uncle."

Yoen's gaze drifted to his nephew's rigid spine. A wave of nostalgia washed over him. Arben wasn't a little boy anymore, the one who used to run to him during their night walks with Nim, eager to be hoisted onto his shoulders and gaze at the stars. No, that little boy was gone. His nephew's shoulders had broadened, and his frame had grown taller. So much time had passed. But how or when, he couldn't begin to understand. When he wore his old Chief Guard's crimson uniform, that little boy used to gaze at him as if he were a mighty wyvern. Not even Ragas could outshine him.

The day Nim and his sister crossed into the forests, Yoen had cradled the twins in his arms so tightly, he didn't know how he could ever let go. That same day, he wore his guard uniform for the last time and swore to the forests and the skies to protect the only family he had left. But there Arben was, drawing closer to the woods that had claimed his mother, and the weight in Yoen's chest grew with every inch. "I wanted a different life for them. I thought I could keep them safe, away from the pain Ka'zan brings," he finally said with a shuddering breath.

"I understand why you relinquished your position as Chief Guard, even against the Regent's wishes. We would all do anything to ensure our children have a better life than us. But these lands—" Gerel paused, his eyes tracing the wall of smoke ahead as if weighing his words. "They require more than hope and perseverance. To shield them and ourselves from Ka'zan's blight, we must learn to wield its shadows. It's a dance of survival. We strive not just to live but to endure, and avoid being consumed by it."

Gerel's mount shouldered closer. "You once had a fire that was hard to tame. I still remember the days the very air around you crackled with energy—as if Ragas himself had ignited your heart. It's no wonder the High Regent wanted you by his side. I believe that's who your boy needs—who we all need, if I may be so bold."

Yoen sighed. "The man you speak of lived a different life, in a time long past." The wind carried ash across the scarred fields where he and Nim once raced their horses through golden wheat. Now they lay desolate. In a matter of days, the land that had watched him grow had transformed beyond recognition. He knew the feeling, one that haunted him since he had lost his wife. He stood a stranger in his own home, in his own mind.

"No, old friend. That fire still burns." Gerel's fingers dug into Yoen's shoulder and their gazes met. "I see its embers in your boy as well. He's shown potential in the few days he's been training with Sumani. Give him time."

With a sharp nod, Gerel's mount spurred toward the weathered line of barricades. The old fences jutted from the earth like broken teeth, standing guard before the curtain of smoke. "Set the new barriers along the major gaps. Strengthen any weak points," Gerel ordered, gesturing to the workers.

Yoen's hands tugged on Inara's reins, and she veered toward a cluster of guards and miners. Across the field, Arben dismounted, hauling a wooden trunk from the supply wagon, his muscles straining beneath his new black archer's tunic. Down the line, Gerel and his guards scrutinized the towering smoke, arms extended.

He stole one last glance at his nephew, remembering when the boy barely reached his waist. With a reluctant tug on the reins, Inara wheeled in the opposite direction.

"Wait, Chief. I'll join you." A guard with a cleaved eyebrow waved.

"No need, I won't take long. Just keep an eye on him." Yoen gestured toward Arben before spurring Inara forward, her hooves kicking up dust.

A line of thorn barricades stretched before him, their spikes jutting toward the sky and toward the distant woods like rows of splintered bones. Dread pooled in his gut at the pathetic excuse for a defense. Zuwena could shred them like parchment. The forest's curse kept the Uláak at bay. For now. If they were to breach the spell—his breath hitched—the city would be lost. The High Regent's power alone wouldn't be enough. Elva's raw talent meant nothing against centuries of hunting instinct, despite of her temporary victory over Garam. The Äktastary would shatter beneath the monsters' onslaught.

Sweat traced a path down his neck. Every muscle tensed against the foreboding curtain of smoke devouring the forest. His fingers tightened then loosened against his mount's reins. His breath grew shallow and uneven. The leather saddle creaked when he dismounted. Even the scorching fires of Garam seemed more welcoming than the massive mantle. The ashen haze stretched endlessly upward, engulfing the mountains and sky in its suffocating embrace. "Great Ragas, save us!"

He inched forward. And he wondered how close to the forest his wife had ventured before its pull became unbearable. He had pleaded with her. Begged her to stay away from those damned woods, to let more experienced guards inspect the borders instead. He had been chained to the Regent as his personal Chief Guard. He should've been with her. Duty failed them both, but she paid the highest toll. The forest claimed her.

The Elders' warnings echoed in his thoughts—tales of the Tanama's curse and its unbearable pull. It ensnared the living, then the Uláak finished the job.

A familiar ache stirred in his heart, one that had lingered since he received the news that Nim had followed his sister into the forest. He scouted the edge of the woods many times, calling her name, wishing the forest would reel him in. When the beckoning never came, he considered walking in willingly. But even after long hours of toying with the idea, the thought of abandoning the twins kept his feet frozen on the ground.

"I miss you." The words escaped before he could catch them.

His feet carried him forward of their own accord, drawn not by the forest's pull but by an overwhelming tide of longing and helplessness. One step closer, then another, until he was inches from the mantle of smoke. The forest was his doom, and at the same time the balm for the gaping wound that would never heal. With ragged breaths, his hand shot to the pit of his stomach, a feeble attempt to anchor himself.

A sharp tug at his hood jerked him backward as warm breath huffed against his ear. Inara's teeth had gripped his cowl. The walnut mare's hooves stamped the earth, her dark eyes fixed on his face while she nudged him with her muzzle.

"Fire-beetle." He pressed his forehead against hers, breathing in the familiar scent of hay and leather that always clung to her coat. One hand traced the soft curve of her neck, grounding himself in the steady rhythm of her heartbeat, and slowly, the frantic pulse in his veins began to ease.

"Thank you, my dearest friend." His fingers found the spot behind her ears that his wife always scratched. Inara's head dipped slightly, ears flicking back. She nuzzled into his hand, muscles softening under his touch.

When he first noticed Nim, she rode bareback through the fields on Inara, swift as the wind and utterly free. He had wonder how someone found so much joy in Ka'zan, in a land that only took, even from those who had nothing to give. But she always carried a smile as bright as a full moon on a summer night. He would surrender himself to the Uláak if it meant watching her ride again. "I know you miss her too," he sighed into Inara's neck. His fingers lingered on her mane, the gentle pull of her warmth keeping him still. Moving felt like a betrayal, yet if he didn't, he feared not even the veil of smoke would be enough to stop him. "We should head back." His feet dragged beside his mare, resisting the urge to glance at the ominous haze again.

At a slow and heavy pace, Yoen made his way back to where miners and guards were still bolstering the defenses, noticing Chief Gerel and his patrol had not returned. In the distance, pickaxes clinked against the thorn barricades where workers shored up the barriers. The guard with the cleaved eyebrow staggered near one of the structures closer to the forest's edge. Before he knew it, his wheelbarrow clattered against the stone, then rolled toward the wall of smoke.

"Let it roll, don't chase it." Yoen's warning cut through the air.

The guard lurched forward, colliding with the wheelbarrow. Tools scattered across the ground, one sliding dangerously close to the dead woods' border, the metal surface grazing the hazy veil.

"Don't get any closer," he bellowed, his voice cracking with urgency. The guard scrambled to collect the scattered tools. "Step away. Get back!"

The guard glanced up. "It's all right, I got everything."

"Guard! Move back, that's an order," he shouted again.

The young man nodded, sweat glistening on his brow. But when his fingers tightened around the wheelbarrow's handles, his head jerked to the side, drawn by something within the forest. Clicking sounds reverberated through the woods behind the cloak of smoke, commanding the attention of every person. Some retreated, others stood transfixed, their eyes glazing over. The disturbing clatter wove an unsettling symphony around them.

"Listen to my voice! Move away!" Yoen yelled, rushing forward, keeping a careful distance from the edge of the woods.

The guard's head shook, as if clearing cobwebs from his mind. His fingers gripped the wheelbarrow again, but his boot slipped on the uneven ground, and he pitched forward, losing his balance. One foot landed inside the dead woods behind the murky threshold. His body went rigid at the predatory growls that rumbled through the space, making the very ground beneath them vibrate.

"Move!"

Before the guard could respond, metal shrieked. His terrified scream split the air as invisible forces dragged him deeper into the shadows. Within moments, half his body was already swallowed by the Tanama, while the other half of him thrashed, his fingers desperately clawing at the unyielding ground. "Something's got me!"

Arben launched himself forward, his hands locking around the guard's wrists. Both men skidded across the ground, drawn relentlessly toward the smoke wall.

"No!" Yoen's world collapsed, his nephew inching closer to the sounds of the Uláak. Only the guard's wrists remained visible through the smoke, Arben's knuckles tightening as he held on. Yoen wrenched a wyvern sword free from a motionless guard's sheath and charged forward.

In one swift motion, he swept the obsidian blade through the air, cleaving through the guard's joints—abandoning him to the Uláak. Then his fingers dug into Arben's tunic, jerking him backward. The guard's screams echoed through the smoke before cutting off in a sickening choke. As abruptly as it began, the cries were snuffed out, plunging them into an oppressive silence.

Arben's chest heaved. "Why?" He stared horrified at the severed wrists in his hands, then flung them aside with a yelp. "Why did you do that? I—I had him! I had him." His brown eyes blazed into Yoen's. "I had him!" He shoved a bloody finger at his uncle's chest before lunging toward the smoke.

But Yoen gripped Arben's tunic firmly, stopping him from taking another step. "The Uláak do not yield," he hissed.

Growls rippled behind the wall of smoke, sending horses into a panicked dance. He thrust Arben behind him, blood-slicked sword raised, waiting for the creatures to emerge, but they remained bound to the forest and behind the haze. Then, from the corner of his eye, he caught Sumani drifting toward the wall, her dark hair flowing behind her like silk in water.

"Sumani!" Arben cried.

He shoved him far from the wall. "Stay!" Yoen barked.

He edged toward Sumani, muscles coiled tight. His calls disappeared beneath a wave of growls. A miner stepped forward, arm extended, but Yoen waved him back, eyes fixed on the rope at the man's waist.

The miner's hands worked quickly, fashioning a wide loop.

"Do not miss," he ordered.

The rope sailed through the air, settling around Sumani's torso. One sharp pull snapped her from her trance. Instantly, the archer shook her head, clearing an invisible fog, then her eyes caught his.

"Sumani! Walk away," Yoen said. She gave a weary nod, her breath coming in ragged gasps.

Behind him, Gerel's voice thundered across the field, calling for retreat. More miners and guards stood mesmerized by the wall. One miner hovered inches from the smoke. At Gerel's call, she turned, but her hand unintentionally brushed the veil.

"Move back," Gerel shouted.

From inside the forests, metal rattled against stone once more. Something seized the miner's wrist, and the smoke swallowed her whole, her screams drowned out by the wave of growls.

A resonant trumpet cry pierced the chaos. Gerel stood, wielding his spiraled wind horn, forged from agni stones. Its martial notes overpowered the escalating growls. Those caught in the enchantment snapped from their daze and hastily withdrew.

"Retreat!" The Chief Guard's voice bellowed. "Back to Drekavog! Retreat!"

Yoen's fingers latched onto Arben's arm, and steered him toward his horse. "Don't let him out of your sight," he ordered Sumani. Miners and guards fled, some doubling up on mounts, abandoning their tools. He returned the borrowed sword, urging its owner to ride.

"Chief Yoen," Gerel called out. "You too! Ride."

He nodded sharply. Inara huddled against him, her nervous huffs matching his racing heart. His eyes scanned for stragglers, but something stirring behind the mantle of smoke caught his eye. A figure with a horned mask towered like a tree, its hollowed eyes a bottomless abyss locked on him. It tilted its head—slow, mechanical, blood-curdling. The void in its sockets never wavered, turning his veins to ice. "Uláak," he gasped.

The creature inched closer to the edge.

Yoen's feet tangled beneath him, sending him sprawling. Inara's frantic neighs filled his ears. Instinct made his fingers fumble for his waist knife, but the weapon slipped from his grasp. His hands frantically scraped the earth, searching for it. When he looked up, the creature had vanished, leaving only the dense wall of smoke. His legs still shook when he mounted Inara. They stood alone against the soaring wall of haze, fighting the urge to flee.

The screams of the two latest victims clawed through his mind, forcing him to confront the brutal truth. What he had just witnessed—the vicious butchery—was exactly what Nim and his sister had endured. Bile rose in his stomach. A corrosive rage scalded his veins and charred his reason. The knowledge that his dear wife and sister had suffered such horrific ends ignited something fierce and unyielding.

His jaw clenched until his teeth threatened to crack, nails gouging bloody crescents into his palms. He glared at the forest that had nearly claimed his nephew. Now he knew, with sickening clarity, exactly how the women he loved had spent their final moments—the terror they must have felt, the pain they couldn't escape. The creatures had fed again, and he craved their extinction. He would not tame the wrath raising in his chest. He sought to weaponize it.

"Ragas be damned. I will purge this land from your chains and shadows. I swear it. Even if it's the last thing I do."

CHAPTER 19

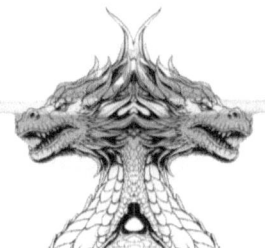

KA'ZAN

YOEN

CROSSING THROUGH DREKAVOG'S GATE, Yoen's fingers dug into his palms. Stone carvings of Regents and wyverns snaked up curved balconies, spiraling above the fortress' hollow heart. He strode through the fortress' indoor atrium, shouldering past greetings and waving hands as the images of the recent incident near the Tanama burned behind his eyes.

His hand found his dagger's hilt, his grip tightening until his veins stood out like ropes. Arben had been so close, too close to being dragged into the dead woods. The guard with the cleaved eyebrow would forever haunt him. But he had to do it—there was no other way. The guard had been lost the moment the Uláak seized him.

The barricades they worked on were strategically placed, positioned at a safe distance from the entrancing whispers of the haunting forests. During his time in the guard force, Yoen had trained many of those troops to resist the pull. But this time, it had been all too easy for the forest to draw them in. Blood roared in his ears, drowning out the rustle of the atrium's trees and the hums of activity throughout the fortress.

He stopped at the High Regent's chamber, forcing air into his lungs until the pounding in his chest slowed.

The atlas chamber door groaned open. Instead of Zohar, three figures stood inside the chamber, their shadows stretching across the table. The High Council, Lord Vardan, and Chief Gerel turned to face him.

"Lord Vardan. High Councilor," he said with a bow.

You're not focusing. A muffled yet resonant voice filtered through the sliding stone wall of the High Regent's atrium.

Vardan made his way past the floor carving depicting the atlas of the entire region. With a fluid wave, he beckoned Yoen to the table. "My father has been training the new Äktastary since dawn." His green eyes lingered on the smooth sliding walls before finding Yoen again. "Our Chief Guard brought the troubling news about the dead forests."

Sweat glistened on Chief Gerel's forehead. The deep lines between his brows betrayed him, despite his square shoulders. "Chief," he acknowledged Yoen with a sharp nod.

"We were just informed the magnetic pull of the Tanama's forest has strengthened," Councilor Hura said. Her chair scraped against stone when she rose and approached the floor atlas. "How many were lost?"

"I lost five of my wardens during our recon. When I managed to gather my thoughts and returned, we lost two more—a young miner and guard," Gerel replied, his hands twisting behind his back.

Realization dawned on Yoen, carving a hollow ache in his chest. Gerel had returned alone from surveying the mantle of smoke. He crossed to his fellow Chief, resting a heavy hand on his shoulders, the gesture speaking volumes his voice could not.

"That makes thirty-six," Hura said, stepping back to the table. The clay teapot rattled as she lifted it, steam curling from the spout in misty plumes. "That's the most we've ever lost in just days. Are you certain the pull is stronger, and not expanding?"

Ice took root in Yoen's veins at the thought of the Tanama's curse spreading to Ka'zan.

Gerel cleared his throat before speaking, his voice carrying the roughness of gravel. "I wish I had answers but all we gathered is that the smoke persists, and we still don't know the cause. For now, it'd be best if our people stay inside Drekavog. This fortress stands as our safest space. No one should wander into the farmlands."

"We do need options," Yoen interrupted, while Hura took delicate sips from her cup. "Garam may be subdued for now, but the mount grows restless beneath us. When it erupts—and it will—this fortress won't stand a chance against it." His gaze drifted to the sealed wall of Zohar's atrium, where the Regent trained the Äktas Enchanter. "Has Elva shown any improvement?"

"My father has spent every waking moment teaching the Äktastary the trait of stone-wielding," Vardan replied, settling into his chair with casual grace, arms crossed over his chest. "But his efforts are futile. The girl needs more than just days." He stretched his legs before him, crossing his ankles. "I still don't see the appeal. The Elders contended that in the past, the ability to wield all three stones could only be granted by the breath of a mighty wyvern. How can an Äktastary hone such power and be so useless? What an utter waste."

Yoen attended those same Elder conclave meetings, and spent countless hours scouring texts for any mention of the origins of the Tristone Enchanters. All he found were fragments about the Emberhearts, from an age when wyverns ruled the skies. The gift of stone-wielding typically bound itself to one's native city. The Ikarites stood apart—their women alone wielded stones, but some transformed into living gems as Sages. Yet Elva claimed no connection to any other city or any Enchanter. With such an ancient and rare ability, she remained the mystery he couldn't decipher.

"The Chief Miner is right," Gerel remarked, pressing his palms against the table. "We need options. If young Elva can't seal the gate on the volcano, why can't the High Regent close it himself?"

"The volcano's unrest is no natural occurrence," Hura replied. Her footsteps traced patterns across the chamber. A metal pin secured her dark hair, gleaming like a captured star. "Zuwena's magic has kindled Garam to its very core. It will continue stirring until a force comparable to the wyvern's power can seal the White Stone Gate and put it back to rest. The only agni gem His Regency can wield with such power is his scepter. But the heirloom fades even more as we speak. The Tristone Enchanter stands as the only solution."

The High Councilor's fingers interlaced behind her back. "Even with his scepter, considering the circumstances—including the Äktastary invasion—it wouldn't be wise for the Regent to wander outside this fortress. He's our only Enchanter," she retorted, her gaze suddenly cutting across the room like an arrow to pierce Vardan. "We can't afford to lose him. We don't know where the Äktastary's loyalties lie, and I care not if their Tristone Enchanter holds an ancient power beyond our understanding. Our city needs its Regent."

She moved toward Gerel, her posture as rigid as tempered steel, the fabric of her robes barely stirring with her approach. "The Äktastary went through a great ordeal to breach our city. If their leaders were willing to send convoys to their death, we shouldn't hesitate to put them to work for our own sake." Her hands came together in front of her, fingers intertwining with a deliberate precision. "The prisoners have yet to disclose their true intentions. Their Commander sent a powerful Enchanter here, and we still don't know why." As she spoke, her hand shot out pointing at Zohar's sealed atrium. "Now our Regent, our only Enchanter is training that girl. We're deliberately creating a powerful and very dangerous weapon, and we don't know if she'll turn against us. If it were up to me, I'd have her seal the gate, then set her free into the dead forest with those creatures. Let her walk back to her city of brutes."

Yoen's fingers drummed restlessly against his leg, sweat beading at his temples despite the cool air of the chamber. "I understand the frustration, High Councilor. But what happens if Elva can't close the gate?" He pulled out a chair, and settled down with his elbows pressed into the polished surface. "I have scanned every possible scroll in our public collections. But I haven't found anything that could help us. We have to figure out a way to help Elva hone her skill. We also haven't discussed what's causing the smoke around the Tanama, and what to do if and when Zuwena decides to return," he insisted, his leg bouncing beneath the table. "If I could gain access to the Sacred Scrolls inside the Arcanum, perhaps I could help you in finding answers."

A muscle twitched in Hura's jaw. She inhaled sharply, nostrils flaring, then squared her shoulders with a rustle of white silk. "The Sacred Scrolls are revered for a reason. They are to be handled solely by the High Regent and his directive council. Need I remind you—you declined that post and privilege when you chose to lead the miners." She drew in another measured breath, her fingers smoothing nonexistent wrinkles from her garment. "You must trust that His High Regency and his appointed councils are doing all we can to safeguard our people."

With the last word, she turned her back on Yoen. Her heels clicked in measured steps until she reached the chamber's far wall. She glared back at Vardan, who rose from his seat without a word. "For the last time, Chief Miner, know your place," she added before the stone wall groaned open.

As it parted, it revealed an atrium bathed in the warm glow of torchlight, mixed with moonlight seeping through the glass ceiling. Through the opening, Elva stood motionless on a wooden platform resting in the middle of the pond, her gaze locked on stones pulsing with a life of their own.

Gerel's firm hand found his shoulder. "The Councilor will come around, Chief. I appreciate your insistence. We could use the help. I'll talk to her," he said, following Hura and Vardan through the opening.

The silence pressed in around him. He slumped forward, elbows hitting the table as his fingers tangled in his hair until his scalp burned. The incident at the edge of the forests shook him to his core. The Uláak had never been so close to the borders. He couldn't wait for things to escalate. No, he *wouldn't* wait. If Elva proved to be the key to protecting his people, he would use her. Nothing would stand on his way. With eyes blazing with fierce determination, he stormed from the chamber.

The iron gates of the barracks loomed before Yoen, rust-flecked metal glinting under torchlight. His muscles tightened around his neck in his struggle to steady his hammering pulse. "Let me through. I've come to talk to the Äktastary prisoners," he demanded.

"We have strict orders not to allow anyone in," one of the two guards replied.

Yoen's eyes narrowed to slits. "I've been sent by High Regent Zohar. It won't do you well to question his orders. Open the gate."

The guard with eyes like the skies swallowed before speaking. "Chief, we need orders from the High Councilor to let you in."

"The High Councilor? High Regent Zohar sent me himself," he lied. "Do you truly believe there's an authority higher than His High Regency?"

The guards shared a brief, tense glance, their scale armor catching the light.

"Would you rather I bring him here and have you both explain to him why you refused to follow his orders?" His eyebrows arched. "Treason would be the first charge. Allow me entry."

With reluctant sighs, they stepped aside. But when they moved to follow him to the cells, Yoen's hand shot up. "Hold there! Hand me the diamond key," he demanded.

The guard with blue eyes swallowed hard, while the other handed him the key with hesitant hands. The small gemstone sparkled against the radiance emanating from the edges of the walls.

His fingers closed around the key before he gestured to the gate. "I need to be alone. Wait at the top of the walkway—do not eavesdrop."

With a piercing gaze, he stalked toward the cell. The diamond key slid into the hidden crevice with a soft click, and the stone door scraped open. Darkness spilled out, broken only by a sliver of moonlight streaming through a high window. A tall figure stood rigid in the shadows, eyes glinting with defiance.

"Come into the light." Yoen's words echoed off the bare walls.

The prisoner's feet dragged with each step forward. His once warm-amber skin now a sickly pale mask, moonlight painting dark hollows beneath his eyes.

"I know you've been questioned several times, young man. This will be your last." Shadows shifted across the prisoner's taut shoulders. "It's Oran, correct?"

Oran's jaw clenched when he met Yoen's gaze, tension visible despite his short beard.

"I suggested the High Regent use his powers to heal you and your friend next door. Consider it a kindness. One that won't be granted again."

A bitter laugh scraped from Oran's throat. "Kindness? After you tortured us?"

Yoen crossed his arms, measuring each word. "One would think an Äktastary knows a thing or two about torture. Your people are notorious for it."

"And Ka'zan isn't?" Oran's words snapped like a whip.

"You're the first ones to have experienced it in many years. Though I suspect you've seen worse. Your own leader's handiwork, perhaps? What do they call themselves?" His steps marked a slow circle around the Äktastary. "The Hand? One council member for each Trade." He halted before Oran, one eyebrow raised. "You should be no stranger to The Hand's methods. A fist would be more fitting, wouldn't you agree?"

Oran's spine stiffened. "What do you take me for? I won't speak ill about my people."

A mocking smile played across Yoen's mouth. "Ah yes, you have all proven to be true stubborn Äktastary. But I thought you cared about that girl, Elva. Or am I mistaken?"

The name struck like a blade. Oran's fingers curled into fists, so tight that tendons stood out like cords beneath his skin.

Yoen prowled forward. "Of course you do. I saw it myself. You cared for her in the caves when she lay unconscious. I was there. It had escaped me, but I remembered. You put the bloodstone box inside her boot. Yet, you keep claiming you didn't know she was an Enchanter."

"I didn't!" The words exploded from Oran's chest.

"You must've suspected something. Are you not friends? I bet you even know who left those marks on her back."

Something flickered in Oran's dark eyes as they met his. His rigid posture wavered for the first time.

"You don't know about her scars?" he asked. Yoen's gaze dropped to Oran's hands—fingers curling into fists again, veins running like angry rivers beneath his warm-amber skin. "Our Chief Healer estimates at least ten gruesome lashes. What do you think would happen to her if she were to return? A Tristone Enchanter in Äktas! Do you think the wildling would be celebrated?"

"Don't call her that," Oran snapped. "How do I know you or your Regent didn't leave those marks on her?"

Yoen's laugh snickered across the walls. "What's your gut telling you? You know it wasn't us. The wounds must've pained her for weeks, left untreated. The scars run deep."

Oran's chest rose and fell in quick, shallow bursts.

"High Regent Zohar won't let her out of his sight," Yoen continued. "You should count your stars it isn't Magnar. You are right to think of Ka'zan's violent history. The late High Regent would sever his enemies' heads and put them on spikes along the shores of the Black Beach. As the tides rolled in, the heads covered in molten silver, would be swallowed by the sea. You might have seen a few of those silver heads when you crossed those treacherous waters. Yours would have been among them by now."

Moonlight followed Yoen's path deeper into the cell, drawing his gaze to the window's narrow slice of night sky. "I can assure you, she'll be safe here. Zohar doesn't employ the same methods his father did, at least not to the people he values. And Elva has become very valuable." His steps paced around Oran until they faced each other again. "Your friend is not progressing in her training and we're running out of time. So, I need you to listen carefully, because I will do whatever it takes to safeguard this city."

His eyes bored into Oran's. "I will bring you to her right now. I think you'll be able to assist her in harnessing whatever power lies within her, better than we can. If you fail, you'll be of no further use to us. And neither will she."

Oran's breathing became shallow. "How can I help her? I'm no Enchanter."

"You seem to know her, perhaps better than she knows herself. We need someone to get through to her. But if you fail..." Yoen's voice dropped to a hiss. "I will go to each of your friends and tear their heads from their shoulders. Then I'll place them by the shore of the beach you crawled out of. I will have your friend Elva watch as you experience the same fate." His heart raced, the sharp edges of the diamond key biting into his palm through a clenched fist. "And when the time is right. By any means necessary, I will personally deliver her into the clutches of your esteemed leader of the Hand, General Commander Buldar. Let him decide her fate. Lashes would be the least of her worries."

Sweat gleamed on Oran's temples, his dark eyes blazing beneath furrowed brows. His chest heaved against his shirt.

Yoen's voice cut through the tension. "Young man, embrace the rage swelling inside you, for it will be your strength. What lies ahead poses a peril that will surpass anything we've encountered. Everyone will witness and suffer its claws. You must've understood that truth when you boarded the metal whale. According to one of your colleagues, you were not officially recruited for this mission. My assumption is that you sneaked in, sacrificing the mission's purpose to shield her. You'd rather face death by her side than let her confront the darkness alone. The mission may not matter to you, but your commitment to her safety does. Help her bring out her Enchanter's powers. Keep her safe."

"Elva doesn't need someone to keep her safe." Oran's voice cracked like thin ice. He drew in a ragged breath before continuing. "She'll leap without a second thought even when she's terrified. She's decisive and impulsive when others falter because she is capable of measuring the stakes when others overlook them. I may not know how to shield her from harm. But..." His gaze dropped to the floor, tears threatening to spill. "No matter what, I will always stand by her." His feet carried him toward Yoen. "Take me to her."

CHAPTER 20

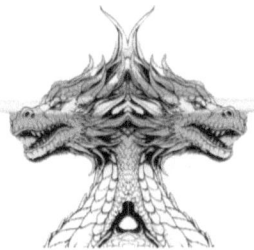

IKARI

ASANTE

S PRAWLED ON THE COLD floor of the outpost, Asante's fingernails scraped over a chipped patch of clay on the wall, each incessant stroke needling through the heavy silence. The miner's lantern flickered, casting thin shadows that faded before they reached her. Beyond the doorway, boots crunched against dirt, back and forth. Tarrak's silhouette stretched and shrank with each pass as his eyes kept sweeping the skies. Time dragged on endlessly since Zama had taken wing over the abandoned city, searching for any trace of surviving Ikarites.

They had settled in an outpost deep within its ruins. Roots had claimed the forgotten place, their gnarled tendrils tearing through the stone walls and floor, creeping into every crevice. The argument with Tarrak still rang in her ears—their heated exchange over not telling Zama about their plan to find the sunken temple. He'd relented eventually, allowing the Sage to help, but only if Asante kept her markings hidden and only if she guarded the wyvern's gem like a buried secret. Yet she'd caught the way her brother's stern words softened whenever he looked at the Avian Sage, how his harsh exterior faltered.

Her stomach growled, the hollow ache sparking a flood of memories, mostly of food. But one lingered. Echoes of her father's flat root-bread danced on her tongue—that perfect crunch giving way to earthiness, the nutty warmth that had once filled their small kitchen in Pālam's lower tiers. Behind closed eyes, she could still see the light streaming through crescent windows, painting patterns on stone walls, swelling like frozen waves. The High Tree's roots threaded through the entire cavern system like pillars. The memory came rushing back to her.

Shavings from a hearty root filled a clay vase. Once drained, her father scattered them onto a hot, circular stone, filling their cavern with an earthy fragrance. Her mother settled into a cushioned chair, Nora's tiny fist curled against her chest. Asante sipped a frothy egg and milk nectar that left a sweet-tangy film on her upper lip. Then her brother burst in, chest puffed out, grinning ear to ear. He clutched a burlap sack that bucked and writhed in his grip, revealing a small rabbit thrashing against its tight restraints.

"Well done, my raven boy!" Their father's voice boomed, his hand reaching for the cleaver.

Her heart sank as she watched the rabbit's head poking out of the sack, eyes wide with terror, tiny paws scrabbling against the burlap.

"Sante..." Her mother's warning filled the air. "Whatever you're thinking, don't."

But Asante was already moving. She lunged forward and snatched the burlap sack from Tarrak's hands, gently pushing the tiny creature safely inside.

The chase that followed transformed their home into a hurdle-strewn passage—over furniture, around her mother and Nora, and up the ramp to the second tier overlooking the main chamber.

Tarrak's yells echoed off the walls. "Sante! Give it back! It's the first one I've caught."

The bundle of fur pressed warm against her ribs. Her bare feet wove around furniture, while their father's laughter boomed through the chamber. In another swift move, she dove back over the open ledge to the lower level, narrowly missing her mother by inches. When she found her footing, her father waved at her, propping the entrance door open. "Run, little Rabbit!" he called, pressing warm bread into her hand and blocking Tarrak's pursuit. "I think the rabbit has earned its pardon, my sweet boy."

"Rabbit," Asante mumbled. In the cold outpost, tears pricked at her eyes. She clamped her teeth down on her tongue—the sharp metallic taste was just enough to hold back the rising swell in her heart. Shaking the memory off, she let her fingers find the jade embryo.

Sitting up, she held the egg in her lap, struck by how something so delicate could seem so vast. "You seem small and big all at once," she said. Then a rhythm emerged from within the gem, a steady pulse like the beat of frame drums during a solstice festival.

Her locs fell forward when she leaned over, getting so close her breath reached the gem. It radiated heat like a burning ember, pulsing against her palms. "Are you—" Her whisper caught as silver light threaded through the egg's veins, matching her own markings in perfect rhythm. Her heart skipped a beat. All this time, she had thought of the embryo as a bloodstone, not a cradle for the life of a creature.

"Are you alive?" The words barely left her lips before the embryo's veins blazed with silver light. She pressed her ear to the smooth surface, tapping it gently. "Are you really in there?" An answering knock sent her jerking backward, the pulse in her mind growing stronger. Light spilled from both her skin and the egg, painting the root-wrapped walls in shimmering patterns.

"What in Ragas' name is that?" Zama's voice echoed from the entrance. She and Tarrak stood frozen by the doorway, their shadows long in the egg's gentle light.

"It's nothing," Tarrak said, lunging for the embryo, only to yank his hand back with a hiss of pain.

Asante caught the egg before it could fall. "Careful with it!"

Her brother stared at his searing fingers, then at her. "That thing is burning hot! How are you holding it?"

She shook her head, wrapping the embryo in Samira's bark mantle before tucking it away. "It's just warm."

"Is someone going to tell me what in the bloody skies is that?" Zama demanded, jabbing a trembling finger at the bag.

Asante's eyes met her brother's. When he shook his head, her teeth found her nail, knowing she had promised not to say anything about the egg. But that came before she discovered it was alive. "It's an embryo, a wyvern's embryo," she blurted out, her voice shaking with excitement.

Tarrak threw his arms up in defeat. "I supposed we had a long argument for nothing." He let out an exasperated sigh and retreated to a shadowy corner of the outpost.

Zama's rapid breathing filled the space between them, her knuckles pressed into her waist. "And how is it that you have a wyvern's egg in your satchel?" Her golden eyes widened, catching the gleam on Asante's arm. "And you have markings! How do you have markings?" The Sage lunged forward, the space between them vanished, then her fingers wrapped around Asante's wrist with surprising strength.

The Sage's gaze traced the argent veins sprawling across her right hand like frozen lightning. Asante's free hand drifted to her satchel, fingers curling around its shape. "We thought the embryo was just a gem... but I think it's alive."

From his corner, her brother's voice carried with a long yawn. "Impossible. It would've hatched ages ago." His words trailed off as he let his head settle back against the wall. He crossed his arms and finally shut his eyes.

Her gaze darted between Zama's intense stare and her brother. "How long do they take to hatch?"

"How can you tell it's even alive?" Zama asked, her hand hovering over the satchel. "May I?"

Once withdrawn from the bag, the familiar weight of the gem settled into her palms. Its soft glow spread dancing shadows across Zama's face while she leaned closer, studying the egg's surface. "Listen," Asante said, and her knuckles tapped the surface three times. The silence stretched taut until three answering knocks rippled through the air. "Did you hear that?" Her eyes brightened with anticipation, searching Zama's amber eyes for recognition.

"I don't hear anything," the Sage replied, her gaze narrowing into suspicious slits.

"How can you not hear the tapping? It tapped back. Three times!" she protested.

The Sage's hand wavered above the gem's surface. "That thing is scorching hot, how are you holding it?"

Asante's fingers danced along the embryo's glowing veins, her own silver markings pulsing in harmony with its light. "It just feels warm to me."

Zama's stance shifted. "When did you get your markings?"

"Same day of the smoke. But I still don't know what they do."

"And how did you get them?"

Asante bit her lip, turning to her brother, who stared at both of them with intensity. A plea shone in her eyes, recalling her promise not to speak of the gem or her markings. He lay curled in his corner, arms locked across his chest like armor. His sigh deflated his entire frame before he turned his face to the wall.

"I don't know exactly," Asante finally said, lifting her arm—the silver veins catching the light. "The gem was glowing. I was afraid Zuwena would see it. When I went to cover it, it felt like I was being engulfed in flames. It was excruciating."

"That's all?" Zama's fingers combed through her braids, stripping away a golden feather.

She replied with a nod, and the egg disappeared into the satchel with a soft rustle.

"And how did you get the egg?"

"It was... given to me." Each word fell carefully measured from Asante's lips.

"Who, then? Who gave it to you?"

She hesitated. The leather strap of her bag creaked under her grip when she caught her brother's burning stare.

"You truly don't know?" Tarrak interjected, surging up from his corner, tension radiating from every muscle of his body. "Your precious Priestess gave it to her," he snarled. "You're going to tell me that you, as a Sage, didn't know the High Tree concealed a damned wyvern's egg?"

"The High Tree?"

"After you left, Samira dismissed the Enchanters." Asante's words tumbled out, recounting the events at Pālam's summit. "It had been inside the High Tree for generations. Samira asked me not to let Zuwena get it. The jade has been keeping the magic in Pālam alive somehow."

Zama's arms dropped to her sides. Her eyes swept the ground before snapping back to Asante's face, storm clouds gathering behind them. "Is that what she inquired about while you were under my wing? The reason for the mind-weaving?"

Asante's fingers found one of her locs' golden beads, rolling it anxiously between her fingers.

Before she could respond, Zama pressed on. "When Zuwena fled Ka'zan, she came straight to Ikari. Why not go to Äktas or Ka'zan?"

"Don't you get it?" Tarrak interrupted again. "It's her embryo. Zuwena's embryo."

The color drained from the Sage's face. "We have to get out of here—now!"

"And where do you suggest we go?" Tarrak's arms sliced through the air. "We're here to find the sunken temple."

"We need to find a safer place than a crumbling outpost. And the sunken temple might be a myth," Zama stammered. "If you had shared your plans with me, I would've told you from the start."

"It can't be a myth—we need answers. My sister needs to figure out her markings..." Tarrak retorted, his shoulders rising in frustration. "We need a way out of this mess. There's no going back to Pālam while the High Sage is there or the shield is up. We definitely won't survive the forests, and on top of that, the bloody lightning fiend will be on our backs for that damned gem."

A heavy sigh escaped Zama before she turned to Asante. "You say the egg is alive, as in it's a real wyvern awaiting hatching?"

"Oh, come on!" Tarrak scoffed. "That's impossible. It's a gem in the shape of an egg. An ignited gem, yes, but it's just a stone."

"Yes, I heard its heartbeat," Asante assured, ignoring her brother's protests.

Zama's fingers dug into Asante's shoulders as she leaned in, narrowing the space between them. "Are you sure? I need you to be certain of this because, if it is true—if there's a creature inside that shell, then..." Her eyes flickered as she swallowed.

"Then what?" Tarrak asked.

"Then our lives are forfeit. Not just ours, but everyone's," Zama said, her chest rising with a deep breath before she continued. "The reason I think the sunken temple could be a myth, is because the scrolls are inside Pālam. Perhaps the temple does exist, but Samira must've ensured all the scrolls were taken into our caves. If we want to figure out Asante's markings, or even attempt to understand what's causing the smoke, we'll have to breach the ruby shield."

Her boots traced restless patterns across the outpost, her gaze fixed on some distant point. "There are mountains of scrolls within the walls of the Great Hall, right behind the carvings of Samira holding the old Ka'zanty Regent's head. The Priestess only allows the five Sages in there. It's an entire chamber filled with our history. There are parchments on all three cities, the Tanama, and even lands far from ours where wyverns took refuge before we destroyed them all."

"You knew about the scrolls!" Tarrak's roar sent both women recoiling. "After all this time, you never mentioned them, not a single word. You knew I was looking for answers for my father, for the city. How could you not tell me after everything?"

Asante's gaze bounced between her brother and the Avian Sage. His teeth ground together, his muscles coiled like a snare, ready to spring. The air crackled with an unspoken past, thick with secrets and shared pain she'd never known existed.

"We are sworn to secrecy by the Priestess," Zama's words cut through the tension. "Her mind-weaving is overpowering. Samira knows my mind better than I know myself. That's probably why she sent me away. She knows where I place my loyalty—that I would've fought against the carnage in the Great Hall." Her gaze lingered on Tarrak. "She probably thought I wouldn't survive flying over the cities, let alone the dead forests. But that's not where we should focus right now."

Her attention snapped back to Asante, her shoulders straightening as she swiped away the shimmer in her eyes. "If Zuwena gets her claws on her offspring, it would mean total destruction. If the story is true, that is no ordinary egg. The scrolls speak of an unfathomable bond between Zuwena and her mate."

"Who?" Asante blurted. "Who was Zuwena's mate?"

"The Great Horned Ragas," Zama's words fell like stones into still water.

Ice flooded Asante's veins, turning her blood to frost.

"That means, if it is true, Sante," Zama placed a hand on her shoulder, "inside your satchel lies the greatest wyvern to have been born, with power like no other. If it connects with its mother, Pālam would be no more. There would be nowhere to hide. I think that's what drove Samira to build that shield."

Tarrak lunged forward, jabbing a finger at the satchel. "Then we destroy the bloody egg."

"No!" Asante cried out, tumbling backward, clutching the bag tightly against her chest.

"One cannot simply destroy an ignited gem, let alone a wyvern's egg. It would take a formidable amount of power," Zama interrupted, kneading the tension from her shoulders.

"Well, good thing there are two Sages in this room right now. Surely you can combine your powers to destroy it?" Tarrak retorted.

"There's only one Sage in this outpost. Besides, it would take a force greater than a Sage to destroy a wyvern's embryo," Zama insisted.

Tarrak's shadow loomed larger as he advanced. "You won't even try? Give me that bag, Sante. I was right from the start. That thing must be destroyed."

She scrambled behind Zama, pulse thundering in her ears. "No! I won't let you."

"I see. You're taking her side?" Tarrak crossed his arms, the muscles in his jaw working with tension.

"I'm on the side of not murdering innocent creatures."

"Innocent?" A bitter laugh escaped him as he jabbed a finger toward the door. "Maybe you should take another stroll around the outer city. Go and inhale all the smoke mixed with burned flesh."

"Firemoon!" Zama interjected, her voice soft, her gaze fixed on Tarrak.

"Don't call me that!" he shouted.

"This isn't her fault!" Zama snapped. "Besides, the embryo is nearly indestructible."

"I don't care, but we're getting rid of it."

While Tarrak's and Zama's voices crashed like waves against rock, Asante edged toward the door. The instant her foot crossed the threshold, she tore into the night, the cold air biting her cheeks as she ran. Her brother's shouts chased after her. A quick glance over her shoulder revealed his tall figure, the distance between them shrinking with each of his long strides.

The root came out of nowhere. Her foot caught, and the world spun. She hit the ground hard, air rushing from her lungs as her satchel spilled open. The jade embryo rolled out across the grass, coming to rest against a small branch with a soft thud.

She reached for it, just as it began to pulse. Light erupted between her fingers, painting the ground in shifting patterns of emerald and silver. Her free arm shielded her eyes as a single beam shot skyward, slicing the night like an arrow.

The roar that followed shook her to her bones. It reverberated through the ground, through her chest, through the very air she breathed. Then came the screeching—a high, piercing cry that needled through her ears. And from the embryo, something else rose—a deeper vibration, not heard but felt, a call resonating beyond sound, reaching into the very core of her being.

Her shoulders tightened as she shoved the embryo back into her bag, its glow fading to a dim flicker. When she turned, Tarrak and Zama stood frozen, their faces turned skyward.

"We can't stay here," Zama said in short gasps.

Asante had barely taken a step forward when her brother slammed into her. White and sapphire flames carved through the night, searing the air where she'd stood an instant before. The blaze cast harsh shadows across the abandoned city, separating them from Zama with a pulsing wall of fire. Above them, Zuwena's massive form soared through the sky, swallowing the stars in her wake. Her eyes blazed with fury, pale-yellow horns catching the moonlight like ancient spears. Another stream of blue flames erupted from her maw, this time aimed at Zama.

Tarrak tightened his grip on her arm, both of them watching the Avian Sage flee and draw Zuwena's attention away from them.

"We have to help her!" Asante's voice clashed with the wyvern's roars. "Zuwena thinks she's the one with the embryo."

Tarrak's breath hitched. He took one step backward even as his eyes remained locked on Zama's retreating form. "Firemoon," he whispered, but his grip on her never loosened.

Tears burned hot trails down her cheeks, watching the battle unfold across her brother's face. His decision to shield her etched itself in every taut muscle of his body. He yanked her away from the flames, their feet scrambling for grip on the uneven ground. Through the fire and smoke, she spotted Zuwena circling the Bloodstone mine like a storm gathering strength before the strike.

Her mind filled with the echoes of missed chances, times when she had faltered, hesitated, and failed. She should've been braver, stronger. If she had been, maybe her brother wouldn't be out there, exposed beyond the crimson shield. She should've done more to protect her mother, her sister, and Lux. Her dear friend, who had once yearned for the markings she now bore. They had all suffered because of her weakness.

A large kapok tree loomed before them, its roots offering shelter from Zuwena's gaze. "Stay low, Rabbit," Tarrak urged, gripping the bark and scanning the sky. "We can't go back to the outpost. Zuwena saw us there. We'll just wait for..." His fists clenched, knuckles pressing against his teeth as if fighting to hold back the words.

"You're in love with her," Asante said. Her heart shattered. The conflict played out on her brother's face, torn between protecting her and being unable to reach Zama. The weight of the choice threatened to break him. He crumpled beside her, his shoulders heaving while he pressed his palms to his eyes.

The embryo's warmth throbbed against her side, a steady pulse echoing her own heartbeat. Her older brother had always shielded her. Now, his need to protect her would be his death sentence. He wanted to destroy the egg, while she needed it. And that alone put him in danger. The path she had been carving in her mind would lead her straight to Zuwena, and perhaps through a more sinister route she couldn't yet dare to consider.

It filled her with dread, though a fierce need for justice warred with her instinct for safety. Outside the ruby shield, no place in Ikari offered true refuge. She was sure Samira was gathering her strength behind it, perhaps at the expense of many more lives. Asante couldn't keep hiding, and she knew Tarrak would only suffer the consequences if they stayed together.

Desperation clawed at her insides. Yet something more ravenous grew, something that knew no mercy. She wanted vengeance, and Zuwena represented just that. The wyvern mother had become her only chance—her means of salvation, the force that could bring the High Priestess down. With Samira gone, maybe the wyvern would relent in her destruction, the smoke would clear, and Tarrak would finally be safe.

With trembling fingers, she gripped her bag and stepped in front of him. Before he could react, she swung the satchel in a wide arc. The strike landed with a solid thud, and he slumped forward, unconscious.

"Forgive me," she whispered, her voice breaking. The words were both a prayer and a promise to her brother, or perhaps to herself. Her cloak settled over his still form. "May the High Tree guide your steps, sweet Raven." *Far from me*, she wanted to say, but the words caught in her throat. "And may your feet follow," she said instead, pressing her lips to his forehead before turning toward the path Zama had taken. Her steps carried her forward, leaving a piece of her heart behind with each stride.

CHAPTER 21

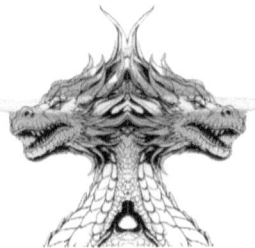

KA'ZAN

ELVA

A DAZZLING BURST OF light catapulted Elva backward. Her spine collided against bark, leaves raining down around her in Zohar's indoor atrium. Stars bloomed behind her eyes, and her muscles seized.

"Stop resisting!" he said, perched on a small bench across the pond. "We've been through this! You must surrender. Allow the essence of the stones to course through you. The stones pulse with the wyvern's breath. Let them sing through your blood. Instruct them, guide them. Fight them, and they will continue to expel you."

Her palms scraped against the rough, uneven surface of pebbles and grass. She pushed herself up, each breath a sharp stab between her ribs. "We've been at this for hours. I can't do it."

The High Regent's shadow fell over her, offering a hand. She jerked back, forcing herself upright. Her glare met his, sharp and unwavering.

Zohar withdrew. "You still doubt me? I promised I wouldn't harm you."

"I don't like being touched," she murmured, her gaze drifting to the garden.

The chamber reminded her of her home. The Regent's lush atrium resembled a sanctuary within Drekavog's walls. A pond rippled at its heart, vibrant fish darting beneath the wooden platform from which she had been propelled.

At its center, a small ceramic case cradled three stones. Two of them had traveled with her from Äktas. The bloodstone box, its crimson glow spilling across the atrium, housed the Äktastary white stone, while an agni stone, rough and uneven, lay beside it. Subtle grays and hints of red marred its surface.

Alabaster arches framed the atrium, opening to other parts of Zohar's chambers. But the room's peaceful beauty shattered against the presence of six guards, their scale armor catching the dim light. Cooperation meant nothing. Their vigilance marked her every breath, every movement. The sanctuary had become her cage, each day dragging longer than the last. Her gaze flickered to Zohar, whose presence commanded the space.

The High Regent caught the sharp edge in her stare as it lingered on his guards. "They're here for my protection," he said, his voice measured, "and yours as well." His bare feet carried him to a small table near a column, where he began pouring tea with deliberate precision. "Must I remind you that you and your Äktastary friends invaded my land? What would you have done if assailants threatened your home?" He extended a small round cup toward her. "Your crew is unharmed, wounds mended. You've even spent some time with your friend Oran."

She accepted the tea, her eyes softening with each sip. "I understand, Sir. I just... I can't do this."

"You've done it before," he insisted. "You must persist. Perhaps the visits with the young man are not helping you after all."

"They are helping," she uttered in one breath. Oran had visited twice, but only for a few minutes. Her heart sank at the thought of losing even those brief moments. "I just don't understand it."

"Understand it?"

"How it all works," she sighed, her fingers tracing the smooth edge of the cup. "I've admitted that I can sense the energy of the stones. It's overwhelming. But, how can a person be the conductor of such power?" Her eyebrows furrowed. "What happened inside the underwater caves is still a mystery to me. And when the Chief Miner and I were nearly swallowed by the earth, I don't even remember exactly what I did. I still don't understand how the bloodstone box is ignited."

Zohar's lips pressed into a tight line. "We've explained it. Doesn't The Hand teach its people about the power of the gems?"

Steam curled from the teapot's spout, rising in delicate tendrils while she poured the liquid into a golden cup. "The stone studies are exclusive to the Enchanters' Trade. I'm an Artificer. All this stone talk feels like trying to hold a reflection in a raindrop. The intricacies of the stones, even the one around your neck, elude me." Her eyes found Sefa, waiting for the subtle nod before offering Zohar the dragon's brew.

The Regent drained his cup in one gulp. He paced between the pond and the table and back again, his fingers absently combing through his thick black beard. The wooden platform creaked beneath his weight with each step toward the center.

Sunlight brushed the surface of the bloodstone box as he lifted it. "Long before the war, the Elder Wyverns chose Ikarite women to serve as vessels for their power. The very essence of the beasts coursed through the Sages' veins. But when others sought to claim this gift and began hunting the creatures for their energy, Ragas decided to bind the magic to our native stones instead."

Elva joined him on the platform, making it sway slightly, ripples dancing across the pond's surface.

"The Ikarite women still carry that enchantment within their blood," Zohar continued, ruby light dancing across his features while he cradled the bloodstone box. "But the stones—Ragas made sure each was unique to its region. An agni stone's wielder commands the elements," he said, taking the rough stone from the clay vase and placing it in her hand. "The ignited lava stones carry the essence of our soil. Born from the molten earth beneath us, tempered and shaped by every force of nature. Those who can fully embrace its power understand the true heartbeat of our land."

With a single breath from Zohar, the stone in her hand kindled, deep oranges and reds swirling like an inner flame. Beneath the platform, the pond rippled and churned, then exhaled steam that coiled around them. The ground gave a slight rumble, making the trees sway and whisper. A gentle spiral of wind danced with her curls. Then, with another breath, silence folded back into stillness.

Elva's breath hitched. Her eyes widened, still unsure how one person could wield such power. Without a second thought, Zohar gestured to the Ikarite bloodstone box and continued, as if the ground beneath them had been still all along.

"As you have discovered, the Äktastary stone inside this case harnesses the vitality of light. It's no mystery that the white stones flourished in the region where the sun and moon rise. You might know this already, there's a legend from long ago, when the Mighty Daemons breathed life into our land—a star fell right where your Iron Tower now stands. Those who wield the power of starlight can conjure shields of unimaginable strength," he added.

Zohar raised his arms, the long, flowing sleeves of his raven-black tunic shifting like shadows. He gestured toward the walls encasing the atrium. "That's why this fortress and our volcano's gate are forged from the white stones of your city. The Äktastary stone was also carved into Ikari's caves and structure."

The Regent paused with a long sigh, his gaze sweeping the atrium. "The people who built our cities weren't seeking to shield themselves from nature's fury. The white stones can withstand even Ragas' raging breath. My father's doing, I'm afraid," he whispered before shifting his gaze to her.

He gave a small nod and a gentle smile, though his dark eyes were filled with sadness—or maybe concern, Elva couldn't tell. He walked quietly across the platform, circling her before continuing.

"Though each stone's power intertwines with its wielder in a unique bond and grants healing abilities, the bloodstone stands apart. Iron is its source, but where it comes from is the subject of many stories. Some of our Elders say Ikari's land is drenched in the blood of the Original Three—the Daemons—Pema, Etzel, and Temsin. Others believe that's a tale meant to hide a far more gruesome truth—a time when our ancestors turned against the wyverns and drenched the land with the creatures' blood." Zohar paused, swallowing hard before he continued. "Despite its origin, the Ikarite gem offers a rarer gift." He inched closer to her, placing the bloodstone box in her hand.

"Its energy merges with the wielder's essence, unlocking boundless potential. It magnifies a talent already within. This is why the Ikarite Sages and Enchanters possess such unique abilities," he said, his fingers lacing together in front of him. "There you have it—the source of the three gems and what ignites them. Their fusion grants you an uncanny ability, unseen for many generations. It is the force we require to put Garam to a complete rest."

The ceramic vase clinked when she replaced the gems. Her shoulders rolled, trying to release the tension coiling in her muscles. Her fingers lingered on the rough edges of the agni stone. "My ears hear them," she said. "I can sense the warmth in them. But still, you are asking me to deliberately engage with a mechanism I can't even see. To pull on imaginary levers. I can't conceive how I can wield them, how any human can—or should."

"We've been over this," the Regent huffed, his fingers raking through his dark hair, leaving furrows in their wake. The skin between his brows creased, and his jaw tightened. "You must tune into the stones' call, focus on their essence. Feel the energy they emanate and let it guide you."

Her lips pressed into a thin line, and she crossed to the tea table, fingers working through her long braid. Zohar's frustration grew heavier each day. His patience, though remarkable, couldn't mask the urgency in his voice or the worry burning in his dark gaze. The volcano's eruption simmered beneath them like a beaker of volatile compounds, waiting for a catalyst to set it off. Time slipped from her grasp, each failed stone-wielding training tightening the noose around her neck. If she couldn't wield the stones, everything would be lost. Including Oran.

The grinding of sliding stone drew their attention. The atlas chamber's walls parted, revealing two familiar silhouettes.

Chief Yoen stepped through, his hair escaping in all directions, waves tangled every which way. Patches of white and dark stubble marked his jaw. Beside him, Oran's figure sent her heart racing. Those brief encounters proved more than simple meetings. They carried proof of his life. He was safe, alive. Even with guards hovering nearby, his presence alone eased the tight knots in her chest.

"What did you just do?" The Regent's voice bounced off the walls as his gaze snapped to the ceramic vase. "The agni stone lit up. What did you do?" His eyes shifted in the same direction she had been staring.

Yoen and Oran sank into low bows, their heads dropping in unison.

"What did you do?" he pressed, ignoring them.

"I'm not sure," she said, stumbling over the words.

"The stones, you made them come to life. What were you thinking about?"

"I just..." Her gaze flickered between Zohar and Oran. "I don't know, Sir."

"Your energy source must be tangled," he said, stroking his beard. "It's in conflict with your emotions for the young man. Your heart. You'll have to release those feelings to properly channel the gems."

Her own brow furrowed, her lower lip caught between her teeth. "This is puzzling. Emotions, by nature, are woven into the tapestry of our physical bodies, changes in our internal system. The notion that such fleeting sensations serve as the wellspring of power defies any logic, Sir. Your Highness."

The Regent released a heavy sigh, stepping over one of the stones in the pond's pathway with effortless grace. His raven tunic draped over the water, creating the illusion of him gliding just above its surface. "Young Elva," he said, spreading his arms wide and meeting her gaze, "the essence of our world—the power coursing through these walls, this entire city, and even the Tanama—is entwined with the very threads that construct our physical tapestry. Simultaneously linked but also separate. Understanding this connection and its subsequent surrender is imperative."

Without breaking his gaze, Zohar reached for the agni stone cradled in the ceramic vase. It blazed to life, amber light flooding the chamber like the breaking of dawn, soft yet intense, wrapping everything in its warm glow. "To wield the magic within these gems, we must sever the ties that bind us to the physical, allowing the radiance that flows within our veins to be embraced. It demands feeling and letting go of the constraints that anchor us to the mundane. Only then can a true Enchanter command the ancient power."

Her gaze darted between the Regent's towering frame and Yoen's watchful stance, then caught on the worry creasing Oran's brow. She struggled to find reason in his words. "Sir, I'm an Artificer. I'm no Enchanter."

With an exhale, the High Regent let his shoulders slump, the amber light of the agni stone dimming in perfect unison, fading slowly as if weighed down by his surrender.

"This won't help her," Oran cut in, his stance rigid and hands clasped behind him. "She needs something more tangible. A methodical connection between an Enchanter and the stones. Any talk of emotions or feelings sends her into a spiral." He chuckled, a smirk curling on his lips. "If you want her to seal your volcano's gate, she'll need a more structured approach, something clear she can grasp."

The chamber fell silent at Oran's unbidden interjection. Even the gentle lap of water against stone seemed to halt. Blood rushed to his cheeks when all eyes turned to him. He shifted uneasily, swallowing hard before muttering. "Your Em-Eminence. Sir."

In a subtle exchange of darting eyes, Yoen glanced at Oran before striding toward the table where she stood. "The young man might be onto something, Your Excellency. Young Elva appears more scholar than a stone wielder. Delving into scrolls and the study of the gems might prove more beneficial."

"We cannot afford to waste more time breaking down the wonders of centuries-old powers." The Regent's voice cracked like thunder. "Garam already threatens with quakes, and we've lost many more lives to the dead forest's growing pull. We must act now!"

Her thumbnail found its place against her index finger, leaving a half-moon indent. The fortress trembled more frequently now. High Councilor Hura's repeated visits weighed heavily, each one bringing more accounts of lost souls to the dead woods. She couldn't stop thinking about her home in Äktas, imagining the threatening smoke engulfing the entire city—her parents and aunt falling prey to the Uláak.

The High Regent, Yoen, Hura, and even Sefa insisted she alone could end it all. They drilled into her that Ka'zan wouldn't survive another eruption from Garam. Her Äktastary fleet waited below in the barracks, unaware that the volcano's wrath loomed over them too. And Oran, who had risked everything to be by her side, shared their fate.

I'm just a wildling. The thought hammered at her skull like a trapped bird battering its wings. She had been forced to board the Underwater Vessels to invade an unknown enemy. Now, she walked another tightrope, forced to wield the magic in the stones.

The thought alone twisted her gut. It was all unnatural and wrong. The stones brought only destruction, not peace.

"Tea?" The offer startled her from her spiral. Yoen stood before her, a delicate golden cup extended in his weathered hands. Steam rose from the dark liquid, carrying the distinct aroma of dragon's brew, a blend of herbs, with a hint of smoky embers and something faintly sweet.

"Drink."

With each sip, warmth spread through her chest, steadying her shaking hands until she drained the cup.

"Perhaps if you'd allow it, Your Eminence," Oran started again, taking a step forward. His eyes darted between Sefa and Yoen before settling on the High Regent, who beckoned him closer. "If just for today, we could examine any scrolls you may have. Let her mind breathe away from the pressure. Allow her to approach this her way. I promise she's a fast learner." He inched closer to Elva.

Zohar tilted his head back, studying the glass panels above, searching for answers. His fingers wove together behind his back.

In the tense silence that followed, Yoen busied himself pouring more tea, the liquid streaming in a thin dark-honey ribbon. His eyes met Oran's in a silent exchange.

"Would that help you, young Elva? Studying the scrolls?" Zohar inquired.

"I—" she began, but Yoen stepped between them, offering another steaming cup. His subtle nod made her glance at Oran, who mirrored the gesture. "Yes, Sir. I think it might."

The Regent's fingers found his beard again. He paced the wooden platform, each step deliberate and measured.

"Your High Regency," Yoen interjected, facing Zohar. "If there's any hesitation, I could be of service and oversee their study of the Sacred Scrolls. Ensure all remain secure."

Zohar's eyes hardened, fixing on the Chief. "The scrolls have been safeguarded for many generations, containing secrets that I have been bound to protect. To allow anyone to rest their eyes on them, especially someone outside of Ka'zanty blood, would be a betrayal of my oath."

"Does the oath outweigh our people's survival?" Yoen snapped, fists clenched at his side. "I still don't understand why the gate was opened if it meant Zuwena could escape from that volcano. We still don't know the cause of the smoke over the dead woods, and the Tanama's pull keeps us in a chokehold. We are in this state because of these guarded secrets. Must we not do all that is necessary to protect and ensure our city survives?"

The lights along the walls flickered wildly, casting dancing shadows across the chamber. In the ceramic vase, the agni stone pulsed with an angry red glow, matching Zohar's glare. "You dare defy me? Question my authority? Chief Miner, you teeter on a dangerous edge. If it weren't for the promise I made to your kin, I would strike you right now."

Yoen dropped to his knees, his face etched with desperation. "Your Eminence, I have been your unwavering servant for countless years. You once entrusted me with guarding your life. My great-grandfather stood by your side, in bonds deeper and more intimate than mere duty required. If my plea contradicts your will and jeopardizes our people's safety, do what you must." His eyes lifted, meeting the Regent's burning gaze. "Yet, I implore you to reconsider. My father shared tales of my great-grandfather, recounting, 'Zohar is the bravest and strongest leader this land has known. His heart overflows with kindness and love for the people he has pledged to protect. Serving him—being in love with him, but ultimately having to let him go, was his ultimate sacrifice.'" The air grew thick with tension. Elva's heart hammered against her ribs while she exchanged nervous glances with Oran.

"Sacrifice." Yoen's voice quivered like a plucked string. "Each soul in this atrium has borne its weight. You've carried it more than all of us combined. It has cost you your children, your friends, your loved ones—your very freedom. It must tear at your soul as it tears at mine each day. Sacrifice—across generations, this land has demanded it. A toll for our survival. But surrendering our people to honor an age-old oath that may hold the key to our salvation—will this become Ka'zan's next tribute?"

Heat flushed Zohar's cheeks at the mention of his children. His measured steps marked time like drumbeats while he fought for composure.

"One day with the scrolls. Just one," the Regent's words cut sharply. Then he locked eyes with Elva. "I will warn you only once. If you use the information against my people, your friend here will suffer another scorching blade. This time I won't stop it." He delivered a final ultimatum directed at Oran. "If she's unable to wield the stones by tomorrow, you won't be seeing her again."

She caught her lower lip between her teeth, tasting copper. Her eyes found Oran's dark ones, trailing across his now smooth skin where Hura's burning dagger had marked him.

"Sefa, escort them to the Arcanum. Keep a watchful eye." Zohar gestured sharply, then walked past the pond pathway and stone arches before vanishing behind a sliding wall. Five guards followed in his wake.

Yoen rose from his low bow, taking long, deep breaths. The charged air seemed to settle with each exhale.

Sefa gathered the ignited stones from the ceramic vase at the center of the pond. "You three, with me!" she directed, shooting a piercing glance at the Chief Miner.

As they crossed to the other side of the pond where Sefa waited, Oran's hand found Elva's, his grip firm and grounding. The warmth of his touch spread through her skin, melting the tension in her shoulders.

"His children, really?" Sefa reproached as Yoen drew near.

"I did what I had to."

The guard moved around the pond's edge. Reaching into her leather waist bag, she pulled out a glimmering square gem and placed it in a crevice next to a small wild purple orchid. "And, you had to bring up your grandfather too?"

"My *great*-grandfather," he corrected, exhaling a weary sigh.

Her hand fell to her sword hilt, then she turned to face Elva and Oran. "If one of you does anything suspicious, I won't be so understanding," she warned. "Step back."

"I thought you were taking us to see the scrolls," Elva said.

The Regent's guard's eyes lingered on Elva and Oran's joined hands. When she tried to slip free, his grip tightened. Without a word, the guard turned to the pond. The central platform groaned, splitting apart like unfurling wings.

Sefa's dark side-braid rested on her shoulder. Her wyvern blade rattled softly in its sheath when she stepped onto the stone pathway. A spiral staircase emerged from the stone silo beneath their feet, each step materializing with a soft grind. The Regent's guard descended first, followed by Yoen.

The moment Elva's foot touched the first step, her entire body seized. The agni stones' energy pulsed through her veins like a second heartbeat, making her head swim. She stumbled against the curved wall, trying to anchor herself.

Oran's hand wrapped around her shoulder. "Are you all right?"

"There are a lot of stones here," she murmured, squinting and massaging her temple.

"Want me to go first? You can hold onto me."

She shook her head. "I'm fine. I'm just not used to it. The agni stones feel strange. It's a bit overwhelming."

From below, Yoen's voice bounced off the cylindrical walls. "Most of our bigger ignited stones are kept here. Take a minute if you must, but make haste. Entering the Arcanum is a great privilege. Do not waste it."

She nodded, watching his shadow vanish down the spiral.

"Ignore that bitter old man. Take your time," Oran said, stepping down to meet her gaze. The dark circles beneath his eyes contrasted with his warm-amber skin, and his raven hair was now an inch longer than she had ever seen it. His jaw bore days' worth of stubble. The sight of him—tired and worried but still present—made her throat tighten.

His fingers brushed her cheek with a feather-light touch, catching a stray white curl and tucking it behind her ear. The simple gesture broke something inside her. The tension she'd been carrying melted away, and she threw herself into his arms. And he caught her, pulling her close with a desperation that matched her own. His face buried in the curve of her neck, his breath warm against her skin. With each deep inhale, his shoulders gradually relaxed, his body softening against hers.

Sefa's voice echoed up the stairwell, shattering the moment. "Are you two love-struck bugs coming, or should I fetch you?"

"We're coming." Oran gently pulled away, carefully studying her. "Do you need another minute?"

She shook her head, her fingers trailing over the rough stubble along his jaw. "I've missed you."

He caught her hand, pressing a kiss to her knuckles. "I've missed you more," he whispered against her skin. "Let's go."

At the bottom, Sefa waited, hands on hips, boot tapping rhythmically.

"Apologies," Elva mumbled, biting her lower lip.

"This way," the guard sighed, leading them through a narrow passage.

The soft radiance of agni stones bathed the corridor, casting long dancing shadows along the walls. Each step sent a fresh wave of pulsing through her skull, the stones' call growing more insistent. Her fingers moved in the pattern Zohar had taught her, thumb touching each fingertip in sequence. She drew slow, measured breaths, her eyes fixed on her moving hands while she walked beside Oran.

The passageway opened into a honey glow, drawing her gaze upward with a gasp.

"Whoa," Oran marveled beside her.

The chamber before them stretched impossibly high, its stone walls rippling like frozen waves caught in eternal motion. A smooth path wound through the vast space, weaving between towering columns housing countless scrolls and files in their carved alcoves. Above, openings in the rock ceiling filtered streams of agni stone light. Each turn revealed new shelves etched into walls, interrupted by clusters of plush chairs and reading tables worn smooth from use. At the chamber's far end, a gentle stream of water trickled through a narrow opening, with patches of forest-green moss cushioning the rocks around it, creating a peaceful retreat.

She stood transfixed. The overwhelming drumbeat of the stones faded to background noise in the face of the breathtaking chamber. Her heart fluttered with excitement, and thoughts of the Academy's restricted access faded away. Here lay more knowledge than Sadfar had ever allowed his Artificers to glimpse, their scroll exchanges limited to past inventions and carefully curated parchments. Her eyes glanced at Oran, finding her own wonder mirrored in his smile.

A whispered exchange between Yoen and Sefa caught her attention.

"You, with me," Sefa beckoned, already moving between the columns.

She followed, casting a backward glance while the Chief Miner led Oran in another direction. He flashed her a reassuring smile, then winked before vanishing into another corridor. A sudden hollowness carved into her chest, his warmth already dissolving like mist. They'd only shared mere minutes together. She craved more. More time to understand the stone magic she'd sworn never to wield, to plot their escape from Ka'zan and return to Äktas. More time to simply be near him. But time remained a luxury she did not have.

A massive wooden door groaned under Sefa's firm push. The room beyond gleamed with walnut floors and wooden columns. A second level wrapped around, its railings polished to a shine, alcoves overflowing with scrolls and parchments. A pendant lantern made of twisted white branches cast soft light from the ceiling onto a large wooden table below.

"The parchments that might help you figure out the stones are on the second level," the guard explained, gesturing upward. "Go up there and rummage. I'll gather what I think might be helpful and bring it to the center. You don't have a lot of time. It's already midday. It'll be wise to remember the High Regent's words," she added, her dark eyes studying Elva's face. "I can't begin to understand the pressure you're under. Just keep in mind what's at stake. It's not just you and your friend. It's an entire city full of innocent children and loved ones." Her fingers drummed against her sword's hilt. "You're going to cut through the skin." She pointed to where Elva's thumbnail dug into its familiar spot.

Startled, Elva wrapped her fingers tightly around it, nodding. She climbed a few steps before turning back. "Earlier, at the spiral stairs, why did you say love-struck bugs?" Her eyes met Sefa's. "We aren't in love."

A chuckle softened Sefa's sharp features, highlighting her high cheekbones. "He definitely is."

"No... we're friends. That's it. Best friends."

"I think I'll venture to the courtship scrolls alcoves and bring you some of those," Sefa grinned. "Perhaps you might learn more than just stone magic." The Regent's guard ignored her protests and moved to scan the shelves.

The guard's comments about Oran muddled her already spinning thoughts. He had been her best friend for many years. Only that. At least that's what she believed. They had been through so much together. If he had feelings beyond friendship, he would have expressed them by now. But contemplating her own feelings left her head spinning, especially with the added weight of mastering not just one stone, but three.

Then, Yoen's mention of Zuwena only added to her confusion. The idea of the lightning wyvern roaming the lands sent a shiver down her spine. Coupled with the smoke surrounding the Tanama and its increasing pull, any thoughts of romance slid far down her list of priorities.

She shook her head, pushing Sefa's comment to the back of her mind. At the top of the staircase, her breath caught at the endless rows of parchments. "There are so many. Where do I even start?"

The first scroll her fingers pulled free, titled *Dance of Flames*, showed two wyverns locked in an intimate embrace, their green and lavender flames intertwining. Heat rushed to her cheeks and she quickly returned it to its place. The next parchment, *The Gift to the Ember Regent*, traced Zohar's lineage as the firsts in Ka'zan to sense the pull from the agni stones. Their unmatched affinity had earned them alone the right to wear Ragas' amulet, now hanging from Zohar's neck.

Several scrolls later, her eyes caught one titled, *Under the Emerald Wings: A Historical Perspective*. It chronicled Magnar's construction of Drekavog, while collections of past High Councilor writings revealed the intricate network of stones powering the fortress, enabling it to withstand Ragas' fury during the Wyvern Wars.

She slid to the floor against the wooden rail, ancient texts scattered around her. Below, Sefa's tall frame moved efficiently between shelves, gathering parchments on the central table, her height allowing her to reach high shelves without the rolling ladder.

"Are those real wyverns' scales? On your armor?" She called from between the wooden rails. "What about your sword—is it true it's made from wyverns' bones?"

Sefa paused, looking up. "You're supposed to be studying ancient stone magic, not my gear."

"There are hundreds, if not thousands in this room alone. And they're not very well organized, if I may add. They should be arranged by time, period, High Regent, and then High Council. But you have *The Anatomy of Feathered Wyverns*, mixed with

Magnar's Transformative Elixirs: A Guide. How can anyone find anything here?"

Sefa's eyebrows shot up.

"I—I mean no disrespect," she stammered, her fingers tightening around the wooden post. "It's just, there's a lot, and I don't have much time."

"No one organizes the texts," Sefa muttered, her fingers brushing over the dusty edge of an old scroll. "Apart from the High Regent, his son, and the High Councilor, no one's allowed here. Not unless it's urgent. Yoen and I were only allowed in here when he was Chief Guard."

Elva's lips curled into a smirk. "And what did you study during that time? The courtship scrolls?"

Sefa cleared her throat, brushing her fingers down the length of her hilt hanging at her side. "No need—my courtship skills are as sharp as my blade."

"You mean, ancient and weathered?" Elva's grin widened.

Sefa's lips quivered before her laughter burst out. "Agile and finely honed," she winked.

The smile tugging at Elva's lips felt like it belonged to a stranger. She hadn't done that since the Sky Lanterns had taken flight. It hadn't been long, yet it felt like ages. A lifetime since she had seen her parents or her aunt. The ache tightened with each passing thought, stealing all joy, casting only shadows. Her eyes blinked rapidly, but the tears gathered anyway, blurring her vision. With a quiet sigh, she returned to the scrolls, turning her back to Sefa.

After scanning several more pages, her arms flew up in frustration. Nothing, she had found nothing about Tristone Enchanters. Nothing that would explain how magic stones connected to stone wielders. Nothing that would help her figure out how to tame the giant volcano threatening to obliterate the city—and Oran with it. "I can't do this," she sighed.

"When I was your age, I almost walked into the dead forest," Sefa's voice dropped to a whisper.

Elva's gaze drifted to where the guard sat surrounded by a pile of scrolls. Her usual rigid posture had softened, her muscled arms resting on the table and her chin supported by one hand.

"It was a senseless game really—who could get closer to the edge of the forests? Two walked in... I was about to be the third when the old Chief Guard tackled me to the ground. Before I realized what was happening, two of my friends were deep in the woods, couldn't hear us calling," Sefa admitted softly, her fingers drumming nervously against the table. "I've carried their deaths ever since. These lands are steeped in sorrow. It feels unnatural to find joy amidst such misery. My friends, like many others, walked into a forest that was condemned by the actions of our ancestors. It's unfair that the responsibility falls upon us to make it right, when so many before us, with far more power, only bred destruction and chaos."

With a scrape of the chair against wood, Sefa stood and crossed the room. She stopped beneath Elva's perch, their eyes meeting in the quiet air. "Crossing those waters and taming Garam's fire rivers shows strength this city hasn't seen in generations. Zohar is strong, but those who have witnessed his might are long gone. The matter isn't whether or not you can do this, but what is stopping you."

Elva pressed her palms against her eyes until spots danced. "Beyond not understanding it—I hate it. If it weren't for those stones and the magic of those creatures, we wouldn't be here. I wouldn't be here. I wouldn't have to face Generals, Commanders, and Regents demanding the impossible. I wouldn't have broken any rules, and Oran..." His name caught in her throat. Her hands fumbled with her high collar, the fabric suddenly too tight around her neck.

"My aunt has this saying: To stop a rogue barrel from sliding down a hill requires understanding the barrel and the hill." Her hand traced an arc through the air, mimicking the motion. "That's why I chose the Artificer's Trade," she added. "In a land where magic does more harm than help, crafting things that could help keep the city running made more sense. My aunt used to let me work in her shop tucked away underneath her dining table, while my parents worked the mines under the Iron Tower. I spent most of my days tearing apart her things just to put them back together," she added with a quivering lip. "Sometimes I think she'd purposefully break things just so I had something to fix. Tools, scrolls, and parchments I understand. But I cannot dismantle and recreate the magic of the stones."

Sefa's hand found the hilt of her sword, her eyes softening. "For being so clever, you seem to forget one crucial thing—the incendiary breath of those wyverns and the magic contained within those gems, helped our land thrive. Just like your artifacts. We forged cities from dirt, fire, and stone." She returned to the table, parchment rustling beneath her hands. "Ragas granted us his essence because, like your engineering, it was a means to evolve. I understand your frustration. But perhaps it'd be wise to recognize that stone-wielding is also a tool. Our doom wasn't brought by a wyvern's essence or its relentless fury—it was our greed," she added, lowering her voice. "Perhaps, one day, you'll see it that way, but for now, there are plenty more scrolls to review."

Elva's attention drifted back to the scattered texts, but the letters slid out of focus like trying to grip a wrench with oiled hands, slipping away from her grasp. Her mind raced back to the first time she sensed the white stone from her city, during a visit to the Academy with her aunt before she enrolled. While her aunt spoke with the General Artificer, she wandered the courts, excitement crackling in her chest.

The allure of the enchanted stone drew her in, more compelling than the thought of one day being admitted to the Artificer's Trade. Her feet moved like they had a mind of their own, carrying her to the window where the General Enchanter cradled it in white-gloved hands, its rhythmic thrum echoing like a heartbeat. A Militia guard's sharp voice snapped her back to reality just in time to avoid discovery.

She quickly learned that those Militia guards served not just to protect but as the Enchanters' shadows, constantly watching and dictating their every move. If anyone discovered her ability to sense the stones, she might as well be in a cage. The irony twisted in her gut. She found herself trapped in enemy territory, drawn not just to the whispers of one stone, but to the stones native to each region, their presence an ever-intoxicating buzz under her skin.

Sefa's words about magic being a tool made her fists clench until crescents appeared in her palms. She trusted the weight of a hammer, the precision of a knife, the scratching of a quill against parchment. But stone-wielding magic promised nothing but a precipice, with a consuming void waiting below. Her fingers traced another ancient text, seeking answers that might help her understand her abilities, but the words twisted in her mind.

She had cornered Oran in the very cage she had dreaded since the first time she sensed the white stone. If she couldn't hone her dangerous abilities, he would pay with his life. The stones demanded a skill and poise she lacked. Her ignorance had become an obstacle, and her fear and recklessness a chain that bound them both.

A raw, clawing unease twisted in her chest. Enchanters like the High Regent or those in Äktas radiated grace and control—qualities of true stone wielders. Buldar had seen right through her—she was, and always would be, a wildling. Impulsive. Feral. Tristone Enchanter or not, Oran and the entire city of Ka'zan had placed their trust in the wrong hands.

CHAPTER 22

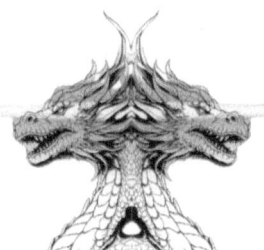

IKARI

ASANTE

ASANTE SPRINTED ACROSS THE cracked cobblestone streets of the abandoned city, her heart pounding in time with her footsteps. Her eyes locked on Zuwena's terrifying figure. The mesmerizing light from the creature's glowing chest pierced through the night sky. Her breath quickened, legs burning with each stride, fingers digging into the strap of her satchel, keeping the jade embryo safe inside.

Glancing back, she scanned the fields behind her, searching for any sign of her brother. Her teeth clenched at what she had done. Knocking him unconscious had been the only way. She couldn't let him follow. Zama needed help, and she needed to get closer to Zuwena. Though she still didn't have a plan, in the end, no matter what, staying away from Tarrak kept him safe.

Past a charred field of grain, the giant wyvern hovered over a group of abandoned stone houses. Her blue belly cast an eerie glow upon the ground as a group of people fled toward the farmlands.

The sight of surviving Ikarites sent a rush of warmth through her, but it vanished in an instant. Zuwena readied her flames, fixing a harrowing glare on the running crowd. Before she could unleash her fiery attack, Asante's hands retrieved the egg from her bag and extended it into the darkness, letting its light pierce the sky. Its radiance stretched until it captured Zuwena.

With rapacious intensity, the creature's gaze locked onto her. Asante's legs stiffened, her pulse hammering in her throat. In the blink of an eye, a dark cloak whipped through the air, snuffing out the gem's glow, and a tight grip yanked her away.

"Have you lost your mind?" Zama barked. "She can't have that egg!"

"She was going to set them on fire," Asante panted.

The Avian Sage pushed her against a tree. "Things will be much worse if she gets a hold of that gem. Where's your brother?" she asked, scanning the ground.

Before she could answer, a ball of white flames hurtled directly at them. Zama lunged, shoving her out of the way. The flames danced and licked at the bark where they had just been standing, engulfing it instantly. Her hand shot up to shield her face from the searing heat, while her other hand gripped tightly around the cloaked embryo.

"Run!" the Sage shouted.

They rushed through the abandoned city. Moss blanketed cracked walls, while overgrown vines snaked between stone pillars. Another burst of wyvern's breath seared the air, turning leaves to ash and sending waves of heat rippling through the air. The creature's shadow grew longer on the ground with each stride, its wingbeats stirring hot wind against her back. She risked a glance over her shoulder—and those amber eyes met hers, slitted pupils contracting to thin black lines, full of fury. Zuwena's nostrils flared, drawing in a deep breath, her mouth opening as fire gathered, ready to strike.

From the shadows, Tarrak lunged, shoving both Asante and Zama aside. Zuwena's flames streaked past, catching his leg. The heat seared through his trousers, forcing him to stumble to the ground. He tore at his cloak, desperate to smother the fire licking at his flesh.

Asante's pulse thundered. Her eyes flicked upward, bracing for another attack. But only silence greeted her. She choked back a gasp. "Where is she? Where's Zuwena?" she whispered, while Zama tended to Tarrak's burns.

A sharp knot twisted in her chest. She had failed, again. There he was, hurt. She had only caused him more pain. The Avian Sage gently cupped Tarrak's face, tracing her fingers over the bruise she had left. Zama adjusted one of his locs behind his ear and pressed her forehead to his.

Asante's gaze turned upward, taking in the river of lifeless trees. A thick layer of haze encased their surroundings, and the ground was drained of all life. Her heart raced—the landscape from her nightmares materialized before her. "We must go. We must go, now."

Zama's eyes raked the area. With a gasp, she hauled Tarrak up. "Let's move, quickly."

A wave of roars crashed around them, followed by the sharp clank of chains scraping against stone. She flung her arm toward her brother, struggling to run, and searched the grounds with desperate eyes. They quickened their pace until the air fled from her lungs. One of the haunting figures from her dreams blocked their path.

Tarrak's bow sang. He released an arrow at the masked Uláak, but the projectile burst into ash before it could strike the hallowed eyes.

The Sage's dagger flew true, embedding itself between the creature's eyes, making its head tilt back with force. As it retracted, its gaze remained fixed on them. Lizard-like hands emerged from the side of the shadowy cloak, plucking the blade free. The metal crumbled to dust like a fragile flower between its scaled fingers.

Still limping, Tarrak thrust his arm across Asante and Zama, shoving them behind his broad shoulders. The Uláak's head tilted at an unnatural angle, a metal chain unfurling from its grip. Her breath hitched when the forest erupted with bone-chilling growls. Hexenbeasts emerged from the shadows, with rows of jagged spines along their curved backs and seething guttural snarls. Through the mist, more Uláak materialized, their gaping snouts and hollow eyes of their masks burning into their prey.

Asante's gaze darted to Zama, her chest heaving. "You can fly. Go! We'll hold them back."

Tarrak spun, breath quick and shallow. His tear-filled gaze met Zama's. "Go!" he whispered, tightening his grip around Asante's hand.

The Sage's amber eyes locked onto the hexenbeasts, unwavering. Rather than fleeing, her hand stretched toward the embryo nestled against Asante's arm. In one fluid motion, Zama seized her cloak exposing the gem. Instead of transforming into her owl form, the fabric morphed into a double-edged sword, its blade shimmering with an ethereal glow. Golden owl feathers adorned the grip that seemed to float in her grasp, humming with quiet power.

Three hexenbeasts closed in with lightning speed, claws scraping against the earth as they dropped low. Spines erupted from their backs, whistling through the air aimed at Zama. The Sage's blade sang with swift movements, each precise arc deflecting the projectiles with practiced ease.

Her sword cut an arc through the air, and three metallic feathers launched from the grip, their edges glinting as they pierced the haze. Each found its mark in the hexenbeasts' corroded shells. Shrieks of rage echoed. The creatures staggered, wounds oozing. They recovered just as quickly. But their snarls grew sharper, claws gouging furrows in the ground as they crouched, muscles bunching beneath their tarnished hides.

Then, the embryo burst into brilliance without warning, forcing a startled gasp from Asante's lips. White light seared outward, driving the hexenbeasts back. Their hisses filled the air, and they retreated, claws leaving frantic scratches in their wake. Tarrak's fingers dug into Asante's arm, pulling her forward through the scorched terrain. "Hang on to that egg!" The words rushed out between ragged breaths.

Asante twisted to look over her shoulder. Zama trailed behind them, her sword at the ready. The embryo's light swirled in a perfect circle, creating a barrier that the Uláak and their hexenbeasts didn't dare breach. "It's keeping them at bay," she shouted in disbelief.

They pushed forward without a clear direction, dead branches snapping beneath their feet. Twisted trees rose around them like ancient corpses, their bare limbs reaching toward a shrouded sky. Uláak stalked between the shadows, their masked forms moving with unnatural grace despite their size. The hexenbeasts' growls rumbled, deep and guttural, as if thunder surged from the very ground beneath them.

Her brother's legs faltered, sending him crashing to the ground with a heavy thud. Asante rushed to his side, struggling to lift him up.

The Uláak's circle tightened, their massive bodies pressing closer, weapons gleaming. "What's our move?" her voice shook. "There are more of them, and I don't know how long the embryo will keep glowing."

Tarrak's fingers wrapped around his injured leg. "Zama, transform and take Asante with you," he said through gritted teeth, sweat gleaming down his temple.

"I'm not leaving you here!" Asante's voice cracked.

Zama's jaw clenched, and her eyes darted to the encroaching figures. She shifted closer to Tarrak, placing a steady hand on his shoulder. "My owl won't do us any good in these woods. Remember what I told you—their whips compelled me out of my avian form," she said, meeting his eyes. "And I wouldn't leave you either."

Tarrak grimaced, his jaw tensing while his hands clenched around his leg. "If the egg is repelling them, we might as well just walk past the Uláak. Get back to Ikari."

The Fifth Sage paced along the barrier of light, her sword firm in her grip. "The Uláak didn't attack. It's like they are waiting for something. Zuwena disappeared too quickly. We were an easy target," she said, her eyes never leaving the gathering creatures. "Something doesn't feel right. What if that's what they want? For us to cross back using the magic of the egg."

Asante's knees dropped beside her brother, tearing a strip from her cloak. The fabric ripped with a sharp, crisp crack. She worked the torn piece around his burned leg, the metallic scent of blood mixing with sweat in the air.

"You think the wyvern did it on purpose?" Tarrak winced when she tightened the makeshift bandage.

"Facing the Uláak means certain death. A terrifying one. Burning us alive would've been merciful," Asante admitted, feeling her insides churn. "Zuwena forced us into a trap. She chased us into the dead woods. Once the Uláak are done with us, she'll be free to collect her embryo."

The circle of light held steady around them, but beyond its boundary, the swarm of creatures grew denser.

"We can't stay here. If they won't approach us with the egg, let's try walking." Tarrak leaned heavily against Asante as she helped him up. Zama moved to his other side, bracing his weight.

Each of their steps drew a chorus of growls that swelled into piercing screeches. Shadows shifted, more Uláak emerged, their hulking forms flanked by hexenbeasts.

"Look!" Asante pointed to a foggy stream that moved like molten silver. She took a few steps, waiting for Zama and Tarrak to follow.

"Sante, don't move. There's nothing there," he uttered with a hint of panic in his voice.

"There's a stream of light," she insisted.

Zama and Tarrak exchanged worried glances but followed closely behind.

The Uláak's masks tracked their movement, heads tilting at disturbing angles as their chain whips dragged furrows in the earth. With each turn along the silver stream only visible to Asante, the creatures' clicks grew more frenzied. Tarrak's grip tightened on his bow while Zama's sword remained poised.

Asante's next step froze mid-air. A massive Uláak towered over them, wielding a whip crafted from three different ignited gems. The white stone hilt gleamed as the chain whip unfurled, its agni stone and bloodstone links marked with the scars of countless victims.

"I know you." The words scraped like metal on stone from behind the mask.

Asante's lungs seized, her body refusing to move. The voice pierced her very essence.

"Get behind me," Tarrak whispered, tugging at her arm, but her feet remained rooted.

"Ah, yes. I understand!" Its voice slithered out like death's exhale. "Your kin has known my weapon. His blood and essence course through my precious stones. I have sensed you for many moons. Such great power. Such a waste, in such a little thing." A deep growl punctuated its words while it advanced. "The matriarch wants her offspring. She shall receive it."

"You stay away from her," Tarrak yelled.

Each note of its laughter rippled through the air, hammering against her chest. The Uláak leader prowled around their barrier of light, slow and menacing, measuring each of them. "Rabbit," it hissed, twisting its mask in slow, deliberate moves as if dissecting Asante before shifting to Tarrak. "Raven." Then it turned to Zama, a guttural snarl dragging behind each word. "Filthy Owl!"

With slow, deliberate sways, the Uláak leader retreated a few steps, its hollow eyes boring into them like twin black moons. With a subtle shift of its lizard-like fingers, the white stone handle of the whip settled into its grip.

The weapon crackled through the air, its agni and bloodstone spikes tearing into the shield created by the embryo, shattering its brilliance until they struck Asante's unmarked hand, slicing clean through flesh. It slipped from her grasp and rolled away, while its protective glow slowly faded. At the same time, a wave of hexenbeasts surged forward, their advances sharp, and voracious.

Tarrak yanked Asante behind him, Zama flanked them. Arrows and metal feathers filled the air, but the creatures barely flinched at the assault.

Without touching it, the leader of the Uláak circled around the fallen embryo. Instinct drove her hand toward her father's knife, and trembling fingers pointed the blade at the approaching fiend.

In a flash, a different whip sang through the air, wrapping around Tarrak's throat. The weapon yanked him off his feet, offering him up as a feast.

Desperate, Asante flung her father's knife toward the Uláak holding her brother hostage. But instead of the knife flying, her markings flared to life, extending from her hand to the dagger, forming a silver tether. The new glowing chain found its mark, severing the metal whip. With a slight tug, it arched back to her marked hand, coiling around her wrist to form an armlet that pulsed with argent energy.

The air stilled. Her eyes darted between her brother's face and Zama's tense expression. A hexenbeast, its towering frame looming over Zama, lunged forward. The impact knocked her flat, driving the breath from her lungs. The Sage's sword flashed, striking true through the creature's gaping maw. Then Asante's blade whistled through the air again, finding its mark deep in the beast's skull. She drew the glowing tether back, watching as the hexenbeast slumped, its bulk forcing the Sage to strain and heave the creature aside.

A chorus of anguished cries rose from the remaining hexenbeasts, making her flinch. Then they swarmed. Zama's sword rang against claws while Tarrak's arrows whistled through the air.

A sudden jerk at her ankle sent Asante sliding, her body scraping against the rough ground. When she turned to look, her heart froze. The stone chain whip that had haunted her nightmares for years seized her foot. Beasts' cries and the clash of weapons echoed behind her as she struggled to break free.

Her glowing line around her arm sang through the air again, meeting the Uláak leader's tristone chain whip with a metallic clash. The weapons sparked and screamed against each other, her blade rebounding without effect. Panic surged through her with each failed strike. She sent the blade flying again and again until, at last, it found the Uláak's flesh. It sliced through the creature's scales, sending an agonized howl ripping through the air. The fiend yanked back the whip, releasing her ankle.

"Grab the egg!" Zama's urgent voice echoed.

Asante crawled with haste until her glowing hand found it. The embryo responded with a massive surge of light, rippling with such force that it sent the hexenbeasts and the Uláak flying backward, putting a vast distance between them.

"We have to get out of here," Zama urged.

Asante used the embryo as a guiding light, following the silver stream she had detected moments earlier. "This way," she said, hurrying. She rushed through the fields of dead trees until the hazy current collided with an invisible barrier, splintering into a web of lightning veins that reached upward. "It stops here." Beyond the shimmer, a sea of green spread out, and a roar of water called from beyond.

"This is not the edge of the forest," Zama protested, hoisting Tarrak up. "We have to move!"

"The stream of light led us here. Maybe we can cross to that forest?"

"What forest?" Tarrak panted.

Asante's gaze flickered to her brother. His hand pressed on his side stemming the gushing blood from a wound. "You're hurt," she gasped.

"We have to move. There's nothing there, just more dead trees," Zama protested.

"The current of silver light connects to a thin veil. Just look! There's a live forest on the other side. Please, you have to believe me." Her eyes bounced between Zama and Tarrak, but the sight of Zuwena's massive form behind them stopped her heart. The wyvern's wings beat, sending gusts of wind, ruffling their cloaks, while her belly radiated a cerulean glow.

Asante's breath hitched. The silver markings on her hand came alive, growing brighter with the humming energy of the embryo. She wouldn't run this time, she had already lost so much. She couldn't lose her brother too. With a shaky breath, she lunged forward, lifting the glowing egg above her head, its power merging with the light on her skin. She ignored her brother's and the Sage's protesting echoes.

In the same breath of time, Zuwena unleashed an earth-shattering roar. It rattled Asante to her core, her knees nearly buckling under the force. But she held her ground, rooting herself as sapphire flames surged from the wyvern's torso, blazing toward her. Heart pounding, she used the glowing embryo like a shield, bracing herself for the searing heat. Instead of flames, an abrasive white light flooded her vision, swallowing the world around her. It scorched her thoughts, twisting everything around her into a haze of radiance. Her eyes blinked, but the light didn't waver. The ground beneath her feet vanished. The weight of wings spread wide, the pulse of blood flowing through scales, all of it foreign, yet intimately hers.

The Tanama forests surged around her feet in a rush. Its ancient trees stood tall, vibrant, alive. Beneath her, the earth pressed against her battered body—no, not Asante's body, but Zuwena's. A weaving of minds took hold, threads of thought and memory intertwining. Her thoughts merged with Zuwena's memories, as if she had lived them herself, a century ago.

Her wyvern wings scraped the ground, the clawed tips gouging earth as she strained to take flight. Exhaustion dragged at her limbs. She summoned her lightning, but the tendrils refused to spark. She sought the warmth of her blue flames, only to find they had abandoned her as well. Her body slithered forward, eyes fixed on the west. Samira had nearly drained her of all essence, and now her offspring would suffer the same fate if she failed to reach it in time.

Her ears twitched at the sound of northern men drifting through the trees. "Regent Magnar, Zuwena's tracks follow this way."

At the sound of the Ka'zanty's voices, her wings gave a feeble stroke, dragging her forward. A stronger downbeat caught the wind, lifting her only a few feet before her body sagged, the air thick and unyielding. With a shuddering lurch, she plummeted, slamming into the ground with a bone-rattling thud as dust and leaves erupted around her.

Their footsteps quickened, their shadowy figures closing in on her. Clad in armor forged from the scales of her brothers and sisters, they wielded swords crafted from wyverns' claws. The High Regent stepped into view, too close to her snout. The arrogance! His braided beard swayed with each movement. She called on her flames again, but only a searing exhale escaped her.

Magnar's fingers traced the length of her scales. "The High Sage nearly finished you. Those fiends will be the end of us, Zuwena," he sighed.

A weak growl rumbled from her belly. She flapped and swirled, but the Ka'zanty fleet didn't retreat. She had been defeated at last, and her embryo would be gone forever. Instead of wielding his scepter to finish her off, Magnar's fingers closed around a binding hanging at his side, tethered to a chain of obsidian stones.

When the Regent secured it around her leg, the power of the chains surged through her core, manipulating her like the strings of a marionette. Her flames, her lightning tendrils, even her wings surrendered to the essence of the powerful stones. With a sharp tug on the dark onyx chain, Magnar pulled her forward, hauling her effortlessly across the ground. "This is for your own good, Zuwena." The High Regent's voice trailed off, fading into silence.

Light ripped through Asante's consciousness, severing her connection to the wyvern's memories. The surroundings wavered, each pulse of light blurring the edges of her vision. Before her, Zuwena perched, her belly glowing in hues of blue, casting faint reflections across a thin layer of water like scattered stars.

Asante's chest tightened at the sight of the creature. The cool water lapped at her ankles, and the High Tree of Pālam loomed above them, its towering ivory roots stretching across the vast expanse.

Your connection to my embryo is strong, and your blood holds a distinct energy. Only one has ever been able to slip into my memories. Zuwena's low, silken voice curled through her thoughts.

The creature's voice made Asante stumble backward, sending ripples through the water. The wyvern's serpentine form glided between the roots with voracious grace.

I sense we share a common enemy, little bug. Surrender my offspring, and I promise to rid this land from Samira and her Sages. They will be nothing but ashes.

"You—you nearly ended us back there in the dead woods," her voice quivered, but her feet planted firmly in the shifting water. Heat bloomed in her chest at the image of Samira being consumed by flames. The High Priestess had stripped everything from her. The craving for revenge whispered through her veins like sweet poison—intoxicating yet tempting. Her fingers twitched at the thought of exchanging the embryo for the promise of vengeance, but she pushed the urge back. The wyvern's words could be a honey-dripped bait waiting for her desperate bite. "How will I know you won't do the same the moment I hand you the gem?"

Relinquish the embryo, Zuwena's voice hummed, low and rasping, as if each word dragged itself from deep within her chest. The wyvern's massive body cut through the water until she lowered her head level with Asante's. Their eyes met, predator and prey. *I will ssspare you and your brother.*

Her knees threatened to give way under the creature's stare. "What about Zama?"

A growl rumbled from Zuwena's throat, vibrating through the water at her feet. The wyvern's nostrils flared, releasing wisps of blue flame. *All the Sages will burn. I offer you mercy alone because of the rare bond with my offspring. My flames will ravage every crevice in Ikari. This entire land will be nothing but a forgotten ruin in the wake of my ssscorching wrath.*

A chill crept up her spine. "You mean..." her voice wavered. "You want to destroy all of it? Everyone?" She blurted the words, her hands shaking at her sides. "But... But there are innocent lives in Pālam. Samira is the one to blame. No, I—I... can't."

Zuwena's laughter slithered into her mind, the sound cold and mocking. *You are a fool.* The wyvern's body twisted in the air, coiling around the High Tree with terrifying grace. *Samira's little puppet,* she snarled. *Too young to understand. You think you've suffered loss?* Her glare pierced through Asante. Drawing a deep, resonant breath, the creature's chest pulsed with bright blue flames, the air thickening with heat.

You humansss, parrrasites! Zuwena hissed. *You all longed for a power you could never comprehend. Then you STAINED it. Through your cursèd greed and arrogance. And now—you, little bug, with a smidge of our essence...* Zuwena's voice sank into a low growl. *You ssseek vengeance—yet you know not its meaning. What it takessss...*

The wyvern's eyes burned with the same rage that had once consumed Asante. Her nostrils flared, a row of fangs bared in a blood-curdling snarl. *What will you sacrifice for the vengeance you ache for? His bonesss and flesh will do.*

"Tarrak!" Asante gasped. In an instant, Zuwena's flames roared to life, threatening to consume everything in their path.

The connection between their minds shattered, and in a heartbeat, the dead woods loomed once more, cold and silent, as if no time had passed at all.

Her arm shot forward, the glowing embryo sailing between her and the engulfing blaze. The collision of blue fire and egg erupted in a shockwave that flung both Zuwena and Asante backward. The ground slammed into her back, driving the air from her lungs. Through blurred vision, she scrambled to her hands and knees, then forced herself upright, eyes darting frantically for her brother. Zuwena lay sprawled in the distance, her massive form carved against the destruction left in her wake.

Her focus turned to the silver shroud ahead, and she motioned for her brother and Zama to follow. "This way, quickly!" The embryo slipped into her bag as she leaped across the gleaming stream. Her boots barely grazed its surface before finding purchase on the opposite bank. The air shifted around her like a curtain being drawn aside. Dead woods gave way to a living forest. Leaves rustled overhead, earth rich with moisture beneath her feet. She charged through thick undergrowth, branches catching at her clothes. Zama and Tarrak's footsteps pounded behind her. A sky full of stars loomed above them. A backward glance revealed trees full of life instead of the dead forest. The threshold they had just crossed shimmered softly with silver light, and Zuwena's roar faded in the distance.

"Stop!" Zama's urgent voice came too late.

Asante's feet left solid ground, and the world spun around her. Her stomach lurched with the shift in air pressure, and she plunged into frigid water. The impact drove ice needles into her skin. The current seized her, yanking her under and spinning her within its grasp.

Wings fluttered above her as Zama circled in her avian form. But before she could reach out, a loud bang rang out, and the Avian Sage's body went limp, spiraling down until she struck the water with a splash.

Asante's legs fought the current as her eyes caught strange figures on the shore. Five silhouettes in gray coats and red armbands hauled her brother from the water, dragging him onto solid ground.

"No! Tarrak!" Water filled her mouth, drowning her cry. Her chest seized with panic, thrashing against the river's swift pull. The red-armband figures retreated with her brother, each step taking him further beyond her reach. The failure settled in her bones, heavy as the day she lost her mother and sister.

With each labored arm stroke, the ache in her chest grew heavier, threatening to pull her under. She had been so focused on her fear, on survival, when she should've been focused on her rage. Each gasp for breath reminded her of her hesitation. Her fingers wrapped desperately around the embryo, willing it to glow, to pulse with life like it had done in the dead woods. But it remained cold and silent. The warmth of her own markings abandoned her, leaving her fighting alone against the merciless waters.

CHAPTER 23

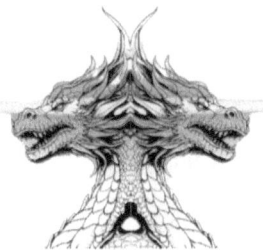

KA'ZAN

ELVA

E LVA LAY ON THE wooden panels within the Regent's study main floor. Her bare feet dangled over a wooden chair while her hands grasped a piece of parchment above her head. After several more texts, she scanned the one titled *Whispers of Wyverns: Chronicles of the Ancient Remains*. Line by line, she examined the descriptions of wyvern remnants scattered throughout the Tanama's dead woods, protected by the Uláak. Her fingers traced the silhouettes of full-body skeletons, wings, fangs, sharp claws, horns, and feathers. All said to be full of the powerful magic still. The remains many humans had fought and died for, lay lost in those dead woods now veiled by dark smoke.

A sea of scrolls surrounded her, all of which she had scanned through, yet none yielded information on mastering the stones. Histories of past stone wielders and the intricacies of various wyverns unfolded before her. The perspective from Ka'zan introduced an intriguing layer to some of the stories she already knew. With a protracted exhale, she let the scroll fall onto her face. "Nothing. There's nothing here that can help me."

"There are more scrolls over there," Sefa said.

"We've been at this for hours! I wouldn't complain about having such vast knowledge at my fingertips, but I'm running out of time. What if the Regent drops me at the center of the volcano's mouth and leaves me there?" Elva muttered, tapping her toes on the chair. A beat of silence stretched between them as she waited for a response. "You don't think he'll do that, do you?" She flipped onto her belly when the Regent's guard didn't reply. Sefa's dark eyebrows furrowed over a scroll, completely absorbed. "What are you reading?"

Elva shuffled over to the table, leaning closely over the Regent's guard to have a look. "Hm, *Silent Peaks, Haunted Valleys: The Tanama's Lament*," she scanned the title, ignoring Sefa's stare. "Is this about how the Tanama became haunted? Does it talk about the Uláak? Does it have illustrations of the creatures?"

"Ahem." Sefa cleared her throat with a hint of irritation.

Her eyes darted from the scroll and to Sefa's intense dark eyes.

"Do you mind?" The guard gestured for her to move back.

Without moving, Elva gently placed her fingers around the edge of the scroll picking it up in slow motion without breaking eye contact.

"Are you always this obnoxious?"

"She is, more if you give her time," Oran's deep voice came from the entrance.

"You should count yourself lucky. Not everyone gets that close to the Regent's personal guard without suffering the consequences." Yoen followed closely behind, carrying several parchments.

A small smile tugged at her lips. The familiar warmth returned to her skin at the sight of Oran's smirk. Her fingers relinquished the parchment, and she inched closer to him instead. He glanced at her bare feet, revealing patches of white and bronze skin. "Did you find anything?" he asked, fingers delicately moving along her ear, tenderly tracing the little curls behind her neck.

"Not really," she replied, her gaze locked onto his.

"Ha!"

She turned at Sefa's sarcastic laugh from across the room. The guard crossed her arms, a smirk playing on her lips, while her eyebrows danced in amusement. Then she flicked her gaze between Oran and Elva.

Elva bit her lip, her eyes turning back to Oran. Her feet stumbled back, heat bubbling in her cheeks as her fingers scratched the spot on her neck where he had touched.

"Everything all right?" Oran probed with a raised eyebrow, his gaze shifting between Elva and Sefa.

"Uh, yes. Did you and the Chief find anything useful?" she blurted, casting Sefa a sharp look. The Regent's guard countered it with a playful smile.

"Here," Yoen interrupted, handing her a scroll before diving into the text Sefa had been reading.

Oran reached for the scroll. With a nod, he guided her to a corner on the wooden floor, leaning against bookcases filled with texts. Settling beside her, his broad shoulders pressed against hers. She nestled into his familiar warmth. Her gaze lingered on the chiseled lines of his jaw and the intensity in his gaze while he reviewed the parchment. Oran's finger traced the text, then paused at his lips, where he gently bit down, deep in thought. Each time he leaned toward her, a flutter rose in her chest.

"Do you want me to read it to you?" he offered, meeting her gaze.

"What?" She blinked, startled. Her head shook then nodded. "No, yes. I mean, I can read it."

"What's gotten into you?"

"Nothing," she nodded, biting her lip.

Oran chuckled. "You're acting strange. And you're still a bad liar."

She frowned, not knowing how to reply... or daring to. Her focus shifted to the pieces of parchment. The intricate illustrations and faded text came into view, along with the title, *Stones Aflame:*

The Emberheart's Scrolls. The scent of aged parchment filled the air. Immersing herself in the text, a wave of unease washed over her. "Emberhearts," she muttered under her breath, "Tristone Enchanters." More of the texts revealed the connection to the three stones and uncanny powers required to wield them. An ancient lineage bound the Emberhearts through blood. The connection to the stones flowed through their veins, and their unique ability to sense the three stones set them apart. "Blood," she whispered, her finger stuck to the word.

The revelation sent her mind spinning out of control, like a handwheel slipping free from its grip. Her parents were foragers and farmers, with a stand selling stuffed cabbage in the main square. They occasionally lent a hand in the Iron Tower mines, living simple lives and never mentioning any ties to an Enchanter or their kin.

Her mind spun. Despite her aunt's trepidation about Buldar, she never discouraged her from joining the Academy. Over two years had slipped by since she last saw her parents, yet her aunt trekked down the mountains to see her every quarter. If they had known of any connection to Enchanters, they would've told her. Her aunt would've told her.

Oran's hands wrapped around her trembling ones. "Hey, hey," he spoke with a gentle voice. "What is it?"

She swallowed. "All of this. It doesn't make any sense. It speaks of Tristone Enchanters being part of an old lineage. Listen to this." She scanned the text with her finger. "The Emberheart's powers stand as a resilient bloodline, a gift from Elder Wyverns, Ragas' ancestors." Her brow furrowed as her gaze darted to him. "This can't be true! There's no way I'm linked to Ragas."

He stared back with wide eyes squeezing her hand.

"This one here! That's the one I saw." Yoen's voice echoed in the chamber, breaking their stare.

Oran pushed himself away from the scattered papers, extending a hand to her. Across the chamber, Yoen jabbed his finger at the parchment spread in front of Sefa.

"What is that?" Her eye caught the illustration Yoen pointed at. A tall figure in a horned mask, gripping a long, spiked whip, stared back at her.

"It's an Uláak," Oran muttered through his teeth.

"It's not just any Uláak," Yoen retorted, his eyes still fixed on the illustration. "It's their leader."

"Those things have ranks?" she asked, leaning closer to inspect it.

Yoen turned the scroll, offering a better view. "It seems they do. This one is mentioned more often in different texts."

Unease crawled down her spine. Her fingers traced the Uláak's weapon, the scars on her back blooming with a lingering ache. The hilt resembled the stones from Äktas, while its links were a chain of ruby and volcanic rocks coiling beneath the figure like a serpent's tail. "What is its weapon made of?"

The Chief Miner's gaze bore into her. "It's a tristone chain whip. And its wielder is an Emberheart. Just like you."

Her breath caught, nails digging into her palms. The words from the parchment she had just read and Yoen's words twisted together, merging into a harrowing truth. Her eyes fixed on the image of the creature gripping the tristone weapon. Like her, it stood as a Tristone Wielder, an Emberheart. And if all Emberhearts shared a lineage, then she carried the same blood as the Uláak staring back at her.

Oran slammed a hand over the illustration. "What are you implying?" he snapped, appearing to have made the same connection.

"She read the Emberheart scroll, didn't she?" Yoen said, darting his eyes between them. "This," he pointed at the Uláak leader, "is her kin."

Elva shook her head. "It can't be," she muttered, her voice barely a whisper. Her heart thumped against her ribcage, wild and uncontained, as if it too wanted to escape the truth. She anxiously wiped the sweat from her palms against her trousers. The horror of the revelation deepened the stabbing in her stomach. Magic had caused the destruction of the land—and now it bound her to the very monsters that had claimed hundreds of innocent lives. Her disdain for the stones consumed her, flooding her senses, a loathing that seeped into her bones. Buldar had been right all along—*I am a wildling*. Just another creature, an Uláak, poisoned by the stone powers that tore her city apart.

A rhythmic pulsing flooded her mind, the agni stones of the fortress beating like war drums—unceasing, overwhelming. The sound surged through her bones and skin until nothing else existed. It rose and fell like a merciless tide, both crushing and pulling, a force that left her drowning in its wake. Heat and cold warred within her, each pulse a collision threatening to tear her apart.

Then came the bloodstone, the one she had grown to fear and hate the most. It tugged at her core, unraveling her from within, weaving its presence through her thoughts until she could no longer separate herself from its power. The white stone's once-familiar rhythm had transformed into a tempest. Steady drums erupted into thunder, bolts of energy crackling across her skin like lightning made solid. Her palms flew to her ears in desperation, but the sound lived inside her. Her eyes squeezed shut. Heat flooded her veins, a wildfire devouring her from within. The violent hums pulsed against her skin, and the more she fought, the deeper they pulled her into an abyss where no anchor could reach.

"Elva," a gentle voice called.

Her eyes blinked open. Oran had placed his own hands over hers, still clinging to her ears, actively helping her drown out the noise. He stayed there, unmoving, as she squinted against the flickering lights. On the table, Sefa had pulled the small agni stone and bloodstone box from her waist satchel, their surfaces flickering with light.

"Take a deep breath, Glowworm." His voice sounded muffled behind their hands.

Yoen and Sefa exchanged hurried glances, their urgent words drowned by her racing pulse. She drew in a few deep breaths, the cool air filling her lungs, realizing her knees had buckled onto the floor. Oran knelt in front of her, his eyes warm as they searched her face.

"There you go," he said softly, taking a deep breath himself for her to mirror. "You're safe."

Staring into his dark eyes, a pang of sorrow washed over her. Shaky breaths escaped her lips as a hollow ache settled in her chest. She slowly moved his hands from her, then gripped her churning stomach.

"She's going to be sick," Sefa grimaced, taking a step back.

"I... I'm fine."

Oran's fingers stretched across the space between them, but she jerked back. Her cheeks flushed, her eyes darting from him to Yoen and then to Sefa. Her lips struggled to voice the words drowning in her mind. "You—you have all lost someone to those creatures. To those—wildlings," she added in disgust.

"Don't say that," Oran reached for her again, but she pulled away.

Yoen took a step forward. His arms folded across his chest, the fabric of his sleeves pulling taut. "At least now we have some answers."

Oran's muscles tightened, his fists shaking at his sides. He scowled at Yoen. "How dare you? Are you implying she's one of those monsters?" He jabbed a finger at the Chief Miner. "If you suspected anything about her being an Emberheart, why not talk to her directly? Why show her this?" His hand seized the illustration, the parchment crinkling under the force. "This is cruel! You did it to get a rise out of her. This whole city would've been swallowed by that damn volcano if it weren't for her."

Yoen approached Elva, who remained on her knees. His shoulders relaxed despite Oran's outburst. "The unraveling of one's own tapestry is a journey that unveils our virtues, but also the wicked side of us," he said calmly, extending a hand to her, but she declined him.

"Don't touch her!" Oran seethed through gritted teeth.

Yoen squatted down to meet her gaze. "While I believe you are capable of great power, I don't see those creatures in you. But, to understand who we are, what we are, and what we are capable of, we must confront every thread we are woven from. You must understand that at least."

Her eyes locked onto him, battling the warmth rising in her cheeks. Before she could speak, a tall figure filled the entrance.

"What is all this? Why are you in my father's study?" Vardan's voice echoed against the walls.

"Lord Regent," Yoen greeted with a low bow. Sefa and Oran's heads dipped in unison beside him. "The High Regent granted us access to some of the scrolls. We're helping young Elva understand her powers."

Vardan directed an intense, expectant look at Elva, his jaw tensed. Sefa nudged Elva on the side.

"Sir—Lord Regent." Elva finally bowed.

His focus remained on Yoen only. "My father allowed this?"

"Yes, Lord Regent."

The silver pleats of his long skirt ruffled against the wooden floor as he entered the chamber. He paused at the table, fingers brushing over the agni stone Sefa had conjured from her satchel. "I take it she has learned how to wield them?" His gaze shifted slowly to Yoen while Oran reached out to help Elva to her feet.

"Not quite yet, Your Highness, I'm afraid she still needs more time," Yoen replied.

Vardan's gaze raked over Elva. "Is that so? Perhaps it's time to pursue a different diplomacy with the Äktastary."

"Lord Regent, there you are," High Council Hura said, her voice cutting through the study. As she stepped inside, everyone bowed instinctively, except for Vardan. "What is the meaning of all of this?" she asked, scanning the room.

"High Councilor, we are here by order of the High Regent," Yoen explained. "Perhaps we can discuss in private."

"After I warned you not to bring up the matter of the scrolls... You *still* managed to push your will into the Arcanum."

Yoen bowed again. "High Councilor, we are seeking a different approach, to help the young lady here."

Her eyes scrutinized Elva while she addressed Yoen. "It'll be wiser if she practiced her powers outside the fortress. We can't afford her bringing this place down with her incompetence," she spat.

"High Councilor Hura, I promise she has been under a watchful eye all this time. Both of them have been," Yoen insisted.

"I'm not speaking of your ability to keep them in place," she hissed. "I'm referring to her uncontrollable bursts that have caused the entire fortress to tremble. Haven't you noticed?" she asked, her arm sweeping in a wide arc. "Several ignited stones—ablaze, flickering like fireflies. The Lord Regent suspected Garam was causing the tremors. But the volcano wouldn't activate the stones in such a way. Why in the skies of Ragas is she in here?" Her hand flicked to Elva. "Her training should be with the High Regent, where he can control the Äktastary."

Blood drained from Elva's face and a wave of nausea surged through her, forcing her hand to her stomach. Sefa was right, she was going to be sick. She had only just started to study her new-found magic, but uncontrollable bursts of destruction presented a new foul riddle. She carried the same curse that plagued the Tanama, forced to contain the monsters within. Wide eyes around the room shifted from Hura to Elva in silent disbelief.

"She didn't even notice the scope of her reach," Vardan scoffed, a hint of a snarl curling at his lip. "Such extraordinary power in the hands of a wildling."

Oran's knuckles tightened beside him. Elva and Sefa simultaneously reached out, catching his arms.

"My sincere apologies, Lord Vardan and High Councilor. We will move our training back to the High Regent's atrium," Yoen said, his voice carefully measured.

"Make sure the Äktastary don't sneak around. Chief Gerel is still trying to figure out the pouches of black dust they brought," Hura remarked, approaching the door.

"Black dust?" The words escaped Elva's lips, and instinct made her step forward. Before she could get any closer to the Councilor, Sefa's hand tightened around her wrist. "Sir, Hura. High Councilor, what—what do you mean by black dust?"

Hura's glare could have frozen a flame.

"She means no harm, High Councilor. She's just not used to our ways. Apologies once again," Yoen conveyed with a bow.

Sefa yanked on Elva's tunics, forcing her to bow. Hura and Vardan's footsteps faded down the corridor.

"Are you out of your mind?" Yoen raised his eyebrows.

"What black dust? We didn't bring any black dust," she cut him off.

"You know what it is?" Yoen asked.

"Where is it being kept?"

Yoen remained silent, darting a look at Sefa.

"Is it in here, inside the Arcanum? Beneath the fortress?" Her eyes flicked between the two of them.

Oran stepped in beside her. "Lyla carried some pouches with black dust around her waist, but no one knows what it is. She won't say either. That's why she was in such a rough state when you first saw her." He placed a steady hand on Elva's arm, gently guiding her to face him. "Do you know what it is?"

The room seemed to spin under her bare feet. Elva pressed her fingers to her temples, squeezing her eyes to clear her vision. "Just tell me the black dust isn't here, inside the Arcanum."

"Speak up," Yoen ordered. "What do you know?"

Her fingers tapped against her thigh. "Every quarter, the Academy hosts tests for the Artificer's Trade. The entire Trade is allowed to participate, but first-years use it as an opportunity to gain rank." She slumped on the chair Oran offered.

Yoen's eyes narrowed. "And...?"

"If they are skilled enough, they are allowed to seek counsel from Sergeant Artificers. I was ordered to assist Fenris, a first-year working on a classified project. These assignments are always kept secret so others can't steal ideas. The first-year called it searing ash. It resembles dust."

"Like black sand," Sefa added.

Elva nodded, her leg shaking beside her. "It's composed of different elements. I was supposed to examine his last findings, but... I was sent here." She leaned forward slightly, her eyes focusing on Sefa and Yoen before she continued. "Months ago, I witnessed the first test. A gentle spark brought it to life, causing it to catch fire and burn a piece of parchment. As Fenris continued to refine it, the ash caused an explosion large enough to obliterate an entire pile of wooden cases." Her gaze flicked to Oran before returning to the others.

"Its success caught the attention of the General Artificer and the Commander General. The boy had been working on making it stronger, eager to impress them. The goal, as expressed by the Commander," she said, repeatedly clasping her hands in her lap, "was to create a more potent substance that, combined with a strong fuel, could combust through larger structures."

"Like walls of stone," Oran muttered, standing beside her, eyes wide in panic.

Elva looked at Sefa and Yoen, giving a subtle nod. The Chief Miner stormed out of the chamber without a word. Sefa followed quickly behind him.

As Elva and Oran moved to follow, the guard raised a finger to them. "Stay put! Don't touch anything." Her hand patted her waist bag, making sure she had the ignited stones. "I'm warning you. Don't break anything. Don't even breathe too loudly. Just stay!" She held their gaze until both nodded their agreement, then pulled the door shut with a decisive click, leaving them alone in the High Regent's study.

CHAPTER 24

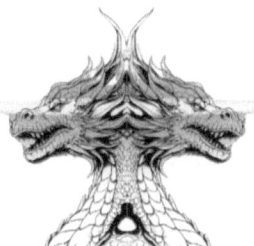

KA'ZAN

ELVA

E LVA STARED AT THE looming oak door in the Regent's study, shoulders tense until Oran's gentle hand found hers, warm and reassuring.

"I helped Fenris with the ash measurements," she said, her voice quivering. "It's on me if something happens."

"You are not responsible for any of this," he insisted, dragging a chair in front of her and sinking into it.

Sprawled across the table, the illustration of the Emberheart Uláak caught her eye, stealing her breath and tightening her chest. Her thumbnail found its familiar groove along her index finger, sinking deep. "Do you think it's possible? That I could be related to that—thing?"

"Yoen was just trying to pressure you," Oran stammered, quickly rolling the parchment away, the creature's image vanishing beneath the layers. His hands reached for hers again, massaging the spot where her nail dug. "He's a self-serving—calculating snake who wanted to get under your skin."

"He's right, though," she mumbled, her eyes darting to a split between the floorboards. "If we're going to make it out of this mess alive, I have to face this damn magic, and learn whatever I can. No matter how disturbing the truth is. In the end, Buldar was right. I am a wildling," she scoffed, the words leaving a sour taste on her tongue.

Oran dropped to his knees before her, his hands cradling hers with an urgency that made her look up. "I can't stand seeing you like this. But you know yourself. I know you too. If it's true, about your kin, it changes nothing about how I see you, how I feel about you. But it cuts me deep to hear you speak like that."

Her teeth caught her lower lip, meeting his gaze. The darkest, most beautiful eyes she'd ever seen brimmed with concern. She hated that look more than anything. Not because it was wrong, but because she had no idea how to fix it. Her fingers traced the spot where Hura's blade had burned him, now fully healed and hidden beneath a short, prickling beard. "This beard," she whispered.

"I'm letting it grow," he added.

"It's ugly."

Oran's loud snort echoed through the study, tugging a smile from her lips and allowing her to breathe easy again. With a long sigh, she let her head fall forward onto the table's cool surface. "I'm so tired. It's weird, but I miss my cot at the Academy."

"I'm sure they all miss your snoring."

She had never noticed how his right side revealed a dimple when he smiled. Even with the short beard, she could still see it. His hand gently cupped her cheek, and warmth bloomed beneath his palm, wrapping around her, grounding her like only his touch could. Her shoulders softened, and she closed her eyes, the weight of the day dissolving with his touch.

"I keep thinking about that time you broke that old lady's weaving wheel. Remember?" he asked, his thumb brushing her cheekbone. "What was her name?"

"Moira, but I didn't break anything!"

A deep chuckle rumbled in his chest. "Yes, you did. The old woman chased you down the hill with a slipper in her hand."

With a sigh, a half-smile tugged at her lips. "She had thrown the other one at me. She had good aim—nailed me right on my temple. But I didn't break the wheel. I fixed it."

"You took the whole thing apart!"

"Taking things apart and breaking them are two very distinct things." The words slurred with exhaustion. "She'd complained to my aunt about how slow the process was. Her business was suffering. I was putting it back together when she found me."

His laugh vibrated through her as his fingers moved to dance with the strayed curls from her braid. "And you ran away with three of the spindles."

"If I recall correctly, you became an accomplice the moment you kept those spindles for yourself. Besides, she didn't need them, and her business picked up after."

Her eyes fluttered open to find his face inches from hers. Heat rushed to her cheeks, and she held her breath, caught off guard by the sudden flush. Each gentle tug of his fingers through her braid sent shivers down her spine. He shifted to hold her hand, his thumb tracing the soft patterns of her bronze and white skin. For a moment, his lips pressed into a thin line, his expression heavy with unspoken words before he averted his gaze.

"What is it?" she asked.

"It's nothing."

"Please, Oran, just tell me."

His chest rose with a deep breath before meeting her gaze. "Why didn't you tell me?"

"Tell you what?" she asked, though she knew what he meant. Her stomach twisted into knots.

"About everything, El," he said, his hand shooting to the back of his neck, fingers digging into the muscle. "We had to cross the bloody sea for me to find out you could sense the stones."

She pulled her hand back, her nail finding the tender skin on her finger. "And what would you have said? If I had told you that I could hear them?"

The chair legs scraped against wood as Oran stood and crossed to the far side of the table. His eyes darted around the study, never settling, his fingers raking through his hair.

Her spine straightened, and she forced herself to meet his gaze before continuing. "Everyone in the city and the Academy throw festivals every time an Enchanter passes the trials. Children grow up wishing they could wield the stones. I wanted to be an Artificer—not many would understand that decision."

"I would've," he objected, his arms crossing over his chest. "If you had only given me the chance, but you couldn't trust me. After everything, you still keep me at bay," he added, his eyes dropping to the floor. "That's why you also didn't tell me about—" The words died on his lips. He spun on his heel, pacing before the table with tight shoulders and a clenched jaw.

"About what?"

"What the Commander did," he snapped. "The marks on your back. Is it true? I had to find out from a Ka'zanty of all people. Why didn't you tell me?"

"I couldn't, all right?" she blurted, her teeth catching the inside of her cheek and her fingers twisted the edge of her sleeve.

"You couldn't or wouldn't?"

"I…" she swallowed, her shoulders stiffening. Her tunic brushed against the marks on her back. "Why would you want to know about that anyway? It's not a day I like to talk about," she added, feeling the heat on her cheeks.

He scoffed, dragging his hand through his dark hair. The new gray tunic the Ka'zanty had given him stretched across his chest with his agitated movements. "Wouldn't you want to know if something happened to me?"

"Of course I would." The words burst out of her. "But that's… that's different."

"How?"

Her fingers drummed against the table's edge before retreating to her lap. "I didn't hide it on purpose. I was embarrassed, maybe.

But I just thought it was part of the Academy life. A normal thing that just happened. The whole quarter burned down. A lot of important scrolls were lost because of a ridiculous oversight, and that was my punishment."

"What part of any of that is normal?" His voice hardened, his gaze narrowing as he stepped back. "I can understand life being hard, even hard punishments. But what he did—what he continues to do," he snarled, fists clenching at his sides. "I could kill him."

Her leg bounced beneath the table. "Perhaps that's why I didn't tell you. That kind of rebel talk is dangerous, Oran. It could be treated as treason."

His lips parted, and his thick eyebrows furrowed with a pained look. "You'd expect me to sit back and do nothing?"

"No! I—I don't know, Oran. But I'd expect you not to act so recklessly. Think about the consequences."

"You're telling me about consequences?" His arms shot upward. "About recklessness? The girl who jumped over the edge of the Sky Lanterns midair."

"Yes, reckless! Look at where you're standing. You're not supposed to be here!" Her heart hammered against her ribs. "Admit it, you didn't even think twice about boarding that vessel. It was different for me. I was ordered. But you went and got yourself in trouble for nothing. Now you're in this bloody mess!"

He crossed his arms beneath his tensed jaw. "You're right. I didn't think twice, and I would do it again!"

"That makes no sense. Why on Ragas' skies did you do that? Why did you get on that vessel?"

"You're really asking me that, after all this time. Isn't it obvious, El?"

"No, it isn't obvious Oran, why risk your life?"

"Are you saying if the roles were reversed, you wouldn't have done it? You wouldn't have gotten in that vessel?"

"Never mind what I would do. What you did is illogical," she sighed.

"Right, because if it's not a machine or a scroll—if you can't find any reason or sense in it," he stammered, his tone growing louder as he jabbed a finger at his temple. "Your brain just can't fathom putting the pieces together."

"It's different because my life is not worth yours!" she confessed, the words bursting from her in pain and frustration.

His shoulders dropped, arms heavy at his sides. As he moved closer, the warmth in his gaze melted the jagged edges of her anger. With a heavy sigh, the tension drained from her, her fists softening in her lap.

"Yes, I would get on that vessel for you. Because I couldn't bear it if anything happened to you," she admitted, her voice trembling. "What you did doesn't make sense. You make lists, plans, and schedules. You never leave anything to chance. I thrive in reckless-ness. You're different. Acting on impulse isn't what you do—look at where it's gotten you. Now, if I don't figure this stone magic out, nothing else matters. This land will consume us all, and you're here in the middle of it all because of me." She exhaled slowly, blinking back the sting in her eyes. "Once again, chaos surrounds me, like the wildling I am, and you're here, bearing its blows."

"I love bearing its blows," he replied with a gentle smirk, trying to ease the tension.

"You shouldn't." Her voice quivered, her gaze flicking down-ward. "At least not because of me. I got you into this mess. And now, the thing I hate the most is the very thing I need or I lose you." She swallowed hard, pressing her lips together to stop them from shaking.

Oran stepped closer wrapping his hand around hers. Her fingers relaxed against the warmth of his touch.

She avoided his warm gaze, fearing it might shatter something inside her. "Most people in this land would welcome the gift of stone wielding with open arms. Instead, it's me who ends up with it," she scoffed. "Zohar is right, the very foundation of our land is built on this one thing that I can't seem to grasp. And you'll pay the price for it, all because you got on that vessel."

"And I would do it again," he admitted.

Her head shook as tears welled in her eyes. "Then you're a fool."

"I'd do it for the same reason you would do it for me," he said before his knees dropped in front of her. "But since you need to break things apart to understand them, allow me to be as clear as I can," he added, cupping both her hands. "Do you remember the first time your aunt took us to the river near her cabin in the woods?"

She nodded, her chest tightening at the mention of her aunt.

"My knees buckled when I saw that cliff, but you sprinted without a second thought. I almost turned back—then your hand found mine. And I knew. I knew I could jump if you were by my side. If you held my hand." The floorboards creaked beneath him as he shifted, bracing himself before letting out a slow, steady breath. "In that fleeting moment, a mere heartbeat, when our feet left the ground and we floated in the air, we were untethered from the pain of this land. Alive, weightless, and free. That's how you make me feel."

Elva's eyes widened. Heat rushed to her cheeks. She shifted in her seat, her heart fluttering, and with a soft breath, she finally let her gaze meet his.

Oran's lips curved into that gentle smile she'd come to know so well, his eyes softening when he drew in a deep breath. With deliberate tenderness, he cradled her face in his hands. As he leaned in, their lips met, and time seemed to still. She melted into him, his warmth easing the burdens she had been carrying.

Her lips moved with his in a dance they somehow already knew, each breath drawing her deeper into the moment. Oran had been right. His touch left her untethered. Alive, weightless, free. But at the same time, his embrace grounded her, anchoring her in ways she hadn't known she craved. He was the rope she searched for as she plummeted through an insatiable abyss. He had been for a long time.

He pulled away slowly, his hands still holding her face. As he withdrew, a soft breath escaped him, and his dark eyes bore into her with an intensity that made her come undone.

"I'm in love with you, Elva. Tristone Wielder, Enchanter, Emberheart," he confessed, his thumb tracing her lips. "Ever since that time when you fixed my father's locket. Ever since that day, you became a beacon in a veil of shadows I didn't know consumed me." He let out another long sigh. "Is that clear enough for you, Glowworm?"

Her feet itched to run from the overwhelming surge of feelings she couldn't fully name or understand. At the same time, her body ached to melt into his embrace and never let go—to let him hold her so close she'd forget where she ended and he began. Instead, her fingers traced along his chin, brushing the edges of his beard. "I still don't like this beard," was all she could manage.

"I'll shave it," he said with a bright smile.

She sat frozen in place, her breath caught in her throat, heart pounding. Only days ago, they had been excited, even celebrated when testing the Sky Lantern. Now, they were prisoners in enemy territory, with no way home and no refuge in sight.

His warm eyes sent her mind spinning. He knew her, accepted her—wildling or not. Even if her link to the Uláak leader held true, he loved her. Instead of embracing it fully, a suffocating tightness wound around her chest. Her world fractured, like the gears of an old wheel unhinging from their axis, scattering in pieces as the whole structure collapsed.

The room spun. Ka'zan's High Regent demanded Elva wield the power of the stones to seal the raging volcano. If she didn't, Oran and everyone else would face its wrath. But her heart continued to recoil against the stones' essence. Oran had given up everything to be by her side, and she had days—hours—to hone her stone-wielding powers. Enchanters spent years learning to control just one type of gem. The thought of controlling three sent cold ripples down her spine.

Even if she managed to put Garam to rest, the threat from the Tanama still loomed. Smoke still clung to the edges of the dead forests, and if the Uláak broke free, nowhere would be safe. And even if the lethal creatures stayed contained in the forests, Ka'zan would never let a Tristone Enchanter escape their grip—she'd remain a prisoner, but as long as Oran survived, as long as he was safe, it didn't matter.

All of her focus needed to be directed on wielding the magic she had avoided for a long time. If she failed, the price would be his life. She couldn't afford to leave room for anything else, even if it tore her heart apart.

"Oran," she finally whispered, as his thumb wiped a tear from her cheek.

"I know," he said, his arms folding around her shoulders. "You don't need to say anything right now. Just let me hold you."

With a trembling lip, she followed his directions, letting him hold all of her.

CHAPTER 25

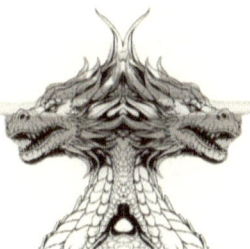

KA'ZAN

YOEN

G ARAM'S VOLCANIC TREMORS SHUDDERED through the fortress, sending ripples across the pond inside Zohar's atrium. Yoen's eyes traced the water lapping against the wooden platform where the Regent stood, bare feet planted wide, loose strands of dark hair falling from his knot. The onyx silk of his skirt caught the dawn light filtering through the high windows.

"You cannot ask me to stay hidden like a coward. High Regents have protected this land for centuries," Zohar's voice boomed. "You can't expect me to sit back while another attempts the duty I am meant to fulfill."

Hura stepped forward, parchments crinkling beneath her vice-like grip. Her silver robes rustled with each movement. "Your Eminence, I implore you to reconsider. Our city cannot afford to lose its only Enchanter."

Across the pond, Vardan sat hunched on a wooden bench. Dark circles under his forest-green eyes had deepened since the Äktastary invaded. His shoulders twitched at the High Councilor's words. For several days, while his father immersed himself in training Elva and studying scrolls within the Arcanum, the Lord Regent had shouldered the burden of leadership. After learning what the eastern invaders' searing ash could do, Vardan had also taken on the task of prisoner interrogation—all except Elva and Oran, who were excluded by Zohar's orders.

On the opposite side of the pond, the other Chiefs and the High Regent's guards stood poised, awaiting instructions. Zohar remained resolute in his decision to journey to the volcano's largest crevice, determined to seal the White Stone Gate he had opened several days prior.

"Your Eminence, if I may," Chief Gerel cleared his throat, breaking into Hura's continuous pleas. "The Äktastary has demonstrated true affinity. Her stone-wielding strength will be enough to seal the gate. We shouldn't jeopardize your High Regency. The plan we have discussed, if executed accordingly, should prove effective."

Zohar's spine straightened. "I can't risk our city's safety on someone with only days of training." His words fell like stones into water. "While she has exhibited strength, alone, she does not stand a chance against Garam in its full might. I must join her. The mount's reawakening this time will unleash its complete power. It'll require the strength of more than just one stone wielder."

"Father." Vardan pushed himself up from the bench and circled the pond, forcing Zohar to face him. "The young girl carries no ordinary power. She's an Emberheart, bearing Ragas' bloodline. The Äktastary only needs to follow the training you have so eagerly provided. Part of the Chief Guard's plan is to haul one of our large stone reserves. The girl should have more than enough resources." He stopped at the water's edge, shoulders dropping into a soft bow. "I implore you, trust the Chiefs you've chosen to take care of your citizens. Let them carry out their plan."

The High Regent's bare feet moved around the platform, his hands clasped tightly behind his back. Another tremor sent ripples across the water's surface. Finally, his gaze settled on Yoen. "I need a private word with the Chief Miner. Leave us." He then addressed Gerel and Sefa. "Ready the soldiers, send for the boy, and bring her to me." His hand rose, halting Hura and Vardan in their approach. "Only the Chief Miner. I'll summon you if needed." Vardan's chin dipped in acknowledgment. Hura's shoulders sank in a low bow while her eyes cut into Yoen like shards of ice.

As the sound of departing footsteps faded, Zohar's composure crumbled. He sank onto the bench, elbows digging into his knees, face buried in his hands. Yoen settled beside him, the wood creaking beneath them.

"I understand the weight of your sacrifice," Yoen said in a low voice. "But your worth exceeds the girl's."

"You sound like my father," Zohar said, dropping his hands. "And you're wrong. This city needs the strength she carries. I have become a relic of older days."

"I spoke of worth, Your Eminence. The people need their leader now more than ever. They hold you in the highest regards, as do I," he replied, crossing his arms and resting his back against the bench. "It'll work."

"How do you know? She still has much to learn."

"I'll make sure of it," he reassured, wiping his sweaty palms on his trousers. "The rest of the plan is sound. Gerel has relocated the Äktastary from the fortress, and his guards have strategically placed more ignited stones around Drekavog. If anything goes wrong," he shifted his gaze to Zohar, "you're the one the city needs. Your scepter might no longer be at its full strength, Your Eminence, but that doesn't render you a relic. You still possess the strength of one of the mightiest Enchanters to grace Ka'zan. The city needs your protection. And if I may be so bold," he took a deep breath, "I wouldn't leave my family alone while I journey to Garam if I didn't believe you could keep them safe."

"Your boldness has surged as of late. Reminds me of your youth before Nim," Zohar said with a soft smirk. "Still, you're not entirely accurate. My father was much stronger than I am, and his strength pales in comparison to Elva's. It makes me question if Ka'zan has ever truly experienced the essence birthed from a wyvern's breath—a genuine Emberheart. I never thought I'd live long enough to witness such power."

"You're certain then. She's an Emberheart, Ragas' kin?" he inquired, his leg bouncing restlessly at his side.

The High Regent nodded. "There are more questions than answers as of late. But her bloodline is strong. Chief Daigo has taken blood samples to the Sanctum for examination and to cross-match them with our Elder's specimens. She's reluctant to believe it still. Especially after your lack of tactfulness in your revelation of her possible link to the Uláak leader," Zohar continued, the last words dripping with mild reproach.

Yoen's shoulders stiffened. "We need bluntness and swiftness in these times, even heartlessness."

Zohar picked his way across. With each step, the platform swayed, fracturing his reflection into rippling pieces across the pond's surface. "My father had similar views. They did not serve him well after all."

"Are your own views the reason you kept silent after my warnings of Garam. The reason you didn't mention the bloody wyvern locked within its walls?" Yoen's unintentional outburst sliced through the air.

Zohar whirled around, muscles tensing beneath his robes, jaw clenched tight enough to make a vein pulse at his temple.

He let out a strained sigh. "My apologies, Your Eminence."

Zohar drew in a deep breath, easing the tension in his shoulders. "Keeping Zuwena captive saved her life amidst the chaos of the wyvern hunts. She must know this or our city would've already been ravaged by her vengeance. Or that's what I tell myself to find solace. Without her, our city would've ceased to be long ago. It is her essence that allowed us to retrieve the stockpile of agni stones we keep tucked away." His eyes drifted upward to where sunbeams pierced through the glass ceiling. "I do regret not telling you."

At Zohar's confession, Yoen's heel stopped mid-bounce against the ground. His gaze followed the way sunlight caught in the High Regent's dark strands, turning them to silk.

The ground trembled beneath them, sending more ripples across the pond's surface as Zohar continued, his dark eyes tracking the expanding circles in the water.

"I let the words of others persuade me into opening Garam's gate. I was convinced the beast had escaped, and that the only way to bring her back was to retrieve the obsidian chains that kept her captive." He exhaled, bitter with the memory. "But the bindings still held when we entered. They broke open with the outburst of her blue flames against my scepter. If it hadn't been for my discretion about keeping secrets, the only threat we would be facing now is the smoke cloaking the forest."

He turned, his gaze meeting Yoen's with sudden intensity. "There is one thing I will divulge, however, given the state of things. I believe I discovered the reason Äktas dispatched their metal whales when they did."

Yoen rose from the bench and closed the distance between them. "You've been spending a lot of time in the Arcanum. What else have you found?"

Zohar's fingers traced the outline of his dark beard. "It appears there are portals that manifest every summer solstice."

"Portals?"

The High Regent's hands clasped behind his back. "Threads linking Ka'zan to Äktas and Ikari. They have existed long before Ragas cursed the Tanama. They manifest every year, but their stability has always been compromised. According to a scroll from my father's late High Council, it was predicted the portals would gain strength around the centennial anniversary of the Wyvern's War. This coincides with the time when the smoke slithered within the Tanama and the Äktas invasion."

Zohar's eyes met Yoen's. "These passages surround the dead forests and water caves. There might be more scattered around the region. Äktas' leaders must've had access to this knowledge."

Yoen struggled to piece Zohar's words together. Something about the Äktastary's plan felt wrong. But he had spent all his efforts making sure Elva could wield the stones, including separating her from her friend and ensuring she spent every waking moment training. Still, he feared the invaders had a more sinister plan.

"Despite the heightened chances of crossing, the stakes were still too high. The Äktastary barely made it out alive. If not for Elva, it would've been a sure death for all of them. Unless..." Yoen's shoulders tensed. "They must be plotting something more significant."

The gentle tap of clay broke the tension. Steam curled up from the spout as Zohar poured two cups of tea, the aromatic blend filling the air with notes of herbs and spice. "There are still questions I have not yet figured out. If they had an inkling their vessels could survive, they sent them here to cause damage. The Äktas Militia members confessed. They indeed had orders to set off the searing ash, but to what extent?" Zohar added, pressing the delicate cup into Yoen's hands, its warmth spreading through his palms.

"You're right, that doesn't explain the aftermath. Even if they had succeeded in damaging the city, what would they gain?" Yoen asked, downing the tea in one swift motion before continuing. "A full armada wouldn't be able to navigate those waters, let alone the dead forest, especially now that it's covered in smoke."

"I'm afraid that's all I've been able to decipher," Zohar said, fixing his gaze on the pond's surface where ripples fractured the stillness.

"Who else knows about these portals?"

"I haven't discussed it with anyone else, but the scrolls have been available to those with access to the Arcanum," Zohar added, his fingers wrapping around the small teacup. "Despite these findings, sealing Garam's gate must be our top priority. While I'm not entirely on board with your plan, I do agree. We must do whatever it takes for the sake of our people. Whatever you do, bring her back safely." Zohar's dark eyes narrowed, boring into Yoen with an intensity that made him shift his weight.

"You've truly taken a liking to her. My grandfather always said it. You have a tender heart," he mused.

Zohar's shoulders dropped, the faintest smile tugging at his mouth. "She is young but once you get to spend time with her, you notice it. Beyond her remarkable mind, her heart is large. It's not only her strength we need," he continued, stepping closer to Yoen. "The darkness we're about to face, young Chief, demands more than the visceral power the stones offer. A strong will, tempered by love, kindness, and empathy will be our beacon. The forces that will set us free." His firm hand settled on Yoen's shoulder. "I pray you keep that in mind when you're out there."

Yoen wanted to tell him he was wrong. This was the moment when they needed to be ruthless and cunning. The stakes were too high. Each moment of hesitation could mean the destruction of everything he had fought to protect. If it had been up to him, he would have extended the tortures against the Äktastary, even to Elva. But she needed her strength. Separating her from Oran had been the only way to manipulate her into wielding the stones. Zohar's kindness, his moral reservations, were a chain, holding them back when they needed to strike decisively. Yoen would gladly sacrifice comfort, dignity, and even humanity itself if it meant preserving a single thread of their civilization—and his children.

He bit his tongue instead. He no longer wore the Chief Guard's helmet. Perhaps, in due time, he'd take it back.

The soft scrape of the sliding wall drew their attention. Yoen's throat went dry, his breath catching as Elva emerged beside Sefa, wrapped in his niece's old coat. The young Äktastary followed the guard's low bow into the atrium.

"Everything is in place, Your Excellency," Sefa assured.

Elva's fingers moved anxiously at her side, her thumb tapping each fingertip in succession.

The Regent's voice softened when he addressed her. "Remember our training. Release the emotions that bind you to the physical, be the conduit of the stones' energy and simply command them. The energy will follow your intentions."

Her eyes widened at his words. "You're not coming with us?"

"The Chief Miner will be joining you instead," Zohar said, gesturing to Yoen.

His chest tightened when Elva's gaze dropped to the floor, avoiding his eyes. Ever since he had deliberately suggested a connection to the Uláak leader, the silence between them had grown. Her disdain had worsened after he separated her from Oran. But he had to do it. He hated how his feelings warred within him every time he looked at her. He couldn't stop thinking about his niece.

"Sumani's waiting with Oran. The other guards are already making their way to Garam," Sefa interjected, her words cutting through the uncomfortable silence.

"You're not coming either," Elva stammered. Her chest rose and fell in quick, shallow breaths.

"Look at me," Zohar encouraged with a gentle tone. "I wouldn't send you alone if I didn't believe you were capable."

"Then, why not join me?" Her fingers absently traced the braid on her shoulder, gears turning in her mind as her gaze drifted, eventually settling on the Regent's. "I see," she added, as if solving a riddle. "My life is of less importance. If anything happens, the city can continue without me, but not without its High Regent." Her brow furrowed and her thumbnail dug into her finger.

Zohar stepped closer. His hand reached out to her but quickly withdrew. "The stakes here surpass the value of both our lives, young Elva. Garam's plight is my burden to bear, and I carry the weight of regret for asking you to rectify my mistakes. I promise you, with every fiber of my being, that I will do everything within my power to ensure your safety and Oran's. All I ask is for you to seal the volcano's gate, just as my father once did. Your strength is our hope, and your courage is the beacon guiding us through this turmoil." With his last word, Zohar bowed his head.

Yoen and Sefa exchanged startled glances before dropping into matching lower bows, mirroring Zohar's gesture.

Tears gathered in Elva's dark-brown eyes, catching the light.

"After today," Zohar went on, straightening and clearing his throat. "You and Oran will be welcome in our city. We'll continue your stone-wielding training, and you'll have access to the Arcanum. A place of rest will be prepared for you in the fortress, outside my quarters. Despite the circumstances of your arrival, I am willing to extend this invitation, as a recognition of your assistance in securing our city's future."

Her hand shook beside her before speaking. "And if I fail?"

Zohar's lips pressed into a thin line. Drawing a deep breath, he let his eyes bounce between Yoen and Sefa. "Then all of our lives are forfeit. It doesn't matter how many stones we have. We cannot face Garam's rage, Zuwena's wrath, and also confront whatever shadows lurk in the forests underneath the blanket of smoke." He leaned forward slightly, adjusting his height to meet her gaze. "Trust your instincts, they haven't failed you. No matter what, I am grateful to have met you, young Elva of Äktas."

At Sefa's gentle nudge, she bent into a low bow.

"Chief Yoen." Concern threaded through Zohar's voice while his gaze followed Elva and Sefa as they exited the atlas chamber. "You cannot fail."

The cold stone pressed against Yoen's forehead as he kowtowed. "I won't, Your Eminence. Even if it's the last thing I do, Garam's Gate will be sealed before the close of day." He raised his gaze but remained on his knees. "Arben and Luan, Your Regency—" The name of his children caught in his throat.

Zohar's warm hand found his shoulder, helping him to his feet. "I made a promise to your great-grandfather to treat his lineage as my own. I'll care for your family as if they were mine."

The ground beneath them shuddered, a low rumble rose from the depths of the earth itself. He cast one final glance at Zohar before turning toward the Blackstone gate. Each step grew heavier than the last. The weight of his mission settled on his shoulders like a shroud. No matter the cost, he'd make sure Elva succeeded.

Sulfuric fumes seeped through Yoen's mask, leading the way across the exposed seabed. Beneath them, Garam's tremors rippled through the ground in increasing waves. The volcano's warnings grew more insistent with each stride closer to its skirts. Sumani followed Inara, keeping a close watch over Elva and Oran, who rode transfixed by the mountain's fury. Three more guards followed closely behind.

At the base of the slope, he slid from the saddle, and his hand found Inara's neck. "Easy, fire-beetle, you know you can't go up there. Knowing you're here and safe already gives me strength." He pressed his forehead against hers, meeting those familiar eyes that had seen him through so many grim days. "You've carried me through everything, old friend. My Nim would've been proud that her Inara is still the best in the city. Stay safe for me. Don't go too far."

Above, threads of steam coiled from cracks in the dark rock. Streams of partially hardened lava still oozed, releasing searing bursts of vapor, occasionally blocking their path on the winding trail. The ground's incessant shakes threw them off balance. Yoen's knees buckled, threatening to give way, but Sumani's firm grip pulled him upright. Oran's hand tightened around Elva's, steadying her steps while his muscles strained with effort. The guards stumbled behind, bracing themselves against the jagged walls, their boots slipping on loose stones, and fighting to remain upright.

When they reached the White Stone Gate, two guards who had arrived before them greeted them. They motioned for them toward a large agni stone they had placed by the gate. Rough and untreated, it loomed almost as large as a small sheep. To non-wielders, it appeared no different from an ordinary porous stump. But Elva's eyes fixated on the stone, like a moth drawn to an irresistible flame.

One of the guards by the gate waved them forward. "Garam is stirring more and more," he shouted through another earth rumble, his long beard dancing in the hot wind. "We should hurry, or we'll be soon facing a rain of fire instead."

"Whatever happens, stick to the plan. Retrieve the three stones from Sumani and place them on the agni stone." Yoen's words sent the guards scurrying into action with quick bows.

His fingers traced Zuwena's scorching marks on the alabaster surface as he edged around the half-open gate. His chest betrayed him again, tightening at the sight of Oran shielding Elva from the falling debris, their fingers intertwined. He dug his nails into his palm until the ache pushed back the memories of Nim threatening to surface.

"We must act now," Yoen beckoned Elva and Oran toward the gate. "I have a feeling Garam might fight back."

After days of avoiding eye contact, Elva stared at him. "You think a mount could sense what we're about to do?"

He nodded and signaled the guards to their positions. "This mount is as old as time. Whatever happens, stay focused on sealing that gate. It will respond to your connection with the stones. Follow the High Regent's advice. They will heed your commands."

He stepped back. With freshly shaven skin, Oran inched closer, cupping Elva's face before pressing a gentle kiss on the white mark on her forehead. Then his eyes turned to Yoen, who directed him with a sharp nod. "Stand by Sumani."

"All right, Elva. The three stones are on top of the large agni stone. You have all you need. It's all up to you now," he shouted over the raging wind.

She gave Yoen a weary look, then glanced at Oran before her feet stumbled toward the opening. The wind howled through the gap in the walls, sending gusts that tugged at her braid, curls whipping loose around her face. Her shoulders rose and fell with heavy breaths. She positioned herself before the agni stone cradling the other three gems and raised her hands.

Nothing happened.

Her fingers flexed open and closed. Another attempt, another failure. A gust of wind rattled the rocks above them, sending a cascade of pebbles tumbling to the ground with a sharp clatter. Elva's gaze darted to Oran and Yoen before she flicked her hands in the air, as if urging them to work.

"Try to stay calm. Breathe. Take your time," Oran called out. Yoen's glare cut him off as the ground buckled beneath them. The long-bearded guard's boots scraped against the crumbling edge. Oran lunged, fingers closing around the guard's coat just before the stone gave way, yanking him back to safety. The others dropped to their knees, fingers digging into the ground to stabilize themselves.

Elva's face drained of color watching Oran too close to the cliff's edge.

"We don't have much time, Elva. You must do it now," Yoen shouted. His hand moved to his waist pouch, his gaze fixed on her shaking hands. "This mountain will unleash a river of fire that will consume us before we can escape. Then it will swallow the city whole, just like you witnessed when you first arrived. Seal it."

"I'm—I'm trying," she choked.

"Try harder." His voice cracked like a whip.

Her fingers spread over the stones once again.

"Make them glow! Now." As his shout echoed off the rocks, Oran took a step toward her, only to meet Sumani's restraining grip.

"I—I can't." Her voice broke again.

"You must." He pulled a long leather string from his waist pouch and wrapped it around his hand. At his nod, Sumani's kick sent Oran crashing to his knees with a grunt. In one swift motion, he looped the cord around his neck. Oran thrashed against the restraint, while the long-bearded guard bound his wrists. Elva lunged forward in desperation, but the guard behind her forced her to her knees.

"What are you doing?" Her strained voice echoed through the falling rubble.

"Seal the gate," Yoen snarled.

Her cheeks flushed, her fingers curling into fists at her side. "Please, don't do this."

Yoen tightened his grip around Oran's throat, forcing a strained gasp. "Seal the gate."

Her feet stepped forward again. And when the trailing guard sprang to stop her, Elva's sharp elbow drove into his gut. As he doubled over, she grabbed his collar and belt, pivoting to send him crashing over her shoulder. In one fluid motion, she snatched his knife and pressed the blade against his throat. "Let him go!" she hissed.

Yoen's jaw clenched. Instead of releasing Oran, he yanked him toward the edge, causing his feet to skid dangerously close to the precipice. Oran's face flushed purple. "He doesn't have much time. Seal the gate."

Hatred blazed in Elva's narrowed eyes. Her chest rose and fell in ragged breaths, but she returned to the gate, the knife clattering to the ground. She shut her eyes and extended her hands over the enchanted stones.

Yoen drew away from the edge, his grip on the cord slackening just enough for Oran to draw a rasping breath. In front of Elva, the stones flickered a pale glow, pulsing once before dimming. At his signal, Sumani's bowstring creaked under her pull while the arrow's obsidian tip tracked Elva's movements. As more tremors sent loose pebbles across the ledge, Yoen slammed Oran into the packed earth, tightening the leather cord until it bit into his flesh. Oran's veins bulged and his face turned purple. The crack of Yoen's fist against bone cut through the rumble, followed by the wet sound of a second blow.

"*Stop!*" Elva lurched forward.

Sumani advanced, her bow drawn tight, warning her to halt. Yoen ignored her desperate pleas, the force of his punch relentless. His fist rose and fell, rose and fell, each impact duller than the last until Oran lay motionless, blood sprayed across Yoen' knuckles.

"No!" The stones flared with a searing radiance at Elva's uneven gasps.

He hauled Oran's limp form upright. "He still breathes. If you want him to live, seal that gate. NOW!"

Elva's angry scream drowned out the rumbling earth. The bloodstone box pulsed with deep crimson light, its surface rippling as if something inside strained to break free. The box surrendered with a sharp crack, unleashing a torrent of starlight from the white stone within. The sister agni stones, small and large, bathed the air in honeyed brilliance. Together, Äktastary, Ikarite, and Ka'zanty's gems merged in deep resonance. The searing light flooded the mount, like kindling catching fire and exploding into a roaring blaze, forcing them to shield their faces.

The enchanted stones pulsed brighter as Elva neared the White Stone Gate. Ribbons of searing white, ruby, and amber light unfurled, tethering themselves to her like iron to a magnet. The glowing strands spiraled up her legs, coiling around her torso in luminous threads. Power surged through her outstretched arms. Ethereal streams wove between them, gathering in her palms to form a turbulence of liquid fire. With a fierce thrust, the energy shot toward the massive gate. It cascaded over the carvings, tracing every line and groove with unrelenting precision.

The ground trembled beneath their hands and knees. Garam's fury raged. Debris rained down, forcing them to scramble against the shifting earth.

The barrier inched forward, stone grinding against stone in a shrieking clash of a century-old resistance. Elva strained against the raw power, jaw clenched tight and tendons taut in her neck.

Garam retaliated, launching another barrage of rocks. With a final guttural scream, she pushed harder. The three currents of light pulsed fiercely, each finding its mark in a crevice on the gate. White, ruby, and amber energy sealed every fissure until, with a bone-deep rumble, the barrier slammed shut. As it settled into place, Garam's fury diminished. Its walls gradually stilled, each tremor softening until silence draped over the mountain like a heavy burial shroud.

Yoen's fingers released the leather cord around Oran's neck. His shoulders sagged with a deep exhale. The stones' light dimmed to nothing as Elva's arms dropped, her strength spent. Behind her, the guard pried the bloodstone box closed with his dagger's point, containing the white stone's light once again.

Yoen lunged forward, catching Elva before she crumbled to the ground. "You've done it," he whispered past the tightness in his throat, "you've done it."

Sumani gathered the enchanted stones, handing them to the guards. "Take these to High Regent Zohar. Report everything you witnessed here," she said with a smile.

Elva's eyes fluttered open, scanning wildly until they locked onto him. Her lips curled back from her teeth. Without warning, her wrist slammed into his nose with a sickening crunch.

Warm blood trickled down his face, metallic on his tongue. In a disoriented moment, he glanced up again. Elva twisted, driving her foot into his chest. The force left him gasping for air before he collapsed onto his back. Yells echoed around him but he couldn't distinguish the voices.

Elva kicked the guard attempting to stop her between his legs, then went back to Yoen, with a wrath he didn't know she had. She seized the front of his coat and with a clenched fist, slammed all her anger into his face. His right eye bore the brunt of the force. His head snapped sideways, and her knuckles found his temple.

Two guards hauled her back. She thrashed and screamed. "Let go of me!" she yelled. "How could you! You vile, wretched man!"

"Elva! Elva!" Oran's voice cut through the chaos. "It was all a setup. I'm fine! I'm unharmed!"

Yoen rolled to his side, wincing as Sumani reached for him. "I'm okay," he said, spitting out a mouthful of blood. He bit through a grunt, clutching his chest and stumbling up. He squinted through the pain, his right eye refusing to focus.

"What do you mean a setup?" Elva grabbed Oran's chin, yanking his collar aside. Her sleeve scrubbed frantically at the blood staining his face.

"Sumani," Yoen gasped, doubled over. "The stones, send them away."

"Yes, Chief," Sumani replied, motioning the guards to depart.

"It's okay, I'm all right," Oran's voice quivered. "It wasn't real. They thought it might help."

"What about the blood? I saw it." Elva's chest heaved, fighting back tears. "There was so much blood."

Oran swallowed nervously, wiping the crimson pigment from his face. "Just pig's blood, Glowworm."

"Pig's blood?" Elva stammered. "What kind of monster thinks of such a plan?"

"A desperate one." Yoen squinted through his bruised eye.

Elva's gaze darted between them. "You were all in on it?" Her gaze fixed on Oran. "Even you?"

Oran managed a small nod. "I'm sorry, Glow—"

Her fist buried itself in his stomach before he could finish. He folded with a wheeze, dropping to his knees.

Elva turned and sprinted down toward the waiting horses.

Yoen motioned Sumani to follow her, then offered a hand to Oran. "Are you all right?"

"She hates me," he coughed.

"Just give her time. She'll come around."

"How do you know?" Oran's hand pressed his abdomen.

"She just sealed an ancient gate to save your life."

Oran sighed. "I just hope I don't lose her in the middle of all this." His gaze flew to Yoen's nose. "I warned you. Her aunt taught her how to fight. You might want to have that checked."

"I've been worse," he said, giving Oran a subtle nod. "You should start apologizing now, go!"

When Oran disappeared from view, Yoen gaze fell on the sealed gate. His heart hammered against his ribs. One hand rested on the familiar spot at the pit of his stomach, while the other reached for the cold white stone.

He sank down before it, facing the distant mountains veiled in their perpetual haze. His fist found his mouth, teeth breaking skin to trap the scream building in his throat. Like the Tanama peaks shrouded in the veil of smoke, Elva's burning gaze would haunt him. Cold sweat beaded on his forehead while relief and guilt warred in his chest. He knew what it would take to force her hand.

He resisted the pull at his heart. The warmth Nim had kindled flickered like a dying flame, one he had to smother, tear from his very soul. Elva was nothing more than a tool, a weapon to protect those he loved. Drawing a steadying breath, he cast one final look at the distant range before making his way to Inara.

Chapter 26

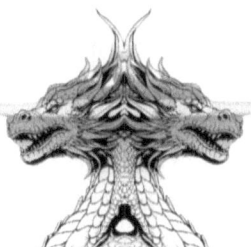

KA'ZAN

YOEN

Inara's hooves charged at Yoen's signal, each stride sending ripples through the seabed. The setting sun cast long shadows across the wet ground. With each gallop, her walnut coat gleamed as she raced toward Sumani's distant figure.

"Chief!" Sumani nodded, her braid bouncing with her mount's gait. Her quiver swayed slightly against her back, filled with arrows forged from wyvern bones. "I thought we'd have to send someone for you."

"I wanted to make sure the seal held its place," he said, his gaze drawn to Oran and Elva's figures in the distance. "How are they holding up?"

"She's not happy, as expected. And the boy's all over the place."

Oran leaned across the gap between their horses, his hand reaching for hers. Elva jerked away, shoving him hard enough that he tumbled from his saddle, hitting the sand with a muffled thud. She rode on, but her head twisted back, teeth catching her lower lip.

"See that?" Yoen let out a soft chuckle. "Even now, she's checking to make sure he's okay. That boy is already forgiven."

As Oran scrambled back onto his mount, Yoen's gaze softened. A familiar ache swelled in his chest. The seabed had once echoed with his wife's laughter when she and Inara raced ahead of him, her dark coils streaming like waves in the wind. His fingers clenched at the pit of his stomach—the same spot where Nim's gentle hands had once eased the storm in his heart. The same spot she had turned his worries into hope and helped him rest. Now, the space she'd filled with sunlight twisted into an all-consuming void, and he found himself welcoming his older self, unable—and unwilling—to stop it.

His fingers locked around Inara's reins, the leather biting into his palm. His gaze tracked Elva's advance toward the Blackstone Gate, Oran trailing behind. From the corner of his eye, a radiant shimmer sliced through the horizon, miles away.

"Sumani!" Yoen urged.

The archer had already nocked an arrow, her bowstring taut. Her mount surged forward as she released it in a fluid motion. The arrow whistled past Elva's ear, finding its mark in an Äktastary Militia member's chest. The force sent him toppling over the gate, arms and legs flailing as he plummeted.

More Militia members vaulted down from the gate, their weight crashing into Elva and forcing her from the saddle. Yoen's stomach lurched. They swarmed her, fists and boots connecting with sickening thuds. His gaze snapped over the chaos—ten Äktastary of the red-armband Trade, the same prisoners who should have been locked away in the posts outside the fortress.

One lunged at Elva's mount, but the horse's hooves slammed into his chest. A sharp crack cut through the air, sending him crumpling to the sand. Oran urged his horse forward, the animal's massive bulk slamming into another with a heavy thud.

Inara's hooves thundered against the sand as Yoen charged forward. Two men pinned Elva down, while Lyla's hands rifled through Elva's pockets and boots.

"They're looking for the stones!" Sumani shouted, her hands already releasing three arrows in quick succession. Two struck their targets, sinking deep into chest and throat. Lyla twisted sharply, dropping low to the ground, and the third arrow hissed past her ear. In one fluid motion, she snatched a staff from the gate, fingers curling around its obsidian surface.

Yoen's breath hitched again. Lyla darted toward the farmlands with the High Regent's scepter in her grasp, the staff catching the dying sunlight. Two Äktastary trailed behind her, matching her stride for stride.

The remaining pair raised their daggers, metal glinting as they aimed for Elva. Oran lunged in front of her, intercepting the strikes. His body jerked from the impact—one dagger lodged near his heart, the other pierced his stomach.

"No!" Yoen gasped, and he dug his heels into Inara's flanks. Sumani's bowstring sang twice more. Two arrows found their individual targets, and the dagger-wielders crumpled just before Oran collapsed into Elva's arms.

"ORAN!" Elva's agonizing scream shattered the air. Her hands pressed against his wounds, fingers trembling as blood welled between them. "No, no, no."

Yoen dismounted, his eyes fixed on the growing blood stains spreading like ink through the gray tunic. Oran's chest heaved with shallow, rattling breaths, his thick eyebrows drawn together in pain. When he reached toward the wounds, Elva's hands slammed against his chest, the impact driving him backward.

"Don't touch him!" The words ripped from her, dissolving into a sob. She thrust out a blood-slicked hand. "The stones—give me the stones," she pleaded, her voice cracking like thin ice. "They were looking for them, but I don't have them. Please..." she stammered, eyes darting between Yoen and Sumani, who had dropped to her knees beside them. "I can try to heal him. Please."

"We don't have them." Sumani's whisper barely carried over Oran's labored breathing.

Elva's gaze pierced through to Yoen's, raw desperation flaring in her eyes. "*Please.*"

Yoen's throat tightened. "I'm sorry."

A wet cough wracked Oran's body. "Glo—Glowworm," he gasped, crimson droplets speckling his lips.

Elva cradled his face in trembling hands, blood smearing beneath her touch. She pressed her forehead to his. "Don't leave me." The words tumbled out between shaky breaths. "Please. I can't... I need you. Hang on!"

Oran's hand, weak and unsteady, brushed a white curl from her face, his fingers lingering on her cheek before falling limply to her lap. His eyes, growing distant and glassy, held hers but the light within them dimmed.

"No, no, no. Oran! Don't." Elva's voice broke, the plea muffled by her face pressed against his chest.

A familiar ache crept into Yoen's core, settling deep in his ribs like an old wound reopening. Before he could speak, the hiss of bone and steel sliding free filled the air. Elva had drawn Sumani's wyvern claw sword. The blade's edge caught the light, and then she bolted toward the farmlands where Lyla had fled.

Yoen's knees dropped beside Oran. One of the silver daggers had buried just shy of his heart, its hilt unmistakably Ka'zan made. He pressed delicate fingers against the wound, searching for any flutter of life beneath.

"He's not gone yet. He might have a chance inside the Sanctum. Get him to the High Regent," he said, thrusting Inara's reins into Sumani's hands. "She'll get you there faster. Mind his wounds. Go—fly!"

Yoen shifted his gaze and bolted after Elva, his boots pounding against the cracks and crevices left by the volcano, sending up small wisps of dust with each step. His legs screamed with each stride, muscles burning, begging him to slow. But he couldn't let her slip away, not now. The thought of the prisoners escaping with

Zohar's scepter sent a chill down his spine. The Regent would never relinquish his heirloom willingly.

His neck muscles tensed, his pulse quickening at the thought of the High Regent being hurt again, or worse. His heart ached for Oran. He even understood Elva's rage. But none of it mattered. If Zohar had fallen, Elva would have to serve as their Enchanter, regardless of her wishes. His fists clenched until his knuckles ached. She would not escape. Could not.

The fleeting relief of sending the volcano into slumber had faded too quickly. The Regent's fate remained uncertain, and the threat from the Tanama still loomed. Ahead, the mantle of smoke mocked him, taunted him. Heat surged through his blood. He needed to find a way to keep his family safe. And for that, he'd have to force her into submission.

His eyes finally caught sight of Elva, darting ahead with the wyvern claw sword pressed tight against her side. She neared the thorn barricades marking the edge of the dead forests.

"Watch out!" The warning had barely left his lips when two Militia Trades crashed into her, driving her to the ground. The sword whistled through the air, missing one Äktastary's head by a breath.

Dark obsidian metal flashed behind her—Lyla swung the scepter. The hilt connected with Elva's skull with a sickening crack. A sharp gasp escaped her lips before her legs gave way. The sword slid into the ground with a dull thud as she crumpled.

The two Militia Trades struggled with Elva's limp form, pushing her closer to the dead woods. Yoen narrowed the distance between them.

"Leave the traitor. Let's move!" Lyla's command thundered across the field.

"There's nowhere to escape," Yoen shouted, jabbing a finger toward the Tanama. "Once you enter those woods, those creatures will tear you apart. Surrender the scepter now, and your lives might be spared."

Lyla's stance faltered, her gaze flickering to the mantle of smoke just feet away. Growling sounds echoed from behind it, making her flinch. With muscles tensing, she abandoned her Trade members and bolted toward Ka'zan's farmlands, tightening her grip on the scepter.

Yoen's eyes locked onto the two remaining Äktastary. His heart skipped a beat, noticing their proximity to the dead woods. One red-armband charged at him, his boot connecting with Yoen's chest. The impact sent him stumbling back. He channeled the momentum into a flip, landing in a defensive crouch. The second guard's dagger sliced toward his eye. Yoen twisted away, the blade slicing close enough to rustle his hair. Behind the mantle, the growling deepened into a vicious rumble, thick with menace, intensifying mere inches away.

The men struck as one, their combined weight driving him backward. Yoen's fingers found the hilt of his knife. With a desperate thrust, the blade sank into one of them. The man's eyes went wide in shock as the steel tore through him. But his expression grew even more horrified when he realized where they had landed.

The force had sent all three of them sprawling onto uneven ground. They froze. Twisted trees loomed overhead, their branches reaching like gnarled fingers. The earth beneath them bore scorched patterns, and a silver mist hung like a mantle around the dead woods.

Twin beasts erupted from the shadows and their fangs gleamed before sinking into the Äktastary's throats. More creatures materialized, their victims' screams drowned by the monstrous growls.

Yoen scrambled backward, his palms scraping against rough stone. Spines jutted from the creatures' backs, sharp as daggers, and masked figures with forward-pointing horns slithered through gnarled roots. "Uláak," he gasped.

A deep, guttural voice boomed through the thick air. "At last, we meet. The one that lurks at the edge of my forest..."

The suffocating voice coiled around Yoen, sending a chill straight through his veins. His skin prickled, his breath quickened when his eyes caught the Uláak's weapon. A chain whip with a white stone hilt, its links glistening with agni and bloodstones. He recognized it immediately, remembering the illustrations he'd studied days before. "You're—" He swallowed hard, his voice faltering while more Uláak closed in. "You're the Emberheart."

The Emberheart Uláak glided forward, like oil on water. The hexenbeasts continued their feast, tearing at the lifeless Äktastary. A low, resonant hum emanated from beneath the Uláak's leader mask, creating a subtle vibration as if inhaling the lingering essence of the fallen youths. Its hollowed eyes fixed on Yoen, unwavering and cold. "You're not one of them. Tell me, Ka'zanty, how did these Äktastary cross into the land of lava stones?"

"I'm not telling you anything!" Yoen spat, fists clenched at his sides.

"Such a strong will. I know you well." The Emberheart Uláak's voice scraped against the air, each syllable dripping with spite. "I have sensed your longing for years now. Many fight the pull of my forest, avoid stepping too close. But you..." The creature tilted its head, twisted horns promising violence. "You linger. You've been wanting the forest to reel you in. Tell me Ka'zanty, who was it you lost? Someone so precious that you'd willingly court death itself?" A twisted, blood-curdling laughter rumbled from the depths of its sinister mask.

At the Uláak's words, Yoen's stomach churned violently. The thought of his wife—lost to those vile creatures and in that damned place—ripped through his chest like a spear. His jaw clenched, the taste of acid rising in his throat. He had failed her in many ways. At least he would meet the same cruel end she had.

It had been reckless to fight the Äktastary so close to the dead woods, but at least Elva was safe. Ka'zan would still have a Tristone Enchanter to protect them from whatever doom awaited. His niece and nephew could still have a chance.

The taste of surrender clung bitter and thick on his tongue. Rage-filled tears burned his eyes, but he refused to let them fall. His voice was a low growl, dragged from deep inside his chest. "Why don't you just get on with it?"

A low, scraping laugh clawed its way from behind the Emberheart Uláak's horned mask. His head tilted again, hollowed eyes raking over him. "Why would I waste such exquisite turmoil on my hexenbeasts?" Mockery laced each word. "No, young soul, that tormented wrath you carry will lead an army of my underlings. That's precisely what you hunger for." His words twisted in the air like a serpent's coil. "You don't fear death—you long to become it."

The words slithered into Yoen's mind, stealing the air from his lungs in shallow, ragged gasps. His fingers found the leather sheath at his ankle, and he reached for his knife. The moment he swung the small blade, metal chains shrieked before cold links wrapped around his wrist, tightening like vipers.

The Emberheart Uláak's laughter echoed. "There's no point in fighting it. You're already mine," it snarled.

With every thrashing against the restraints, the chains dug deeper. More metal hissed through the air, constricting his throat. His other hand clawed at the links in a futile attempt to break free.

"Surrender your heart, Yoen of Ka'zan. Let the twilight become you."

As an Uláak underling inched forward with claws ready to tear at his chest, a wyvern sword sliced through the air. It carved into its lizard forearm, forcing an ear-splitting shriek from the creature.

Yoen's blood froze. Through the haze, Elva surged into view, retrieving the weapon she had hurled. The obsidian blade struck the chains—each blow ringing hollow through the forest—until the final link burst apart. She hauled him upright, sweat and blood glistening on her brow, her chest heaving with exertion.

"What in the wyvern's skies are you doing here?" Relief and remorse tangled in his voice.

"We have to move!" Elva's voice cracked. Her gaze darted to the lifeless bodies of her fallen colleagues, then froze on something in the distance. She took a step toward it—but her body stiffened, color draining from her face as the Uláak leader emerged into view.

"Another Äktastary!" The Emberheart Uláak's reptilian hand rose, and a hexenbeast lunged—a tide of fangs and spines.

Her grip tightened on the wyvern sword as she swung in a fluid arc. The curved blade cracked through bone, slicing the beast's snout. With a final twist of her wrist, she severed its head completely, watching it roll to the ground with a sickening thud.

Without a word, she thrust the weapon into Yoen's palms and darted toward the fallen Äktastary.

His arms shook with every strike against the enclosing fiends. Just as the blade could find its mark, something metallic wrapped around his ankle. The wyvern sword seemed to grow heavier in his hand as claws tore into his flesh, his blood running hot against the chilling air.

The clatter of stone, bone, and metal echoed from where Elva had vanished. Light flickered at the edges of his vision while the chains tightened their grip. A beast's jaws snapped toward his neck, but an urgent neigh cut through the chaos. Inara galloped into the onslaught, her hooves pounding the earth before she reared, kicking at the creatures swarming him.

His heart sank. "Get out of here!" The words rasped past his lips. But Inara circled closer, thumping her hooves and rearing at the encroaching beasts. "Go! Leave!" he choked as another chain tightened around his neck. Then another yanked at his ankle, pulling him in opposite directions. His muscles seized. The pain carved through him—a white-hot blaze spreading with each strangled breath.

Inara's defiant whinnies tore through the air, each one louder than the last in her battle to drive back the beasts. Their claws raked her flanks, but she held her ground.

"Inara, get out of here! Please!"

Claws slashed into his hand, breaking his grip on the blade. Fangs gleamed inches from his throat. As he braced for impact, the tristone chain whip cracked through the air, its sharp links ensnaring the creature's neck. The weapon yanked back with brutal force, severing the beast's head in one clean motion. White, seething blood splattered onto Yoen—the sickening crack echoed through the chorus of snarls.

Two more strikes of the tristone whip freed him from the chains. He stumbled upright as Inara limped toward him.

Bloodied and reeling, Elva staggered toward them—clutching the tristone chain whip. Her breath came in ragged bursts, each inhale making her wince sharply. She lashed the Emberheart Uláak's weapon at another encroaching hexenbeast, piercing through its hide.

"Move!" She tugged on Inara's reins. The Uláak leader's weapon trailed behind her, its stone links scraping the ground with each pull. "This way," she panted, guiding them deeper into the dead woods.

The ground cracked beneath their feet, dry and brittle. A murky haze thickened around them. Gnarled trees loomed, their charred branches twisting like crooked fingers reaching for the sky, concealed by a suffocating veil.

Yoen's gaze flicked from shadow to shadow, each breath a painful drag through his ribs. More Uláak emerged from the fog, circling them. His fingers tightened around Inara's reins while his other hand searched for his missing knife. He braced for the onslaught, eyes darting, trying to spot which creature would finish him. Their horned masks tilted ominously over their bodies, weapons clicking against the ground. Still, none attacked.

Ahead, Elva swung the tristone whip with brutal precision, the white stone hilt flashing in the dim light. Each crack of the whip rang out like thunder, sending the creatures skittering back. Low growls and high-pitched shrieks filled the air, but the beasts hesitated, slinking away from the weapon's bite.

Elva's steps quickened as she darted toward two pillars standing like sentinels among the dead woods. Yoen's eyes flicked over his shoulder. His heart skipped a beat. The Emberheart Uláak closed in, missing one arm. It hissed, stretching the other toward him, claws aimed for his throat. He lunged after Elva, slipping through the gap between the stone pillars. The Uláak's claws swiped at empty air—jerking back as if striking an invisible barrier, unable to follow.

His heart pounded. The salty tang of the sea invaded his nostrils as the chaotic sounds of the hexenbeasts faded behind them. He glanced around, taking in the landscape—no twisted trees, no dead forest. The cool, familiar scent of Ka'zan's Black Beach wrapped around him like a blanket. "We're back home!" he muttered. His gaze shifted back, searching the path they'd just taken. There was no sign of the dead forest. Instead, jagged basalt columns rose before him, gray and towering against the purple sky. "She got us through a portal." It dawned on him. "You got us through a port..."

When he turned around, a cold dread seeped into his bones. Elva lay face-first in the sand, unmoving. His legs wavered beneath him. Sharp stings of pain overwhelmed his senses, making him aware of the damage the hexenbeasts had inflicted. Deep gashes across his arms and torso bled fresh crimson onto the black sand. Inara circled Elva's still form, nudging her shoulder.

Something glinted near her arm. His pulse quickened. A wyvern fang lay beside the Emberheart Uláak's weapon, its jagged edge larger than his own hand. "Skies!" he whispered, his voice trembling. He carefully turned Elva onto her back and cradled her head. "You even managed to grab a wyvern's remains." A tightness gripped his chest. His fingers traced the bruise on her forehead. "So smart... so brave." She had risked everything to pull him from death's claws—the same woman he had sworn to use as a weapon to protect his people.

While examining her wounds, a heavy thud drew his attention. Inara's legs had buckled, her body sinking into the sand. "Fire-beetle, are you all right?" He moved Elva gently aside and approached his mare. His breath caught. The hexenbeasts' claws had sliced through her walnut hide, exposing strips of muscle and bone underneath. Yoen's knees gave out beside her. A lump formed in his throat as Inara's breath shuddered against his skin.

"I told you to run, stubborn girl." His voice cracked. He ran shaking fingers through her blood-matted coat.

Forcing himself to move, he gathered the wyvern fang and tristone weapon, then settled Elva against Inara's side. "Wake up," he pleaded. "Elva, wake up." He shook her, a little harder each time, until her eyelids fluttered, one eye bloodshot and unfocused.

His hands trembled as he pressed the fang into her palm, guiding it to Inara's flank. "Heal her," he begged, his voice breaking. "I'm sorry. For everything. She can't die. Please."

Wavering between consciousness, Elva's fingers twitched against Inara's side. A tear tinged with blood escaped her eye. "I'm... I," she croaked before losing consciousness again.

"Elva! Elva!" He shook her again, but the abyss she fought overcame her.

Grief surged through him, striking his chest like flint against steel, flaring into a blaze he couldn't control. His breath hitched. Every moment of loss he had buried crept back, threatening to consume him. As he struggled for breath, Inara nuzzled his leg with a soft whine.

"My fire-beetle."

His gaze rose to where ribbons of lavender and amber bled together, painting the sky in a fiery dance during the final moments of daylight. He leaned his forehead against hers. "You always liked sunsets. They remind me of Nim, too." He choked on each word.

"Now you'll ride with mighty wyverns at your side. May Ragas grant you strength and illuminate your path. If you happen to see Nim, tell her I miss her." He ran his hand through her walnut mane. "My sweet Inara. You have been an extraordinary companion." He bowed his head as her breaths grew shallow. "Good night, fire-beetle." He tapped her side gently as she drew her last breath.

A sinking stillness pressed in around him. His shoulders trembled with silent sobs. His teeth clenched, biting down hard on his tongue, fighting the guttural scream that clawed its way up. The last tie to his dear wife, now gone. And he was responsible for it. No. It was those cursed woods, those vile creatures—this damned land had taken everything from him. Tears carved hot trails down his face as the sun merged with the Great Sea, draining the warmth from his body.

With quivering hands, he draped his coat over Inara's eyes. "Thank you, my old friend," he managed between sobs. "Your spirit kept me from the shadows."

His feet dragged through the sand until he reached Elva. He wrapped her coat around the wyvern fang and Uláak's tristone weapon before lifting her onto his shoulders. Yoen's gaze fixed on Drekavog miles away, but his vision blurred, his chest rising and falling in ragged gasps. The void at the pit of his stomach seethed, oozing into his very bones. He pushed past the basalt columns, each step heavier than the last. He didn't dare look back—afraid he wouldn't be able to take another step forward.

CHAPTER 27

ZAMA

DRIFTWOOD BUMPED AGAINST ZAMA'S feathers. She bobbed on the river's surface, her owl form pressed against a waterlogged trunk. Sunlight pierced the morning haze, casting sparkles across the stream. Something slammed into the log, launching her into the current. The river yanked her under, then up, then under again. The roar of rushing water filled her ears, drowning even her own panicked heartbeat.

The Avian Sage summoned the magic from her markings until the energy stirred beneath her feathers. One wing broke free, then the other. Her talons treaded against the current before she finally thrust herself above the surface. Three powerful wingbeats carried her to a nearby boulder, where water streamed from her sodden feathers.

Her horned ears swiveled toward the symphony of awakening land. Leaves rustled overhead. Birds called from distant branches. Wind whispered through the trees. She filtered out the animals, focusing on anything that might resemble humans—past the occasional snap of twigs beneath cautious hooves, the subtle creak of tree limbs, and the soft hum of insects. Despite her acute senses, no sign of human presence emerged.

With a powerful thrust, her talons scraped against stone, launching her skyward. Wind rushed through her wings, and she climbed higher, higher, until the river that had nearly claimed her life shrank to a silver thread below.

Where are you, Tarrak's and Asante's names echoed in her mind, tugging at her while she soared through unfamiliar skies. The recent events weighed on her.

Zuwena would have finished them in the dead woods if Asante hadn't led them across that invisible thread. The sudden plunge into the cold river had twisted her insides. She saw Asante struggling in the current while guards with red-armbands hauled Tarrak toward the shore, before something struck her hard and knocked her unconscious. The stars still lit the sky when they crossed, but now the sun blazed overhead, its light mocking her disorientation and the hours she had lost.

Her owl body struggled to hold a steady flight, causing her wingbeats to grow uneven. Her gaze swept over the river, but she found no sign of Tarrak or his sister. Asante, the girl with a heart as big as the skies, now bore markings of the kind she had never seen before. A knot tightened in Zama's chest. She couldn't lose them, not now, not after everything.

Her golden owl eyes swiveled, locking onto the distant murky mantle of smoke, engulfing the Tanama. It blanketed its three serpentine tails, like ink spilled on parchment, its edges sharp and unmoving. With a powerful sweep of her wings, Zama soared higher into the blue sky, her gaze fixed on the encroaching shroud. Even from above, the veil halted at Rengō's towering peak, as if the land itself had drawn a boundary the smoke dared not cross. The sight sent a shiver through her feathers.

Having flown over Ka'zan and back to Ikari, the source of the smoke still eluded her. When it spread over Rengō, Ka'zan's volcano lay dormant and untouched by the chaos. Zuwena had still been trapped inside when it all began. Samira's actions against her people meant she truly fear the worst. Her stomach twisted at the thought of her attendant, Lux, her life stolen by the High Priestess. *I'm so sorry, sweet child.* Guilt pressed against her chest, thick and suffocating. Knowing Tarrak's mother and sister had met the same fate sent her mind spiraling, but she had to focus. Hours had slipped away with no trace of Tarrak, Asante, or Zuwena's embryo.

In silent flight, her body rolled with the wind, one wing dipping as the other rose, her movements smooth as she banked toward the city nestled between mountains.

Her gaze flickered to miles of wilderness, the landscape unfolding like a familiar painting. The town lay nestled between the undulating green peaks, a place she knew from the Sages' scrolls housed within the walls of the Great Hall. Her heart sank. *We crossed into Äktas. How is this possible?*

With the realization came a shift in the wind, thick and hostile. Her golden wings flared swiftly, catching an upward draft to steady her just before she plunged. If Asante and Tarrak had fallen into merciless Äktastary's hands, her whole world would vanish into shadows. Time bled away with every beat of her wings.

Stone walls rose from the earth ahead, embracing a city perched on a hillside. Courtyards lay empty, their silence broken only by the wind whispering through cracks in the walls. Limestone houses huddled together in neat rows beneath fourteen sandstone towers. Maroon banners crowned each spire, their fabric barely stirring in the breeze. Each standard bore the same mark—a raised fist clutching a stone, encircled by a flame and edged with a gilded border. *The Hand*, Zama thought, rushing forward.

Below, the market square gaped empty, its stone fountain surrounded by abandoned stalls and scattered goods. A crude barricade stretched across the square—broken benches, splintered wood, and twisted metal piled in desperate haste. Beyond it, flames licked at a building's skeleton, but the destruction lacked Zuwena's scorching signature. Zama's stomach churned, staring at the raw aftermath of civil unrest. *Äktas is at war.*

The Avian Sage's gaze followed the downhill path leading to an unfamiliar structure. Sandstone walls enclosed it, five banners hanging above its bridged entrance—the center one blazing red, each bearing The Hand's symbol.

Limestone pavilions stood in rows, their white stone gleaming in the sunlight. Tall, metallic wyvern sculptures loomed over the courtyards like silent sentinels. Meticulously manicured gardens and rows of greenhouses stretched across the landscape, all carefully arranged. At the heart of it all, a grand staircase swept upward, leading to different quarters, guarded by figures in gray coats and red-armbands.

On one side of the grounds, bare mounds of sand snaked their way until they met the dead forests. On the other, near the stone walls leading to the harbor and the Great Sea, the Iron Tower loomed, its shadow long and unyielding. Zama's owl head pivoted, eyes scanning the ground around the tower, keeping a safe distance. She followed several Äktastary guards until a whisper, faint but unmistakable to her owl ears, cut through the air.

"Firemoon."

Her wings faltered. The mere gentle sound of his voice sent warm ripples through her skin, her heart racing in response. She swiveled mid-air, searching through the sea of red-armbands.

To one side of the Iron Tower, she saw him. The amber eyes that could melt any frozen heart locked onto her. Her breath caught in her throat, her body trembling despite herself. Tarrak stood within a cage of gleaming metal, its bars pulsing with an eerie white glow, casting cold shadows around him.

Her owl form hovered, her eyes sweeping the area for any signs of prying eyes. When the coast cleared, she slipped behind the cage, her wings cutting through the air with utter silence. As she neared the ground, her talons pulled back, replaced by her Sage feet.

"Firemoon," she whispered, reaching through the bars. The moment her hand brushed the glowing metal, a searing burn shot through her skin, forcing her to recoil with a gasp.

"It's enchanted," Tarrak whispered, straining to turn toward her, his bindings only allowing him a slight tilt. Sweat trickled down his forehead, a few of his locs slipping from their half-knot. Torn pieces of Asante's cloak clung to his burnt skin. Relief flickered in her chest when she noticed his stomach wound, now crudely bandaged. Amidst the shadows of the dead woods, he'd been slashed by a hexenbeast. The memory clawed its way back to her—the chaos, the wyvern, the relentless creatures. Still, she couldn't fathom how they survived it all, and ended up so far from Ikari.

His warm eyes met hers through the bars, steady even in his exhaustion. She blinked hard, forcing back the sting of tears.

"Asante, where is she?" she asked through trembling lips.

Tarrak's eyed widened in horror. "She's not with you?"

Zama shook her head, swallowing hard to prevent her voice from breaking. "I've been searching for hours." Her gaze took in the imposing stone walls. "What is this place?"

"It's the city's Trades Academy," a strained voice muttered nearby.

Zama spun, meeting the gaze of a prisoner in the adjacent cage.

"You're not from around here, are you?" the woman whispered, inching closer. "My name's Anani."

Without a word, Zama drew her cloak tighter around her, her fingers slipping into its folds as if reaching into shadows. Her hand emerged with a glinting metal feather, seemingly called forth from fabric itself. Her gaze swept the grounds before she crouched, steadying her breath to slide the feather into the lock.

"That's not going to work, bird lady," Anani said, leaning against the bars, her voice barely reaching Zama. "They've bound it with white stone magic. The Commander carries the only key on his belt. Where are you from?"

She ignored Anani's words, wrestling with the lock as the feather slipped deeper into the groove. Each time her fingers brushed the stone, heat flared against her skin—like the angry scorch of a burning ember. She pulled back, steadied her breath, and tried again and again.

"Firemoon," Tarrak pleaded softly. "You have to go. Find Asante. Please."

The words stilled her. She gripped the feather, its sharp edges biting into her palm. She blinked away the sting.

Anani's voice cut through the moment, her brown eyes fixed on Zama. "The girl seems important to you, I might know where to find her."

Zama's head snapped toward the woman, eyes narrowing. "Where? Where is Asante?"

Anani raised a finger, metal bindings wrapped tightly around her wrists. "One question first," she said, standing tall despite the cage. Disheveled dark curls draped over her shoulders, her sun-kissed skin damp with sweat, a bruise marking her lip.

Zama's jaw clenched. "Don't test me," she snarled. "Tell me where she is."

Anani inched closer to the bars. "When the smoke stirred up over Rengō, our Commander General sent water fleets to invade Ikari and Ka'zan. My niece..." she faltered, her lips pressing into a thin line. "She went with them. I don't know which fleet. But maybe with your bird eyes... you've seen her? She has skin like moonlight and warm honey mixed together, with a streak of silver-white hair from her forehead."

Zama's eyes caught Anani's shaking fingers against the bars. "No fleets invaded the city we're from," she admitted.

The fight drained from Anani's body. Her body caved into the metal bars, her knees buckling beneath her. "Right around the Academy's main staircases," she sighed in defeat. "The Commander's meeting quarters are just between Zuwena's and Ragas' metal sculptures. If your girl is captured and not here, she's certainly there," she added, her hands clenched on her lap.

Zama's feet dragged around Tarrak's cage, as though invisible chains tethered her to him. When she reached through the glowing bars, the searing magic branded her flesh, yet her fingers stretched further, seeking his warmth. Through the tears blurring her vision, she memorized every line of his face. Her eyes stayed fixed on his, as if looking away would shatter something fragile between them. Every part of her screamed to stay.

"My Firemoon." Her heart thundered so loud she could barely hear her own whisper. With shaking fingers, she pressed a metal feather into his hands, letting her touch linger on his warm skin, wishing she could hold him forever. Her breath hitched when she pulled her hand away. Even if her body ached with the need to stay, they had promised each other to put Asante above everything else.

Before turning to the quarters, her knees sank beside Anani's cage. "These fleets... you say they were sent through the waters?"

Anani nodded slightly, fingers tightening around the metal bars.

Zama gave a long sigh, measuring each word. "Could they have been in some metal creatures?"

"Yes!" Anani's breath hitched. "They call them Underwater Vessels. Large metal containers, big enough to fit ten Trade members."

"I'm uncertain of what I saw." Zama's eyes flickered to the ground, her jaw tightening. "I was under distress, and I can't guarantee that it is what you speak of. I thought I imagined it at first. But—I think I might've seen two of those metal vessels up north, near the caves of Ka'zan's Black Beach."

Anani's brown eyes widened, a soft smile curling at the edges of her lips. Zama's fingers conjured another metal feather and placed it in the woman's hand. Her feet shifted, toes leaving the earth as golden feathers erupted across her skin, her form rippling and shrinking until an owl hovered where she had stood.

By the time she reached the General Commander's meeting quarters, the midday sun blazed overhead. Her feathers melded with the stone, gliding effortlessly through the air. She perched on the edge of a half-moon window above, and scanned the room. But her eyes found no Commander with keys at his waist. Instead, a towering figure in a cerulean coat drew her attention.

He lingered until the last echoing footsteps faded. His hand traced the edge of a tapestry adorned with three Elder Wyverns, pulling it aside before slipping a small ring from his pocket and sliding it onto his index finger.

Zama glided in, silent as moonlight. The man pressed the ring against the limestone, and the wall shuddered apart with a deep, vibrating rumble. As he slipped through the narrowing gap, she followed like a shadow, finding purchase in a crevice above.

A thin layer of water stretched across the smooth dark obsidian floor, its surface a perfect mirror, undisturbed by even the slightest ripple. At the heart of the circular room, a stone figure of a woman loomed. Her crown of thorns cut sharply against the dim light, while wyvern wings, etched across her back, swept outward in intricate patterns. The statue extended her hands in offering, cradling a large gem that pulsed with honeyed hues, spilling across the water's surface.

The gem's glow grew brighter. Three beams of light shot outward, forming a golden triangle that spread to three points around the statue—north, east, and west. The radiant shape reached the walls, bathing the chamber in its brilliance. The man in the cerulean coat, hood now drawn, stood at the eastern point. With a flash, two hooded figures appeared, one on the north side, the other on the west.

"It's been several days since our last convocation!" The northern man's voice boomed off the walls. "Do you realize who you sent to cross over the threshold?"

"Please, accept my apologies," the man from Äktas said. "Our people have been consumed with pressing matters."

"The rebels must be really making The Hand sweat! A city of brutes in ruins—who would've imagined it?" A familiar woman's voice rang from the west. Her words carried a sarcastic smile, but Zama struggled to place her.

"Did you not hear me? You sent the wrong person through the portals. I should've known better than to trust an Äktastary!" the northern man spat.

"Measure your words," the Äktastary rumbled, his voice deep and controlled. "Must I remind you that I've given you both a chance to lead, where you had none. Be mindful of your place!" With his last word, a ripple surged through the chamber, sending waves through the thin layer of water. His spine straightened. His fingers brushed the lapels of his coat, adjusting it with deliberate care. Then his gaze fixed on the north point. "Now tell me, who do you speak of? You informed us two vessels crossed successfully through the portals and reached your Black Beach. A pity none made it to Ikari."

The northern man's voice thickened with restraint, a growl barely contained. "The Artificer girl. Her bronze skin marked with patches of white. The one with the streak of white in her hair."

"Ah, yes," the Äktastary mused. "I told you she's clever, but she poses no threat."

The northern man exhaled sharply. "The girl's a bloody Tristone Wielder. You sent us a pure Emberheart."

At his words, the woman from the west gasped, the sound rising and spiraling up the walls of the round chamber.

The Äktastary tilted his head, shifting the weight of his stance before replying. "You must be mistaken. There were no Enchanters in any of the Underwater Vessels. The Artificer wields no power."

"Not only did you send an Emberheart, you sent her with two ignited stones. A white and a bloodstone," the northern man retorted, his words sharp and jagged. "The wildling wielded three enchanted stones to seal Garam's Gate. Your plan failed—Äktastary. All of your hard work, wasted." His voice cracked. "The beast didn't kill Zohar," he hissed. "We released the wyvern for nothing. To make matters worse, the incompetent Shroudmist lost the gem." His words came faster, clipped and furious. "Now there's no way Zuwena can break through the Ikari shield," he yelled, his voice reverberating through the chamber. "This is a damn disaster."

Shroudmist. Zama's mind spiraled. The voice from the west had sounded familiar after all. But for it to be Narisa's, the First Sage. Her heart raced. A cold dread settled in her chest as the implications hit her. Confusion clouded her thoughts as she considered the possibility that the oldest Sage might be working with Samira, or worse, had betrayed them all, including the High Priestess. If she, with these two men, were responsible for the smoke on the Tanama, it meant the Shroudmist Sage had plotted against her own people. The thought twisted in Zama's gut.

The man in the blue coat shifted his weight, his finger tapping lightly on the ring. After a moment's pause, he leaned forward, his voice measured and controlled. "Where is the Artificer now?"

"She hasn't returned. Word has it she followed your incompetent Militia members to the edge of the dead forest. They managed nothing except taking Zohar's scepter. I doubt they could cross any other thresholds. The portals grow faint as we speak."

Narisa's laugh cut through the air before she spoke. "Why is the Ka'zanty even in our convocation? The man with no Enchanter's powers—all he seems to do is whine like a baby goat looking for mother's milk. The only valuable thing you've managed to discover is that there's an Emberheart in our midst."

"How dare you!" the Ka'zanty shot back. "You lost the gem we seek. And tell us, how much longer can you hold that smoke? Even now the sentient woods grow stronger. If the Uláak escape the forests, we are done for! I was promised that gem. Without it, all of this was a waste of time."

Narisa's laugh rang out again, harsh and biting. "You mean to say you have a Tristone Wielder—the kind this land hasn't seen for generations. An Emberheart at your beck and call, and you've let her wander to the edge of the Tanama? You haven't figured out how to use her, have you?" she scoffed. "Surely the late Regent Magnar had more sense."

Her voice dropped, now a soft snarl, each word laced with spite. "You complain too much, Ka'zanty, for having done absolutely nothing. Yes, it is true—the High Sage sent the gem out of Pālam without my knowledge. But had you been more observant, northerner," she hissed, "you would've noticed what crossed into Äktas several hours ago."

Another laugh escaped from her, cruel and sharp. "And as for you, Äktastary General, if you were so keen, you would've noticed there's an infiltrator hovering above you."

The First Sage spun on her heel, her figure flickering like a candle flame before vanishing into the stone wall. As she disappeared, the man from the north also dissolved into a spectral wisp.

The golden triangle's threads shattered, and shadows crept from the edges, leaving the chamber with a single faint source of light. The gem cradled in the statue's hands glimmered with amber light, brushing the stone wings.

Zama's talons scraped against stone as she spread her wings to flee, muscles coiling for flight. But the Äktastary man was faster. His gaze snapped upward as his hand thrust skyward, and the ring on his finger erupted in blazing light. The radiance struck her like a physical blow, overwhelming her senses. White-hot light consumed her golden feathers, searing through every bone. Her wings collapsed, folding uselessly against her sides, and she tumbled as the world dissolved into an endless void.

ARCHIVES

WHEN FIRST WE EMERGED from the void, stone gathered where our essence passed, and storms claimed the still-forming land. Fire fell sideways through the sky. Gas and lightning twisted like serpents over molten earth. There were no oceans then, only rivers of flame.

Storms were once simple things—measurable in their violence, fleeting in their hunger.

But we soon learned how humans became storms made flesh. Raw, ever-moving energy. Always becoming. They carved through time, unaware of what they carried—or what they left behind.

Ragas, too, became a storm. Once.

When he believed Zuwena and their offspring lost, something within him ruptured. He turned toward Mount Rengō, and there, in the shadow of his grief, love became its own opposite. Where his nature was to nurture and sustain, he chose instead to drain and hollow. From the highest peak of the Tanama, he leeched the life from root and branch, from water and ash. He tethered his essence to the land and, as Uzoma once taught the High Priestess of Ikari, he took more than the earth was willing to give.

Decay followed. And from that hollowing, new and deadly shapes rose.

Bound to the stripped forest, the Uláak awakened—twisted and vast. Their hexenbeasts were shaped by anguish and rooted in the dead bark of what once sang. What was human in them fell silent.

But energy, even corrupted, does not vanish.

Many storms have come since, and many more are brewing.
Not all announce themselves with thunder or rain.
Some carry sorrow—quiet, unyielding.
Some spill blood—raw, searing, relentless.
And some carve their mark so deep into the heart of the land, no eye will ever see the wound.

Fragment xlii: The Hollowing
—From *Daemons Archives, The Original Three*

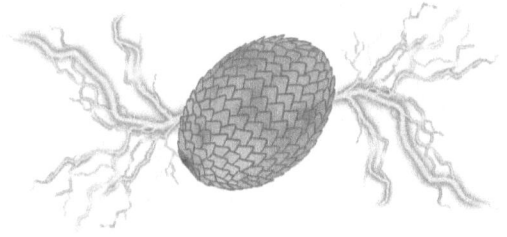

Epilogue

THE CRASH OF BRANCHES behind Asante faded, her pursuers' shouts muffled by a labyrinth of thick underbrush. Her lungs burned with each ragged breath, feet pounding against the unfamiliar forest floor where roots twisted like gnarled fingers. The satchel at her side bumped against her ribs. She couldn't risk a glance, not now. The embryo had to stay hidden.

Towering trees loomed overhead, their thick canopies shimmering with life. Moss and damp earth filled her nostrils, a stark contrast to the lifeless woods they had fled hours before. The silver veil had transported them from the haunted forests and thrust them into a place she didn't recognize.

The river had hurled her far from Tarrak and Zama, beyond any hope of finding them. Her desperate scans of the churning waters revealed nothing. No trace of Tarrak, no sign of life. Only Zama's horned owl form had flickered briefly above the river's churning waters. But before she could signal the Fifth Sage, the red-armbands spotted her. They moved with predatory precision.

They fired at her with hand cannons unlike anything she'd ever seen. The blast broke through the stillness of the forests, red and orange sparks flashing toward her, tiny metal palettes skimming past her arm.

The guards narrowed in, heavy boots snapping twigs and rustling leaves with each heavy step. Her pulse pounded against her temples, drowning out everything else. A cold grip seized her chest, the thought of Tarrak's possible demise at the hands of the strange hand weapons clawing at her mind. Warm tears blurred her vision, her fingers clutching the satchel tight against her body.

A root rose like a serpent, hooking her ankle. Her shoulder struck packed earth first, roots and stones gouging into her skin. The impact knocked the breath from her lungs. Another failure. Another moment of being hunted.

The smoke above Rengō had started it all. Then the Priestess, urging her to take the embryo hidden in the High Tree and flee. But those moments paled against the raw horror of watching her mother and sister fall, cut down by Samira and her Sages. Now Tarrak's fate burned in her chest, a wound more visceral than the dirt grinding into her cheek. The memories spun like fractured glass, each shard slicing through the last threads of hope.

The crack of a branch snapped her attention. She melted behind an old oak, her body flattening against the gnarled bark. Her fingers dug into the strap of her bag, tightening with each frantic heartbeat.

Shadows ahead rippled as five figures emerged, their gray coats shifting with the warm air. Red-armbands stood out against their sleeves. The shine of a lapel pin, a hand gripping a stone with a wheel of fire etched around it, caught the dim light. Deliberate breaths circled closer. Hand cannons glinted, their barrels raised and ready.

Leaves rustled behind her, but the warning came too late. The sudden blow sent her sprawling. Her feet skidded over tangled roots, throwing her off balance before she hit the ground hard. She scrambled forward, crawling away. She had to get away.

"Stay where you are!" A stern voice cut through the chaos, sharp and threatening. A man stepped into view, black leather markings branding his shoulders.

"Oi, look, another one," a second guard jeered, leveling his weapon at her. "You've got the same face as the man by the river-bank. But prettier," he added with a grin.

"Tarrak," her voice cracked. "What did you do to my brother? Where is he?"

The guard's words painted unbearable images in her mind. Her brother could be anywhere covered in blood, his body broken and abandoned. In the hands of those guards, those metal cannons meant destruction—to take life, not protect it.

The loss of her family carved hollow spaces in her chest. First, her father, following the Priestess commands until the forest and the Uláak claimed him. The creatures' leader had reminded her of that fate, the tristone chain whip delivering the final blow. Then her mother. Her sister. Her dearest friend. And now Tarrak. All sacrificed to the Priestess' endless hunger for power. The High Sage took and took, devouring everything until nothing remained.

Her feet inched backward. "Where's my brother? What is this place?"

A rough sack dropped over her head, cutting off her vision. The fabric scratched her cheeks as hands tightened it around her throat. She thrashed. Her elbow slammed into soft flesh, but too many hands pinned her down. They tore away her bag, then her father's dagger. "No! Give that back!" Her cry rang out, only to vanish into the trees.

"This one's got strange silver markings on her arm, Sergeant. How much do you think we'll get for her?" Rough hands yanked her wrists in front of her and bound them together, coarse rope biting into her skin. "Where'd you come from? The other one had no idea we're in Äktas."

"Where's my brother!" she yelled, heat blazing through her markings. The realization sunk in. They had crossed into the White Stone City, the land of violence and brutes.

"Our orders are to capture, not ask questions, Squire." She rec-ognized the voice of the one with the black leather markings as he barked. "This marked one goes straight to the Commander. Move out! The shots from earlier gave away our position. Any moment now, these woods will be crawling with rebels," he ordered.

"Let go of me!" Her breath hitched, raw and uneven. She twisted and kicked, but their grip held firm.

"Check the bag," one of them said.

Asante's heart skipped a beat. She couldn't let them have the embryo. The Priestess orders meant nothing now. But the embryo couldn't land in Äktastary hands. She remembered how her markings had pulsed in the dead woods, their energy threading into her dagger. But her father's weapon lay beyond her reach. Her body tensed hearing the unlatched strap. If the embryo sparked to life, Zuwena would find them and finish her once and for all.

Again and again, she found herself in the same predicament, always tracing it back to the same catalyst. Samira. The High Sage and every city leader, all of them hungry for power.

The memory she shared with Zuwena in the dead woods before crossing into Äktas still burned in her mind. Ka'zan's leader Magnar had captured her, imprisoned her for a century, feeding off her power. Her mind stirred, remembering the first time their minds had connected, when she fled through Pālam's secret tunnels. Zuwena's fury had nearly swallowed her whole. That need for vengeance, for blood, and carnage.

Asante leaned into it, made it her own. Let it settle into the space grief had hollowed out. Her markings blazed beneath her skin, not a glow, but blood heating to match her rage. She twisted with force, breaking free from one guard's grip. Eyes-shrouded, she fought like a cornered animal. She clawed and kicked, ramming her knee into flesh and bone.

An arresting bang of a hand cannon split the air, and something hissed past her ear.

"Don't move!" One of the guards shouted, his deep voice promising death.

Beneath her skin, her silver veins awakened. The power that once terrified her now flowed like molten metal through her blood, her last remaining ally.

The ground shuddered beneath her feet.

"What's happening?" The guards' voices cracked before dissolving into wet, gurgling screams. Wood groaned and splintered, the deep rumble coursing through Asante's chest. Earth shifted and broke apart with sounds like hundreds of bones snapping. The grip on her arms disappeared with a sickening crunch, sending her staggering backward. Her fingers curled around the cloth blurring her vision and yanked it away. Only then did the speckled sunlight revealed nature's bloodthirsty violence.

Tree roots erupted with life of their own. Tendrils wrapped around her captors' limbs, pulling until flesh gave way. Bodies shattered against trunks. Branches constricted until bones cracked and blood-stained bark.

Her markings drank in each death, power coursing through her veins, intoxicating as sweet nectar. Natural as breathing. She recognized the connection. She had it all along. The forest whispered around her, a song she'd always known but never truly heard. Like the High Tree's voice. But this was—visceral—untamed.

The roots beneath the soil reached for her, seeking her touch, claiming her with subtle affection. The forest's strength and whispers merged with her grief, her rage, and loss. And she surrendered to it.

Movement flickered at the forest's edge. New figures approached with bows drawn, dressed in ordinary clothes, no armbands in sight. They didn't look like guards, but she had no intention of staying to find out if they posed another threat.

She snatched her bag and melted into the shadows of the Äktastary forest. As her feet took flight, she opened it slightly. A faint light spilled from within. Her heart nearly gave out, noticing the spider-web cracks spreading across the embryo's shell. "I'm so sorry, little one," she whispered, clutching the bag to her chest, as if she could hold the breaking pieces together.

The forest parted before her like a reverent crowd, roots smoothing her path, and branches lifted to guide her deeper into the welcoming embrace of ancient soil.

Her mind wandered back to the beginning of it all, the same day the smoke started. Samira had warned her about the wrath and misery this land had seen. The Priestess insisted that loyalty and sacrifice were their only salvation. But Asante's loyalty had died with her family—both sacrificed to Samira's hunger for power. Zama had been right all along. The High Sage needed the strength of those women, including her mother and sister, to create the crimson seal around Pālam. Without it, Zuwena would have ended all of Ikari.

The matriarch wyvern had offered destruction in exchange for her embryo. Asante would deliver both, and more. With Tarrak gone, nothing else mattered. If it meant standing beside Zuwena... or even the Uláak, then so be it. The Priestess, along with the leaders of every city, had sealed their own fate. They had stripped away everything that tethered her to humanity, everything that gave her hope, and that kept her kind. The fury searing in her heart would become her weapon.

She would become wrath itself.

To be continued...

Acknowledgements

Though it has taken a few years, I feel my journey as a writer has only just begun. It has been filled with many ups and even more downs. I don't think I would've come this far without the unwavering support of those who not only inspired my story but also encouraged me to keep pushing forward.

First and foremost, my gratitude goes to my parents. For the first time in my life, I had to lean on you to make this dream a reality. Thank you for your support.

Thanks to the friends I neglected for MANY months while I focused on my story, yet who still welcomed me with open arms and cheered for my journey. I am blessed to have you in my life.

Nicole, beyond my admiration for you, I am deeply grateful for your constant encouragement and for loving my characters from the very beginning. During these very heartbreaking years, buddy reading with you kept my spirits high. Sharing this story with you has been an honor. I know without a doubt that none of this would have been possible if you hadn't believed not just in me, but in the story itself. P.S. I'm still waiting for our podcast—Hagug!

Emer, you are a true inspiration. Believe it or not, you helped me rediscover my passion for writing. It all started small with our five-word challenges, but reading your stories and seeing your talent made me want to write again. You were one of the first ones to see potential in my story and not only believed in me, but encouraged me until the very end. Your faith in me and in my characters was a light that guided me through MANY waves of self-doubt. Thank you, from the bottom of my heart.

Heartfelt thanks to my first editor, Nicolette Beebe, who took my infant story and kindly pointed out all the plot holes. I only stressed out about it for a few months... But your insights ultimately helped the story grow in many ways. Thank you for taking such good care of it.

To my beta readers, your honest and thoughtful feedback made this story so much stronger. Thank you!

A special thank you to A.J. Torres, CY Harold, Jade Hernandez, and Michael LaBorn for your unwavering support—not just on social media, but also for helping me navigate this indie author journey so I didn't feel so alone or end up hiding under my desk and cry!

To my social media followers and ARC readers who embarked on this adventure with me, thank you for giving these characters a home in your e-readers, your bookshelves, and your imagination. Your feedback as ARC readers meant the world to me, and I took it to heart as I made changes to the story. Thank you, from the bottom of my heart.

And finally, heartfelt thanks to the reading community that continues to inspire me. I'm especially grateful to my Black, Indigenous, and Latine besties, as well as the Queer community and people with disabilities, who have shown me the importance of not only reading stories from diverse voices, but also embracing my own voice without apology. Thank you for creating spaces where we uplift each other. You are all truly inspiring.

About the Author

Maldonado (she/her) is an introvert at heart. When she's not writing, she's likely lost in a book or spending an arguably unhealthy amount of time scrolling through social media. She enjoys reading fiction across genres, as well as nonfiction on neuroscience, astrophysics, social issues, and anything that helps her become a better human.

Her love for storytelling began in childhood, when she would imagine alternate endings to her favorite TV shows, movies, and books. Born and raised in Puerto Rico, M. Maldonado draws inspiration from her culture and travels. Exploring new places and cultures has deeply influenced her world-building and character development in Whispers of Emberstones. She enjoys traveling, spending time with friends and family, and dreaming up her next story.

www. authormimaldonado.com
instagram.com/m.maldonado_writes

ISBN 979-8-9985347-1-3

90000>